THE CINDERELLA SECRET

by

Bethany Maines

Blue Zephyr Press
2661 N. Pearl, #360
Tacoma WA 98407

Cover art by **LILTdesign.com**.

ISBN-13: 978-1-7332813-2-4

DEDICATION

With many thanks to Juel Lugo for her support and enthusiasm.

CONTENTS

THE CINDERELLA SECRET

Ella Zhao

"Pick one," hissed Sabine, her breath already heavy with alcohol.

Ella could feel her mother's fingernails digging into the soft underside of her arm. The Mexican night was unseasonably hot for the end of the rainy season, and Ella felt herself sweating. Sabine dragged her along the line of fighters, each one in a Mexican wrestling mask and not much else. Ella stumbled on her high-heels. She had known the shoes were a mistake. But for one moment, staring into the mirror, the enormous silver-blue poofs of her skirt going out in every direction, her hair piled high above her Day of the Dead skull mask, she had dared to think that she might enjoy this party. Dared to dream of being a pretty, seventeen-year-old Cinderella. Dared to think that she didn't need to be on guard. Ella had put on the shoes, costume, and mask, and gone out to her mother with a smile.

"Look at you!" her mother had exclaimed, circling her shark-like, kept at bay only by the enormous skirt of the Cinderella costume. "Don't you look sweet?" Somehow Sabine had made *sweet* sound like an insult.

Ella had thought that would be the worst of it. Her mother's Day of the Dead parties were legendary, and this year Sabine had married her favorite passions—costumes, sex, and illegal fighting. Ella had thought Sabine would be too distracted to focus on her. And Ella had been even more relieved to see that Sabine had dressed in a barely-there Egyptian goddess costume that somehow meshed well with the Day of the Dead skull masks she had commanded everyone to wear. As long as everyone was looking at Sabine, then they weren't looking at Ella. For a few brief hours, Ella thought she would be free to simply enjoy herself. She had been wrong.

"Pick one," said Sabine. Ella looked away from the fighters, but her mother grabbed her by the chin and forced Ella's head back around. "Pick one," she growled directly into Ella's ear.

Some of the men were openly leering at her, but most of them were looking anywhere but at her. Only Number Nine was glaring at her mother with an intense hatred, which rivaled Ella's own.

"You're losing it tonight," said her mother. "One way or another. Pick one or I will."

Ella tried to pull away, but her mother dragged her back.

"Fredrico wants you because you're *pure* and *innocent*." Sabine hissed the words into her ear, sneering at the very concepts. "You think I don't know what he likes? So we're going to fix that. You pick one or I will."

Ella looked down the line again. She knew which one her mother would pick—Dulce, the giant brute with the scar running down his chest and the tattoo of a Mexican god over his heart. She'd seen her mother going down on him at the previous fight night. Her mother had no investment in monogamy or faithfulness; what she had were simply investments. She owned people. She owned Ella. And she owned her current lover, Fredrico. Sabine could sleep with whoever she wanted, but the idea that Fredrico would want someone else—and Ella of all people—was unacceptable. Tonight, for the first time, her mother had caught Fredrico looking at Ella. It wasn't the first time he'd looked, or the first time he'd tried to grope her—it was only the first time Sabine had caught him. And instead of being mad at Fredrico, Sabine had blamed Ella.

Sabine shook her hard. "Pick one."

Ella was silent.

"Fine," said Sabine, raising her hand.

"Number Nine," Ella gasped.

Sabine shoved her at the wrestler and Ella teetered on her shoes and crashed into him. She was face first against his naked chest, her mouth dragging against the skin of his neck, her breasts rubbing against him. The only thing keeping her from feeling the size of his cup was her massive skirt. His arms folded around, held her upright, kept her from crashing down, holding her safe.

"There's the room," said Sabine, pointing to the guest bungalow. "Don't come out until you've fucked her."

The party noise picked up again and Ella could hear everyone dispersing, but what she was mostly aware of was the beat of her heart in counterpoint to his.

"It's OK," he whispered. "We're just… going to go over here. It's going to be OK."

His accent was American. They'd been in Mexico too long—she hadn't realized how much she missed American English. If she was honest, what she really missed was her father's British accented English and his Chinese bedtime stories, but she tried to bury memories of her father. He was dead, and without him, she wasn't going to be able to escape her mother or Mexico anytime soon. Number Nine half-carried her into the bungalow and sat her down on the bed. Then he squatted down in front of her, looking her in the eyes. His skin was pale and he smelled of soap and sandalwood. She wondered how old he was. His eyes behind the mask looked young.

"Hi, Cinderella," he said, smiling at her in a way that made her think everything actually *might* be OK. His black mask only covered the top half of his face and had a purple number nine on the side. It made him look a little like Zorro. "Who can I call?" he asked.

"What?"

"To get you out of here. Who do I call? Parents? Mom? Dad?"

"Dad's dead. And that was my mom," said Ella.

He paused and his head kind of jerked like he was displeased with that information, but was biting his tongue around his opinion. "OK. Well, in that case, you will have to come with me. Do you need anything? We'll go grab it from the house and then we'll get the hell out. You can't stay here."

"Do you live in Mexico?" she asked.

"No, I live in the US. It'll be OK. I have family there. And lawyers. You won't have to come back to her."

"I can't go with you," said Ella. "I'm not eighteen yet. Mom will call the police. If you get stopped at the border with an under-age girl…"

"Fuck." He rubbed his chin. "Um."

"Also, she keeps my passport locked in the safe in her room."

"There has to be someone you can go to," he said.

"My uncle," said Ella, nodding. She'd thought all of these thoughts before. "My father's brother," she clarified, in case Number Nine thought her entire family was like Sabine. "But he's in Europe, and last time I checked, the ticket price was at least fifteen hundred dollars. That's why she won't let me have any money or my passport."

He sat back on his heels as if thinking, then a smile quirked up the sides of his mouth.

"But the passport is in the bedroom," he said.

"Yes," agreed Ella. She felt stupid and slow and embarrassed. Embarrassed to have her problems laid bare before this total stranger. And even more embarrassed that he wanted to help. How bad did her life have to be when a complete stranger thought it was total shit?

"The bedroom that no one is in because everyone is out by the pool?"

Ella straightened her spine. "I have the combination," she said. Then her shoulders dipped again. "I still don't have any money."

He grinned. "I've got an idea about that," he said. "Give me a couple of minutes. I'll be right back."

Ella watched as he slipped out of the bungalow. She thought about getting up and leaving. She didn't know Number Nine. How could she trust him? What would she do if he came back? What would she do if he didn't?

She could leave.

But she didn't.

She sat on the bed and waited for him to come back. She'd never waited for a boy before.

Aiden Deveraux

Aiden Deveraux slid out the door of the bungalow and checked to make sure no one was watching. A last-minute trip to Cancun against his grandmother's wishes had seemed like a lark. And taking his friend Harry's place at an illegal fight after Harry had drunkenly dislocated his shoulder jumping off the hotel balcony had seemed like the height of hilarity.

Keeping to the shadows, he made his way across the compound to the gravel parking area. The bus the fighters had been brought in on was locked, but it took him only moments to scramble to the roof and slither in through the unlocked emergency hatch that had been cracked for ventilation.

But the whole thing had stopped being funny the moment Slutty Cleopatra had lined all the fighters up and demanded Cinderella pick which one got to rape her.

In the bottom of his bag was an emergency fund meant to keep him out of trouble. He'd dipped into it twice already this vacation for random purchases, and he now regretted it. It wasn't that he couldn't get more, but if he pulled out too much cash, his grandmother would probably assume he'd been kidnapped and put a freeze on his bank account. Neither he, nor his sister Dominique or their cousin Evan would receive their full inheritances until they turned twenty-five. When the Deveraux children—Uncle Randall, Uncle Owen, and Aiden and Dominique's parents, Genevieve and Sam Casella—died in a plane crash ten years ago, the last thing on Aiden's mind had been money. He could never have predicted how annoying it would be to have his grandmother still controlling his life at twenty-one. He supposed Evan had known. But then, Evan was older and he understood a lot of things that Aiden somehow missed—things that Aiden probably didn't want to understand, if he was being honest. Aiden pulled the cash out of the bag and hurried back to the bungalow.

He slipped back through the door, making sure that none of the other party goers were looking his way. Cinderella was waiting for him. She was a tiny little thing, with a swirl of black hair and a Day of the Dead mask covering half her face. The dress pushed her boobs up in a way that was probably too adult for her, but he had to admit looked good.

"OK," he said, kneeling down in front of her and counting out the cash with quick fingers.

"You don't have to do this," she said. "It's only six months. I can make it another six months until I turn eighteen."

He looked up at her and with a clarity that surprised even him, he knew that she wouldn't.

"No," he said. "No, Cinderella, you won't. I've known people like her. Or rather, I was related to people like her." There was no way of summing up the cruelty of Randall and Owen Deveraux, but it was clear that Cinderella's mother would have gotten along just fine with Aiden's uncles. The fact that Cinderella wasn't coping with her abuse through drugs and alcohol like his cousin Evan was a miracle.

"Those kind of people don't change. They want power and they don't let it go. You're going to turn eighteen and nothing's going to change. In fact, it will probably get worse. She's not going to give you your passport. She's never going to let you go."

Aiden knew he had to rescue this princess—he could *not* let her stay here—and as he spoke, tears sprang up into her eyes and she swallowed hard, but didn't say anything.

"All I've got is five hundred bucks." He held out the cash and her fingers closed around it, but she stopped.

"No," she said, pushing it back at him. "I can't take your money."

He looked at her in surprise. He had never had anyone turn down his money before. He was a Deveraux, and to everyone he'd ever met, that meant he was a walking black card. For most of his life he'd had to figure out how to tell people he wasn't going to pay for their shit.

"Yes," he said, pushing it back at her, "you need it."

He could tell by the way her fingers almost took it that she wanted it. He could also tell by the stubborn set to her mouth that she wasn't about to take it. "That's all your money," she said. "No."

"Oh," he said. He was torn between laughing in her face and giving her a hug. He managed not to do either. "Um, no, Cinderella, I've got more. This is just what I have on me. And we're going to need it to get you your plane ticket. I have a plan."

Her expression weakened. "What kind of plan?"

He tucked the money into her hand and she didn't resist this time. "I've scoped the competition. I'm pretty sure for the first three brackets—after that it gets a little fuzzy—but I'm pretty sure I'll win. You're going to take this and you're going to bet on me. And then you take the winnings and you'll bet again. You'll do that every time I fight."

Her head tilted back and behind the mask he was pretty sure her eyebrows had gone up. "You seem…confident."

"Cocky, you mean?"

"If the shoe fits," she said tartly.

"No, that's *my* line for you. Like I said, it gets fuzzy after the first three match-ups. I don't know the competition well enough to be really certain, but I'm yeah, I'm fairly confident."

She shook her head. "Dulce's fighting tonight. He always wins."

"Which one's Dulce?"

"Big one. With the tattoo and the scar." She drew her finger across her chest mimicking the scar pattern.

"Ah. That guy. Met him on the bus. He's an asshole."

"Yes. He's also good. Most big fighters just lumber around and try to squish people. He actually fights, and he likes left hooks."

"Helpful," said Aiden. "But either way, I'm new, so I'll fight at least three times before I get to him. And that ought to get us enough cash."

She took a deep breath and let it out slowly. "OK," she said, but didn't look entirely convinced. "I'll do it. What about the passport?"

"I was just out there. Everyone's down at the pool watching Jell-O wrestling."

"Oh, right," she said, nodding. "Mom really debated over lime or blue raspberry."

"Somehow, I wish I didn't know that," said Aiden.

"There's lots of things about Mom I wish I didn't know," Ella said drily, and once again Aiden wanted to hug her, but this time out of sympathy. He wondered how long she'd been living in this hell hole. How had anyone let Slutty Cleopatra procreate? And how had she managed to produce someone nice?

"I'm sure that's true. But I think we should go get the passport now as fast as we can."

"You'll get in trouble if they catch you," she said.

"Like you won't?"

"She'll lock me in the basement for a couple of days," she said with a shrug, and he felt an overwhelming urge to punch Slutty Cleopatra in the face. "But they will *hurt* you."

"Then we'd better not get caught," he said with a smile.

She led him into the main house and he stepped warily across the threshold, uncertain of what to expect. Most of the lights were off, but it wouldn't have mattered—most of the walls had been painted in midnight shades of blue, purple and crimson that swallowed all light and made the room's ceiling close in on them. The house had the weird, grandiose, unfinished shithole vibe that came with vacation homes in third world countries.

"Jeez, who's your mom's interior decorator?" He glanced at Cinderella, hoping she wasn't going to be offended. He never could seem to keep his mouth shut.

"She says it's chic," whispered Cinderella, looking amused as she went up the stairs ahead of him. He decided that Cinderella thought he was funny.

"It's not chic. It's depressing as fuck." He pushed a little further, wanting to make her smile.

Cinderella flashed a grin at him over her shoulder as she made it to the second floor. She really was about the cutest thing ever. He wondered what she looked like without the mask. She went down a hall and he followed close on her heels. The sounds of someone having sex could be heard emanating from in front of them.

"Someone's in the game room," she said, sounding annoyed. "It's probably Rolo. He likes to fuck while watching porn."

"That's so not cool." Aiden was horrified that she knew Rolo's fucking habits.

"Particularly when I'm trying to do homework," she said bitterly.

"I have that same problem with my roommate," he said.

"Noise-canceling headphones," she said. "It cuts it down, but it's not really enough, is it?"

"Not really," he agreed. He couldn't believe he was having this conversation.

She tip-toed forward and peered around the corner into the TV room, her dress making a soft shushing noise against the wall. She gestured to him to follow and then quickly dashed across the open doorway to the other side of the hall. They came to an open area, with several doors opening in every direction. One door was surrounded by bright white paint and over the door was a mural of a bird.

"What's wrong with that door?" he asked. "Did she forget where to find the devil's paint chips?"

Cinderella giggled. "That one's mine. She disapproves."

"Nice bird," he said. It was Chinese in style, swooping with a calligraphic dive toward the door. He liked the line of it.

"Thanks. My middle name means…" she hesitated, as if looking for the right word. "Bird. Come on, let's get this over with."

She went to the large double doors and tried the handle. It clunked hard, without moving. "It's locked!" She turned to him, panic hovering in her eyes, all of his effort to make her laugh gone in an instant. "She never locks it!"

Aiden hesitated. Behind them, the couple in the TV room were getting louder, and someone must have rolled over on the remote because the porn on the TV suddenly joined them in a rising cacophony.

"Fuck it," said Aiden, and he kicked the door open.

They both froze, waiting for the inevitable yelling, but nothing happened. The woman in the TV room came with a loud shriek, but nothing else in the house moved.

With a grimace, Cinderella stepped inside the room and gently shut the door. "We'd better leave tonight or I really am in such deep shit."

"I'm more worried about how we're going to get past the porno fans," he said.

"We can climb down the balcony, but I'm going to need some help due to the…" she gestured at the poof ball of a skirt.

"Right," he said, grinning.

She moved a painting and opened the safe within moments. She hiked up her skirt, revealing a tantalizing flash of thigh, and tucked the passport somewhere he probably shouldn't think about. At the last second, she reached in and pulled out a necklace with a ring on it.

"Belonged to my father," she said, dropping it over her head and settling the ring into her cleavage.

She put the painting back and they went to the balcony. He looked over and was relieved to see she was right. A vine covered trellis extended all the way up to the balcony—getting down would be easy for him. He glanced back at the princess. She was looking doubtful.

"Wait for me to get down," he said, swinging himself over. Once he was on the ground, he looked back up at her, a slender figure glimmering in the moonlight. "OK, drop over the edge and hang down, and when I say *now*, let go and I'll catch you."

"Are you sure?" she asked, sounding skeptical.

"Once you're dangling, it's barely one story. It'll be easy."

It was easy. Except for the dress. It took him twice as long to get free of it as it had taken to catch her. By the time he was done, they were both laughing. "I don't think you needed me to catch you in that dress," he whispered as they made their way back to the bungalow. "I'm pretty sure you would have bounced."

She covered her mouth, smothering a giggle, and then froze. "Mom!" she whispered, pointing urgently. They ducked behind a shrub.

He risked a glance over the greenery. Slutty Cleopatra was

getting closer. "We wait until she walks by," he whispered. "Then you go back to the bungalow and I'm going to the fighter's area."

"Don't be ridiculous, Fredrico," said Slutty Cleopatra, slurring slightly. "I'm sure she's enjoying herself immensely. I'm just going to go check on her."

Cinderella stared at him in panic. There was a call from another female voice and Slutty Cleopatra walked away from the shrub. Aiden grabbed Cinderella's hand and they sprinted for the bungalow, trying to stay low behind the shrubs.

"OK, what do we do now?" gasped Cinderella, as they shut the door behind him.

"Um? Get in the bed?"

"Do you know how long it takes to get in and out of this dress?"

"So leave it on!"

"I think she'd notice the giant lump under the covers!"

Aiden grimaced and looked around the room. No ideas were springing out to meet him. Outside the bungalow they could hear Slutty Cleopatra getting closer.

"Kiss me," ordered Cinderella.

"What?"

"She'll look in and she'll just think we're... slow or whatever."

"That works," agreed Aiden and grabbed her around the waist. "Sorry," he said, feeling like a kiss between strangers was a little bit awkward and some apology ought to be offered.

"Whatever," she said, and she flung her arms around his neck. He liked her practicality.

Aiden was good looking enough and rich enough that he had kissed what he considered to be a pretty good number of girls. And kissing was not, nor did he think it ever would be, earth-shattering, fire-work inducing or magical. He suspected that the people claimed that were lying to themselves, or someone else, to justify the fact that kissing was a very pleasant pre-game warm up to the main event—sex.

He angled and went in for a pleasantly chaste kiss, but kissing Cinderella was different. Cinderella made his head go hot and his fingers cold. Cinderella tasted like chocolate and smelled like spices. Her lips parted and he leaned in further, their tongues meeting hesitantly and then more urgently. Cinderella made the blood pound in his ears with a roar like the sea. Cinderella made him forget that this was just a show. He kissed her like he meant it, and she responded in kind. Somewhere he registered that a door opened and closed, but ignored it. They finally broke apart and Aiden stood, staring down at her, his arms still around her waist, hers around his neck. Her brown eyes were wide behind her mask.

He cleared his throat. "Um. Right." He forced his hands to let go of her. "Right. I was... Uh..."

Cinderella had turned him into an idiot.

"You were going to the fighter's area," she said, sounding breathless.

"Right," he said, nodding. "Right. OK." He tried to pull himself together. "You know how to make the bet?" One hand went to her hip and her chin dipped down. "Right," he said again, this time with a grin. "You got this."

Ella – The Chance

Ella could feel the fistful of cash in her bra making an awkward lump, but she was too afraid to be seen holding it in her hands. It had been hard enough to sneak over to the betting pool without her mother noticing. She was allowed to make small bets. Sabine approved when Ella took part in the entertainment, but she would never approve how much money Ella was now holding.

In the empty pool, Number Nine dodged out of the way of Dulce's meaty paw and dove in for a front kick and a flurry of punches. He was in and out quick as a bird, and Dulce roared in rage. She'd tried to get close to Number Nine before the fight had started. She had nearly five thousand dollars shoved down her dress, and for this fight, she'd only placed a token bet to make it look like she was sticking to her pattern. He didn't need to fight, but when she'd tried to signal him, he only grinned and winked at her.

Dulce swung again and this time connected with a sickening thump to Number Nine's ribs. She was as close to the edge of the pool as she could get, which wasn't actually that close. Being the daughter of the host got her privileges, but not front row. She was forced to peer between the wide shoulders of the fight organizer and his bodyguard, who was clearly an ex-fighter with a historically pummeled face.

Number Nine launched himself off the wall of the pool and landed a flurry of blows and then took Dulce down to the cement floor, splashing in the residual pool of water at the deep end. She heard the organizer's sharp intake of breath and he turned to his bodyguard with a furious expression. She heard him hiss something in Spanish and only understood the words after the other man began to move.

Not supposed to win.

The fight organizer's bodyguard was headed for the ladder into the pool. It had been blocked off as the fighter's entrance. It would have the clearest view of the fight.

Do something.

She realized, as the man reached into his jacket, what *something* he was planning on doing. She began to bully her way through the crowd, pursuing the bodyguard. She stomped on three more feet and shoved a man. There was a wave of drunken, stumbling reactions to her push and someone fell into the pool. She saw the bodyguard take out an enormous pistol.

"Gun!" she screamed. The crowd began to churn away from the pool just as she finally arrived at the bodyguard. Raising her skirt, she kicked out and sent him flying over the edge. The gun went off with a shocking bang. There was a spark and an explosion as the bullet struck a generator near the pool house. With a sharp crackle, the generator sparked and burst into flames.

The crowd began to run, and Ella found herself carried with it, unable to turn or find her way out of the mass of running people. In front of her, a woman tripped and went down, and Ella leaped to avoid her. The crowd was running on instinct, headed for cars parked along the desert road behind the estate. As tires began to screech out onto the pavement and the crowd thinned, Ella was finally able to stop running. She stopped and turned, looking for Number Nine.

Instead, she saw her mother. Sabine was screaming in fury at everyone, but mostly at Fredrico. Illuminated by the now engulfed pool house, she looked like the devil incarnate.

Closer to the house, she saw Number Nine. He was twisting

this way and that as if looking for her. She held up one hand, and by some miracle, he saw her. She saw him look from her to her mother.

"Everyone in the van who's getting in the van," bellowed someone who sounded Australian. She turned and saw a man holding open the door to a minivan taxicab.

She looked back at Number Nine. There was no way she could get to him without her mother seeing. He pointed to the road. Ella found herself backing up toward the van. Climbing in, Ella looked back one more time—Number Nine waved, and she waved weakly back. She had the cash. She had her passport. She had her opportunity. She had to take it. Getting in the van, Ella took a deep breath and hoped she was doing the right thing.

Aiden – Axios Partners

"Um, Aiden," the secretary's voice squeaked, and twenty-seven-year-old Aiden Deveraux paused in his brisk walk through the halls of Axios Partners, looking up at the woman in surprise. Jenna was a cheerful thirty-something who handled phones and appointments for himself and the three other lawyers in his department with ease. Too much ease, actually. Jenna was smarter than the job. He kept trying to angle her into a law clerk position, but so far, the partners had blocked him.

He liked Axios well enough. It was the easiest job he could find that met his grandmother's criteria of making the family look good. But when he'd selected corporate law as his area of interest, he hadn't realized how boring it would be. It did leave him plenty of time for his extra-curricular activities, but it also meant Aiden frequently spent his days spacing out in boredom, which only contributed to his air-head reputation.

"What's up, Jenna?" He wondered what he'd managed to miss this time. He'd spent most of his morning prepping a brief for the ACLU. Jenna was the only person at the office who knew about that particular extra-curricular. She approved of his volunteering for the ACLU, even if it was time that Axios Partners paid him for. Jenna usually sent up warning flares if he was about to miss something important.

"Um," she said again, "your brother is in your office."

Aiden didn't have any brothers. He had one younger sister and two cousins, either of whom could have been mistaken for brothers.

But between his cousins Evan and Jackson, Jackson was far more likely to drop by unannounced.

Jackson was the illegitimate child of Aiden's uncle, Randall Deveraux. Jackson had been in prison when they discovered his existence, and Aiden had expected Jackson to conform to his resume of burglary and armed robbery. But Aiden could not have been more wrong. Jackson had changed the Deveraux family for the better. Jackson was endlessly supportive, occasionally prying, and generally went out of his way to ingratiate himself to support staff.

Aiden's cousin Evan, on the other hand, was the victim of an entire childhood of abuse at the hands of his father, Owen, and Evan had spent most of his late teens and early twenties following in his father's footsteps. The idea that Evan would pop in for a visit seemed far-fetched, even if his behavior over the last year had been...better.

"I brought him a water," said Jenna. "You don't need me to do anything else, right?" She was twisting her fingers together in front of her.

Evan it was, then.

"No, we won't need anything else," he said. "Thanks."

Aiden opened the door and saw that his guess had been correct—Evan was in his office. His thirty-year-old red-headed cousin was always impeccably dressed and today was no exception. Hand-tailored Italian suits were Evan's signature look, and with the classic Roman profile, Evan, of all the cousins, looked the most Deveraux-ish.

Evan was currently frowning at the bottle of water in his hand. "Do I owe your secretary an apology?"

"I don't know," said Aiden, surprised. Evan was not known for apologizing to anyone, let alone secretaries. "What did you say to her?"

"Nothing. I asked to see you and she put me in here and brought me a water."

Aiden shut the door and went around to his desk, shuffling through the various folders in his hand. "You didn't want water?"

"I didn't ask for water. She just brought it. But the way she practically ran out of the room made me think maybe last time I was here…" He trailed off, looking embarrassed. "I don't remember her."

Evan had spent a lot of time under the influence of various substances. Aiden had the feeling that sobriety for Evan was one prolonged morning after. Unfortunately, when it came to those kind of messes, Aiden was the one in the family who had to do the cleaning up. So far, cleaning up after Evan had involved some minor fender benders and damages to a hotel room that Evan refused to discuss. The idea that Evan had been in any way abusive toward Jenna made Aiden's stomach clench. He didn't want to have to choose between the two because he knew what the answer was going to be, even if he hated himself for it.

"Well," said Aiden, brusquely, "whatever you did, as your lawyer I'm going to advise you not to say anything. Apologies can be construed as responsibility."

"That's a dickhead thing to say," retorted Evan and Aiden felt relieved. If Evan thought apologizing was the right thing to do then perhaps nothing bad had really happened.

"It's a lawyer thing to say," replied Aiden, easing his tone a bit. "Frequently, those two are the same thing. Did you need something or did you just pop by to call me a dickhead?"

"Sorry," said Evan, coloring up. "I needed to talk to you about DevEntier."

"Didn't you get my report after the last board meeting?" asked Aiden, sitting down at his desk and gesturing to the empty chair on the other side. DevEntier Industries had been founded by their grandfather Henry and his partner Charles MacKentier Sr. It was started as a research and development firm, originally focusing on aviation innovation, but had moved into alternative energies. After Henry's death, Randall and Owen had filled his shoes. Owen eventually left to work in finance and real estate development, but Randall had still been working there when the Deveraux plane went down. Jackson and Evan had split a twenty-five percent interest in the company and ostensibly sat on the board. Not that they ever went to the meetings. They sent Aiden instead.

"Yes, of course," said Evan, sitting down and carefully placing the bottle of water on a coaster at the edge of Aiden's desk. "Thanks for doing that. I ought to go myself. I just…"

Aiden felt a pang of sympathy. Evan was just enough older that he had memories of DevEntier from when Randall and Owen were alive.

"I don't mind," said Aiden. "It's fine."

"No, I'm trying to work on some of these Dad and Randall… things. I ought to go. But being there makes me…" Evan flexed his fingers a few times and ended up making a fist. Then he carefully flattened out his hand on the armrest. "I should probably go."

"No rush," said Aiden. "I don't mind going." Mostly. Going to the board meetings meant dealing with snide comments from Charlie MacKentier Jr. He was a pain, but it wasn't unmanageable. Aiden usually just gave him his patented dumb-rich-kid stare and a smile before wandering off. "Besides, it's not like Jackson ever goes."

A rare smile flashed over Evan's face. "I'm thinking he would not be comfortable at a board meeting."

"I'm thinking he would stick gum under the table," said Aiden.

"I blame that on you. He says you're the one who made him quit smoking."

"I didn't know he'd take up terminal gum chewing!"

Evan laughed at Aiden's outrage.

"And it is definitely not my fault that he periodically reverts to juvenile delinquency and sticks it under a table," continued Aiden. "It's so embarrassing!"

Evan shrugged. "Only if he gets caught. Which he never does. And with his skill set, it could be a lot worse. Besides, we all have our rebellions."

"I don't know what you're talking about," said Aiden, adjusting the ceramic Mexican sugar skull paperweight on his desk. "I'm too lazy to have any rebellions. Insurrection takes too much effort."

"Mm," said Evan, giving him a skeptical look that made Aiden nervous. The problem with sober Evan was that he could be more observant than Aiden wanted him to be. "Well, Jackson's gum habit aside, I actually wanted to talk about the DevEntier stock."

"What about it?" Aiden really didn't know where this was going.

"Well, between Jackson and me and Charlie MacKentier, we own fifty-one percent of the stock."

"Controlling interest," agreed Aiden with a shrug.

"But I keep an eye on the publicly traded stock."

"Sure," said Aiden. That didn't surprise him. Evan, despite drug problems and depression, had always been good at his job and conscientious about looking after the family money. Aiden might go to extra board meetings and clean up messes, but he never had to think about his investment portfolio. Evan took care of it.

"And recently there has been a... disturbing trend. Some of the portfolios I've been watching have had some interesting splits and subsequent sales."

Aiden felt his eyes start to glaze over. It wasn't that he couldn't follow Evan through the loops of higher finance if he really put his brain to it, it was just that he never, ever, ever wanted to.

"Do we have to do this?" moaned Aiden. "Can't you just tell me the end result?"

"Don't you want to know how I came to my conclusions?" asked Evan, raising an eyebrow.

"No. You say it, I believe it. You got all the numbers and you smushed them together with your brain things and then you found out new things."

Evan looked like Aiden had lost his mind. "My brain things?"

"Just cut to the chase before my brain melts."

"Someone is buying up DevEntier stock. A lot of it, and I'm concerned," said Evan.

"OK," said Aiden. "Who and why?"

"What do you know about Zhao Industries?" replied Evan.

Aiden made a dissatisfied grunt and ran his hand down his tie, enjoying the sticky smooth feeling of silk. What *did* he know about Zhao Industries?

"They're an energy company founded by Bai Zhao," said Aiden. "Mostly. They are generally considered one of the solar energy power houses. And they're poised to be huge. From what I've seen, they seem to be trying to put together a complete pipeline for solar power manufacturing. They want to own every stage of the process. Which is smart. It would insulate them from some of the ups and downs of the marketplace, but it's a global proposition. And as a result, they hire a lot of lawyers. I've run into one or two of them in the last few years—they tend to be hyper-competent bastards who specialize in international contract law. And possibly I'm overly reading into things, but I would characterize their attitude toward the Deveraux name as… chilly."

Evan nodded. "That wouldn't surprise me. Bai Zhao had a brother who worked at DevEntier with Uncle Randall."

"Really? But Bai is a Chinese national, so his brother must be as well. DevEntier has defense contracts. Wouldn't that be a problem?"

"I have no idea," said Evan with his trademark dismissiveness. "I think Bo Zhao was married to an American. It's been a long time. I really don't remember. But what I do remember was that Bo was killed in a mugging shortly before our parents died."

"Bummer. But Bai Zhao can't blame us for that, can he?"

Evian looked at him pityingly. "It has been my experience that most people who worked for Randall and Owen blame them for any number of things."

Aiden frowned. "Do ex-employees actually say things to you?"

"Not much anymore," said Evan, avoiding eye contact. "It was worse right after they died."

"No one ever says anything to me," said Aiden and instantly wished he hadn't.

"Your parents were nice," said Evan. "Anyway, my point is that it would not surprise me to learn that Bai Zhao doesn't care for us. And that would make his recent moves in stock acquisition more concerning."

"Yeah," agreed Aiden thoughtfully. He picked up the sugar skull and leaned back in his chair. He loved the smooth, cool feeling of the ceramic, and it always gave him a sweet twinge of nostalgia for Cinderella. He wondered what she was doing now. He hoped she was happy and safe. He tossed the skull up in the air and caught it. He knew it made people nervous to watch him throw a breakable object around and he'd used that nervousness to his advantage on more than one occasion, but Evan didn't appear to notice. He wondered what that said about Evan.

"I think I should probably do a little reading up on Zhao Industries," said Aiden, sitting up and setting the skull down on the desk. "Even if they bought all the remaining stock, there isn't much they could do though, right? How much is available?"

"If they could get enough, they might be able to demand a seat on the board or force a board turn-over," replied Evan.

"They can't get rid of us or Charlie though."

"That's more your department than mine. But Dad and Randall once talked about forcing Charles Senior out. If I remember right, they could have forced him off the board, but he would have still owned shares and voting rights."

Aiden sucked air through his teeth. "I'm going to have to go back and read the partnership agreement, the wills, and the incorporation paperwork. Thanks."

Evan laughed. "Thanks? I just handed you a pile of homework."

"Meh," said Aiden. "It's not hard and I've read all of them before. It's just a brush up. But if we're exposed to some potential risk from Zhao, I want to know now rather than when he's camped on our front doorstep." Aiden tapped his fingers a bit more. "I'll see what I can pull together and then we'll compare notes at Sunday dinner?"

Evan looked surprised, although Aiden wasn't sure why. "Yeah. Yeah, sounds good. Let me know if you need anything," he added, standing up.

"Probably the names of the companies buying stock."

"I'll send you what I've got when I get back to the office," said Evan.

"Great, thanks."

"See you Sunday," said Evan, opening the door.

"Yeah, see you Sunday," said Aiden, already logging onto his computer intending to run a search on Zhao Industries. He looked up again in time to see Evan lean down to say a brief sentence to Jenna and then depart for the elevator. Jenna looked shocked, but smiled tentatively after him. Aiden waited until he heard the elevator ding and then went out to Jenna's desk.

"What did he say?" Aiden asked, bracing himself for the worst.

"He said thank you for the water," said Jenna. "Every time he's been here before he's been… I've never had anyone make me feel so incompetent in my life. And he's definitely never said please or thank you before."

"I'm sorry he was rude," said Aiden. "I didn't realize he'd done that. I would have said something to him."

"It was only a few times," said Jenna, looking embarrassed. "He didn't actually *do* anything."

"He can be really horrible," said Aiden. "I'm sorry."

"It's not your fault," she said. "And this time he was fine. Sort of nice even? I thought maybe you'd already said something to him."

"No," said Aiden. "That was all him."

Jenna shrugged. "Well, then… I don't know. Maybe he found a better therapist?"

"I think he found *a* therapist," said Aiden and then realized that she had been joking and that Evan would be mortified to have his problems publicly discussed. Why could he never learn to keep his mouth shut? Jenna looked uncertain of how to respond.

"That is really great, then," she said eventually. "I would send his therapist a massive bouquet of flowers."

"I'll add her to the Christmas list," said Aiden with a laugh.

He was barely back at his desk when his cell beeped up a text. Last minute cancellation on tonight's fight. Torres broke his hand. You want in?

Aiden looked at the sugar skull with the painted lines and flowers that always reminded him of Cinderella's mask. Did he want in?

Yes. But fighting this close to home was definitely against the rules. But on the other hand… He was fucking bored off his ass. But she hadn't been at any of his fights for the last six years and he was out of clues. She was probably happily living in Europe somewhere and never even thought of him.

Aiden hesitated, then typed in his response.

No. BETTER NOT.

He knew way too many people in New York to risk it and Cinderella wasn't going to be there.

Ella – New York Fight

Twenty-three-year-old Ella Zhao hurried through the parking garage. It had taken her too long to slip free of her uncle's security. If she missed this moment, she was going to have to wait, possibly months, for another opportunity.

An entire section of the parking garage was blocked off with plastic sheets, and two large trucks were parked in front. Three hulking men loitered by the trucks in yellow reflective gear. Ella fished in her bag for her invite. She held out the card with green devil face and the barcode on its tongue. The man in front pulled out a scanner and scanned the card. He gave a nod to the second man, who held open the divide in the plastic sheeting.

"Have fun," he said, and Ella smiled perfunctorily.

Fights in the U.S. generally weren't as good as the South American fights. The rise of legal MMA fights pulled the talent away. In other parts of the globe, where leagues and rules were rare and fighters had fewer opportunities, the fights were better quality. Ella didn't specifically want to attend illegal fights. She enjoyed MMA, she enjoyed her own training, and she liked people with skills. But what she wanted, even six years later, was to find Number Nine.

Her uncle disliked illegal fights, disapproved of her attendance, and had instructed his security not to let her go to them. Hence her quick exit through the back entrance of the penthouse apartment her uncle had rented. She had never dared to tell him about Number Nine. She suspected that if she involved Bai and his security, Bai would certainly find Number Nine, but he would also go out of his way to make sure that Ella never did. So she was left with chasing slender clues and rumors and sneaking out to the occasional fight.

Number Nine rarely fought in the U.S. She was aware of only three fights in the States in the last six years, one of which was last year in Mississippi. She'd been three minutes too slow there. By the time she'd managed to get through the crowd, she'd only caught a glimpse of him and his car pulling away. But she'd gotten a better look at his trainer—an ex-fighter with a build like a bull and a rough thatch of hair like a dandelion. It had taken her a few months to track the trainer down to New York. He trained a few other fighters, legal and illegal. His roster was skilled, and Ella was certain that he would lead her to Number Nine.

The intervening years had not been exclusively dedicated to hunting for her luchador. Mostly they had been dedicated to law school, and now working as a lawyer for her uncle's company. She knew the other lawyers at Bai's firm were annoyed, as her uncle insisted that she take lead on certain cases, but it wasn't her fault that she was better than they were.

She'd been excited when Bai had announced that they were moving to New York for the year, and even more excited when he'd presented her with the DevEntier problem. She'd known the moment he gave her the file that it was what he'd been grooming her for. Her father had worked for DevEntier and Randall Deveraux. They owed the Zhao stock shares and a seat on the board for the work he had done. Ella's one job was to go and take those things away from the Deveraux.

She smiled just thinking about it. It was going to be a cake walk.

The air grew warmer as she went further down into the garage. Music played at deafening levels, but she could hear the crowd cheering. The host for this evening was an ex-Golden Gloves boxer who knew how to put on a good show. He'd brought in out-of-country talent and a few up-and-comers for the fights. Then he'd completed the set-up with a complete bar, and the local gang as the designated drug vendor. It was everything rich people could want when betting on the physical devastation of another human being.

Number Nine's trainer's name was Josh, but went by the fight name Bull and she had it on good authority that Bull had a fighter on one of the undercards tonight. Ella got as close as she could to the fighter's area. It was literally just an area blocked off with pipe and drape. Security guards stood like statues at the entrance. She saw one of them notice her and she moved to a less conspicuous spot along the wall. The best part of pipe and drape was that even though people acted like they were real walls, it was literally just curtains. Ella waited until the fight pulled everyone's attention and then she slipped through the fabric. She came through into a prep area, and face-to-face with a startled Latino looking fighter.

"I'm looking for Bull," she said.

He shrugged and then pointed further back. Ella followed his finger.

"Hey," said a grumpy looking older man with cauliflower ear and a crooked nose. "You're not supposed to be back here."

"I've got a message for Bull," said Ella.

The man scrutinized her. Her sneakers, jeans, and baseball cap didn't look like she was attending the fight as a guest.

"He's prepping his fighter," he said.

"Yeah, Torres," said Ella knowledgably. "I know. I just have to give the message and then I'm out." That was actually the truth. She had to meet her uncle's family for dinner in forty-five minutes. The move to New York had been fortuitous and had saved her months of scheming to figure out how to coincide a visit with a fight, but it came with its own set of time constrictions.

"Yeah, all right. Third room back on the left."

"Thanks," said Ella.

She went back toward the third doorway, a loose term since there was only a different color curtain in front of the area. At the back, she glimpsed an open area with a line of water coolers and a table of snack food. Ella was preparing her opening statement when she saw Josh come out carrying a water bottle. He turned away from her and went back toward the snack table and Ella hurried after him.

"Josh?" she asked hesitantly. Now that the moment was here, she was feeling less confident. It had seemed so easy in her head. Just go ask Josh for Number Nine's information and then she would find him and she could say... something. This was the part where her fantasies and plans got mixed together. In her most private thoughts, he pulled the mask off and he was gorgeous and dashing and promised to give up fighting and devote himself exclusively to her. She knew that she was probably in for a severe disappointment or, at the least, someone with cauliflower ear who barely remembered her, but at minimum she wanted to say thank you and give him back the five hundred dollars he'd loaned her. It wasn't everyone who'd give up their last five hundred dollars and risk life and limb for a scrawny seventeen-year-old they just met. Number Nine was a hero—her hero—and she wanted him. To find him. She wanted to *find* him. Ella let out a nervous breath as Josh looked up from filling the water bottle.

"Yeah?" Josh scanned her from head-to-toe with a frown.

"Hi, I'm looking for someone and I hope you can help." She held up the five hundred dollars in cash that she'd been able to pull from two ATMs on her way here. She really needed to start keeping cash on hand. If he wanted more she was going to have to PayPal him, and that wasn't exactly untraceable.

"Depends on who it is," he said. He didn't look too impressed with her cash.

"Number Nine," said Ella.

Josh was silent and Ella waited. "Never heard of him," he said at last.

"Please," said Ella. "This isn't… I just need to talk to him."

"Don't know the guy," he said.

"I can get more money."

"This isn't about the money," he said firmly. "I don't know your Number Nine. Now you need to leave before I toss you out on your ass."

"Can you at least get him a message?"

"Read my lips, girly, I don't know him."

Ella opened her mouth to argue further when she heard the bellow of the security guard. "Hey! You're not supposed to be here!"

"Tamade!" Ella swore in Mandarin and ran behind the nearest curtain. While the security guard ran after her, she cut straight through the next curtain. Three curtains later she was outside the fighter's area. She decided that discretion was the better part of valor and headed back up the ramp to parking garage. Now that she was living in New York, she could try again later. She would find Number Nine if it was the last thing she did.

Jackson Deveraux – Sunday Dinner

Jackson sat in the study of Deveraux House and watched Aiden and Evan flip through papers, their voices quiet but intense as they pulled apart whatever they were working on. The fact that he didn't know what that was bothered him. That they were getting along so well ought to have made him happy, but what he really felt was jealous. He looked across the room at Dominique to see what she thought. She stuck her tongue out at him and he cracked a smile, trying not to laugh loud enough to disturb Evan and Aiden. Youngest of the Deveraux cousins, Dominique was tall, like all of them, and slender. None of them were ever going to be heavy weights. Aiden was the thickest and he hid it behind tailored suits and casual wear with stretchy properties—as if admitting to muscles was a fashion sin. Dominique took another look at Aiden and Evan and then held up a bottle of wine and waggled it at Jackson. He nodded. She poured them both a glass and came over to him on the couch.

"I feel left out," she said quietly, handing him his glass.

"Mm-hmm," he agreed.

She sat down and carefully balanced her wine glass on the arm of the couch—something their grandmother would not approve of. He knew the second Eleanor entered, Dominique would whisk it away or find a coaster. Her rebellion had not yet stretched to obvious endangerment of the furniture. He also noticed that she still mostly wore slacks and formal clothes to Sunday dinner. He wondered how much longer that would last.

"Do you know what they're working on?" she asked.

"No," said Jackson.

"And we're not worried about that?"

"We're definitely worried about it," said Jackson.

Aiden went out of his way to never appear serious about anything. His nickname in the society pages was Prince Charming. He was known for being fun, a little bit of a dumb blond, and always up for a party. Never mind that his partying had drifted to a stop the year after Jackson had arrived. Or that he had been on the dean's list in college and currently worked for one of the top law firms in the city. Some reputations were harder to shake than others. Not that Aiden tried very hard to shake it. If anything, Aiden played into the reputation. But if Aiden was being serious, then whatever troubled his cousins was probably something that Jackson ought to know about.

Dominique removed a rubber band out of her pocket and pushed and pulled her long blonde hair into a pony tail, watching her brother and cousin with a frown. Odds were that she was thinking along the same lines as Jackson. Of all of his cousins, he and Dominique were the most on the same wavelength. He suspected that wavelength bothered her US Marshal boyfriend, Maxwell Ames. Society girls probably weren't supposed to get along so well with their convicted felon cousins.

"Where's Max today?" Jackson asked.

"Dinner with Grant. He's decided to copy our family dinners and try to bully his dad into behaving like a parent."

Jackson chuckled. Dominique's boyfriend had a textbook passive-aggressive relationship with his father. "Well, good luck to him."

"It's been working for Grandma," said Dominique. "We're almost like actual grandchildren at this point. I mean…" She gestured to Evan and Aiden.

Jackson nodded, looking at his cousins again.

"Jacks…"

He looked back at Nika, who chewed her fingernail. He raised an eyebrow. "What's up?"

"I want to move in with Max. Or rather, I want him to move in with me."

"His lease is up in a couple of months. It would be the time to do it," agreed Jackson. She gave him an annoyed look.

"Do you have to know these things?"

"I like to be able to predict the future," said Jackson. "It makes me look cool. Plus, I dislike surprises."

Dominique chuckled. "You like to have your minions keep tabs on us."

"I'm in charge of security, and like I just said, I hate surprises. What's Max say about moving in?"

"I wanted him to move in months and months ago, but he gets stuck on the finances and doesn't like to look like he's taking advantage. Which is stupid because I don't want or need him to help pay my mortgage."

"He's a stand-up guy," said Jackson with a shrug. "And you wouldn't like him if he just did everything you wanted when you demanded it."

Dominique tried to look stern and then laughed again, but this time it was the entirely unrepentant giggle of happiness that was specifically tied to Max. "Yeah, that's true. Anyway, I've finally persuaded him that we're starting to look ridiculous and that him paying rent is a waste of money which would be better saved and used toward his other goals. But now… what do I say to Grandma? What do you think? Is she going to get all old-fashioned and weird?"

Jackson considered that. "I don't think so. You want me to float the idea and see what she says?"

"Can you? I can't strategize appropriately without a trial

balloon. And none of you jerk-faces will do me the favor of bringing a girl home to take the heat off me."

Jackson laughed. "Sorry," he said. "I don't think that one special girl is in the cards for me."

"Yes, you feel like everyone is always working an angle on you, which you detest," said Dominque. "I sympathize. And I can't say I think you're even entirely wrong, but I also don't think you're really making an effort."

"I don't have time to make an effort," said Jackson. "All of you keep me too busy. Not to mention Eleanor. Bug your brother or something. He's the stable one."

Dominque rolled her eyes.

"So we're saying he could fucking do it," said Aiden, standing up and angrily throwing down a stack of papers onto the tabletop.

"No," said Evan. "I don't think so. There aren't enough shares on the market."

"And what if someone decides to sell?" demanded Aiden. "We can't predict that. We're tip-toeing up to the line here."

"I've put in standing orders to buy whatever becomes available. And I can make some calls," said Evan calmly. "I can get a heads up if someone with a large percentage decides to sell."

"Evan!"

The shocked exclamation drew all eyes to Eleanor Deveraux standing in the doorway of the study. Eleanor never dressed casually. Today, as usual, she was wearing a carefully stylish, but not overly fashionable skirt, blouse, and low-heels. She came from the generation where a woman dressing for power had to tread a careful line to avoid the dreaded criticism of *unfeminine*. As if only by appearing soft, vulnerable, and in a skirt could she blind everyone to the fact that she was a United States Senator with over a decade of experience and political clout.

"Evan, we do not admit to insider trading!"

"Grandma," said Dominique, taking a sip of wine, "exactly which one of us do you think is going to be reporting him?"

Eleanor looked at Dominique and appeared to be at a loss for how to answer the question—or at least answer it when it was being asked by Dominique. Eleanor really seemed to think that Dominique was a fragile little girl.

"Someone is always listening," Eleanor said at last. "You never know when the house is bugged."

"I checked last week," said Jackson. "We're fine."

"Really?" asked Aiden.

"What?" said Jackson. "She's right. She sits on two different committees that have increased security threats from foreign powers. I'm sure Russia would like to have some dirt on all of us that could be used as leverage against Grandma."

"Well, you might warn a fellow," said Aiden, looking affronted. "I say all sorts of crap here."

Jackson chuckled. "I got your back. Here is probably the safest place *to* say crap."

"Oh, well, then," said Aiden. "Rubber baby buggy bumpers and nertz to Russia."

Dominique giggled into her wine and, if anything, Eleanor looked more annoyed.

"Regardless," said Eleanor sternly, "insider trading is still rather a bad idea and I'm surprised that you have not reminded Evan of that, Aiden."

"I'm his lawyer, Grandma," said Aiden. "It's confidential. And actually, I'm kind of hoping he's serious about it because the future of DevEntier might depend on it."

"What are you talking about?" demanded Eleanor.

"Bai Zhao is buying up stock," said Evan, sorting the papers on the games table into piles. "We think he might be trying to leverage his way onto the board of DevEntier."

"Bai Zhao… didn't he die ages ago?" Eleanor was frowning.

"You're thinking of Bo Zhao," said Evan. "Bai is his brother. He's the head of Zhao Industries."

"Ah, yes," said Eleanor, glancing up at the portrait of her husband on the wall. "Hmm. That would not be ideal."

"No, it damn well wouldn't," said Aiden. "It would throw off the entire balance of power at DevEntier. And he would probably force a board turn-over and put in a more pliable board to do… whatever it is he wants to do. And since Jackson and Evan are the least involved, they're the obvious targets to flip."

"Do I care about being flipped?" asked Jackson.

"Yes!" said Evan and Aiden at the same time.

"It's a hostile take-over," said Aiden, which clarified things by only a tiny measure for Jackson.

"Just asking," he said. Jackson sometimes had a hard time telling which things were truly important and which were just things that rich people cared about. He glanced at Dominique and she gave him a nod. Three out of three meant he actually needed to care. "OK," said Jackson. "So, who is this guy and what does he want?"

Aiden and Evan looked at each other. "Um," said Aiden, scratching his head.

"He wants to take over DevEntier, right?" Jackson tried again and they nodded. "OK. But why?"

"His brother Bo worked with Randall," said Evan. "But he died in some sort of mugging before our parents did."

"That's right," said Eleanor going to the bar and pouring her own glass of wine. "He was married to that horrible woman."

Evan shrugged as if to say he had no idea, but that all things were possible.

"Since Bo's death, Bai Zhao has built Zhao Industries into one of the leaders in solar power manufacturing," said Aiden.

"OK," said Jackson, nodding. "But who is Bai? Where does he live? Does he have other family? What's his angle? Why is he interested in DevEntier? So what if his brother used to work there. That's pretty ancient to hold a grudge. There has to be something else."

Aiden and Evan looked at each other again. "I have no idea," said Evan.

"DevEntier has a number of patents pending on solar innovations that would be valuable to Zhao Industries," said Aiden. "But DevEntier is playing most of those pretty close to the vest, so I'm not sure how he would know about them. And as for Bai himself... Last I heard, Bai was in Germany. I think? He's a Chinese national, though I don't think he lives there much. But that's just the impression I have from some of his lawyers."

"You said he didn't like us," said Evan.

"I said his lawyers were not thrilled with the name Deveraux," said Aiden. "I actually don't have any evidence of how Bai Zhao feels. And, for all I know, this isn't coming from Bai. Maybe it's just someone in Zhao Industries with a bug up their ass."

"No," said Evan, shaking his head. "I can get that far. Some of the accounts buying stock are directly tied to Bai Zhao."

"All right," said Jackson. "What I'm hearing is that we need a complete profile and background on this guy. Give me a few days. I'll see what I can do."

"Oh," said Aiden, looking like this was the first time the idea had occurred to him. "Right. That's a good idea."

"Oh, my God," said Dominique. "You two geniuses forgot that you could ask Jackson, didn't you? What do you think he does for Grandma?"

"Security?" Aiden didn't look like he was terribly certain of his answer. "He's responsible for the punching of people and whatnot."

"Whatnot?" repeated Evan, sliding his chair further away from Aiden, his eyes dancing. It was the first time in a long time that Jackson had seen Evan look amused about anything.

"Well, I don't know," said Aiden. "He's just annoying about safety and always pops up to tell me not to go places."

"Oh, good grief," said Dominique.

"That's your brother," said Evan.

"Rub it in," said Dominque. "Aiden, darling, Jackson practically *is* Grandma's opposition research team. Not to mention the other security things, such as making sure the house isn't bugged and no one kidnaps us."

"To be fair," said Jackson, "I *do* also punch people and whatnot."

"I wish you wouldn't though," said Eleanor. "It's so terribly gauche."

"But periodically necessary," said Jackson.

"Speaking of kidnapping us," said Aiden, walking over to steal Jackson's wine. Jackson let Aiden have it. Aiden had given up partying and tended not to pour his own glass of anything, but he still seemed to enjoy small tastes. Jackson kept an eye on it, but the habit didn't seem to go any further than occasionally stealing his cousin's drinks. Jackson suspected it wasn't about the alcohol, but more of a way to claim ownership on the rest of the family. "Does anyone know what's going on with Granger?" continued Aiden, taking a sip before returning the glass to Jackson.

"Bastard is still CEO of Absolex," said Evan bitterly. "That's what I know."

"I do not understand how that is possible," complained Dominique. "They have the mercenaries he hired to kidnap us. They have the evidence that Grandma's Senate hearings turned up about the falsified research and the drug his company was selling to the VA. What more do they need?"

"A paper trail," said Aiden. "I told you at the time, nailing Big Pharma for anything is difficult. Absolex has a ton of expensive lawyers to make sure the blame and the buck gets passed down the food chain to someone else."

"They're starting to call him the Teflon CEO," said Evan.

Jackson heard the anger in Evan's voice. For the last year, Evan had been generally silent when the conversation had turned to Absolex. Apparently, his silence had not been due to any amount of forgiveness. "It's been a year. Absolex stock is higher than it's ever been. The market thinks he can weasel out of this."

"He can't," said Eleanor, startling them all into looking at her. "I have been getting official and unofficial reports on the matter for the last year. As of two weeks ago, the reports have stopped."

"Isn't that bad?" asked Aiden. "If they're not returning your calls…"

"They return them. They have just been very carefully telling me that they cannot tell me any news."

"Ah," said Aiden. "*Cannot tell* is very different from there is no news to tell."

"Precisely," said Eleanor. "It's my guess that sometime within the next month they will hand down at least one indictment."

"It had better be good," said Dominique. "I did not appreciate having my family threatened. And I certainly didn't appreciate the amount of furniture they broke when they came to my house."

"Yeah, but they *did* break Great Aunt Claudia's vase," said Aiden.

"Well, yes," Dominique admitted. "That *was* nice of them. But the Venetian glass lamp was extremely difficult to replace."

"That was a *really* ugly vase," said Evan.

"That was a valuable antique," said Eleanor, glaring at all of them. "Claudia gave it to me as a house warming present and I thought Dominique would appreciate me passing that sentiment to her."

"Then why did you always keep it in the third-floor bathroom?" asked Evan, which made Jackson laugh and then choke on his wine. Dominique giggled and thumped him on the back, and Evan looked pleased at having made them laugh.

"You children are sadly lacking in the appreciation of good furniture," said Eleanor firmly, but her eyes twinkled and they all saw the smile hovering at the corners of her mouth.

The door to the study opened and Theo, the Deveraux House butler, entered. He scrutinized the family and Jackson thought he caught the ghost of approval on his face. Theo had a master-level poker face and although Jackson had lived at Deveraux House for the last four years, he still hadn't deciphered all of Theo's micro-expressions.

"Dinner will be served in ten minutes," said Theo.

"Thank you, Theo," said Eleanor. "Perhaps if their faces are full of food they will stop spouting such utter nonsense."

"That seems unlikely, Grandma," said Aiden. "I can talk a lot of nonsense with or without food in my mouth."

"We're all aware of that, dear," said Eleanor. "But we can try."

Aiden – Follow the Leader

Aiden sat in his car and tried to picture how his conversation with Jackson was about to go. It had been four years and he still had trouble believing that Jackson was on his side. He had several reasons to believe in his cousin and Dominique had become impatient with his vacillating. In her opinion, Jackson was to be trusted before Grandma or Evan, and sometimes, Aiden suspected, before himself. That annoyed him, but the price he paid for keeping his secret life a secret was never really being able to open up to his family. Before Jackson come along, that had seemed fine, because that was how their family operated. But Jackson had changed a lot of things. Sometimes with his fists.

Aiden snorted, remembering how fucking drunk he'd been for Jackson's come-to-Jesus conversation. Did it count as a conversation if it started as a fist-fight? It was the year after Jackson had come into the family and Aiden had spent most of that year and the previous one being miserable and drunk and partying with people he hated or taking fights that he knew weren't good for him.

The part he remembered the most clearly was when he'd come to lying flat on his back in a lounge chair on the roof deck of his brownstone.

Jackson had been sitting on the end of one the other lounger and smoking. The rest of the roof was empty of everything but trash. Above him an airplane glided across the night sky, a tiny blinking red dot in a field of white stars.

That night had solved a lot of problems, but it hadn't been able to really solve the main one—Aiden had secrets and he wasn't about to share them.

Aiden took a deep breath and got out of the car. This was Jackson's area of expertise. He was in the right place, doing the right thing. Mostly. He had to admit, he'd been dying to poke around in Jackson's business the way Jackson poked into his. Aiden approached the building with the fading, peeling sign that read *Cheery Bail Bonds*, which he thought of as the Deveraux satellite office, and tapped the swinging number nine of the building's address above the door as he entered. He never asked why Jackson hadn't changed the sign. For one thing, he got the distinct impression Jackson would prefer that he and the rest of the family forget that Cheery Bail Bonds existed.

"Well," said Aiden, entering the front office and looking around, "this looks exactly as shitty as I thought it would when I read the purchase agreement."

Pete Schalding, the private investigator responsible for finding Jackson in that hellhole jail, stood by a desk with a cup of coffee halfway to his open mouth. Aiden wasn't sure what caused his shock, though it was enough to make Aiden question his choice of a pale pink shirt. Aiden had thought it was fun and sure to annoy the partners at Axios.

"It's got that original bail bonds funk," agreed Jackson, spinning around in a desk chair to eye Aiden.

It occurred to Aiden that his statement might have been misinterpreted. "That wasn't a knock. It feels very authentic and seems exactly suited to its purpose."

"So glad you approve," said Jackson, opening a desk drawer and searching for something. "What's up? You lose your phone?"

"No, after your comment about the house being bugged, I'm paranoid and I needed to talk to you. Besides, I wanted to see Cheery Bail Bonds in person."

"OK, I'm off—" A large black guy with dreads came out of

the back and cut off whatever he'd been about to say as soon as he saw Aiden. "Uh, laters," he said with a quick wave at Jackson and ducked around Aiden and out the door. It was exactly the kind of thing that made Aiden think all of Jackson's employees had the Deveraux faces memorized.

"I like how everyone you work with looks guilty when they see me," said Aiden, just to needle Jackson. He was also fairly certain that none of the Deveraux were supposed to know what Jackson's employees looked like.

"Most of them have residual PTSD from every lawyer experience they've ever had," said Jackson, finally finding a pack of gum in the drawer and taking out a piece.

"That doesn't make me feel really positive about your employees," said Aiden, laying the criticism on between a bemused tone and a smile. Most people couldn't figure out which part to respond to and said nothing.

"I'll be in the back office," said Pete, turning to head down the hall.

"No, I think Jackson might want you to stay," said Aiden, making Pete stop. As the words had left his mouth, he recognized that he sounded arrogant. "And there's no sense in hearing it second hand." He added, hoping that softened it.

"Hearing what?" asked Jackson, leaning back and kicking the nearest desk chair toward Aiden.

"Coffee?" asked Pete, turning around.

"Thanks, I'd appreciate that," said Aiden, taking off coat and hanging it on the hat rack next to the Burberry scarf that Dominique had gotten Jackson last Christmas. By the time he'd seated himself, Pete was back with a mug for him. Aiden eyed the green mug with its fish handle in amusement.

"So," Aiden said, putting his feet up on the nearest desk. Pete sighed and Aiden looked at Jackson in surprise.

"Ignore him," said Jackson. "I'm convinced he got this job because he and Eleanor share deep feelings about feet and furniture."

"But," said Aiden, looking at the desk critically, "it appears to be made of sawdust and plastic."

"It is," agreed Jackson, leaning back and putting his own feet up. Aiden found himself grinning at his cousin. Jackson's interference in his life might be annoying, but the rest of Jackson was funny.

"Heathens," said Pete, shaking his head and leaning against the wall. "All right, can we get to the problem?"

"I'm being followed," said Aiden. "His name is," he fished in his pocket for his phone and checked a photo, "Chang Huang." Jackson glanced at Pete, who grunted unhappily. "News that appears to surprise neither of you," said Aiden, scrutinizing them. "Hm. Well, it should probably go without saying, but I dislike being followed."

"And what condition did you leave Mr. Huang in?" asked Jackson.

Aiden debated how honestly to answer that. "In exactly the same condition I found him in," he said. "I don't punch people. We decided that last Sunday. Punching people is your department."

Aiden knew Jackson didn't believe him. Even if Jackson wasn't a naturally suspicious person, the fist-fight on the roof deck of Aiden's brownstone was too much evidence to the contrary.

"Uh-huh," said Jackson, and he snapped a bubble.

"I'm glad you stopped smoking," said Aiden.

Jackson had been sitting on the end of one of the loungers on Aiden's deck, breathing out white puffs of smoke and watching the blinking track of the airplane in the dark sky. The air had felt cold, but Aiden had felt hot and sweaty and every part of his body ached or stung or creaked.

"Me too," said Jackson, eyeing him across the desk with a twinkle in his eye, running a middle finger across his lip where Aiden had split it.

"It's nice to have things settled," said Aiden.

"Did we settle that you didn't punch things?" asked Jackson. "I don't think we settled on that at all."

Aiden remembered the way his ribs had felt like they'd been pummeled by a horse and how Jackson had looked completely fine. He'd been so annoyed.

"What the fuck happened?" he had asked, using the nearby BBQ to claw his way upright.

"You drunk-dialed your sister," said Jackson. "She sent me to get you. You tried to kick my ass."

"How'd that work out for us?" asked Aiden, standing all the way up. The world had spun.

"Not that great," said Jackson. Aiden focused on Jackson's face, finally seeing that Jackson's lip was split and there was blood on his shirt.

"Well, fuck you," said Aiden. "You earned that."

"Did I?" asked Jackson.

"Yes! You keep trying to steal my sister. She's *my* sister."

"No one's saying she's not," said Jackson.

"Yeah, then where the fuck is she? I called *her*! She's supposed to be here!"

"Unavoidably detained. She sent me," said Jackson.

"Fuck you. I hate you. You're ruining everything."

"Am I? How?"

Aiden swayed on his feet. He'd felt like he was thinking

through a wall of cotton balls. "Evan might have voted you in, but I didn't. I don't even know why he wants you here."

"He wants a brother."

"Then go be his brother. Stop trying to… You're trying to make us…"

"Yes?"

"She's supposed to be here!" Aiden fell back on what he was sure of. He staggered to the trio of chimney stacks, one of which had a cooler on top of it. He plunged his hand inside, searching for a beer, and felt the gliding kiss of ice against his fingers and the frigid sting of water on his scraped knuckles.

"You know, one of the first things Dominique told me was that you were disappearing. She needed me because you weren't there."

Aiden stopped, one arm still in the cooler, his fingers going numb. "I have stuff," he said. There was no way he could tell Jackson about Number Nine or Cinderella. He would sound insane.

"Apparently," said Jackson, inhaling from his cigarette. Aiden hated those cigarettes. They were matte black with gold filters.

Angrily, Aiden yanked out a bottle and discovered it was some sort of lemonade shit meant to make the girl guests happy. Aiden decided he didn't care and opened it.

"But I think she also meant it in the metaphorical sense," continued Jackson. "You're not happy at your job. You're not happy in your life. And you keep disappearing, one way or another."

Aiden closed his eyes and stared at the sparks on the inside of his eyelids as he leaned against the tallest chimney stack. He took a drink and tasted the sugary sweet over the sour alcohol and lemon.

"I was never supposed to end up like this. I never wanted to be here."

"I do," said Jackson.

"Well, good for fucking you," said Aiden. "But you can't just come in here and be all, bam, mine. Dominique is my sister. I need her. I can't be out here on my own. It's always been her and me."

"Yes," said Jackson, "Evan noticed."

"Fuck you. Evan is abusive."

"Absolutely. Doesn't mean he doesn't feel shut out by the two of you. You know he used to live with Eleanor about half the year before he turned twelve. Then he went to boarding school and was with his father. Then your parents died and suddenly it was the perfect two of you hogging up his grandma's time."

Aiden blinked. "No. That's not… It wasn't like that. He used to target Dominique. He was the one who was always perfect. Never a hair out of place. Come when called. Smile at the right time. Fucking robot on parade."

"Sure. Just the way his father made him. Didn't you used to play with him when you came over to Eleanor's? But then you moved in and it was just you and Dominique against the world. No room for three."

"Stop," said Aiden. "Stop trying to rewrite history."

"I'm not. I'm saying there's more than one history."

"Evan is not my fault!"

"No, Owen, Randall, and Eleanor all had a hand in that mess."

"And you think you can fix him?" asked Aiden sarcastically. "If you want a sibling so bad, go take him. Stop trying to steal mine. I may be the only one who notices, but I see it. You can just admit it. You're trying to steal her."

"Yes," said Jackson. "I am."

Aiden stared at him. "What?" he croaked.

"And Evan too. He's a little more challenging in some ways, but I'll worry about him after I worry about you."

"What?" Aiden repeated.

"Well, it's no good to just have a Dominique," said Jackson, breathing smoke out of his nose and Aiden found his shoulder blades digging into the chimney bricks. It was the smoke. He finally saw the family resemblance. It was like Randall stared at him through the haze.

"I need an Aiden too," said Jackson. "I want the complete set. But so far you've been very resistant."

Aiden dropped the bottle of booze and stumbled forward to knock the cigarette out of Jackson's hand.

Jackson looked surprised.

"It's bad for you," said Aiden. He couldn't bring himself to say the truth.

"OK," said Jackson.

Aiden fell onto the lawn chair next to him.

"You need to stop with the drugs," said Jackson.

"Evan does them."

"Evan's damaged. You're not. You're just trying to escape. Go look for a different escape."

"I'm allowed to have bad habits," complained Aiden.

"Certainly. Just not ones that will kill you. Dominique would be very upset."

"Like you care what she wants!"

"Of course, I care," said Jackson, reaching into his pocket. "What good is having a sister if I don't care what she wants?"

Aiden stared at Jackson angrily. "You make no sense."

"This is where you're going to go," he said, handing him a card. "I made you an appointment for Monday at six."

"I'm not going to rehab."

"It's more like rehab light. You don't have to stay there. You just have appointments after work."

"Fuck you," said Aiden, but he didn't let go of the card. Jackson didn't think he needed full rehab, so maybe he wasn't a total fuck up?

"And this is the card for a guy down at the ACLU. You're going to volunteer legal services for them."

"No," said Aiden sitting up. "No, I'm not part of Grandma's bullshit. I don't go in the fucking newsletter."

"Eleanor's not going to know."

Aiden paused. "You're going to tell her."

"Why would I tell her?"

"That's why you're here, isn't it? To keep us in line for her."

Jackson grinned and his head rocked back in an almost laugh. "This is why I need the complete set." He leaned back, lying down on the lounger next to Aiden's. "You're all so smart. And yes, that is why Eleanor came to get me."

"So you're going to tell her," repeated Aiden gloomily. He would have liked helping the ACLU. He'd enjoyed the criminal law he'd done on Jackson's case.

"No," said Jackson.

Aiden looked at his cousin. Jackson was draped across the lounger and looked relaxed as he stared up at the stars. "Why not?" Aiden asked tiredly. "Why wouldn't you tell her?"

"Brothers first," said Jackson.

Aiden considered that. He felt tired and bruised. He was fine with that feeling physically. His body was used to it. But he was reaching the end of his rope emotionally.

"You can't fix Evan," said Aiden.

"Why not?" asked Jackson.

"Dominique…" Aiden began hesitantly.

"You don't think she would prefer to have him be better?"

"There's a lot of stuff," said Aiden. "It's not just the decade of shit with Evan, but all the shit with our parents. I'm not even sure he wants to be better."

"I'm absolutely certain that he does."

"Why?"

"Because he is never alone with Dominique."

"That's because we make sure…" Aiden trailed off. When was the last time Evan had even gone into the house when it had just been Dominique? "We used to make sure…"

"You set the rules," said Jackson, "and Evan obeys. You don't obey if you don't care. He rages and snaps, but he obeys all the same."

"What if I don't want a brother?" Aiden demanded, knowing he sounded childish.

"Then you should have thought of that before you got me out of prison," Jackson said calmly.

"I just want it to be like when we were kids," said Aiden. "I want my mom back. I want my dad. I want Evan to be OK. I just want… I didn't want it to turn out like this."

"And I don't want to be alone anymore," said Jackson.

There was the sound of feet on the stairs and then Dominique burst through the doorway wearing a black cocktail dress. She walked quickly over and looked down at them.

"You have a black eye," she said accusingly to Aiden.

Aiden put his hand up and touched his face. "No wonder that hurts."

Dominique put her hands on her hips and looked exasperated. "You're a fucking idiot! What the fuck are you trying to do? Do you think I want one less family member? What the fuck is wrong with you?"

"I'm fucked up?" he offered.

Suddenly she dropped down onto the lounger and hugged him, squishing painfully against his bruised ribs.

"I'm sorry I'm late," she said with her face on his shoulder, "but I was at a party with Grandma and I didn't think you'd want her to know."

Aiden processed that. "Brothers first?" he asked, patting her back.

"Right," she said, sitting up. She gave a sniff and wiped her eyes. "You can't keep doing this," she said. "Please stop."

"Decision time," said Jackson.

Aiden looked at Dominique, then over at Jackson, who was pulling a pack of Sobranie cigarettes out of his pocket. Jackson didn't want to be alone. He looked at Dominique. Their parents were never coming back. But at least Jackson *wanted* to make Evan OK. Maybe Aiden could get some of what he wanted. But that meant that Jackson had to get his wish. "I've decided…" said Aiden. He transferred the business cards Jackson had given him to the other hand and then reached out and took the pack of cigarettes away from his cousin. "I've decided I'm going to go to"—he looked at the card—"New Beginnings on Monday. And that Jackson is quitting smoking." He threw the pack overhand and they all watched it arc over the edge of the building. Getting a new brother didn't mean he had to be the little brother.

"Well, that's probably good," said Dominique. "It makes him look like Uncle Randall and it creeps me out."

"Reason enough to quit," said Jackson with a wry smile.

After that night, Aiden had spent months waiting for his grandmother to make some comment on his ACLU work and demand that he write up something for the newsletter. The request and the commentary never came. But it was another year before he really believed that Jackson hadn't told her. He supposed that he could have told Jackson the other stuff then. Or told him any time in the two years since. But he'd never even told Dominique. Number Nine and Cinderella were a secret that was all his, and Aiden liked that. On the other hand, he also liked that Evan was civil at dinners, laughed a little these days, and came to see him at the office when there was a problem. Evan might not be entirely better, and Jackson might pry too damn much, but life was infinitely better than four years ago.

Jackson had earned some amount of honesty.

"I really don't know what you're talking about," said Aiden with a smile, ignoring the way Pete was watching them with raised eyebrows. "I did not touch Mr. Huang. But it is possible that I may have dropped his wallet in a urinal."

Jackson laughed in the whole-hearted way that always made Aiden smile. "How did you manage that?"

"It's easy," said Aiden with a shrug. "I used to do it all the time with photographers. If you stay at a place long enough and the photographer is determined to wait, they will eventually get cold and go into the bar across the street. Apparently, the same is true about other people who follow you. So I waited until he went into a bar, then I ducked out the back of the art gallery and went into the bar and grabbed his wallet from his back pocket. He chased me into the bathroom and I told him to not show up again and tossed the wallet in the urinal. While he was busy trying to retrieve it, I went back outside and caught a cab."

"Nice," said Pete with a nod.

"Thanks," said Aiden, feeling genuinely complimented. "But meanwhile, you didn't look surprised. Who else are they following?"

"Evan called me this morning and said I should do something about the Asian person following him around. I just sent someone over. And Dominique says Max dropped a bag of garbage off the deck and onto someone's head last night. Although, either they aren't following me or they are better than I am. I haven't seen anyone. I'm not sure if my feelings should be hurt or not."

Aiden chuckled, but then frowned. "I don't like this. People should not be allowed to follow my sister around and Evan has enough problems without adding a bullshit stalker to the list. Can't you"—he waved a hand at Jackson—"squash them in some way."

"I was going to ask if you wanted me to. Odds are that it's Zhao related."

Aiden grimaced. Of course it was. "What do you think they're doing?"

"Opposition research," said Jackson with a shrug. "Looking for something they can use for leverage or just getting to know us."

"I would think," said Aiden, "that by now people would have gotten the message that we don't want to be known."

"You would think," said Pete, looking amused.

"What have you found about the Zhaos?" asked Aiden.

"Bai Zhao, fifty-eight, father of three, married to Liu. The family recently moved to New York. Took a year-long lease on a penthouse on the west side. He founded Zhao Industries the year that Bo died. He used investment capital from a small contingent of investors and built up the manufacturing side of the business first. Rumor has it that about ten years ago he fought off a take-over from some of the original investors for control and leveraged his clout within the Chinese political party to do it. That makes him anchored to China pretty heavily, but at the same time, he hasn't been back to China since. He even moved his mother out of China to live with him and his family. His oldest daughter recently married a German businessman. Middle daughter is at Oxford. Youngest daughter, Lilly, is in high-school. Just enrolled at St. Lucius. Then we get to the interesting one—his niece, Ella Zhao."

"Niece?" asked Aiden. Jackson nodded to Pete, who took a cautious sip of his coffee before speaking.

"Yeah. Niece. Ella Zhao is Bo Zhao's daughter. The most info I can find on her is that she moved in with them five or six years ago. Said to be living with her mom before that. Not sure where. Bai put her through law school, and she's spent the last year terrorizing everyone who dared to step into a courtroom with her. She's my bet for who he'll put in charge of whatever they're planning."

"Bo's daughter... This is starting to feel more and more personal," said Aiden.

"Agreed," said Jackson. "I'm going to reach out to some people in the police department and see what I can dig up on Bo's death."

"Do we want to know?" asked Aiden.

"What do you mean?" asked Jackson, taking his feet off the desk.

Aiden hesitated. "I mean, what if we find out that the reason they're mad at us is because Randall or Owen actually did something?"

"Are you saying that Randall or Owen killed this guy?" asked Pete.

"No," said Aiden. "I mean... probably not. But if even half the stories I've heard about them are true, the two of them were walking HR-violation nightmares. If they weren't dead, they'd be getting hashtag Me Too'd the fuck out of town. Legally speaking, it might be better if we had plausible deniability."

Jackson popped another bubble, but if bubbles could be thoughtful, this one was it. "I'll keep that in mind," he said at last.

"What does that mean?"

"There are times when it is better for Eleanor if Eleanor doesn't know things. I'm used to making that judgement call. I'll keep that in mind with this issue."

"But you'll still know about it," said Aiden.

"Not that you'll know," said Jackson.

Aiden stared at his cousin. "How many secrets do you keep?" he asked.

"At least as many as you," said Jackson.

"I don't have any secrets," said Aiden, plastering on the sunny smile that was his usual armor. "Everyone knows everything about me. My biography is practically on page six."

"Uh-huh," said Jackson, who looked like he didn't believe the sunny smile one bit. "Meanwhile, what do you want me to do about our special new friends? You said squash them, but is that really what you want? Legally speaking."

Aiden thought about it. "Yes," he said at last. "Fuck them. This is our town and our family. They've come here to take what belongs to us and I don't give two shits if one of their dogs of war gets his nose swatted."

Jackson smiled. "Nose swatting. Check. I can do that. What's our next official move?"

"Nothing," said Aiden, shaking his head. "We have to wait for them. They'll do something. Probably small. A letter of some kind. And if we were clueless and stupid, we might just give them what they want to make them go away."

"But we're not clueless and stupid?" asked Jackson.

"Not generally," said Aiden. "I mean, periodically yes, about women, booze and that forty-eight-piece box of McNuggets."

"Yeah, McNuggets," murmured Pete, nodding sympathetically.

"Oh, please," said Jackson. "Like Rico lets you eat McNuggets."

"Of course not," said Pete. "Why do you think I had to eat all forty-eight in one go and destroy the evidence?"

"Yes!" exclaimed Aiden, pointing emphatically at Pete. "He understands."

"Both of you need to stop dating vegetarians," said Jackson.

"Rico is not a vegetarian," said Pete. "He's a pescatarian."

"Oh, totally different," said Jackson, rolling his eyes.

"It is," said Aiden. His diet had gotten thrown completely out of whack when dating the Channel Four weather girl, who should have come with a warning label for eating disorders. "They eat fish." Jackson raised his eyebrows. "Which you already know but were being sarcastic about. Right. Anyway. What was the question? Whether or not we're stupid or clueless?"

Jackson nodded, looking enormously entertained at Aiden's expense.

"When it comes to matters like legal matters?" asked Aiden, trying to muster his dignity. "No, we're neither stupid nor clueless."

Ella – Declarations of War

Ella looked at her reflection in the full-length window of the conference room. She had put her hair up and wore what she thought of as her Bette Davis pantsuit. It was cut like 1940s menswear, and she usually liked it because it made her feel like one of those broad-shouldered dames who took command of everything. But looking at herself in the wavy reflection, she wondered if it had been a mistake. Maybe she should have gone for something frothy and feminine. She had wanted the Deveraux lawyers to take her seriously, but maybe she should have allowed them to misjudge her. She decided probably not. She had a hard enough time getting respect in a courtroom already. She probably didn't need to feed into it.

The other Zhao lawyers were sitting to the right of Bai. Their backs were ram-rod straight and they sat with perfect formality, hands folded over their briefing files. They might as well be robots. Ella thought of them as Tic, Tac, and the bald one was definitely Toe.

In her brief, post-law-school career she had worked only for her uncle, and she was aware that he had dropped her like a shark into bigger and bigger pools of water, testing her skills against larger and larger problems. She had met each challenge with ease. It had not been until they had arrived here that she'd understood. What he'd been training her for was this—claiming a controlling spot on the board of DevEntier Industries for her uncle.

There was just one teensy little problem. The shares necessary to get on the board were never going to become available. Charles MacKentier Jr. and Evan and Jackson Deveraux had controlling interest of the company and there just weren't the shares needed in the marketplace to force his way onto the board. But when her uncle found a decades old email from Randall Deveraux to Bo Zhao buried in the Zhao Industry servers, it had felt like the winning lottery ticket. It was thin, at best. The words were vague and the promises merely implied, but it was enough to do what Bai wanted—wrestle shares away from the Deveraux cousins.

"Who do you think they'll send?" asked Bai. "They won't actually come themselves."

Ella knew who the *they* was in that statement. He meant Jackson and Evan. But sometimes she wondered if he meant Randall and Owen. It was becoming increasingly apparent that Bai hated the deceased Deveraux brothers.

"No," said Ella. "Odds are they'll send Jerome Strand. He's Harvard Law. Good at contracts and cheating on his wife. They might also send Aiden Deveraux for the look of things. He goes to the board meetings for them."

"The stupid one," said Bai, nodding. He had read the same background reports she had.

"Our research indicates," said Tic, "that Strand will negotiate and settle on *some* amount of shares, but not all. We doubt that he is aware of our share purchases, so whatever he gives us should be enough. We do not think anyone at DevEntier has been aware of our efforts."

Bai stared at the lawyer, who promptly went back to sitting quietly.

"What do you think Ella?" asked Bai, still watching Tic for movement.

"I think it depends on how annoyed Evan Deveraux is," said Ella. "The background file indicates that Evan can be… territorial. Jackson does not appear to care about DevEntier or follow the stock market at all. I think Evan is the one we have to worry about. I put in a few calls to people who have worked with him that are also in our contact list. They say he can be hell to negotiate with."

"Who did you call?" asked Bai, looking up at her in surprise.

"Eizo Matsuda in Tokyo. He said Evan was an ice-cold bastard who he really liked."

Bai snorted. "Sounds like the kind of person Eizo would like."

"It was his estimation that if we're going up against the Deveraux, we should prepare for war."

"That was all he said?" asked Bai, looking skeptical.

"No. He invited me to dinner next time I was in Tokyo and then said that you should go fuck yourself," said Ella.

Bai grinned. "He's still pissed about the Cormoran deal."

"Yes," said Ella.

"It's not my fault he underestimated you," said Bai, looking entirely pleased with Matsuda's anger.

The conference room door opened, and the secretary bowed in Aiden Deveraux, followed by Jerome Strand.

"Thank you," Aiden said, smiling at the secretary, who blushed and smiled back.

Prince Charming was everything that the society pages said he was. He stood at probably just six feet, with hair the color of brightly polished brass, and shoulders that proclaimed a substantial workout regimen. Aiden Deveraux was utterly stunning. Ella blinked. Pictures had not at all captured his radiating attractiveness. Now she wished she'd gone with frothy and feminine.

"Hello, everyone," said Aiden, beaming. "It's so nice of you all to be here today."

As if he had called the meeting. His ego was so staggering that she was speechless.

"Sorry I'm late," he said sweetly. He beamed around the table, turning the laser beam of his blue eyes on each of them. Ella found herself not only speechless, but holding her breath as he turned to her, eyeing her with more than a spark of curiosity.

"No, scratch that," he said turning away from her. "I'm not sorry. I'm never on time. You probably ought to get used to it. Is this for me?" He gestured to the chair at the opposite end of the table from Bai and sat down without waiting for an answer. Jerome stood behind him but didn't sit down.

Ella took a deep breath, preparing to regain control of the meeting and her emotions. Whatever momentary and ridiculous flutter of attraction she felt for this egotistical asshat was clearly merely a product of his physical beauty.

"So," he said, looking down the table. "Let's see you must be…Li, Chen and… Chang?" He pointed to each of the lawyers in turn and Ella watched their eyes widen in shock. "And you," he focused on Ella and smiled. It was a good smile. She was willing to bet he had girls falling over themselves with that smile. Ella steeled herself to look unimpressed. "Must be Ella Zhao."

She felt Bai stiffen as Aiden ignored him entirely. The insult was carelessly delivered, but she doubted it was an accident.

"Mr. Deveraux," said Ella coolly. "I take it you are here to respond on behalf of your cousins?"

"I am," he said, nodding. "And the response is… no."

"I don't believe the question was yes or no," said Ella. "The question was: *when* will you be handing over the stocks that were promised to Bo Zhao?"

"That decades old email you provided was cute. It really gave me a chuckle. But considering that Bo Zhao was never more than a contract employee of DevEntier, and that email is vague at best, the answer is: no. We will not be giving the Zhao any shares or financial compensation at this time or in the future."

Ella frowned at Aiden. She wasn't sure where to start with the entire truck-load of bullshit that he had just shoveled at her. She had expected push-back. She hadn't expected complete repudiation. The idea that Bo hadn't been employed by DevEntier was ludicrous. She remembered his business cards sitting on the shelf in his office at home. They had all read: DevEntier, Bo Zhao. He'd made them put his name in Chinese too.

"Bo worked for DevEntier," said Bai. "He worked for Randall."

"Lots of people worked at DevEntier with Randall," said Aiden with a shrug. "That doesn't entitle them to stock."

"It was promised," barked Bai, slamming his hand down on the table. Tic, Tac, and Toe jumped at the noise.

"Even if it was promised to *him*, a story we strongly take issue with, that entitles *you* to exactly nothing," said Aiden.

Bai opened his mouth to respond and Ella stepped on his foot. "And that is a position that *we* strongly take issue with," replied Ella.

Aiden grinned at her and she got the feeling that it wasn't in any way forced. "We thought that you might."

Her uncle's lawyers were quaking in their loafers and Aiden Deveraux was enjoying himself.

"Are you saying that you do not intend to negotiate?" she asked, keeping her tone coolly disinterested. Showing that she was the least bit impressed would undercut everything she was trying to do.

"We have no intention whatsoever, Ms. Zhao. This visit is simply a courtesy to respond to your letter in person." He leaned back in his chair, a cocky smirk on his face, as if daring her to come at him.

"Hm," said Ella, tilting her head slightly and giving him a soft smile. "And did you make this decision?" she asked.

"Excuse me?" his eyes narrowed, and Ella let her smile widen. Men hated it when she questioned their decision-making capabilities.

Even the most confident could lose control of their tempers and go off script.

"Are you sure you don't need to run this course of action by someone? I hesitate to suggest that perhaps someone with more experience might be better suited to taking control of the situation." She turned her smile on Jerome Strand who stared back at her impassively. "But you might not be as familiar with matters as perhaps you should be."

The fact that Jerome didn't take the bait was what she expected from a lawyer of his experience, but the fact that he didn't even twitch made her suspect that Aiden's behavior was *not* a surprise to him. Ella began to get a very bad feeling about their background research on Aiden Devereaux.

"Hm," said Aiden, his smile fading to a patently fake concerned expression. "Well, maybe you're right. I suppose you'd know better than I would. Maybe it *does* help to have your relatives holding your leash while you're trying to do your job." He glanced at Bai, then back at Ella. "Not that I mean to imply that anyone is holding your leash. Or that you have a leash. Sorry, don't pay any attention to me. I always say the wrong thing. Well known fact." He ended on another dazzling smile.

This was exactly why she hadn't wanted Bai to attend this meeting. His very presence undercut her authority. And Aiden Deveraux had spotted the weakness easily. Fortunately, it was not the first time someone had made that accusation and it probably wouldn't be the last. Ella had already put her feelings on that insult aside. She couldn't even hate him for it—she had started the war after all.

"You are—" Bai's voice came out in a growl.

Aiden's words might not have bothered her, but they had angered Bai. Ella put her hand on his shoulder, and he subsided into his chair, but she could feel the angry bunching of his muscles under the suit jacket.

Aiden was watching them closely and she was suddenly aware that she was in the presence of a fighter. Someone cunning and smart who moved quickly and could hit hard. It would have been sexy as hell if she hadn't been the one on the ropes. But she was. She needed the bell to ring so she could regroup.

"To clarify," said Ella, "you are rejecting our claim to DevEntier shares?"

"We are," said Aiden.

"Well, then it would seem, Mr. Deveraux, that we will be seeing each other in court."

"I look forward to it," said Aiden, standing up. "Oh, and"—he waved at Strand—"these are for all of you." Strand placed a stack of envelopes on the table in front of the lawyers and then went to the door. "Have a nice day," said Aiden with a sunny smile.

Jerome held the door open for him, as if Harvard Law grads always acted the part of a doorman, and Aiden sauntered through it. The door swung shut behind them and Tic tentatively opened the letter on top. "We've been served," said Tic sourly.

"What the hell was that?" demanded Bai, looking up at Ella.

"That was a serious error in our profile on Aiden Deveraux," she replied.

"I don't understand why he would bother to show up if he wasn't planning to negotiate," said Tac.

"He wanted to see if his background research was accurate," said Ella. "Which, apparently it was. Or at least, more accurate than ours. He also wanted to let us know what kind of response we would be facing."

"What kind of response are we facing?" asked Bai.

"The kind Eizo Matsuda predicted," said Ella. "This is going to be war."

Aiden – Home Again

"How'd it go?" asked Evan as Aiden shrugged out of his coat and handed it to Theo. Jackson was at the far end of the hall on his phone. From the hard set of his mouth, it was probably something security or Grandma related.

"About as expected," said Aiden. "Bai was surprisingly emotional. Ella was reserved."

And gorgeous. Abso-fucking-lutely gorgeous. Ella Zhao was so hot he felt sunburned just looking at her. She'd been dressed with a man-ish formality that somehow just made her look even more feminine. The contrast between her sharply cut suit jacket and her curves had been sexy as hell. He'd taken one look at her and nearly forgotten what the hell he'd come to say. None of Jackson's background research had indicated she was a perfect ten. It said she was a holy terror in the courtroom. Being gorgeous hadn't even made the list, and after meeting her, it really seemed like it rated a mention.

"Grandma," said Jackson, and his voice had the flat quality that meant he was annoyed. "I think you're overreacting."

Evan and Aiden exchanged looks of trepidation. Aiden was never entirely sure how Jackson managed to persuade their grandmother to do, well, anything. He was aware that Jackson's success rate was far better than his or Evan's, but that didn't mean that Jackson batted a thousand.

"She's an adult," Jackson continued. "It's perfectly reasonable."

"Dominique?" whispered Evan, and Aiden was surprised to see that Evan looked genuinely concerned.

"I don't know," Aiden whispered back. He didn't think

Dominique was up to anything that Grandma could be upset over, but lately he hadn't exactly been as plugged in to life as he should have been. He felt bad about that, but she had Max and Jackson to rely on and every time Aiden had tried to connect, it seemed like he ended up with a black eye or some other noticeable injury and had to cancel.

"We will discuss it when you get home," said Jackson. "No. We will *discuss* it. You're not going to call her. This is me predicting the future, not Nika making an announcement."

"Did he just tell Grandma not to do something?" asked Evan, looking thrilled and slightly shocked.

Aiden nodded. "I feel like I need popcorn." They turned to watch Jackson, who rolled his eyes at them and turned his back.

"I think he's trying to tell us the show's over," said Evan. "Do you think—" he began when there was a knock on the front door.

Theo answered in his usual brisk manner and Charlie MacKentier entered, handing Theo his hat and jacket without looking at the butler. Instead, he surveyed the main hall and grand staircase and then the three Deveraux cousins.

"God, it's been age since I've been here. I need to start making it to the Christmas parties again." Charles MacKentier Jr. was sixty-three with a wide jaw and a face that was settling into hard crags. "Jesus, Ev, you're starting to look like your old man."

Aiden felt himself bristle. Usually he could deal with Charlie's crap, but he was unprepared to have it directed at Evan.

"Hi, Charlie," said Evan, putting a hand on Aiden's shoulder. "How's wife number four? Or is it five? I forget. They all blur together."

Charlie barked out a sharp laugh. "Now you even sound like him. God, he was such an asshole. It's wife number four. She's fine. I assume. I sent her and the kid to Aspen for a couple of weeks.

They were getting on my nerves. I'm getting too old to have toddlers around the place, but the wives all seem to want them. Utterly useless, really. At this point I can't imagine why my father had me."

"Neither can anyone else," said Evan. "Come in and have a drink. Aiden was just about to tell us about his meeting with Zhao."

"Aiden," said Charlie, looking him over. "As usual, you look like someone who listens to his sister about fashion."

"Could be worse," drawled Evan. "He could be listening to *your* sister. Jackson, stop talking to whoever and come pay attention to your money."

Aiden blinked at Evan. It was all textbook Evan, except this particular Evan hadn't been around in so long Aiden had forgotten what he was like.

"If you insist," said Jackson, dropping his phone into his pocket. "But I reserve the right to space out and run off when I get what I'm sure will be an urgent text."

"No," said Evan, leading the way into the formal living room. "We already have Aiden for those things. If you want to leave, you will have to be epically classless and completely street."

"*Brat, ty ubivayesh' menya,*" said Jackson, in Ukrainian.

"Yes, exactly like that," said Evan, flashing a smile that was real enough that Aiden wondered what Jackson had said. Aiden glanced at Charlie and saw an angry expression cross his face. Apparently, Charlie didn't like being cut out of the conversation. Or maybe it was just that Evan sounded a little *too* much like Owen.

"Theo," said Jackson, as he closed the drawing room door behind them, "don't worry about the drinks. I'll pour."

The drawing room was decorated in a sort of sixties rendition of classic that included a tan wood sideboard where Grandma kept the snooty liquor. Jackson set himself to the task of pouring while the others seated themselves.

"None for me," said Aiden, choosing to play into his own stereotype. He opened the door and bellowed out into the hall. "Theo, can I get a Coke?"

"Yes, Mr. Aiden," called Theo as he returned from hanging up Charlie's coat.

"Right," said Aiden, smiling at all of them. "Now that caffeine is on the way, we can chat."

"I'm awfully sorry you boys are having this trouble," said Charlie, settling into the middle of one of the opposing couches. It was an asshole position to take. It meant that either someone had to crowd onto the corner of his couch, that the three Deveraux had to crowd onto the other couch together, or that one of the cousins had to take the awkward slipper chair that was too low for any of them. Jackson filled a scotch and Aiden took it over to Charlie, dropping it into his hand.

"If it wasn't us, it would be you," said Aiden. "DevEntier holds the patent on that solar array linking system and a few other innovations. I think that's what they want."

"I didn't think you were paying attention to that," said Charlie, eyeing Aiden sternly.

"Do you think we just send him to the board meetings to look good and chew gum?" asked Evan. "That would be ridiculous."

"Particularly since that's my job," said Jackson. He brought a drink to Evan and sat down on the opposite end of Evan's couch, leaving Aiden to fiddle with the knick-knacks and lean on the fireplace mantle. Aiden adjusted the clock to the correct time and tried not to stare at his cousins. Sometimes they really did look like brothers. Not just in the arch of their noses, which he knew he shared, but something in the way they made space for each other as they moved around the room—like large predatory cats on the hunt. They seemed to do it instinctively and Aiden felt like it was something he didn't know how to do. It gave him an aggravating twinge of jealousy.

Charlie took a careful sip of his drink, his eyes on Jackson. "Gum chewing? Is that your job?" he asked. "It seems like you must be doing a bit more. What are you up to these days?"

"Oh, Charlie," said Evan, before Jackson could answer. "You've known the Deveraux for how long? Why would you think there was something new to learn?"

Evan's answer surprised Aiden. It was a beautifully executed deflection that simultaneously played to Charlie's ego—assuring him that he knew more about the Deveraux than any outsider—and also made it difficult to persist in questioning without being rude or exposing his lack of knowledge. Evan had also managed the neat trick of neither lying nor making any statements on what exactly Jackson did for the family. Not that it was a secret exactly. Anyone who dealt with Eleanor knew that Jackson handled her security, but Dominique said that most of the people in Charlie's kind of society assumed that was just code for sponging off the family money.

"I just don't hear much about any of you these days," said Charlie with an easy smile. "Randall and Owen were so much easier to keep tabs on. They did like to make a splash."

"Evan and Jackson have a better lawyer," said Aiden.

"Point taken," said Charlie, with a chuckle.

"Your Coca-Cola, Mr. Aiden," said Theo, entering the room with a tall glass on a silver tray.

"Thanks, Theo."

The butler nodded and exited. Theo was well known for his impassive façade, but Aiden thought he caught a side-long look at Charlie. Aiden wasn't the only one who disliked having him in the house.

"So you think it's about our solar patents? You don't think it's personal?"

"Why would it be personal?" asked Jackson. "The paperwork you sent over showed that Bo Zhao was only a contract employee."

"Randall could make enemies out of just about anyone if you gave him long enough," said Charlie with a shrug.

"Are you sure there weren't any other records?" asked Aiden. "That file was pretty thin."

"We had a server crash about ten years ago and we lost a lot of the older HR records. There might be more in project record storage, but they wouldn't pertain to his work status—just the projects he worked on. Bo Zhao was a contract employee doing project management. China had just started into big manufacturing at the time. Randall needed someone who could speak the language and who could make sure our parts didn't come back fucked up."

Evan frowned. "I knew he was Chinese, but I remember him sounding British."

"That's how I remember it," agreed Charlie. "I think he learned English in Europe. He was multi-lingual. Like I said, that's probably why Randall wanted him. But we would never have made him a full hire. Like you said—he was Chinese. And we were chasing a lot of DoD contracts at the time. A Chinese national on the team would have been a problem."

"Do you think Randall ever promised him shares?" asked Jackson, and Charlie snorted in derision.

"Ask your brother. Cousin. Whatever. Randall might have *said* all kinds of things, but I doubt he meant it. And he certainly wouldn't have put it in writing."

"We'll be staking our case on that," said Aiden. "If there's anything else, you need to tell us now. We can't afford any surprises and you can't afford for us to lose."

"Aiden, you almost sounded like a real Deveraux just then," said Charlie, turning to look at him with a grin.

"Couldn't possibly," said Aiden, taking a sip of his soda. "Everyone knows I'm the nice one. Practically famous for it."

"Yes," said Charlie with a laugh. "Prince Charming. What does that make those two?"

"Evil step-sisters?" suggested Jackson.

Evan gave Jackson a genuine look of amusement but turned back to Aiden. "If you say a word about frogs, I will tell Grandma about Stacy Kasich."

"Wasn't going to!" exclaimed Aiden, laughing in surprise.

"And I'm going to suggest you keep it that way," said Charlie, earning an angry look from Evan. Charlie put his glass down on the coffee table and stood up. "Anyway, it sounds like you've got everything well in hand, but let me know if you need anything else from me."

"We'll do that," said Evan without getting up.

"Aiden," said Charlie, turning to him and holding out his hand, "I'll see you at next month's board meeting?"

"See you then," agreed Aiden with his usual empty smile while shaking Charlie's hand.

Evan and Jackson were silent until they heard the front door close.

"He didn't answer the question," said Jackson. "You asked if there was anything else we needed to know and he avoided."

"My fault," said Aiden. "I didn't phrase it as a question. I left him too much wiggle room."

"What do we think it means?" asked Evan.

"At a guess?" said Aiden. "There may have been a promise for shares, and he knows it."

"The paper trail is on our side though," said Evan. "We could try project record storage or whatever bullshit Charlie just said, but I wouldn't even know where to start or what projects to ask for. I'd probably have to dig up any records from Randall that we have before we could even start looking at DevEntier. And I'm not sure we want to."

"Agreed," said Aiden wholeheartedly. The last thing he wanted was to send his cousin down a rabbit hole of old family memories for what was possibly a wild goose chase but would certainly be an entire zoo's worth of unpleasant memories for Evan. "Everything else Charlie said is consistent. I think we have to proceed as planned," Aiden continued, but Jackson was noticeably silent, and Aiden raised an eyebrow at him. "You have other thoughts?"

"When do I not?" asked Jackson, seeming to rouse himself. "Although, at the moment my thought is to ask about Stacy Kasich."

Evan began to laugh, and Aiden glared at him.

"That is *very* ancient history," said Aiden, "and I don't think it needs to be revisited."

"Let us just say that the Three Stooges have nothing on a teenage Aiden trying to sneak a girl out of this house."

Aiden shook his head. "It was like Grandma was everywhere. It was enough to give a guy nightmares."

Evan chuckled, then subsided, scrutinizing Aiden critically. "You met with the Zhao. How ugly is this likely to get? If this is going to be an exercise in dredging up Randall and Dad's finer moments, I'd almost rather give them the shares. Grandma doesn't need that."

"Forget about Grandma," said Jackson swiftly.

"I don't really think that's an option," Evan replied, looking startled.

"Randall and Owen aren't going away," said Jackson. "As a threat, I mean. And it might be uncomfortable for Grandma, but she's had a long time to prepare and practice for having them thrown in her face. They don't affect her."

"They might not affect her work," said Evan. "But it will still upset her."

"And again," said Jackson, "I'm telling you to ignore her. Take her out of the equation."

Evan looked like he didn't know what to say.

"I think what Jackson is getting at," said Aiden, more gently, "is that you shouldn't steer your course by what Grandma wants. What do *you* want to do?"

Evan frowned. "What I want doesn't really…" he trailed off. "Well, what do you want?" he asked Jackson.

"I want to do what you want to do," Jackson replied, and Evan looked annoyed.

"Stop trying to bully me into making a decision."

"Then make a decision," said Jackson.

"I feel weird telling Aiden what to do."

"Since when?" asked Aiden. "I think you told me what tie to wear for every fucking public appearance that Grandma ever made us go to when we were kids."

"That was for your own good," said Evan. "I let you pick *one* time and you came out in a turquoise clip-on bow tie. Where you even found such a thing, I will never know."

Aiden grinned. "Came in a joke kit with a matching boutonniere that sprayed water."

Jackson snorted.

"Evan," said Aiden, "this is what I do. If you want me to protect DevEntier, I can do it."

"I'm not Grandma," said Evan. "I don't want to…" He frowned, seeming to search for words.

"Use us," supplied Aiden. "Thank you. I appreciate that. But I am good at my job, and honestly, I would rather be good at my job for you than for my jackass employers."

Evan looked embarrassed. "All right," he said slowly. "Then, no, I don't want to give the Zhao one inch of DevEntier."

Ella – J.P. Granger

"Ella, Ella, Ella," said Lilly, skidding around the corner on the tile floor of the hallway as Ella stepped off the elevator. "Mom's going to ask you if I talked to you about Nora's party and you need to say you thought it was a good idea."

Ella looked skeptically at her younger cousin. "Uh-huh. And why do I think it's a good idea?"

"Because I need to socialize and make friends and I'm not going to do that if I don't go to Nora Lieberman's party."

"Are there going to be boys there?"

"God, I hope so," said Lilly.

"You know your dad's going to flip a biscuit if there are boys there."

"Dad flips a biscuit every time he thinks one of us is possibly getting near a penis. But, I mean, like, half the world is made up of penises, so it's going to happen sooner or later. Also, as daughter number three, I don't see how come he's not used to the idea already."

Ella had to admit that Lilly had a point. She also had to admit that the older she got, the more horrified she was by the things she'd seen at her mother's parties, and she wasn't particularly sure that she wanted sixteen-year-old happy-go-lucky Lilly exposed to anything similar.

"How big is this party?" Ella asked, heading for the kitchen entrance of the apartment. She still wasn't used to the idea that there was a staff entrance on an apartment. It seemed weird. "Is it a 'my parents are away, let's burn this place down' party? Or is it, 'my mom's upstairs doing blow and pretending to be a chaperone?'"

"Those are your only two options?" asked Lilly. "Those are horrible options. I think it's a: my dad is feeling guilty for divorcing my mom so there's a pool party and it's being mostly catered while my dad pretends to grill."

"That's a slightly better option."

"Ella, please," begged Lilly. "You've got to help me. This cannot be like Germany. I was a total outcast in Germany."

"You were thirteen," said Ella. "Everyone is an outcast at thirteen."

"Ellllllllla," whined Lilly, throwing her head back, and slumping her shoulders.

"I'll talk to your mom," said Ella. "We will discuss it. I'm not promising anything."

"OK, cool," said Lilly, immediately perking up. "Do you think you could talk to Dad about it too?"

"Lilly!"

"What? You're the only one he actually listens to. I don't understand why you get to have boyfriends and the none of the rest of us do."

Ella sighed. The reason she got to have boyfriends was because she was discreet and she never bothered to ask Bai if she could or not. Also, with Sabine as a mother, Bai rather obviously assumed that Ella had arrived in a de-virginized state. And Bai, while phobic about discussing matters of sex with all the female members of his family, was practical when it came to matters of barn doors and horses.

"I will think about talking to him," Ella said, taking off her coat as they walked through the kitchen. Liu was working on hiring staff, and soon she wouldn't be able to sneak in and out this way. "Maybe. If it comes up. Where is Uncle anyway?"

"Uh… I think he was talking to some guy in the living room? I don't know. Are you coming to dinner with us? Or are you going to spend more time on case prep?"

"If you roll your eyes any harder, they will fall out of your head," said Ella.

"That's all you do since you got here," complained Lilly as Ella paused to hang her jacket in the hall closet. The Zhao family was used to moving. Any new apartment or house could be home within a week—it was simply a matter of putting up the right decorations. But at the moment, what Ella missed was carpeting. She disliked the slick, cold feeling of the tile in all the halls.

"Well, that's because…" Ella trailed off. Aiden. It was because of Aiden Deveraux. Golden, beautiful, horrible Aiden Deveraux. "This case is really important."

Lilly sighed in disgust. "There are more important things than case prep," she said. "You need to hang out with me."

Ella laughed. "Yeah, all right. Tonight. I'll come to dinner and then we'll stay up late and Fortnite the shit out of some stuff."

"You are such a dork," said Lilly, but she looked happy. The living room door opened just as they arrived in the foyer. "There's Dad," whispered Lilly. "Peace out. Good luck."

"I'm not…" began Ella, but she shook her head as Lilly was already gone.

"Ah, Ella," said Bai, opening the living room door fully. "There you are."

"Well, there's the little lady who's going to take a chunk out of the Deveraux," said the man with him. Ella took one look and instantly disliked him. He was about Bai's age and tall, at least taller than Bai. She thought he was not as tall as Aiden Deveraux. He was hiding a bit of paunch across the middle with a long tie and she suspected he dyed his hair. It was too uniformly dark brown. But it was the eyes that caught her attention—they seemed flat and bitter, as if he were never truly happy with anything he was looking at.

Ella smiled politely, as she did at all her uncle's guests.

"Ella meet J.P. Granger," said Bai.

"Nice to meet you," said Ella, keeping her face impassive. She and Bai would have words later.

"I'm following the DevEntier case with interest," said Granger. "The Deveraux need to be taken down a few notches."

"You dislike them?" she asked.

"You've been out of the country, so maybe you didn't notice the queen bitch Eleanor trying to use her seat in the Senate to interfere with my company."

"Ah," said Ella. "Yes. Absolex." She didn't add that she'd seen enough of the hearings and read enough of the news articles to believe that Eleanor Deveraux's crusade against Absolex had been absolutely justified. J.P. Granger had sold PTSD medication to the VA based on falsified research. "The hearings didn't come to anything?"

"They're still wrapping up their report or whatever," said J.P. dismissively. "Who cares? Politicians should stay out of business. But trust me, every single one of those Deveraux are lying snakes. I mean, hell, one of them has even done time and she's got him running security. What does that say about them?"

"I couldn't speculate," said Ella.

Granger laughed. "Lawyers. All the same no matter what size or how pretty they are. But trust me," he said with a smug grin, "you are going to love me."

"Lawyer," said Ella. "Remember? We're all the same and we don't love anyone."

Granger laughed heartily. "Your uncle has my info. Give me a call sometime." With a cocky little salute Granger showed himself out.

Ella waited until the door was firmly closed before turning to her uncle. "What the hell was that?"

"I've known J.P. for years," said Bai. "

"You've bumped into him at parties for years," corrected Ella. "Why was he here?"

Bai looked a little guilty. "Well, he obviously doesn't like the Deveraux and when he heard that we were going after them he called me."

"And?" demanded Ella.

"He's offering us his opposition research," he said.

"No," said Ella firmly. "We do our own research. That way we know where it comes from and we can assess the risks. Granger is poison."

"He could have good information!" objected Bai.

"If he had anything legal, he would have been using it already," said Ella. "We don't need his kind of help."

"We need any kind of help," snapped Bai.

"No," said Ella. "No, we do not. I want to win as badly as you do, but I am not going to align this family with someone like Granger."

"I make the decisions for this family!" barked Bai.

"Then get yourself another lawyer," said Ella. "Because I won't do it."

"*Nihao*," called Liu, cheerfully, entering the foyer through front door. "We're… back." Liu paused, surveying Ella and Bai with a wary look. Behind her, Bai's mother entered slowly, walking with her cane and bundled up to the ears.

"Bai," said her grandmother in Mandarin, "Leave Ella alone

and come take my coat." Nai only spoke Mandarin, although she understood a fair amount of English.

Bai grunted and went to do as ordered. Liu gave Ella a questioning look. Ella grimaced and headed for her room. His anger at the Deveraux was starting to complicate matters. Her phone beeped in her pocket and she pulled it out to check the text. It was from one of her fight friends. Although *friend* was a loose term. Reluctantly, she opened the message.

Just got a last minute invite – Number Nine is fighting tomorrow night in Jersey. Thought you'd want to know.

Ella's heart took a giant leap in her chest. It seemed like a sign. The trainer had to have told him about her. He was fighting in the States. It had to be for her. He wanted her to find him. This time she would not be late. This time she would get to him in time and then she could stop thinking about Aiden Deveraux.

Aiden – Jersey

"Kid," said Josh as Aiden pulled on the Number Nine mask. "This is a bad idea. I told you about that girl, right?"

Aiden felt the same nervous flutter of excitement as he had the first time Josh said the words. "Yeah, I heard you. But I need this."

"You need to get caught? This one is close to home. And with someone looking for you, it's a bad idea."

"You don't think I can beat this guy?"

"That is *not* it and you know it. You're going to fuck him up as long as you don't get cocky and do something stupid. But this whole thing is cocky and stupid."

"Josh," said Aiden, adjusting his cup and then rolling his shoulders. "I'm going fucking nuts. I have barely left the house in weeks except to go to work or court. My cousin is watching me like a hawk and I'm starting to get weird and talk to house plants."

"Lots of people talk to their plants," said Josh reassuringly.

"But I don't *own* any house plants. I'm talking to the neighbor's ficus, and what's worse is that I think it's starting to resent how much of its time I'm taking up."

Josh chuckled. "We're going to have to get you a cat or something."

"Do we really think I'm ready for that kind of responsibility?" asked Aiden and Josh laughed again.

"Maybe a Roomba then," said Josh. "We'll put ears on it. But either way, this girl is looking for you and that's not good news. No one should know to look for you in the States. This is a sure-fire way to get caught."

Aiden didn't want to explain that if it was the right girl, he wanted to get caught. And a short, dark-haired girl with five hundred dollars… That sounded like a glass slipper shoe-in for Cinderella. He needed to find her. He wanted her to find him. If only so that he could stop thinking about Ella Zhao.

"Not to mention your fucking cousin," continued Josh.

Aiden grunted. Jackson was a different problem all together. Leverage was difficult to acquire with Jackson. But after four years, Aiden thought he had a pretty good bead on what Jackson wanted. Jackson wanted a family. He'd been absolutely clear on that. And Aiden thought that if Jackson tried to put the squeeze on him about fighting, his leverage was to remove the one thing Jackson wanted—closeness. He could freeze Jackson out and he was pretty sure he could get Dominique to follow suit, at least long enough to get Jackson to cave. It wouldn't be pretty, but Aiden wasn't about to give up the one thing that made him feel really alive outside of a court room. The tough part would be making Jackson believe that Aiden could be enough of an asshole to do it. What no one really understood was that all the Deveraux were assholes. Even Nika. Maybe especially Nika. Aiden tried not to think about that.

"Jackson's guy thinks I'm in my house tucked up safely in bed," said Aiden. "Get me home by dawn and it'll be fine."

Josh looked unconvinced. "Showing up at work with bruises is going to be a problem for you. Not to mention court."

Aiden looked up guiltily.

"What?" asked Josh, clearly reading Aiden's expression despite the mask.

"It's not like I was putting maximum effort into my job before, but with this DevEntier mess in my lap, I've been blowing it off worse than ever. Honestly, I've been thinking about quitting."

Josh let out a whistle. "That's a big step. Are you sure?"

"No," said Aiden. "Not at all. But it's like this case has given me a serious case of the I-don't-wannas at work. I'm not sure what I'm going to do."

Josh shrugged. "What's your family going to say if you quit?"

"Don't know," said Aiden. "Grandma might blow a gasket. We'll have to see about the others. Maybe if I do it right, I can get Jackson to smooth it over with Grandma."

Josh laughed. "Why don't you just tell Jackson what you're doing? If you trust him to help you smooth the road with your grandma, why not this?"

"Because…" Aiden petered out. "Because this is mine," he said at last.

Josh shook his head. "Well, good luck, I guess. Did I tell you I talked to a friend of mine that knows Jackson?"

"No! What did he say?" Aiden was fascinated. Getting information on Jackson was so rare that he'd generally stopped trying.

"This guy I know, he's ex-Navy SEAL and he goes shooting at the same range as your cousin. He says not to get in front of him… ever. Apparently, Jackson's a dead eye. If you don't want to get shot by Jackson, you'd better sneak up behind him."

Aiden chuckled. "I think you'd have to get up pretty early in the morning for that. Or better yet, do what I do, and make sure he doesn't want to shoot you in the first place."

"Yeah, easy for you to say, you're not sending out his favorite cousin to get pummeled."

Aiden flashed a grin. "Don't worry. Nika's his favorite. I'm probably ranking third. You'd barely get a flesh wound."

"Ha. Ha," said Josh sourly.

"Look," said Aiden. "Fighting in Jersey for a bunch of mob guys and Italian Stallions isn't my favorite plan either. But I need something and there's no way I can get out of the country until this court case is over, so this is it. Just make sure the car is ready to go and we'll get the hell out of here before the guy even hits the ground."

"Yeah, OK," said Josh, nodding. "I'll have Donny ready with the car. But I just want it on record that I'm not happy about this."

"The court stenographer is typing it in right now," said Aiden.

"You're so full of shit."

"Dude, I've been talking to a ficus. I don't know what you expect."

Josh shook his head. "Come on, genius. Let's run some drills. Get you warmed up."

Aiden pulled his focus to the drills, trying to put expectations of anything else out of his head. Even the worst opponent could trip up a good fighter who wasn't paying attention. He only had to be unlucky once and everything would come crashing in on him. Josh's mantras echoed in his head: do the drills, do the work, do what winners do. He kept his earbuds in, trying to block out the sounds of the other fights and the crowd. It was never good to look too closely at the crowds. If he did, he'd realize how much he despised them. They weren't fans of fighting, they were fans of violence, and he was feeding it. Aiden tried not to think about what that meant about him and what he liked.

Finally, it was his turn. Since he didn't fight in the States very much, he was an undercard. That didn't bother him, except that he usually didn't get good fighters that way. And he liked good fighters. He liked to have at least the chance of losing.

Tonight's fight was in a construction site for an unfinished office building. The wide cement columns had been strung with lights and paper lanterns. The crowd was Jersey Shore all the way and the ground was littered with red solo cups. The ring, if you could call it that, was a square of concrete that had been marked off by un-padded jersey barriers. There wouldn't be any advantage to hitting the side of the ring tonight. He could see that several of the cement edges were already smeared with blood. Aiden started to wonder if Josh was right and maybe this wasn't the best plan ever. But then, he thought that about every fight.

His opponent tonight was someone going by the name Tear-gas. He was tanned and buff in the rounded, unchiseled way that indicated steroid use. He was an inch or two taller than Aiden and probably had a good twenty pounds over him. Aiden took a long stride and hopped up on the cement barrier for a moment, looking down at his opponent and the ring before dropping inside. There was one ref—a greasy looking goomba with a pistol tucked in his waist band. That wasn't totally uncommon, but it didn't mean Aiden liked it.

The ref offered to let them shake hands—Teargas declined. Aiden shrugged. Shake or no shake, it was all the same to him. Then the fight started. From the roar of the crowd, Aiden could tell that his opponent was a crowd favorite. Teargas strode forward, his hands low around his middle. Aiden kept his guard where it was, high around his face. He could hear the jeers. Caution was appar-ently for sissies. He let Teargas swing first—a big left and a wide right as he advanced forward.

Aiden slid off to the side, ducking under the long meaty paw and drove two sharp punches into the mid-section. Teargas grunted and pivoted, swinging again. Aiden circled, stepping closer, advanc-ing in tighter. He feinted with a jab and threw his other hand high and wide, then bringing it down hard in a ridge-hand. Teargas stag-gered back and Aiden kicked out in a front kick, advancing in his turn. Teargas stumbled from the impact, nearly sitting down on a jersey barrier, but he was pushed off by the crowd and shoved back toward Aiden. Teargas lunged forward and Aiden tossed out a hard cross to his jaw just for being stupid. But he'd underestimated the sheer mass of Teargas and found himself being ensnared in a tackle. Aiden went down, feeling the hard bite of concrete on his exposed back. He rolled swiftly into an upper position, and swung his legs away, then drove a quick knee into Teargas's ribs and was quickly back on his feet.

Teargas came up fast and mad, spitting out his mouthguard and swinging for Aiden in fury. Aiden blocked and avoided, circling the ring. The music was blaring, and Aiden found himself moving in rhythm to the heavy bass. Josh always yelled at him for this. If his opponent figured it out, moving to the rhythm was too easy to predict. But Aiden had found his groove and shifted his footwork to move faster. Teargas was a bully and Aiden didn't like bullies. He dove in, tagged Teargas in the ribs again and bounced out. Same spot. Just to piss him off. Aiden couldn't stop himself from smiling. This was exactly what he needed.

Teargas saw the smile and roared in fury. Teargas took a step forward as the bell rang. Aiden backed up toward his corner, not taking his eyes off Teargas.

Aiden spit out his mouthguard into Josh's hand and took a swig of water from the bottle Josh was holding in the other. "Well, now that you've pissed him off," said Josh, "go finish him off and let's get out of here."

"I'm just starting to have fun," said Aiden.

"When you have fun, nothing good happens," said Josh. "Just get in there and get it done. Don't get fancy." He shoved the mouthguard back in and swabbed Aiden down with a towel. It was only then that Aiden felt the warm trickle of blood on his back from his early trip down to the concrete. The bruises and lumps sucked, but it was the stinging scratches and tears that hurt the most the next day.

The bell rang again. Teargas and he both advanced out into the ring, but before either could throw a move, there was a scream from the audience and a woman tumbled over the jersey barrier and into the ring. She scrambled up and attempted to run, but a man came over after her and grabbed her by the hair. Aiden took one look at her terrified eyes and did what he knew he shouldn't—he took two swift steps and punched her attacker in the face. The guy went down like a sack of potatoes, blood gushing from his mouth and nose, but before Aiden could do anything else, he heard a roar from Teargas. Aiden managed to only half pivot and brace for impact before they went down in a wild tangle. Aiden wrapped his legs around Teargas and hugged his head, pulling the man tight to him, leaving no room for punching. Teargas struggled and above them, Aiden caught glimpses of the crowd swarming the ring. This was about to become a total shit show. The smell of Teargas—Axe body spray and tanning oil— filled his nose. His vision was now filled with dark hair, and his lungs were flattening with the pressure of the heavy weight on top of him. Aiden could feel the clock ticking. This was about to go all kinds of bad and he was on the ground.

Aiden released Teargas and the fighter sprang up, preparing to punch, but Aiden kicked out, shoving Teargas away from him. Aiden back flipped to his feet. He could hear Josh yelling. He turned, trying spot Josh. Teargas came back and Aiden completed his turn, jumping out in a side-kick. Teargas was unprepared and took the kick full in the face. There was a thud as Teargas hit the floor twitching. There was a moment of silence and then someone came charging at him out of the crowd. Aiden punched him and then ran for his corner, hoping that Josh would meet him.

Josh and Donny were both there. Aiden crashed through them

and as a group they began to make their way toward the back where their car was parked. They were nearly to the car when he became aware that someone was yelling for him.

"Number Nine!"

It was a woman's voice and he turned back toward the sound. The crowd parted for an instant and he saw Ella Zhao smash a guy in the head with a beer bottle. The blood began to pound in Aiden's ears, and he took a step toward her. He needed to help her. She couldn't be here. Another guy lunged at her from the crowd and Aiden snatched up a folding chair and flung it at him. It bounced off, but the man hesitated, turning toward Aiden. But Ella didn't pause, she snatched up the chair and cracked it into the man's skull, then she dropped it, stomped him in the gut, before turning back toward Aiden. Suddenly two guys in black appeared at her side— Aiden recognized one of them as the man whose wallet he'd left in the urinal. Josh grabbed Aiden by the arm, pulling him toward the car. Ella took a last look at Aiden and then seemed to deliberately turn her back. She pointed toward the exit and the security guards began pushing their way through the crowd, following her directions. As usual, Ella didn't need help. She had everything under control. Aiden turned and dove into the car, Josh right behind him, Donny scrambling to hit the gas.

Ella Zhao. At a fight in Jersey. Did she know? She had to know. She couldn't know. What the fuck had just happened?

"What the fuck just happened?" asked Josh, sitting up.

"I'm not entirely sure," said Aiden, trying to play it cool. It was a little hard to do when his heart was hitting his ribs like a damn bongo player.

"We lost out on our prize money," said Donny, from the driver's seat. "That's what happened."

"Fucking Jersey," said Josh.

Ella – Lilly

The judge made his way out of the courtroom as Ella reloaded all her papers into her brief case. She glanced up, pretending to scan the crowd, and took another look at the two gray-suited bodyguards at the back of the courtroom, hoping Aiden hadn't noticed them. She couldn't help feeling that the presence of bodyguards was a massive embarrassment. She was now paying for going to the fight in Jersey with security guards loitering in her shadow.

In all her years of searching for Number Nine, it was the first time that she'd gone home and cried. Six years had only made Number Nine a better fighter. He was graceful, fast, harder than ever and achingly beautiful. Watching him had brought everything rushing back, every tumultuous feeling, every mixed up, heady delirious and crazy dream about him she'd ever had. And he had been right there. She'd been within twenty feet of him and, once again, even if he hadn't known who she was, he'd still tried to help her by throwing that stupid chair. Number Nine was, as always, her hero. And she'd left him behind. Again.

Ella had woken up determined to try to find his trainer again. If Number Nine had gone to the fight in Jersey and if his trainer was in New York, it meant that he had to be close by. She was not going to be deterred.

Except she was being deterred. She wouldn't be doing any investigating any time soon because she had goddamn babysitters dogging her every step. Not that she had time for investigating anyway. Not with Aiden Deveraux countering her every move.

Across the aisle, she heard Aiden make a comment to Jerome and she stole a glance at him from under her lashes. As usual, he looked carelessly fashionable and utterly, annoyingly gorgeous.

It was possible that Aiden might not notice that his *respected opposition council,* as he occasionally termed her, was being followed, but considering all the things he noticed in court and pointed out with maddening persistence, she really couldn't count on it. And if Aiden saw those two bodyguards, then he would know for certain that her uncle really was holding her leash.

She took out her phone and dashed off a message to her uncle.

TELL THEM TO STOP FOLLOWING ME.

Bai's reply was almost immediate.

YOU NEEDED THEM LAST NIGHT.

She hadn't needed them. They had been nice to have, but she could have gotten herself back to her car just fine without them. And because of them she'd missed Number Nine.

I DIDN'T NEED THEM. THEY SCARED OFF THE DEVENTIER EMPLOYEE I WAS TRYING TO FIND.

It was a lie, but at least it justified why she had been there. Not that Bai would believe it.

CALL THEM OFF. THEY ARE EMBARRASSING AND IT MAKES ME LOOK WEAK IN FRONT OF THE DEVERAUX TEAM.

I WANT YOU TO BE SAFE.

IT'S A NEW YORK COURTHOUSE. WHAT DO YOU THINK IS GOING TO HAPPEN?

IF I CALL THEM OFF YOU HAVE TO PROMISE NOT TO GO SOMEWHERE DANGEROUS.

That was Bai, always willing to negotiate. On the other hand, she actually couldn't think of anywhere else she would go that would be dangerous. At least not until she got a lead on the trainer or Number Nine. Currently, she had zero leads, so it was an easy promise to make.

FINE. I PROMISE. BUT I WANT THEM TO LEAVE NOW.

A moment later, the security guards stood and exited the courtroom. Ella felt smug, until she saw Aiden looking thoughtfully after them.

"So, Mr. Deveraux," said Ella, stepping out into the aisle, hoping to distract him, "will you be in attendance at the bank?"

"Of course," he said with a smile. She hated that damn smile. It was too nice. Too charming. Too… Aiden Devereaux. Why did he have to be so good looking? "Were you thinking I didn't belong there?" There was something chilly in his tone that hadn't been there the previous day and it puzzled her.

"Well, considering your track record of late arrivals, I had you marked down as a maybe at best," she replied tartly.

"I beg to differ," said Aiden. "My timing is impeccable."

Ella actually laughed in surprise. "Your notion of perfect timing is… unique."

"I'm always there for the exciting bits," said Aiden, giving one of his lazy smiles that she was beginning to think he only used when he didn't feel like smiling. She frowned, perplexed. Was he mad at her? In the entire time that she'd known him, she didn't think he'd ever actually been mad—even when she'd surprised him with the stack of DevEntier records earlier in the week that indicated that Bo had indeed been an employee.

"Well, better to be lucky than good," said Ella with a shrug. "I suppose."

"I specialize in being both," said Aiden, taking a step closer to her, using his height to loom. Whatever was going on he was definitely aggravated about something. "Do you always travel with bodyguards?"

Ella tried not to react. "New York is a dangerous city," she said with a fake smile of her own. "My uncle likes to make sure I'm safe."

"And he thinks they're necessary in the courthouse?" asked Aiden, and Ella knew that this time her irritation showed on her face.

"He thinks they're necessary everywhere. He's a very caring uncle."

"Then why did they leave?"

"Am I on the witness stand? How are my security arrangements any of your business?"

He took a half-step back and added another one of his smiles. "They're not. He's right. Better safe than sorry."

Ella felt as if Aiden had very carefully put the kid gloves back on.

"Mr. Deveraux," said Ella, startled into blurting out her real thoughts. "Are you not trying your best?"

"What?" He looked surprised.

"Have you been treating me differently because I'm a woman?" she asked, her eyes narrowing.

"What? No?" he looked uncertain and Ella felt the thrill of having him on the ropes for a change.

"Do not insult me by giving me less than your best," she said, deciding that she actually did feel insulted and more than a little bit worried. Because if this was his B game then she was in some seriously deep shit.

"Ms. Zhao," said Aiden leaning in, and Ella was suddenly very aware of what a very perfect mouth he had. "Trust me, you are getting the varsity team."

Ella realized that she had worked herself into a very awkward and somehow intimate conversation with her opposing counsel and she had no idea how to get out of it. She also realized how good, and also somehow familiar, he smelled and that made her feel very confused.

Ella's phone rang and she glanced down and saw that it was her cousin. Ella hesitated. She really didn't want to take a call from a teenager in front of Aiden. How was she supposed to look cool while doing that?

"Are you going to answer that?" asked Aiden when she let the phone ring. He was so cocky, and she longed to wipe the smug off his face.

"With you standing right here? That would seem unwise."

"And yet you let it ring. Not worried about being annoying?"

The phone stopped ringing and Ella breathed a sigh of relief.

"Why would I worry about annoying you?" asked Ella, trying to look as arrogant as he was.

He stopped and she couldn't tell if he was truly pondering the question or if he was astounded by her rudeness.

"I actually can't think of a reason," he said.

Then a text popped through and Ella glanced down at the message.

EMERGENCY. CALLING.

"Well, keep thinking," said Ella, moving away from the cluster of lawyers, answering her phone this time when it rang.

"Hey, what's up?"

"I need you to come get me and I need you to not be mad." Lilly's voice was tense and urgent.

"Chún?" asked Ella, switching to Mandarin, hoping that no one on Aiden's team understood the Chinese dialect. Ella glanced over her shoulder and moved further away from the crowd of Bai's lawyers and the Deveraux team.

"Yeah, OK, fine, alcohol," said Lilly, sticking to English and sounding both sarcastic and scared. "I will totally cop to half a bottle of hard lemonade, but I need help."

Ella managed to separate herself from both sets of lawyers, but kept her voice low as she slung her bags over her shoulder.

"OK, where are you?"

"Coffee shop on someplace and someplace?"

"What?"

"I don't know!" snapped Lilly. "We just moved here. I don't know where anything is! Give me a minute and I'll ask and text you."

"Are you safe where you are?"

"Yeah, I'm fine. I just needed to leave the party quickly."

"Text the address and I'll be there as soon as I can. Stay put," said Ella.

Ella snuck one last look at Aiden as she hung up. He was discussing something with Jerome Strand, who nodded. It was so blatantly obvious who was in charge. She utterly failed to understand how their research could have been so wrong.

Ella shook her head and left the courtroom. Her Aiden obsession just about rivaled her Number Nine obsession. Only in this case, thinking about him didn't give her that pleasant little erotic charge. There weren't any fantasies about Aiden Deveraux like she had with Number Nine. Mostly. He might work for the weird fetish one where she tied him up... No. Nope. There were no fantasies about Aiden Deveraux. There was just the spinning angry buzz of having to constantly think about him and what he was doing. Why couldn't he just have been stupid like the research said? Why did he have to be... himself? He was so frustrating and handsome and smart. He was wrong. All wrong. Wrong. Wrong. Definitely wrong.

Ella drove to the address Lilly texted. It was a crappy diner that looked like it had been at that same location for about hundred and fifty years and probably cleaned twice in all that time. She walked in and took a look at her cousin, who sat at one of the vinyl-wrapped tables looking glum. Ella took another look and realized that under her sweatshirt Lilly was wearing a towel around her waist, and flip-flops.

Ella sat down across the table from her cousin.

"So," said Ella, "I take it the day off from school slash parents getting divorced pool party was not a success?"

"One of the older boys groped my friend Kacey," said Lilly. "And I punched him in the face. And then her dad yelled at me for overreacting and being too aggressive and Kacey wouldn't back me up. So I called them all fucking rapist pigs and I ran out of the house."

"Yikes," said Ella. She got up and went around to Lilly's side of the booth. She put her arm around her cousin and Lilly leaned into her with a sniffle.

"What was I supposed to do?" Lilly asked, her voice tiny and muffled by Ella's shoulder.

"What you did," said Ella. "Although it would have been preferable to do it without the alcohol."

"Chet brought it," said Lilly. "I didn't want him and Bret to think I wasn't cool. I guess I shouldn't have worried about it considering he was clearly just using it to get to the groping part."

Lilly sat up and wiped her nose.

"He's the one you punched?" asked Ella.

"Yeah," said Lilly, she took a sip of water. "I left my clothes there. I just ran out. I felt... gek."

"That's not a word," said Ella.

"Icky," said Lilly. "I didn't want any of them looking at me. Kacey just kept apologizing. She didn't do anything wrong and she was the one who apologized. I wasn't going to do that. Everyone was all in my space. I had to get out of there."

"Good job," said Ella. "You kept your friend safe. You kept yourself safe. You told an adult and when that didn't work you got out of an unsafe situation and went to someplace public and called for help."

"That's the check-list," said Lilly, a tear rolling down her cheek. "You gave me the check-list. I thought it was stupid. I wasn't supposed to need it."

Ella felt her own eyes well up. "I know, baby," she said putting her arms around her cousin. "None of us are supposed to need it."

"Hope for the best, plan for the worst," whispered Lilly, repeating one of Ella's sayings. "Why do boys make us live like that?"

"It's not all of them," said Ella, thinking of Number Nine and even Aiden Deveraux, who might be a thorn in her side, but still treated her with the utmost respect. "And some things are just basic principles of self-defense for men or women."

Lilly gave her a bitter, cynical look that aged her about a decade.

"Because life isn't fair," said Ella. "I'm sorry. There are people, most of them men, with more power than you and sometimes you're going to lose. Learn to fight now. Learn to protect yourself and learn to come back when you can't."

"I'm going to have to see them at school tomorrow," said Lilly.

"Yes," agreed Ella. "It will take courage for you to show up."

Lilly looked like she was thinking this over, then she smiled. "Chet's still going to have a black eye."

Ella grinned. "It does take a little of the sting out of it," she agreed.

Aiden — Axios Partners

Aiden watched Don's lips move and let the sound wash over him. Don was working up to a point, but it was a good five minutes away. Aiden was certain of this because he'd heard this story three times already. It was Don's go-to story for teaching the maxim of working smarter not harder. Don deployed it on all occasions when he thought some junior lawyer wasn't working the right kind of hard enough. To date, Aiden had never had it used against him, but there was a first time for everything.

Don's lips were still moving and all Aiden could think about was Ella Zhao. Their last encounter in court had left him confused and more than a little turned on. He still wasn't sure if she knew he was Number Nine. She challenged him on so many levels in court—he had the hardest time not feeling like they had more of a relationship than they did. He felt like he understood her, but he didn't understand where her being at the fight in Jersey fit in.

"You see where I'm going with this?" demanded Don, and Aiden nodded automatically.

Don was a partner at Axios with the kind of spotlighted career that made him well known on a statewide level. He was mid-fifties, well-dressed, and basically the kind of person who intimidated others simply by having his shit epically together. Aiden, when he bothered to think about Don at all, generally liked him. Although, he suspected that Don's feelings were not reciprocal. It had never been stated, but Aiden thought Don had voted against him in the hiring process.

The story reached the part about the goats. Aiden had never been able to figure out what that part meant, but it did mean they had passed the halfway mark. Aiden wasn't sure he was going to actually make it to the end without drooling. He could zone out for a while longer, but the beautiful and legally lethal Ella Zhao had just dropped a pile of briefs on him and he needed to get to those.

"Don," he said when Don took a breath.

Don looked startled and paused.

"Skip to the end. You're pissed at me about something, spit it out. I don't have time for all of the goats today."

Don looked angry, but like a true professional he swallowed the anger and smiled. "Your family's case is taking up too much of your time."

Aiden nodded. Don was right. His work had been slipping. Jenna had been trying to warn him. Something had been bound to fall through the cracks and it had definitely been Axios. He didn't like underperforming, but he was feeling the pinch. Something had to give.

"You're not doing your work."

Aiden nodded again.

"You're right," said Aiden. "I've really let some stuff slip here. That is unfair to Axios."

Don looked surprised and then puffed up as if the goats were personally responsible for the admission. "Look, we're sympathetic. It's obviously a tough spot to be in. But MacKentier has a stable of good lawyers, and good lord, we know a few. And I know this isn't exactly Jerome's wheelhouse, but he's hardly a back bencher. You should lean on him more. I'm sure you can find a co-counsel to take care of DevEntier."

"Oh," said Aiden. "No, you've misunderstood. In the pecking order, my family is here," he held up his hand at about head height, "and you are here." He put his other hand at about chest level.

"There's a lot of space between those two," said Don, looking as though he wasn't certain how he'd arrived at this point in the conversation.

"Yes," agreed Aiden. "Probably best not to investigate that gap too much."

"We're your employer," said Don, seeming to fall back on an argument that he was certain of. "And you've been shirking."

Aiden thought *shirking* was an unnecessarily pretentious word. It wasn't as though Don was British. What American went around saying *shirking*?

"Yes, I understand that's frustrating for you. I'll resign."

Don gaped at him. "That's a stupid decision. What about your career?"

"Don, I haven't checked my bank account lately, but generally speaking I have fuck tons of money and a law degree. I'm fairly certain I'll be OK. Anyway, I'll clean out my desk and be out of your hair by the end of the day." Aiden stood up and looked around the office. Not seeing any of his belongings, he nodded and prepared to exit.

"But your cases…" stammered Don.

"Yeah," said Aiden. "If only you had promoted Jenna to law clerk, you'd have someone who was up-to-date on all of my stuff." He shook his head sadly. "Tsk. Well, too late now. See you around, Don."

Aiden ambled out of the open office door and smiled at the secretary, who was sitting at her desk with wide eyes. He took the long way back to his floor. Jenna was waiting for him when he got there.

"Did you just quit?" she demanded.

"Yeah, I think I kind of did," he admitted.

"Son of a bitch. Do you know how bad this is going to suck with you gone?"

"Sorry," said Aiden. "But as much as I hate to admit it, Don's right. I've totally been slacking on Axios and it's not fair to the company."

"You've been slacking for years," said Jenna drily.

"Well, I've achieved a new level," said Aiden. "I hate to admit it, but I can't do it all, and of all the balls that I'm juggling, I think this is the one I'd prefer to drop."

Jenna shook her head. "Yeah, I get it. I just…" she sighed. "I liked not having a dickhead for a boss."

Aiden grinned. "Thanks. I think that's the nicest thing you've ever said about me."

Jenna sighed again. "Come on. I'll help you load up your office."

"Thanks," he said. "Can you help me come up with what to tell my family? I think Grandma is going to blow a gasket."

"Just text them," said Jenna confidently. "That way they're not there to yell at you."

"Brilliant as usual," said Aiden.

Jackson — Deveraux House

Jackson watched the footage of Aiden fighting on his phone again. Four years of waiting for Aiden to slip up and here it was. Jackson had gone sprinting out the door when he'd gotten the call from Aiden's minder. A high-speed drive to Jersey had him there just in time to watch Aiden pummel the shit out of Teargas. Never mind the riot that had happened moments later. But he still couldn't believe it. He hit play again and watched Aiden jump, spin and kick Teargas in the face. His cousin was a goddamn action star. He had suspected that Aiden's interest in MMA extended beyond a passing fancy, but somehow he really hadn't expected this. Pete was now digging into Number Nine's past. Jackson was interested to see what came up, but he really wasn't sure what to do about it.

Or if there was anything to be done.

Aiden clearly had been managing this aspect of his life for quite some time. Jackson didn't actually object to secrets. He just objected when they didn't tell *him* the secrets. However, Aiden's text this afternoon had Jackson wondering if, at the very least, a conversation was in order.

The front door slammed, and Jackson reflexively took his feet off the sofa before looking up from his phone.

"It's just me," said Dominique, entering the study and flinging down her bag. "You can put them back up."

"You sounded angry," said Jackson, slipping his phone into his pocket before putting his sock clad feet back on the green velvet couch. "So I assumed you were Eleanor."

"I am angry," said Dominique, stripping off her gloves. "Didn't you see my stupid brother's text?"

"Yes," said Jackson. "I am contemplating my response."

"Is your response going to be: go back to Axios and beg for your job back?"

"No," said Jackson. "It is not."

"Why the hell not?"

"He hated that job," said Jackson with a shrug. "He was bored all the time. And a bored Aiden is an Aiden who gets himself in trouble. Now that he's busy with the DevEntier case, he wasn't actually doing his job. I can see why they were putting the pressure on him to get a co-counsel to handle DevEntier."

"He should get a co-counsel!" snapped Dominique.

"Why?" asked Jackson.

"Because he…" She paused and took a deep breath. "My brother is a darling. He's very smart, but you said it yourself, he gets bored easily. This is really important to the family and I'm not entirely sure that he should be in charge of important things."

Jackson frowned and sat up, slipping back into his shoes. "You don't think he can do it?

"Oh, who knows," said Dominque in exasperation. "Probably he's capable. But will he? That's the question. And I would love to say yes, but to be perfectly honest, I have not been able to rely on him to show up for very many things since… I don't know, college? He wanders off. He disappears. Christmases, I can count on, and that's about it."

"Like what?" asked Jackson.

Dominique sighed impatiently. "I really wanted his help on that scholarship review to help pick the winners for the Genevieve Fund. He went once and then no-showed for the final panel. I wanted him to help me review the contract on that building I invested in and he took the contract and then he disappeared for two weeks.

Not even a damn text. I ended up having to ask Evan. Evan! I mean, really!"

"Did Evan help you?" asked Jackson, trying not to laugh at Dominique's outraged tone.

"Well, yes, he did. He was actually completely civil, helpful and thoughtful. Which is just weird. I didn't know what to do."

Jackson grimaced. "Yeah, I had a taste of the old Evan a couple of weeks ago. I remembered how much I wasn't a fan."

"What did he do?" she asked, finally sitting in the armchair next to the sofa. She spared a moment to glare at the portrait of her grandfather, who had more than a passing resemblance to Evan, on the far wall. "Was he awful to you?"

"No," said Jackson, "he was awful in defense of Aiden and I, and aimed at Charlie MacKentier. I've never seen the full Deveraux deployed as an offensive weapon against outsiders. It was kind of impressive."

"Ugh," said Dominique. "I hate that guy. He used to look at me when I was fifteen."

"What?" asked Jackson, sitting up straighter. "Where?"

"I don't mean he was a peeping Tom or anything," said Dominique. "Charlie's just one of those pervoids who looks at anything with boobs, and age and relationships don't mean much to him. I mean, it's not shocking—he was friends with Randall and Owen after all. He never did or said anything to me, but I could always feel him looking. It was icky. Anyway, my point is… Aiden: not that reliable."

"Mm," said Jackson. Dominique clearly didn't know about Aiden's alter-ego. Otherwise she wouldn't have been this annoyed.

"That is distinctly not an answer," said Dominique. "It's barely even a response. You disagree with me?"

"Yes," said Jackson.

"Why?" demanded Dominique.

"I'm not in prison," said Jackson. "Eleanor didn't let you go to my court stuff or the prison, but Aiden showed up. Which, since he didn't even want to be there, I have always found impressive."

"He had help," said Dominique.

"He had to," said Jackson. "It took too long for the Illinois bar results to come back. I don't think that guy did that much though."

"Aiden disappears," said Dominique. "You know he does."

Jackson debated what to tell Dominique. Unlike Eleanor, Dominique wouldn't mind the illegality of Aiden's secret life, but she would not approve of the danger and he doubted that she would accept that he was managing it successfully.

"Do you know," said Dominique thoughtfully, "I've been saying that he disappears, but lately I've begun to think that he literally does go somewhere. Like at Easter when he was tan and he said it was spray on, but it definitely was not."

"Yes," said Jackson, "he makes semi-frequent, unannounced trips to South America and Europe. Something I'm extremely uncomfortable with."

Dominique looked shocked. "Like... He really goes out of the country?" She blinked rapidly as if trying to assimilate this new information. "Dear God, please tell me he's not running a drug cartel."

Jackson burst out laughing. "A minute ago you didn't think he could run a court case and now you're fitting him up to be a drug king pin?"

"I told you—he's very smart, but distractible. Maybe that's what he's distracted by."

"No," said Jackson. "It's not that."

"OK, but... He's had problems with partying too much in the past. Is that what he's doing? It doesn't seem like he's doing drugs."

"It's not drugs," said Jackson, reassuringly. "I had him tested."

"What? How did you get him to do that?"

"He doesn't know I did it," said Jackson.

Dominique laughed. "How did you manage that?"

"With difficulty," said Jackson. "But nope. He's clean. Flying colors. Extremely healthy."

"He *is* kind of obsessive about fitness," said Dominque with a nod. "Ooh!" She sat bolt upright, her hand slapping the arm of the chair. "Is he gay?"

"You sound way too excited about that possibility," said Jackson.

"It would be *so* good for Grandma's LGBTQ platform," said Dominique, flopping back.

Jackson snorted in laughter. "I really don't think he's gay."

"Are you sure?" complained Dominique, looking disappointed. "He wouldn't be the first in the family. In retrospect, now that I'm older and understand such things, I'm fairly certain that Uncle Owen was into guys. At least partially. Maybe. No one ever talks about it. But that could be Aiden's secret."

"No," said Jackson, firmly. "That's not it."

"He wears a lot of pink shirts," said Dominque.

"What's wrong with pink? Didn't you try to convince me to buy a pink shirt?"

"Yes, you would look gorgeous in pink. I'm just saying, Aiden likes to look fashionable. Perhaps too fashionable?"

"Fashionable has nothing to do with being gay! That's fucking gender identity and expression. How was this covered in like Prison 101 and the bougie elite can't get it?"

Dominique chortled in laughter and he began to suspect that she was fucking with him.

"Aiden just likes to annoy people with his clothing choices," said Jackson. "Also, stop trying to make him conveniently gay for your next list of talking points for Eleanor. You do realize that if he was gay, that being good for Grandma's politics would be exactly why he wouldn't want to tell us?"

Dominique chuckled. "Yeah, that's true." Her phone beeped and she picked it up. Her face lit up and he knew that it must be a message from Max.

"Good news?"

"Halloween costumes have been procured. I have a boyfriend who doesn't mind dressing up." She looked incredibly smug. "Someday I'm going to throw a Halloween party like Grandma throws a Christmas party."

"You'll go full bat-shit crazy," he said. "Got it. Thanks for the warning."

"Shut up," she said, glaring at him. "You are just jealous because you don't have anyone to dress up with."

"I prefer dressing down."

"What I have learned is that if you wear the right costume, you get to do that later and it is *loads* of fun."

Jackson considered that. "Well, OK, fine. Now I'm little jealous."

Dominique cackled happily, but quickly returned to serious. "I'm still worried about Aiden and whatever it is that he's up to."

"I hear you," said Jackson, "but I'm handling it."

Dominique skewered him with a hard stare. "Meaning that you already know what he's doing but you're not telling me."

"Meaning I want to try and talk to him again before I do anything. I have hinted several times that I would like a conversation on the topic, and he has given me the patented Aiden smile and jazz hands. Like I'm supposed to believe that. But I don't think it's a crisis and I want to try again before we elevate to intervention levels."

"He's my brother, you know. You shouldn't be keeping secrets about him from me."

If Aiden had delivered the line, Jackson thought it would have been filled with anger and hurt feelings, but it was Dominique, so she was about as irritated as if he was not sharing cookies.

"I don't think he wants us to know," said Jackson.

Dominique sighed. "He probably can't bear the idea of actually talking about himself. He has always hated being the center of attention. Which I know sounds weird because he likes going to court."

"He hates being vulnerable," said Jackson. "Court is a show. He's good at doing a show. Being real is a lot harder for him."

Dominque looked sad. "I just wish he didn't feel he needed to do that for us."

"Work in progress," said Jackson with a shrug. "We'll wear him down."

Dominique laughed. "And you always accuse me of too much long-range planning. All right, fine, we'll back burner that. And since you're keeping tabs on the situation, I guess we'll ignore the fact that my brother is an international man of mystery slash male escort or something for the moment. But doesn't that support my point? Do we really think he should be in charge of the DevEntier mess?"

"He wants the mess. He point-blank said he could do it," said Jackson. "I think you should trust him. It's my money anyway. Mine and Evan's. What do you care?"

"Thank God," she said casting her eyes heavenward. "Frankly, I could not be happier that Owen and Randall left the two of you that mess. I'm quite happy that Mom sold her shares to Randall after Grandpa died. Although, Evan may have bought me back in. I should ask. Is it bad that even after he's gone to the trouble of explaining those dratted reports to us that I still don't bother to read them?"

"You know he's looking after things," said Jackson, amused by his cousin's apparent stream of consciousness. "But if you think I'm going to forget I asked a question, you should think again. What do you care if Evan and I lose a bunch of money?"

Dominique looked annoyed, then shrugged. "Fine. Theo isn't eavesdropping, is he?" she asked craning to look through the door in the hall.

"Wouldn't matter if he was. Pretty sure Theo knows where all the bodies are buried."

"OK, but you can't tell Grandma this. I have thought... I mean, just in the general scheme of things, as one ponders the future."

"Sure," said Jackson, grinning. He knew what happened when Dominique pondered the future: plans got made. "As one does."

"Well, Grandma will have to retire eventually, and I don't think any of us want to go into politics exactly. But wouldn't it be nice if Aiden were to do something like, I don't know... run for State Attorney General?"

Jackson hadn't thought that far ahead, but now that she mentioned it, that might be an option. At some point Aiden would have to go public with his ACLU work and he would have to...

"But he has to have a high-profile job and the high-profile donor base that goes with it?" asked Jackson, realizing where Dominique was heading. "In other words, Axios Partners?"

"Attorney General does require a certain resume. But it would sort of fill the niche that Grandma is filling now. And that would be convenient for everyone."

"So, it's really our needs that you're thinking of?"

Dominique shrugged innocently and Jackson laughed.

"You're not wrong, but I don't think Axios is the only way to get there and I don't think that Aiden should have to be at some job that bores him to death to make it happen."

Dominique frowned unhappily and picked at the crease in her slacks and Jackson sensed that they were narrowing in on the real reason for Dominique's distress.

"I've asked around about this Ella Zhao girl," she said after a moment. "She's really good. What if he loses? He's set his heart on this. If he loses, he'll be heartbroken. And quitting his job is so public. If he loses after quitting… I think you're right. I think he hates for people to see that he's vulnerable and this will be exactly that. I'm worried for him, Jacks."

"Yeah," agreed Jackson. "Me too, but I really think he can do it."

She didn't look convinced, but she didn't argue any further, so Jackson decided it was as good a time as any to bring up the next awkward topic.

"Although," he said, clearing his throat, "if we're discussing cousins I'm worried about, we should probably switch to you."

"Me? Why? What have I been doing? Have I been doing something?" She appeared to think for a moment. "If I am, I've forgotten it."

"The whole moving in with Max thing. I floated the trial balloon with Grandma and she promptly brought out the large artillery, shot it down, and then possibly set it on fire and curb-stomped it."

"Good grief. I guess she does feel some kind of way about it. Does she not like Max? She's always seemed to get along with him in person."

"I asked that, and she says he seems quite nice and liking him isn't the issue."

"All right, so what is the issue?" Dominique looked perturbed.

"I'm not entirely sure. She's very resistant to being questioned on the topic. His work seems to be a large part of it. And… I don't know. It's this feeling I get like she doesn't want any outsiders."

Dominique frowned. "Grandma places a great deal of importance on appearances. Does she think he's not good enough? I swear if that's it, I will… Well, there will be words. Words will be said."

Jackson laughed. "I don't think that's it."

Dominique frowned. "Grandma is annoyingly secretive. And I can't help feeling that whatever it is she's freaking out about, it would be better if she would just tell us. I mean, no one told me that Uncle Owen abused Evan as a child and look what happened. I never understood any of his behavior or why Aiden ever wanted him to be part of the family, and poor Evan, he practically went all… well, he got very depressed."

Jackson didn't bother to illuminate that *very* didn't actually cover the depths of Evan's depression. Suicidal would have been closer to the truth.

"He seems like he's getting better, right?" she added anxiously. "He's been very… Did I tell you he tried to apologize to me?"

"No," said Jackson, blinking in surprise. "What did you say?"

"I freaked out. I did not handle it all well. Which I feel bad about. He sort of stumbled around and I could see that he was literally sweating. So then I started to try and get him to calm down. But then I felt angry that I was trying to make him feel better while he was trying to apologize for being abusive toward me when we were kids. I mean, he should feel horrible. He *was* horrible."

"I think he does feel that way."

"Yes, that much was obvious," said Dominique. "And, after some day drinking and meditation, I really, really, really appreciated his attempt, but him having honest emotions completely threw me.

This sounds peculiar, but I'd rather he not try it again. I'm glad he tried, but I really can't talk about it without completely spazzing out and probably ugly crying and I'm not ready to be that vulnerable in front of him. Anyway, I kind of waved him off and ran out of the room and I think we're fine. I think. I don't know. I spent like three weeks worrying that my poor handling of the situation would lead to some sort of relapse for him."

"You can't put that on yourself. Evan is responsible for his own behavior," said Jackson, and Dominique sighed impatiently.

"Yes, he is. And I know that. But there is a lot of pressure in this family to be perfect. And I think Evan has had that pressure even more than Aiden and I have. I didn't want to be the snowflake that leads to an avalanche. Dealing with him, a lot of times, it makes me tired just from having to think about him. I used to worry about him. And now I mostly worry *for* him. But I have to admit that sometimes, I worry that this is just one long stretch of Christmas and that sooner or later he'll go back to being an asshole."

"He has his moments," said Jackson with a shrug. "And then he course corrects. He's working really hard."

"I know. I see that. And the fact that he lets me see that he's working is actually more reassuring than just having him be nice to me. And now that I know about Uncle Owen, I can understand the kind of hole he's working out of. Grandma and Aiden shouldn't have kept that from me. Now that we all know, he doesn't have to spend any energy trying to hide—he can just work on getting better. And he *is* better. Everything isn't perfect, but God, he is so much better."

"Right?" asked Jackson. "He's showing up. He's communicating. He's not taking drugs."

"He's doing so well! I'm really looking forward to Christmas this year. He's always been better at Christmas and I bet now that he's less depressed and less of a dickhead it's going to be even more fun! Anyway, my point is… What was my point?"

This time, Jackson thought Dominique wasn't faking because her eyes flicked toward the ceiling as she tried to recall the conversational thread.

"Grandma and people not keeping secrets?" supplied Jackson.

"Yes! Whatever she's bottling up, it would be better just to spill it. Because I'm doing this one way or another and it's going to get super awkward if I have to threaten to withdraw my marketing expertise support to all her campaign stuff."

"Ooh, full worker strike," said Jackson. "It's serious now."

"It's about to be," said Dominique. "I guess I'll have to formally announce soon. Max has started packing and his lease is up in a couple of weeks. It's going to be a thing."

"Wait for Sunday dinner," advised Jackson. "That way we'll all be there to support you. I'll tell the guys."

"Thanks. I think—"

Both their phones vibrated, cutting off whatever Dominique was going to say next.

YOUR OFFICIAL STANCE IS NO COMMENT. FUNNEL ALL QUESTIONS TO MY PRESS SECRETARY.

"It's from Grandma," said Dominique. "No comment on what?"

"I don't know," said Jackson.

"Mr. Jackson," said Theo as he came in to the study. "There are some undesirable persons on the lawn. They have dislodged the decorative pumpkins." He looked affronted.

"Really?" Dominique looked equally affronted, like she wasn't a certified pumpkin kicker from way back. Nika went out to the hall and peered through the narrow window by the door.

"Looks like press," she said. "Oh, yeah, totally. There's a van.

One of them is going to come up to the door. I think he's trying to figure out the recording app on his phone. Did they send the junior brigade? Come on, get it together people. We deserve seasoned reporters."

Jackson's phone rang. "Hey, Ev."

"Did you see the fucking news?"

"No, just the text from Grandma. And now we have reporters on the front lawn. Theo is very peeved."

"Kicked a gourd?"

"Precisely."

"He'll spray them with the hose if you want him to."

Jackson laughed. "No, probably not. What *is* the news by the way?"

"They just indicted Granger! Absolex is placing him on temporary leave, but I called some people and they say they'll be moving to request that he resign in an emergency board meeting tonight."

"Ha!"

"Ha?" asked Dominique, still looking out the window by the door.

"They just indicted Granger. Evan says he'll be fired by the end of the night."

"Is that Evan? Let me talk to him."

Jackson handed over the phone with a feeling like he'd pulled a straight flush in poker. He now knew Aiden's secret, Dominique and Evan were genuinely doing all right with each other, and Granger had just gotten indicted. It was a damn good day.

"Ev, are they going to fire him or make him resign?" Jackson couldn't hear Evan's response. "Well, what did the news say? What are they charging him with? Do you think Aiden will let us go to court and gloat?"

Jackson could hear Evan's laugh, tinny through the speaker.

"Put it on speaker," Jackson said. "I want to hear what they're charging him with too."

"—one count of conspiracy to defraud the U.S. government." Evan's voice picked up as Dominique switched to speaker. "There are a couple of different counts of conspiracy to blah blah—I need Aiden to translate—I think that's us. Then there's four other things including securities fraud. Idiot. They're charging him in federal court, but I can't tell if that's good or bad. The news is saying that the defense will most likely try and separate some of the indictments and move them to the state level."

Their phones vibrated again. "Grandma again?" asked Jackson, looking at Dominique.

"Aiden," she said holding her phone up.

SERIOUSLY. NO COMMENT. DON'T SAY SHIT.

"I have half a mind to text him back that I can't talk because I'm about to go on camera," said Dominique.

Evan snorted.

"Well, really! Who does he think he's dealing with? I can say *no comment* in three different languages. This family practically comes out of the womb saying *no comment*."

"I've only got two languages," said Jackson sadly. "Unless you count sign language, and Aiden says I shouldn't use that one."

Evan laughed. "No, don't use that one."

"Well, this is just great," said Dominique. "I was only popping in to talk to Jackson. Max and I were going out to eat. Now what am I supposed to do?"

"They won't follow you," said Evan. "Just have Jackson give a polite *no comment* and escort you to the car and go out to dinner."

"You don't think they'll pester Max too, do you? He will *hate* that."

"I doubt it," said Jackson soothingly.

"I can give my own *no comment*," she said, looking at Jackson. "You don't have to do it. I know you hate being on camera."

"It's fine," said Jackson, taking back his phone. "Ev, are you going to come over for dinner and watch the news with me?"

"It's not a sporting event," said Evan drily. "But… I mean, I could. If you wanted."

"I believe we have just taken possession of a few bottles of the 2015 Antinori Tignanello," said Theo, walking by with a dustpan and broom.

"Yeah, I can come to dinner," said Evan, and Dominique silently laughed.

"Great," said Jackson. "See you in a couple of hours."

He hung up and looked at Dominique. "Theo's my secret weapon," he said, and Dominique chuckled out loud this time.

Ella – Chiropractic Adjustments

Ella lay on the floor of her office and hated Aiden Deveraux. Above her, Aiden's stupid headshot with his stupid smile from his stupid law firm was taped to the case board. She crossed her leg over her body and popped a vertebra. This is what he had done to her. He'd made her tense enough that she had to do her own chiropractic adjustments. She put her leg back down, but didn't get up.

What was the point? There was nowhere to go. She had missed her chance at Number Nine in Jersey and now all she had to occupy her mind was stupid Aiden Deveraux. And she did not want to think about Aiden.

The only good thing to have happened the last week was the indictment of J.P. Granger, which had forced her uncle to admit that *not* using any of his research was the right thing to do. She felt like she had narrowly dodged a bullet with that one. She wanted to win, but it had to be on the merits of the case. There was no way that Bai could force himself onto the board of DevEntier and not end up having to work with the Deveraux. It wasn't like they would magically disappear. If Bai wanted a future with DevEntier they needed the Deveraux to concede that the Zhao had a right to be there. But stupid Aiden Deveraux was making that very difficult.

Her grandmother came into the room, hobbling with her cane and tiny steps to loom over her. The glory of downtown Manhattan was having a beautiful apartment that was only a block from the offices. The downfall of downtown Manhattan was that all of the relatives knew where to find her when she was hiding in the office.

"Why are you glaring at the cute boy?" asked her grandmother in Mandarin.

"He's not cute, Nai. He's an evil plague of boils," replied Ella.

Nai Nai looked amused. "And he has stricken you to the floor?"

"Yes! Yes, he has!"

Her grandmother looked skeptical and went to settle herself into the desk chair, wheeling it around the desk so she could look at Ella on the floor. "Who is this lady killer then?" She squinted at the photo. "He looks so happy."

"Lies! All lies!" said Ella from the floor. "He is a dissembler. A fraud. A fake. A phony."

"Oh my."

Ella hauled herself to her feet and dropped into the chair opposite the desk.

"This was supposed to be easy. He was supposed to be stupid! A charming, but ultimately ineffectual rich boy, playing at being a lawyer, with all the intelligence of a tree frog." She leaned forward and snatched the Deveraux dossier off her desk, shaking it angrily. "All of Uncle's research says he's an idiot. His cousin Evan is the smart one, but cold and vindictive. His cousin Jackson is a violent ex-con. His sister is… well, honestly, she's just pretty and smart and I hate her because she's tall. But he"—she pointed at the photo—"was supposed to be stupid!"

"Not stupid?" asked Nai Nai.

"No! Oh, he pretends to be. He bumbles along, with that stupid smile of his and he charms everyone into believing that he's some sort of adorable, funny puppy, but he is not. I'll quote statute and he, just pops up and says, *thank you for clarifying that, Ms. Zhao, but I thought the rest of the statute stated…* and then he just quotes from memory. Who does that?"

"Besides you? I don't know."

"And then, he'll tie it back to some sort of case law. And say something chummy like, *well, of course, Judge, you would know better than I, but that was my interpretation.* And then, he doesn't even…"

"Doesn't even what?" Ella was silent. Her grandmother raised an eyebrow.

"I'm not proud of this, but it's desperate times in that courtroom. I wore some shoes the other day that have generally resulted in stupid lawyers staring at my legs and ass. Which means they're not listening to what I say."

"He didn't look?"

"No!"

"Rude."

"Yes!"

"But perhaps he's not interested in such things?" Nai Nai widened her eyes to make a significant expression and indicate that Aiden was gay without ever saying such a word.

"His last girlfriend was the Channel Four weather girl. She comes with her own storm fronts." Ella spread her hands in front of her to indicate how big the double-D storms were.

Nai Nai clicked her tongue in sympathy.

"He's killing me out there. I can see the judge is swinging in his favor. I can't compete with that *let's all go golfing next Tuesday* thing that he does."

"You golf."

"I know how. But I mean the social event of golfing. Like he and the judge move in the same circles. They've met each other before."

"You knew coming in that this wouldn't be a home court advantage."

"Yes, but I didn't count on it being someone else's home court.

I thought it would be more neutral. And I certainly didn't count on giant stupid face over there being smart."

"And funny."

"Don't get me started. He thinks he's hilarious, but he is *not*. I have not laughed once. The rest of the courtroom can go ahead, but I'm not going to."

"Stand firm," advised Nai Nai, nodding her head.

"I cannot lose this case, Nai Nai."

"You'll have to lose some time," said her grandmother. "Nobody is perfect."

"I could maybe stand losing," said Ella. "But Uncle could not. Getting on the board of this company is crucial to his future plans."

"So he can buy an interest like a normal person. Not try to force it down their throat."

"He was promised those shares. He should get them," said Ella firmly.

"Your father was promised them twenty years ago—not your uncle. And the evidence is… not convincing."

"Whose side are you on?"

"Your uncle hates the Deverauxes. Are we sure he's not set his heart on this company because he wants to hurt them?"

Ella was silent.

DevEntier had several innovative solar patents that were about to come through. Having access to them would be extremely useful to Zhao Industries. But DevEntier wasn't the only fish in the sea. Zhao Industries didn't need DevEntier. Her grandmother was right—this was very, very personal to Bai. Ella supposed it should have been personal to her too, but it really wasn't. She could see that Zhao Industries had been her father's dream. His hand was all over the founding documents. She could feel it in the way that Bai would sometimes wax nostalgic and say *we were going to…* She never had to ask who he meant—he meant Bo. For Bai, Zhao Industries was supposed to have been a family proposition and she knew that Bai wanted her to be next in line for the throne. She would probably do it, she supposed. She was trying not to think about it. Zhao Industries was a mammoth and being CEO was all consuming. She wasn't sure she wanted that for her life. But while she couldn't focus on Bai's dreams for the rest of her life, she could try and bring him a tiny bit of revenge and peace—she could bring him DevEntier.

Only Aiden blocked her at every turn. It hadn't occurred to either Bai or Ella that the Deveraux would deny that Bo had ever been a full employee of DevEntier. As a contract employee, he wouldn't have been eligible for the stock shares of an employee, and that meant Randall's nebulous email was her only weapon. At least until she'd turned up a box of records that showed that Bo was getting a 401k contribution removed from his paycheck. That had allowed her to subpoena bank records that she hoped would conclusively prove he'd been employed at DevEntier.

She hoped. Maybe. Fingers crossed. As long as Aiden didn't manage to come up with something else. Her uncle was counting on Ella to bring him his white whale. And Aiden Deveraux stood in her way.

"I owe this to my uncle," said Ella quietly. "I can't lose."

"Why?" asked Nai Nai.

"Oh, I don't know. The last six years of food, housing and college, for starters."

"Meh," said her grandmother, with a shrug.

"Zu mu!" Ella was shocked enough to use the formal term for grandmother.

"Ella, you listen to me. Just because he hates the Deveraux doesn't mean you have to. You've already discovered he was wrong about this one. What makes you think he's not wrong about the others?"

Ella bit her lip. The thought had already crossed her mind, but she had tried to bury it.

"And if it comes down to who owes what, maybe you should consider what he owes you. He built his empire on the work your father did. Maybe he should have tried a little harder to find you when your father died. You should not have had to show up on our doorstep like a beggar girl. He should have found you earlier."

"I've seen the file, Nai Nai. He tried. Mom changed our names and moved like eight times to four different countries. Not exactly an easy trail to follow."

Nai Nai snorted, clearly unswayed by Ella's argument. "I'm simply saying," she said as she heaved herself out of the chair, "that your life is your own. You don't have to do everything to please him."

"Well, generally, I don't mind," said Ella. "The only problem is that this time, I may not be able to. Aiden Deveraux is good. He's really, really good."

"Yes, I understand. That's why you like him."

"No," said Ella, firmly. "That's why I hate him."

Nai Nai shook her head. "Time to go home. Your aunt says we're going to a party."

Aiden – Cousins & Kindness

Aiden ran his hand through his hair and scanned the room. Jackson had convinced him to come to the stupid party based entirely on the fact that the Zhao's would be here and if he didn't show up it would show weakness. Jackson was right, but it didn't cover the hours that he was missing in prep for his next court appearance. He looked around the room again. None of his relatives were looking his direction. He thought he'd been seen enough. Everyone could go jump in a lake if they didn't like it. He made a break for the back elevators.

Ella Zhao was kicking his ass up and down the courtroom. Which was remarkable for someone that petite. He hadn't burned this much midnight oil since college. He also hadn't spent this much time fantasizing about a woman since he'd discovered girls. Ella Zhao had dropped into his consciousness with the force of an atom bomb. Her dark eyes, curves, and fuck-me pump collection were torturing him on a daily basis. Nightly too, for that matter. He couldn't decide which was worse, the days he saw her in court or the days he didn't. At least when they weren't together, he could pretend that she might like him. When they were in court, she made it perfectly clear that she found him underwhelming at best.

But his fantasies had all been upended by the stupid fight in Jersey. What had she been doing there? She couldn't know about him. If she knew about Number Nine, then why hadn't she approached him? It was the perfect blackmail material. If she knew, then she was waiting for the most painful moment. And if she didn't know, if she really was just the kind of person who went to illegal fights… His train of thought stopped there. He had always believed that facing someone in court gave insight into a lawyer's personality—it was like sparring—he could tell what kind of person someone was by how they fought. Ella was logical, aggressive, and above all, fair. She hadn't pulled in any of Randall and Owen's shit. She wasn't trading on the grime of the Deveraux family—she was fighting with the law. That just didn't seem like someone who liked the blood and filth of illegal fighting. So what the hell had she been doing there?

He rounded the corner to the service elevators and came face-to-face with Ella Zhao, clutching a mostly unconscious teenage girl. They stared at each other. What was he supposed to do?

"Keep walking," said Ella.

Aiden recognized the girl from Jackson's dossier's as Ella's younger cousin. The teenager chose that moment to thrash and Ella nearly dropped her. He took an urgent step forward intending to help, but she glared at him.

"I have this," she said.

"She's taller than you," he pointed out.

"Who isn't?" she snapped.

The teenager thrashed again, and Aiden decided he couldn't watch the slow-motion crash that was coming.

"Would you just let me help?" he demanded, reaching for the girl.

"No!" Ella exclaimed.

The girl chose that moment to try to stand up and then promptly fell into Aiden. There was a ding as the elevator door opened.

"Right," he said. "I'm taking her in here. You can come along if you want." Ella made an angry noise but gave up as he hefted the teenager into the elevator. Ella followed, collecting a dropped shoe and a purse.

"Hey!" demanded the teenager looking up at him angrily. "Who're you?"

"Uh…" He looked at Ella, whose expression told him that this was his problem. "I'm Aiden. I'm a friend of your cousin's."

"My cousin Ella? Isn't she the bessht?"

"Yes," he said, trying to restrain his laughter.

"Lilly," said the girl, patting her chest.

"Hi, Lilly," he said. "Did you enjoy the peppermint schnapps?"

"I did! How did you know?"

"Everyone in a ten-foot radius knows," muttered Ella.

"Where's Ella? There's Ella. I love you, Ella."

"I love you too, Lilly," said Ella, looking as if she was nearing the last straw.

"I love Ella," said Lilly switching back to Aiden. "Ella's the besht."

"Yes," he agreed.

"It'sh jusht so mush better sinch she came to live with ush. You know what I mean?"

"I do actually," he said. "I have a cousin like that too."

"Isn't it the besht?"

"Yes," he agreed. On the other side of Lilly, Ella frowned thoughtfully, although he wasn't sure why. The elevator jerked to a stop and Lilly tried to fall over. Aiden heaved her back upright.

"Give me a second," said Ella. "I'll have the car pull up."

She disappeared out into the parking area and Aiden had a sudden fear that she was going to ditch him with a drunk underage girl, and it was going to be all over the papers in two seconds.

"I think maybe I shouldna had the lasht sch-sch-sch-drink."

"Oh, I'm pretty sure you should have stopped way before then," said Aiden.

"Kacey ditched me," said Lilly, with a sob and a tear rolled down her cheek. "I stood up for her. I stood up for her and she just ditched me in front of everyone."

"Oh," said Aiden, feeling his heart drop at the level of heartbreak in her voice. "Oh, kiddo, I'm sorry."

"I should have…" She petered out and looked up at him in desperation. "I don't know what to do. I don't want to be an outcasht but… I can't hang with Brett and fucking Chet. I know what they are. They're fucking wannbe rapists." The final word came out crisp and clear and sober. "How can Kacey just pretend that they didn't do what they did?"

Aiden tried to come up with something that a sane adult full of wisdom would say. He did not feel like he was qualified to be having this conversation. He looked around, hoping that Ella would return soon.

"I know Kacey's freaking out," continued Lilly. "I jusht… How could she ditch me?" Tears leaked out the corners of her eyes and she leaned heavily on his arm. He wasn't sure what all had happened with her friends, but it sounded bad. He also hoped Ella knew about it, because he didn't think Ella would want him involved in whatever this was. He didn't think he could step into whatever was going on with Brett and Chet, but emotionally the real damage seemed to be coming from Kacey's defection. He tried to remember what he would have wanted to hear when he had been seventeen and Evan had ditched him to hang with the college assholes.

"She's doing her best," Aiden said. "Right now her best is pretty sucky. But sometimes people that are hurt make stupid decisions. For instance, sometimes they drink an entire bottle of peppermint schnapps." Lilly looked at him suspiciously, but he continued. "Think of it like an injury that she hasn't recovered from, only you can't see the bandage. And when people are injured, you try to be kind. You don't have to take shit from anyone, but just… be kind to hurt people. That includes yourself."

Lilly looked up at him, her expression miserable. He wasn't sure how much he'd actually helped.

"Plus, you're lucky," he said, a little desperately. "You have an Ella. Kacey probably doesn't have an Ella. I didn't get my Ella until much later."

"You have an Ella too?"

"Yes. He did punch me in the face and tell me to stop being an idiot, of course. So your Ella might be better."

Lilly giggled. "My Ella can punch you in the fashe too. She's good at it. And then she'll tell you to get your guard up and then you're like… well, fuck."

Aiden laughed at the unexpected color commentary and tucked the information away for later consideration. "I think you've just described every training fight I've ever had," he said.

Lilly swayed on her feet. "I'm gonna be in so much trouble."

He heard the sharp click of high-heels on concrete and looked up as Ella returned. Lilly looked at her and gave a little hiccup and a sob. Ella looked from Lilly to Aiden, questioning. "She's worried she's going to be in trouble," he said, hoping she believed him.

Ella sighed. "No, honey. We're just going to go home now."

Lilly sobbed again. "I'm such a screw-up."

Aiden winced in sympathy. He remembered that feeling all too well. It felt like he'd spent all of his teens and early twenties trying not feel like the family idiot.

"Hey, now," he said pulling Lilly's attention back to him as the car arrived, "remember what we said? Kindness, right?"

Lilly blinked at him. "Right. We're kind to hurt people."

"That's right," said Aiden. "And that includes you. You're not a screw-up. You are someone who made a mistake and we all make mistakes. Ella's going to take care of you. And you are going to be OK. Tomorrow is going to suck a bit, but you can't be that big of a screw-up if you've got people like Ella who love you."

Lilly wiped her eyes. "Ella loves me," she repeated, but it was as if she was repeating a lesson she didn't quite believe.

"Yes, of course I do, sweetie," said Ella, rubbing Lilly's back. "You need to stop drinking alcohol, which we will be talking about in the morning, but I love you."

"I shouldnahavea done the drinking," said Lilly. "I'm sorry. I just… I don't understan' how everything got so fucked up. I thought it would get better with schhhhhnapps." Her head wobbled around on her neck until she was looking up at Aiden. "It didn't."

"Schnapps never solved anything," agreed Aiden. "But you're going to be OK."

"I'm going to be OK," she said.

"Yeah, you really are," said Aiden, aware that Ella was staring at him. But what was he supposed to do? He couldn't let poor Lilly think she was a total failure.

"Thanks," Lilly said with another sniff. She looked up at him, and for a moment, sober Lilly peaked out. "I mean it. Thanks."

"OK, then let's get you and Ella home and you can go to bed," Aiden said. She nodded and, judging that the waterworks were dammed, at least for the moment, he half-carried her to the limo. Ella opened the door and Lilly crawled inside, flopping face first onto the seat.

"Good luck," he said with a half-smile at Ella. He wasn't sure what else to say. Everything else seemed like it would lead to a conversation they weren't supposed to have. Then he turned and headed back to the elevators.

"Hey," hissed Ella, and he heard her high-heels, hurrying after him. He turned around and found that they had both misjudged and were now standing too close to each other. "Um. Look, I know this probably just a funny drunk teenage thing to you, but…"

"But what?" Her lips formed a perfect little cupid's bow and her eyes had flecks of amber in them. He'd never been close enough to see that before.

"It will be a big deal in my family. Can you not…"

He realized he'd been staring at her eyes and not really listening. She was asking him not to tell her secret. That almost made him laugh. There was no way she knew he was Number Nine.

"Oh. Uh. Yeah, forget it," he said, backing up. "I never saw the two of you. We were never here. Top secret."

She bit her lip and glanced over her shoulder at the car.

"You didn't have to be that nice to her."

"Oh, come on," said Aiden. "She's really upset. Her friend ditched her, and I don't know what went down with Chet and whoever, but it sounds like someone needs to punch them in their faces."

"Lilly already did," said Ella, looking startled.

"Oh. Well, good for her," said Aiden, trying not to laugh. "But I mean… she needed… Well, she needs a hug. But I figure that's definitely not my department. So I just…"

"You were nice to her," said Ella, smiling at him, something that made him catch his breath. "Thank you." She hesitated and then glanced at the car again, before turning back to him with a frown. "Did you mean that? In the elevator?"

"Mean what?" he asked, trying to remember what he'd said.

"I estimate that acknowledging Jackson cost all of you millions of dollars. Did you really mean that having him here is for the best?"

He thought about how to answer that. There had been other people who had asked him what the hell the Deverauxes were thinking to recognize his Uncle Randall's bastard son. He had punched at least one of them. But there was something in Ella's face that made him want to answer. But giving her an honest answer meant trusting her with a part of him that he didn't like to share.

"Why don't you ask Lilly? She seems to have the answer."

"Lilly's drunk off her ass," said Ella impatiently.

"Doesn't mean she's wrong," said Aiden.

For a moment, Ella Zhao looked vulnerable and alone. Aiden wondered how hard it was to try and integrate into a family that was only kind of hers. Maybe he should ask Jackson.

"See you at the bank tomorrow?" he asked.

She pulled herself together. "Of course," she said. "Like I would let you collect the evidence on your own."

"It's going to show I'm right," he said.

"You hope," she said with a saucy little toss of her head, and suddenly he grinned. Her cuteness knew no bounds.

"I do, actually. See you tomorrow, Ella," he said, returning to the elevator before this moment got completely out of hand.

"Good night, Aiden," she said as the elevator doors closed. He looked up just as they did, she was watching him with a thoughtful expression. He realized it was the first time she'd ever used his first name.

Aiden – The Man With No Fear

Aiden went back upstairs and grabbed two drinks. Then he went over to the Deveraux table and set the second drink down in front of Jackson.

"Thanks for making me come tonight," he said. "It definitely beats my other plan."

"You mean, staying home and freaking out that you haven't studied enough?"

"Who told?" demanded Aiden, only half-joking. Aside from the bodyguard Jackson had shadowing him since the thing with the Zhao watchdog, he was also fairly certain that Jackson was bribing one of his neighbors to keep tabs on him.

"Pretty sure that's mostly what you've been doing for the last month," said Jackson. Aiden tried to decide if there was a hidden meaning in *mostly*. "Where are you with the case anyway?"

Aiden grunted. "The Zhao implied that the loss of the HR records was deliberate. Seems unlikely. DevEntier lost other items as well. But whatever. Then they produced some evidence that showed that not only was Bo working on multiple projects—not that I know where they managed to find a crap load of internal DevEntier documents—but that he was getting money withdrawn from his paycheck for a 401k. Which wouldn't happen with a contract employee. So now there's a subpoena out for the bank records during that time and we're going over to witness them being collected tomorrow morning at the bank."

"If they show that he was an employee, does that mean we lose?" asked Jackson frowning.

"Not even close," said Aiden. "Even if, and I say if, he was employee, he still died before the stock went public. I don't think the promise of stock options to employees extends to an employee's heirs. Ella will, of course, disagree. But we can argue about that next."

Jackson grinned. "Not that you're enjoying arguing with the very pretty Miss Zhao or anything."

"I'm not actually," said Aiden. "She is too smart to argue with."

Jackson shook his head. "Sometimes I cannot believe I'm involved in this mess."

"Neither can I," said Aiden. "It's not like Dominique or I actually even own any shares in the damn company. I'm only involved because you idiots put me in charge."

"I know," said Jackson, "it's great."

Aiden glared at him and Jackson grinned.

"Hey," said Dominique, walking up with Evan. It was still weird to see them getting along. Dominique rarely talked about her relationship with Evan, even with Aiden. He knew she still felt uncertain about their cousin, but he hoped she didn't feel like they were glossing over Evan's past behavior. On the other hand, what were they supposed to do? Talk about it at every family dinner? "So, what are we talking about?" she asked, giving Aiden a little head tilt that meant that his expression was worrying her. He straightened his face into a smile.

"How happy we are that Jackson came to live with us," Aiden said.

"That's true," agreed Dominique, nodding, then sitting down next to Aiden and stealing his drink. He tried to steal it back, but she insisted on drinking half of it first.

"Yes, but why are we talking about it?" asked Evan, watching their tug-of-war with a bemused expression. "I'm fairly sure that talking about feelings isn't allowed for Deveraux."

"Really? Because this evening you told me you felt strongly that my suit was too *on trend*," said Jackson.

"My therapist says it's good to express my emotions," said Evan, and Aiden couldn't help but laugh, which earned him a skeptical look from Jackson. But the fact that Evan could even joke about having a therapist was a massive step forward.

"I'm not sure those are the emotions she was referring to," said Dominique.

"He can't help it," protested Aiden. "Evan has always had deep-seated feelings about our sartorial statements."

"It's a suit," said Jackson. "I'm not making a sartorial statement. I'm wearing a suit. It's a nice suit. I like my suit."

"You look very nice," reassured Dominique.

"I look like *Reservoir Dogs*," muttered Jackson. "It's cool."

"I'm just jealous," said Evan, and Aiden almost spit out his scotch. "If I wear black, I look like a cadaver."

"Mm," said Dominique, nodding. "Curse of the ginger. On the other hand, navy makes you look dreamy. Jackson always has to shift to a more royal blue to make it look right. And Aiden is the only one of us who can actually pull off brown."

All the eyes turned to Aiden. "I…" said Aiden. "I like tweed."

"And on that non sequitur," said Jackson, standing. "I think I'll pack it in. Anyone need a ride?"

"I was riding with Grandma, but maybe I'll go with you," said Dominique. "Has anyone *seen* Grandma, by the way?" asked Dominique, surveying the room.

"I thought she went off with some horde of women," said Evan.

"Her entire reason for being here was to connect with the Junior League," said Jackson. "And once she did, I was told that my services were no longer required due to the fact that the Junior League would only be socially vicious at her."

"The Junior League," said Dominique, looking horrified. "Oh God. Please tell me she's not trying to rope in Althea Redmond? I don't want to join the Junior League!"

"I'm not sure those are connected," said Evan.

"Yes, they are. The only reason I sit on half the boards I do is because Grandma wants me to be her proxy. And I hate the Junior League."

"Get Jackson to tell her that you wouldn't be a good match or something," said Evan. "She'll listen to him."

"You may over-estimate my influence," said Jackson.

"Not really," said Evan. "Aiden, can I catch a ride with you?"

"Sure?" said Aiden. "I mean, sure."

It took them a few minutes to say the appropriate farewells, but when they finally made it out to the valet, Aiden thought Evan looked awkward. Aiden's Aston Martin arrived in front of the three other people who had been waiting ahead of them. Aiden pretended not to notice their dirty looks and tipped his usual amount. He thought Evan did notice, but he didn't say anything, so Aiden certainly wasn't going to say anything.

"Do you mind if we make a stop before we go home?" asked Evan, looking, if possible, even more uncomfortable.

Aiden opened the door to his Aston Martin and wondered what Evan was up to. "Sure," said Aiden, cautiously. In the back of his mind he had a horrible fear that Evan was going to make him stop to buy drugs. Not that Evan had ever done that even when he was using, but Aiden couldn't come up with anything but unpleasant reasons for Evan to make a stop.

"OK, good," said Evan and pulled open the passenger door.

Aiden watched with amusement as his lanky cousin tried to fold himself into the passenger seat of the vintage vehicle.

"Why, Aiden, why?" asked Evan, finally getting all his limbs inside, and Aiden laughed.

"It makes me feel like James Bond."

"So buy a modern one with actual leg room. Did no tall people exist in 1964?"

"It would appear not," said Aiden. "Where are we going?"

Evan gave him the address and Aiden found himself navigating to a neighborhood of office buildings, shops, and bars. It was a good area, with lots of people out even at this time of the evening.

"Just up ahead," said Evan, pointing. "Park anywhere."

Aiden did as instructed and pulled into a space as another car left. "You want me to wait?"

"No," said Evan. "Come up."

Evan led the way to an older building and then jogged up three flights of stairs. Aiden liked the building. Like the Aston Martin, it had a vintage look, with 1960s futuristic light fixtures and curves. Evan went down the hall and stopped in front of a door that had Murdock Esq. painted on glass.

"Murdock," said Aiden with a laugh. "That's the Daredevil's real name."

"I know," said Evan with a grin and Aiden, despite being suspicious, smiled back. He and Evan had always liked comic books. It was nice to be able to connect with him on a *good* childhood memory. Evan reached in his pocket and pulled out a key, then unlocked the door to the office. "Come on in," he said, holding the door open.

"OK," said Aiden. "What is this place? He stepped across the threshold and looked around. It was an office suite. Front desk area, two offices, and a conference room. Nothing fancy. Just a nice office space. It was empty except for a coffee-maker with a bow on it sitting in the middle of the floor.

"This," said Evan, "is your new office. I mean, if you want it to be."

Aiden looked back at Evan in confusion.

"You quit your job," said Evan. "But if you try and run this case out of your house, you're going to go stir-crazy."

He was already stir-crazy. Jersey was evidence of that.

"I thought that you could work here. And if, when you get done, you want to hang up your shingle as a consultant, or whatever lawyers call it when they go out on their own..."

"They call it being a lawyer," said Aiden.

"Well, OK, but I thought you'd at least have some place to do that. If you wanted to, that is."

Aiden hadn't mentioned to anyone that he'd been thinking about that. How had Evan known? Aiden turned in a circle looking at the office and ending facing Evan.

"I love it," said Aiden. "I love it a lot."

"It was the name that sold me," said Evan, looking embarrassed.

"I'm totally leaving that. I will be the fucking Daredevil."

Evan chuckled. "Good. Um, also..."

"What? Seriously, there can't be more."

"I may have called Jenna at your office and asked her to come be your clerk secretary thing person."

"You did what?"

"She said she's in. You just have to call her tomorrow and she'll turn in her notice."

"What?"

"She hates it without you, and she wants to be a law clerk."

"She should be!"

"Well, if you hire her, she can be."

"Can I afford to hire her? I mean, what about benefits? She'll need benefits and things, right?"

"Aiden…" said Evan, with a sigh.

"What?"

"Do you have *any* idea how much money you have?"

"No," said Aiden. "I never look. I just put my money in the bank and then I buy things. Or invest in whatever you and Dominique tell me to."

"How can you not have any clue about your money?"

"You take care of that," said Aiden. "And I make a lot of money, plus we're rich and I don't buy a lot of stuff, so I figure it works out."

He didn't add that he usually paid for all of his day to day expenses with cash from his fight wins. He actually had an entire suitcase stuffed with cash. He really wasn't sure what drug dealers did with cash. He always found it somewhat difficult to get rid of since he didn't party that much. He'd taken to tipping exorbitantly.

Evan looked like he was struggling for words. "Yes, it works out," he said at last. "It also works out that you can afford Jenna. You'll probably want other clients after a bit, but it'll be fine for at least a year."

"Cool," said Aiden, looking around the office again. "This is going to be awesome. You'll help me put together a business plan at some point, right?"

"Yes, of course," said Evan.

"So awesome," said Aiden again. "What did Jacks and Nika say?"

"I didn't tell them," said Evan, rubbing the bridge of his nose. "I didn't want them to know, in case you didn't like it."

"I love it," said Aiden, grinning. He wanted to hug Evan, but he wasn't sure where Evan stood on the physical contact thing. "Thank you."

Evan shrugged. "Just make sure that you don't get caught running around in red pajamas and fighting crime."

"I promise nothing," said Aiden, deciding to take a risk and tossing an arm around Evan's shoulders. Evan looked embarrassed but didn't pull away.

Ella – The Bank

Ella waited at the bank and checked the time on her phone. Aiden was late. As usual. Behind her, the contingent of her uncle's lawyers sat with stiff backs on the hard benches of the bank office. Ella stood, staring out the window at the bustling city street seventeen floors below them, and tried not check her phone again.

The elevator dinged and the door slid open. Aiden strolled out, looking as if he'd just rolled out of a menswear magazine—custom suit in dark blue, a pin-stripe shirt, and a tie with a pink fleck that tip-toed up to the line between quirky and stylish. Those damn blue eyes of his had never looked better.

Last night, she had tucked Lilly into bed and gone to lie down next to her grandmother.

"I think you were right," Ella had said into the darkness. "I think I do like Aiden and, even worse, I think he's a good person."

"Nobody's perfect," said Nai Nai.

"It's very inconvenient," said Ella, not mentioning that she also felt like she was cheating on Number Nine.

"Meh," said Nai Nai.

"That's not helpful," said Ella. "What am I supposed to do next time I see him? Or the other fifty times I see him in court? How am I supposed to beat him when I can't even be mad at him for being a stuck-up rich bastard?"

Nai Nai had shifted in bed, itching her scalp with one bony finger. "I don't think you have to be mad at someone to win an argument with them."

"If I beat him, he'll never like me back. It will cost his entire family a lot of money."

"Better lose then."

"But if I lose, Uncle will never forgive me."

"Better win, then."

"Nai Nai!"

"You young people always panic about things. You're smart. You'll come up with another solution."

Ella had gone to bed buoyed with that advice but woke up with the leaden truth that Aiden Deveraux was not meant to be hers. No matter the outcome of the case, Aiden Deveraux was never going to be any more acceptable to her uncle than Number Nine was.

"It's a crush," she said to her reflection as she got dressed. "Just a crush. You'll get over it."

And then he walked off the elevator and her heart gave a funny little bounce.

He hadn't gotten two steps off the elevator and someone called his name. Aiden pivoted and smiled in his easy way, going toward the young man who'd called his name. Ella watched in annoyance as the two laughed and joked and went back toward an office and then disappeared further into the bank's interior toward the vault.

Ella thought about going to stand next to her team. There was no point in loitering. He obviously didn't feel the need to seek her out. She glanced at Tic, Tac, and Toe and decided to stay where she was. It wasn't like there was going to be small talk.

She was checking her email when he returned. She heard him inhale as if to speak.

"Are you really going to try and talk to me?" she asked without looking up.

"I thought I might attempt it," he replied.

"Without all parties to witness the communication? Do you really believe that's a good idea?"

"Believe it or not, I do know a little something about the law," he said, sounding annoyed.

"Yes," she said, finally looking up. "That is what I believe. You know a *little* something about the law."

His expression froze. "Walked into that one," he said, and he nodded thoughtfully.

Ella bit her lip and looked away to keep from laughing and was certain that he'd noticed.

"How do you know I wasn't just going to say good afternoon and hello?" His tone was challenging.

"Were you?" she asked.

"No," he said, shaking his head. "Not even close."

Once again, she found laughter bubbling near the surface, and once again she was certain he'd noticed, because his eyes were dancing in amusement.

"If you must know, I was going to ask how Lilly was."

Ella was caught off guard. She'd been facing him in court for months. She knew he was brilliant. She knew he was respectful. But his kindness was startling.

"She's hung over like you wouldn't believe and grounded and swearing that she'll never touch alcohol again. And my grandmother is making her write out all one thousand poems of Lǐ bái in calligraphy."

"Ooh, calligraphy *and* poetry. Harsh," said Aiden. "Grandmother punishments are always the worst."

Ella almost took offense to that and then realized that he was speaking from experience. She wondered what it would have been like to be raised by Eleanor Deveraux. It couldn't have been easy. Eleanor Deveraux always seemed rigidly perfect in interviews. Maybe she was softer in person.

"I think she feels lucky to be getting away with only one thousand," said Ella.

"Well, I have—" began Aiden, then the elevator dinged, and they all looked toward the new arrivals.

"Nobody move!" A masked gunman stepped into the lobby. Three more came out after him. They were all dressed in black and carrying large guns. "Hands where I can see them!"

Ella stared at the gunmen in disbelief. This wasn't a standard bank branch—there were no tellers, no cash on hand. What were these people thinking?

"What the hell?" said Aiden. "They don't have any cash here." The thought so perfectly mirrored her own that Ella would have laughed, except that it attracted one of the gunmen's attention.

"Hands up!" the man yelled again, shoving the gun in Ella's direction. Ella put her hands up and he snatched her phone out of her hand and threw it on the ground before stomping on it. He shoved Ella in the shoulder, pushing her toward the far wall.

"Hey!" barked Aiden, taking a step forward.

The gunman held up the gun and Aiden halted.

"Against the wall. Everyone against the wall!" yelled the gunman, but his eyes were locked on Aiden, who reluctantly followed orders.

The gunmen herded everyone against the wall, shoving the bank personnel with callous indifference. They heard screams from the inner office as two of the four went into the back. Ella looked at Tic, Tac and Toe. They looked scared shitless. She looked up at Aiden. He looked wary and tense. She frowned as she felt a funny tingle of familiarity in the curve of his nose. He glanced down at her and smiled as if to say *can you believe this shit?* She smiled back. No, she couldn't really believe it, but she liked that Aiden was standing next to her.

"Phones!" the head bank robber was yelling while the third one went down the line with a sack. "Put your phones in the sack."

They reached Aiden, and he smiled cheerfully. After weeks in court with him, she recognized it as one of his fake smiles. This was the smile he usually reserved for her after she just served him some damaging point.

"I left mine at home," he said.

"Put it in the sack," growled the bank robber.

"I can't," said Aiden.

"Give him your phone," snapped Ella. He was going to get himself shot.

Aiden actually laughed. "I can't. I really left it at home. I'm very forgetful. Ask anyone."

The bank robber flipped his gun around and jabbed Aiden harshly in the stomach. Aiden doubled over and the bank robber ran his hands through Aiden's pockets. Finding nothing, he growled in frustration, which made Aiden laugh again, and Ella glared at him.

"Sorry," said Aiden and for a moment Ella felt like they were the only two in the room.

"Did you get them all?" yelled the head bank robber. The man holding the sack didn't immediately answer. "Ringo! Did you get them all?"

"Yeah," growled Ringo, stepping away from Aiden with a disgusted look.

There was more yelling from the two bank robbers in the back and the final bank employees, including Aiden's friend from earlier, was pushed out with the others to line up in the main foyer.

"Ringo, George," snapped the one that seemed to be the leader, "you're up. Get to the vault."

There was a tense few minutes of quiet in the foyer, and Ella could hear sniffling from one of the employees. Into the silence they heard the very faint, high-pitched whine of the siren.

"Fuck!" snapped the second bank robber, his eyes going to the leader. "They're early."

"Shut up, Paul," said the first bank robber. "We don't know that's for us."

"Because there's another bank robbery happening right now?" demanded Paul.

"Shut up, Paul," snapped the first one.

Ella was aware of Aiden's head turning back and forth between the two bank robbers. His face had the intense expression that she'd come to dread. He was about to figure something out and make her regret whatever she'd just said. Only in this case, she wasn't the one he was aiming at.

"You're not going to make it, John," said Aiden, straightening up and taking a half-step forward.

"What'd you say?" barked the leader, who put his gun directly onto Aiden's chest.

"You can't crack the vault fast enough," said Aiden.

"We only need ten minutes," said the second man.

"That's at least five minutes two long, Paul," said Aiden. "But I can cut it down for you."

"Oh, you can? I suppose you know the combination?" asked Paul sarcastically.

"Yes, I do. I was just back there, and I saw someone open it," said Aiden.

"Aiden!" gasped his friend, from a few spots down the line.

"Let the hostages go," continued Aiden, as if his friend hadn't spoken, "and I'll give it to you."

"Yeah, right," said Paul.

"Shut up, Paul," said John.

"That's not part of the plan," hissed Paul. "He said stick to the plan."

"Well, he's not here, is he?" Suddenly, John wheeled around and looked at the line of bank employees. "All right, all of you on the right side of the desk, you're leaving. Down the stairs." They stared at him in disbelief. "I said move," he yelled and fired a shot into the ceiling. There was a panicked stampede for the stairwell and Ella gestured for her team to join the group as it ran past them. Tic made it, but Paul snagged Tac and Toe.

"No, you Chinks stay right where you're at. You have to stay."

"How lovely," drawled Aiden. "Racist and stupid."

"Fuck you, cracker," said John. "Give us the combination."

"The first three numbers are eighteen, six, and forty-eight."

"And the rest?"

"I said all of the hostages," said Aiden. "And that *does* include the people of color."

The sirens were getting closer.

"People of color," sneered John, then stomped to the hall. "Ringo! The first numbers are eighteen, six, forty-eight. How long is this going to take?"

George came jogging out to the foyer. "We need at least six more minutes. Do you have any more of the combination?"

"I have two more," said Aiden, with a smile. "Too bad I can't remember them with all these people here."

Paul flipped his gun around and rammed it into Aiden's stomach. "Give us the numbers!" he yelled.

Aiden looked up at Paul and grinned. "Is that all of you've got? Because I promise that you don't have time to break me if that's case."

Ella glared at him. Was he trying to get himself killed?

"You don't need a lot of hostages," she said. "You just need a few. Let everyone else go, and the cracker and I will stay."

"No, she goes too," said Aiden.

"Shut up, *gwáilóu*," said Ella.

"I really don't see the need for the use of racial slurs," said Aiden.

"Stop being a patronizing agent of the misogynistic west then," said Ella.

"Really?" he looked hurt, which was adorable and made Ella want to kiss him. She smiled involuntarily and shook her head.

"I'm sorry," said John, "are we interfering with your ability to get your flirt on? Give us the fucking numbers or I shoot your girlfriend in the head."

"Shoot her and I will rip your throat out," said Aiden. There was something about the calmness and speed with which the comment flew out of his mouth that made it sound like a very plausible threat and the room was silent, as if shocked that Aiden—silly, soft, sweet Aiden—would say such a thing. Aiden smiled and once again Ella was aware of a mask of humor and niceness sliding into place. "You're running out of time. You don't want hostages. You want to get out of here. Let them go and I'll give you the numbers."

"This wasn't the plan," muttered Paul.

"Yeah, well, the plan said we would have twelve minutes before they responded. Those sirens don't sound twelve minutes away to me," said John. Then he looked down the line of hostages. "All right the gwáilóu wins. Everyone out."

The remaining employees made a quick shuffle for the door and the remaining two lawyers pulled on Ella's arm.

"Everybody but you two," said John, grabbing Ella by the arm. She saw Aiden tense, but Paul had him well covered and he didn't move. Aiden waited until the last person was through the door into the stairwell. "Last two numbers?"

"Thirty-six and twelve," said Aiden.

"That's ridiculous," said Ella and he glared at her. "Sorry," she said, feeling embarrassed.

"Problem?" asked John, tightening his grip.

"It's ridiculous that we have to do this. I should shut up now."

"Uh-huh," said John and he walked the few steps to the hall, dragging her with him. "Thirty-six and twelve," John yelled down the hall.

"Seriously?" said George's faint voice.

"What?" John yelled back.

"Got it!" bellowed Ringo.

"Multiples of six for the win," said George, running to the entry way. "Get the bags. Let's load up and get out of here."

"You don't need us," said Aiden. "Let us go and get out."

"Maybe we'll just keep her," sneered Paul.

"No," said Aiden, and once again the mask slipped. Aiden's expression was hard and brutal, and she felt John's grip on her shift, his palm slippery with sweat.

"Just go load up," said John to Paul. He walked her toward Aiden. "Get the hell out," he said and flung her at Aiden. The rug skittered out from underneath her on the marble tile, and she fell face first into Aiden's chest.

And she was seventeen again.

The scent of soap and sandalwood filled her nose. His arms were around her, holding her up, keeping her safe. The pounding of his heartbeat in her ear.

Aiden backed up, pulling her into the stairwell. He let go of her then and stared down into her eyes.

"Are you OK?"

She nodded, not feeling capable of speech.

"We're going to go downstairs," he said, putting his words into actions. He was holding her hand. She didn't let go. She kept trying to catch a glimpse of his jawline and match it to her memory. How was it possible? It couldn't be possible. She was mistaken. Number Nine had been poor.

No, Cinderella, I've got more. This is just what I have on me.

He hadn't been poor?

I live in the US. It'll be OK. I have family there. And lawyers.

He had *not* been poor. But… he had been a fighter? She'd seen him fight. He was good. Tall, pale skin, same number nine mask. Six years of fighting. That could not have been Aiden Deveraux. He was sweet and funny and… stupid. Absent-minded. Bumbling. Everyone said so. Only, she already knew that wasn't true.

Number Nine had been willing to help. He'd been kind. He'd been funny. And just a little bit cocky. Wasn't that Aiden?

They reached a landing several floors down and found themselves running into a wall of guns. Police were shouting at them. Or it seemed like shouting. There was a lot of loud talking. Aiden maintained his grip on her hand. It wasn't until they were on the street and all of her uncle's lawyers surged forward to pull her away that he released her.

Was she really going to leave him again?

"Ella!" Bai called. She looked at her uncle striding toward her, ignoring police officers, who were trying to block him. He'd been waiting for them in the car. He was always anxious to see any new evidence she turned up. Today had been no exception.

She looked back over her shoulder at Aiden. He was still watching her. She wanted to run back and fling her arms around him.

"Ella!" Bai yelled again, then he was hugging her and barking orders as he pushed her toward the car. She looked back again, and Aiden was gone.

Aiden — Berdahl-Copeland

Aiden idly flipped through the pile of documents that Ella had submitted into evidence last time they'd been in court. He stared blankly at a Berdahl-Copeland report that was part of a compiled stack of papers showing that Bo Zhao had worked for Randall Deveraux in 2006.

Every time he closed his eyes, Ella's face appeared on the inside of his eyelids. They had pulled her away and he had let them take her. They were her family. That was the right thing to do.

He kept repeating that to himself.

But her face... She hadn't wanted to go.

It had taken every ounce of strength not to simply start peeling lawyers off of her like wrapping paper, scoop her up and run for the hills. He couldn't shake the feeling that she was supposed to be with him and that she hadn't wanted to leave.

He stared again at the Berdahl-Copeland report. From 2006.

His brain was trying to tell him something, but all he could think about was Ella. The police had taken up the rest of the afternoon. The bank robbers had made it out of the building seconds before the police closed the perimeter. Currently, they were in the wind. And he had come out of police questioning to an annoying blockade of press. The damn hostages in the bank had given him credit for saving their lives. That was not how he was supposed to be in the news. He was supposed to be saying *no comment* for other people or giving a prepared statement about his undying support for his grandmother. He wasn't supposed to be the focus of any news stories. He was finding it massively embarrassing. He'd retreated to the safety of Deveraux House, but Jackson and Evan's unrepentant glee over the situation had driven him back out again. He'd finally had Dominique drop him at his new office so he could catch up on all the work he'd missed during the day.

He'd dropped off his boxes of files earlier in the morning, but he returned to find it fully furnished with notes from Dominique and Jackson. And the conference room was now home to a massive antique table from his grandmother. He loved his stupid family. If nothing else, it was nice to not have to sit on the floor.

Not that he was getting much work done. He was mostly just staring at the damn Berdahl-Copeland report from 2006 and trying not to think about Ella.

2006. A Berdahl-Copeland report. From 2006.

He stood up. Knocking over the chair with a loud crash. Fucking 2006.

Forty-five minutes of pacing his office later, he found himself in front of the palatial apartment the Zhao's were renting. He raised his hand and knocked with a nervous feeling that he was entering the jaws of the enemy to do a very stupid thing.

A butler answered and, just like butlers everywhere, did not look surprised at either the late hour or Aiden's request to see Ella. After a few minutes of waiting, the butler returned and gestured that Aiden should follow him.

The apartment was decorated in Chinese antiques and the occasional piece of colonial Victoriana. The butler opened the door to a smaller living room area and Aiden stepped in. Ella was by the window wearing some sort of green robe covered in a pattern of gold dragons, and her hair fell in a long black wave down her back. The wide collar of the robe exposed her neck and delicate collarbones.

"Holy shit, you're a princess," he blurted out. "I mean. Um. You look like a…"

She looked down at herself. "I look like what you think a princess should look like?"

"Yes, um, sorry. My sister had a book about a Chinese girl with a talking fish…"

She looked amused. "The story of Yen-Shen. Yes." She hesitated for a moment and then her mouth twisted into a smile. "It is the Chinese version of Cinderella."

"I don't remember," he said, feeling awkward. "I shouldn't have said anything."

She took a few steps toward him, stopping at a side table with a jade sculpture on it. "Why are you here, Aiden?" she asked, one finger tracking the spine of the jade tiger. Her voice was soft, but her expression was hard to read.

"I… We need to talk," he said, trying to get a handle on the situation. "There's a—"

He stopped talking as an old woman came in and began to drag a chair across the floor to a nook area where a TV had been placed. Ella and the old woman exchanged some words in Chinese and Ella looked perplexed.

"Should she be moving that on her own?" he asked. The woman looked like she was about a hundred and ten.

"Moving it? That is a matter of some debate," she said.

He looked from Ella to the old woman. Finally, unable to take it anymore, he went over and lifted the chair. "Over here?" he asked gesturing with the chair, and the old woman nodded. He set the chair down near the TV and she patted his cheek with a pleased smile and then handed him a candy from her pocket.

"I got a candy," he said, returning to Ella. Which was a stupid thing to say, but he thought it might make her laugh.

"Yes, you did," she agreed, her expression still puzzled.

With a shrug, he popped the small round ball of hard candy into his mouth. The feeling of sugar gave him a little more confidence.

"I do need to talk to you though. Can we go someplace?"

"No," she said, looking up at him.

He stared at her, uncertain of where to go next conversationally.

"Grandmother is not here for the TV," Ella said. "She's here for you. We are being chaperoned."

He found the ball of candy suddenly very sticky in his mouth.

"But, you did get a nice piece of cricket candy," she added.

"Cricket?" he repeated.

"Yes. She has them sent from China."

"It doesn't taste like cricket."

"It will when you get to the center."

He crunched the ball of candy between his teeth. "Oh. Yeah. There it is. Crickety." He swallowed.

She put her hand up to her mouth, hiding a smile as her eyes danced. "Would you like some water?" She was standing too close to him and her body sort of curved in his direction. He wondered what it would be like to slide his arms around her waist and kiss along her throat as his fingers traced the swell of her breast under the silk robe.

"Maybe a little," he said. He cleared his throat, reminding himself that her grandmother was sitting less than fifteen feet away. He felt like he had bungled the entire conversation so far. He was supposed to be polite and formal. None of his behavior had been remotely in the ballpark of formal. Why was he so bad at this?

She went to a buffet table by the wall and poured him a glass of water from a pitcher on a tray. Her robe made a soft slithering noise against the carpet as she walked. "What did you want to talk about?" she asked, handing him the glass.

"It's case related," he said, swallowing quickly. "I'm not

sure…" He glanced at her grandmother, still watching them and the TV from the other side of the room.

"She's fairly deaf and doesn't speak much English," said Ella taking a step away from him. He felt like he'd missed some sort of moment, but he wasn't sure how or why.

"I'm relying on your judgement in this," he said.

"You can," she said, going back to the table with the sculpture.

"Actually, I'm not really sure…" He suddenly had doubts about this entire enterprise. He thought she was honest. Her team, he wasn't sure about. But Ella… He wanted to trust her.

She was watching him, with a questioning expression. "Did the police say when we could get access to the DevEntier files at the bank?"

"No," he shook his head, momentarily diverted from his mission, "they're locked down for the next couple of weeks while they process the scene. We'll have to wait."

"Oh." She looked disappointed. "Then what is it?"

"Um… OK, I was going over the evidence you submitted last court session."

She nodded. Her expression remained unchanged.

"It was the DevEntier financial information from 2006."

She nodded again.

"It contained a Berdahl-Copeland report."

"Yes? To be expected."

There were no nervous ticks, no hedging. She really had no idea where he was leading.

"Yes," he agreed. "I would expect to see it in a quarterly report generated today. But the date was 2006. And," he took a deep breath, "I thought you might want to retract it before court on Monday."

She frowned at him, clearly puzzled. "Why would I do that?"

"2006," he repeated.

"Yes, I checked all of the reports," she said. "They were all generated around the eleventh of June 2006."

"Including the Berdahl-Copeland report," he said.

She stared at him as if trying to fathom what he was talking about. "Yes. Berdahl-Copelands are mandated reports from any corporation with defense contracts. They certify which employees have been vetted for DOD work. They've been required since…"

She trailed off, going pale.

"2011," he finished for her.

She stared at him and her hands lifted up slowly and she began to touch each finger to her thumb in rapid succession as if counting. Her expression became intensely focused, but not on him. He waited for her to speak, but instead, she walked slowly around the room, her fingers still moving rapidly.

"It's obviously a forgery," she said.

"Agreed," he said.

"But who would want that?" She was drifting around him in a circle and he turned to keep track of her. "And why?" Her tone was one of complete befuddlement.

He couldn't believe he was having to state the obvious. "Well, if someone wanted to win a court case…"

She lifted her head and stared at him and he realized that none of the last few moments of commentary had been addressed to him. She was blinking at him as if she had only just now remembered he was there. "Oh!" Her expression shifted into one of horror and she took a few rapid steps toward him, waving her hands as if to erase something. "No! No. You can't really think…" She blinked again and her expression shifted to pained embarrassment, and she stopped, standing too close again. He could smell something sweet and little bit spicy. Was it a perfume or a lotion? It tickled his brain with a memory that wouldn't surface.

"Oh, my God, you're being so epically polite about this," she said. "That is just so you. But no! I didn't fake evidence."

"Well, I don't think you did," he said. He wasn't sure if he'd just been complimented or not. *That is just so you* could go a lot of ways depend on who she thought he was. "But someone on your team…"

"No, you don't understand. *I* got those records. And I got them from—"

The door to the room slammed open and Bai Zhao stormed in.

"Get out!" he screamed, fury suffusing his face. "How dare you be here with her?"

Aiden glanced at Ella for a cue on how to handle this. She looked as shocked as he felt.

"Sir," said Aiden, instinctively angling his body slightly between Ella and the screaming man. "I'm speaking with Ms. Zhao about the case. You need to—"

"Get out!" Bai yelled again, pointing toward the door. "Get out or I will have you thrown out!"

"Bai!" The old woman smacked the edge of the TV with her cane making a cracking noise. Bai spun in surprise. Ella's grandmother rattled off a few sharp sentences in Chinese and whatever she said brought Bai back to earth, but it did not make him any less angry.

"Get out," he said through clenched teeth. "You are not permitted here. If you wish to speak to my niece, you will do it at the office."

Aiden looked at Ella. She pulled herself up straighter and met his eye. "Thank you for bringing this to my attention, Mr. Deveraux. I will be in communication with you about the matter."

She held out her hand.

"Before Monday," he said, shaking her hand because that's what she wanted him to do.

"Count on it," she said with a polite smile that was nothing like the one she'd been hiding behind her hand earlier.

Then he walked out of the apartment, and he couldn't help feeling that every step was a mistake.

Jackson – Nowitsky

"Look, you didn't hear this from me," said Nowitsky, "but the whole thing is fucking weird."

"Fucking weird isn't a secret," said Jackson, signaling the waitress. "I got that from Aiden."

"OK, but…" Nowitsky looked around the diner. There weren't any cops in the place, but Nowitsky still leaned in closer. "CSI is still processing the scene, but I don't think they're going to turn up anything new. It was a four-man crew. Called themselves John, Paul, Ringo, and George."

"I always went with the Stones myself," said Jackson with a shrug. "But whatever. As long as no one wants to use the Backstreet Boys, it's cool."

"Beatles are probably easier to remember though," said Nowitsky.

"For your generation," said Jackson, taking a sip of his coffee.

Nowitsky was a solid police detective who technically did not take bribes. What he did take was letters of recommendation to his kid's college of choice where the Deveraux name carried weight. Eleanor was now watching young Ms. Nowitsky's progress with interest and Jackson thought she might be interning with Eleanor's office during the summer.

"Fuck you," said Nowitsky. "Anyway, the aliases suggest they're professional. Then there's the fact that they made repeated references to a male person who told them that the response time would be twelve minutes."

Jackson thought about that. "That's bullshit. The response time in that neighborhood should be five minutes tops. I mean, maybe it's bit longer for SWAT, but a uniform should be there way faster than twelve minutes."

"I dislike that you know this," said Nowitsky sourly.

"The location of police substations is publicly available information," said Jackson.

"Uh-huh. Anyway, one of the employees managed to dial 911 and say *robbery* before tossing her phone into a garbage can and out of sight. So the response time was fast, but even if it hadn't been, it was never going to be slower than six minutes. The suspects came up in the elevator, avoided cameras for the most part, put their masks on in transit and went straight to the vault. They knew the floorplan and they knew who the manager was. They had an exit route in place and a driver waiting for them. They also knew exactly what to take: bearer bonds."

"So what are you saying?" asked Jackson frowning.

"I'm saying it's weird. It was a good plan. Except for the thing with the response time."

Jackson sipped his coffee and eyed Priscilla, the waitress, who was probably in her thirties, but still definitely qualified under hot. She gave him extra whipped cream on his pie every time he was in the diner. "I don't see the angle for it," he said at last. "So they've got a Geppetto. He puts the team together. He gives them mostly good information. Why not all good information? Does he want them to get caught?"

"This is what I'm saying," said Nowitsky. "It's weird. Also, weird was the fact that they wanted to keep the Chinese guys."

"What do you mean?"

"A couple of the witnesses said the suspects didn't want to let the Chinese hostages go. They weren't supposed to let anyone go, but then your cousin pulled his Prince Charming routine and talked them into it. Only when they were letting the hostages go, they still didn't want to let the Chinese ones go."

Jackson frowned. He didn't like that. That meant that the mysterious string-puller who set up the gig had expected the Chinese to be there. And if they had expected the Zhao, then they had to have expected Aiden.

"What would have happened if Aiden hadn't…"

"Hadn't given them the combination to the vault and convinced them to let all the hostages go?"

"Yeah."

Nowitsky appeared to think about that. "They wouldn't have been able to crack the vault. They would have had to leave without the money. And that's *if* they left. It's possible that there would have been a stand-off inside the bank."

"Aiden said everyone could hear the sirens."

Nowitsky nodded. "OK, so they leave without any money. They maybe take hostages with them?"

"Chinese hostages?"

"Possibly. If you've been told to target those ones, then yeah. Maybe a shoot-out. Stand-off in the lobby? Who knows?"

"But they're not getting out of the building?"

"No," said Nowitsky. "I don't see that happening."

Jackson drummed his fingers on the counter. Priscilla arrived with two slices of pie. His had much more whipped cream than Nowitsky's.

"Thanks," said Jackson smiling up at her. Nowitsky rolled his eyes.

"Judging from the weaponry, do we think that they wouldn't have gone quietly?"

"You can never tell," said Nowitsky with a shrug.

"Everyone thinks they're *Heat*. Most people turn out to be *Dirty Rotten Scoundrels*."

Jackson laughed, surprised by the unexpected joke.

"Anyway, my point is that it's weird."

"I feel like we're missing the Plan B," said Jackson. "I think Aiden disrupted all the plans and they improvised. And I'm guessing that whoever the Geppetto behind this little shindig was, he's now pissed. Because you don't accidentally tell someone twelve minutes." He paused. Something was missing here, and he couldn't, for the life of him, figure out what. "I think he was counting on his guys to *have* to move to Plan B."

"Yeah, well, if I'm John, Paul, George and Ringo, I'm also pissed," said Nowitsky, "because no matter how dumb these guys are, sooner or later they're also going to realize that twelve minutes wasn't an accident."

Nowitsky's phone lit up and vibrated on the speckled Formica of the counter. Nowitsky picked it up with a thoughtful expression.

"Nowitsky," he said while cutting a forkful off his pie. "Go."

Jackson dug into his own pie and made eye contact with Priscilla, who smiled at him. He liked waitresses. The problem was that, with his bank account currently at maximum green, waitresses tended to want to move straight to the end of the fairy tale. But Jackson was not Aiden. He was not going to be sweeping anyone off their feet. He liked girls with their feet firmly on the ground, who didn't need him for anything, and only occasionally wanted him to show up with wine, condoms and three hours to spare. He had a few friends like that, but one more couldn't hurt.

"Uh-huh," said Nowitsky, putting down his fork without taking the bite. "Yeah. What did you—"

There was a tenseness to his voice that pulled Jackson's attention away from Priscilla.

"OK, so you shut down the building? Good. How long until they can get the damn thing out?" There was a response to Nowitsky's question that Jackson couldn't quite hear. "Well, good thing it's the weekend, I guess." Nowitsky nodded as the caller on the other end spoke again. "OK, well, keep me updated. I'll circle back to the scene in a few hours."

Nowitsky hung up and looked at Jackson. "I think we found our Plan B."

"What do you mean?"

"The Beatles left the vault a mess. CSI was finishing up, moved some papers and found, guess what?"

Jackson shook his head. He really had no idea.

"A bomb. It's wired into the electrical system. If they had blown it, it would have fried most of the building's systems and of course put a big fucking hole in the floor. CSI is shutting down the building and calling in the bomb squad, but due to the way it's wired, they might not be able to get it out until at least tomorrow."

"It's *Die Hard*," said Jackson. "The bearer bonds. The bomb that covers the escape of the thieves. It's fucking *Die Hard*."

Nowitsky gave a dry snort of laughter. "Not a genius mastermind at work, I guess."

"So if the cops had shown up, they would have said they had a bomb, and then what?"

"We would have cleared the building and negotiated."

"Then they blow the bomb and either get killed or escape in the confusion?"

"I don't really think they would have escaped," said Nowitsky.

"But they probably would have been convinced that they would." Jackson tapped his fork on his plate in a shave and a haircut rhythm, thinking. "You need to find out what would have happened if the bomb went off."

"I told you—fried systems, hole in floor."

"That's generally. What specifically would have happened? If we're right, then whoever put this plan in motion really wanted the bomb to go off. That was the real target."

Nowitsky grunted and reached for his phone, then stopped. "Jackson, this isn't good. The Beatles were also told to target the Chinese. If that's the case…"

"Yeah," said Jackson standing up and tossing down some cash on the bar. "I know. The Zhao are in danger. You need to warn them."

"Not just the Zhao," said Nowitsky. "Aiden…"

"Aiden is my problem," said Jackson. "Call me if you get anything else."

Ella – DevEntier, Brooklyn Office

Ella sat on the sanitary napkin garbage and braced her feet against the opposite wall of the bathroom stall. She was waiting for the security guard to finish his rounds. The guard was late. She supposed, since it was Saturday, he was being lazy, but she was annoyed by his lax behavior. And also, she was bored and not sure how much longer the tampon disposal unit could carry her weight.

She stared up at the fluorescent light and sighed.

She had hoped, just for a few seconds, last night that Aiden had come to see her because her moment with him in the bank had been *their* moment. That he had realized she was Cinderella, and he'd come immediately to sweep her off her feet. And then he'd told her that he thought she'd faked evidence and she'd come crashing down to earth.

She shouldn't be surprised. She was obviously not the only girl he'd ever kissed. And it really had just been one kiss. She might have spent the last six years wistfully fantasizing about meeting him again, but he had been dating the Channel Four weather girl.

Her own thoughts checked her at that. It wasn't like she hadn't dated anyone in the last six years. There had been several someones. It was just that she'd always wanted Number Nine. And now, here he was, and not only did he have no clue who she was, he thought that she was the kind of person who would forge evidence. And do it badly, at that.

She sighed again and shifted on her metal perch. That wasn't fair either. He'd point blank stated that he didn't think she'd done it. Just that someone on her team had.

He also thought she looked like a princess. That made her smile.

The door to the restrooms swung open and banged against the wall. Ella held her breath. The guard flipped off the bathroom lights and she could hear him walking away as the door slowly swung closed, the draft strip dragging across the tile with a soft noise.

Aiden was right—the evidence helped her case. So it was logical that her side would be responsible for forging it. The problem with that theory was that she knew she hadn't done it.

When she had received an offer of "some records" from a disgruntled former DevEntier janitor, she had been hoping for something showing that her father was an employee. She hadn't been expecting an entire box of records. The box, as far as she could tell, was untampered with, and she had been the first to go over every single piece of evidence in the box. She had pulled out the Berdahl-Copeland report herself. But if she hadn't faked it, that left only one option: it had been done by someone at DevEntier.

And the only reason she could come up with for someone at DevEntier to do that, was if they were planning on pointing it out in court after she had entered it in evidence. But Aiden wouldn't do that. He certainly wouldn't point it out to her before he did it.

She hoped.

There was only one way to be certain. She knew the date on the box. All she had to do was sneak into the DevEntier warehouse.

DevEntier had started life under Henry Deveraux and Charles MacKentier in the seventies in Manhattan proper, but in the early eighties they had relocated to Brooklyn and a brand new building fresh from the desk of a newly minted architect with all the futuristic pink stucco anyone could ask for. DevEntier corporate headquarters had eventually gone back to Manhattan, but the research and development—the actual work of DevEntier—was still in Brooklyn along with the records warehouse. So here she was perched inside one of the women's restrooms of DevEntier Brooklyn, admiring the forest green tile, wondering if the grout had ever been white, and hoping that she could sneak out and locate the records room without getting caught. Thanks to her uncle's research team and a very helpful breakdown of the building's security patterns, and mention of a particularly bribable employee at the front gate, getting into DevEntier had been easier than getting out of the apartment without her security detail. Now she just needed to find anything near that date and look to see if they also contained Berdahl-Copeland reports with her father's name on them. Then she was back out the door and back home before anyone realized she wasn't in bed. Of course, if she did find records with her father's name on them, that gave her with a whole new mystery to deal with, but at least that was a mystery she could take to Aiden.

She waited another thirty seconds and left the bathroom. The record room was in the opposite direction of the guard desk. As long as she didn't do anything monumentally stupid, she should be able to sneak a peek at the records and then be out the side door that the Zhao security team claimed was never alarmed because it was inconvenient for the employees.

She walked on tip-toe so that her heels wouldn't make a racket, and wished she'd worn flats. But heels went with the DevEntier lab coat and the sensible pencil skirt that she hoped made her look more like an adult and less like a child playing at dress up, which was what she felt like. She made it to the records room and slithered through the door, cringing at the creak it made as she opened it. She waited just inside the door, listening for anything besides the pounding of blood in her ears, but nothing moved.

The records room held metal shelves full of white boxes, each labeled with two stickers—one yellow, one white. The white sticker contained a list of what was in the box and the yellow contained a date for when someone made adjustments to the contents. Or at least that was the idea. The yellow sticker could easily be ignored.

Ella located the shelf that her box should have come out of and went down the aisle. She walked quickly, trailing her finger along the boxes, checking the dates. She stopped in the center of the aisle and stared at the blank spot where her box belonged. She scanned the shelves and, taking a deep breath, she grabbed the box from two years later, the year of her father's death, and slid it off the shelf. Resting the box against her stomach, she flipped through the papers, and found a Berdahl-Copeland right where she would expect to find it—right where it shouldn't exist.

"But why?" she murmured, staring at the pink sheet of paper.

"Exactly what I want to know," said a voice and she jumped, dropping the box. Aiden swung down from the top of the shelves and landed with a light thump.

The box dumped its contents onto the floor in pile like a November blizzard of leaves.

She stared at Aiden. He looked angry.

"This looks bad," she said.

"Oh, you think?"

"But it's not what it looks like."

"So you didn't get your evidence from the box that goes here?" He pointed to the blank spot.

Ella hesitated. "OK, yes, I did."

"You stole it!"

"No!"

She hadn't seen him this angry before. At least not at her.

"It fell off the turnip truck?"

"In a manner of speaking," said Ella.

"It may have, but I didn't. You stole it."

"No! I didn't." She knelt down and began to shovel the papers back into the box.

"Stop touching those!" he ordered. She looked up at him and in a fit of childishness, picked up a piece of paper and licked it.

"Ella!"

"Oops," she said and shoved it back in the box. "I guess now it's contaminated with Zhao DNA."

"I can't believe you just did that."

"I can't believe you're yelling at me!"

"I am not yelling!" he yelled.

"You're both yelling," said a sour voice. She looked up and saw a man in a black jacket and pants. Unlike the security guard, he was carrying a gun and it was pointed at them. "Hands up."

Ella put her hands up.

"Put the gun down," said Aiden. "Neither of us is a threat."

"Neither of you is supposed to be here," said the man coming toward them. Behind Aiden, she saw a man approach from the other direction. He was dressed the same as the first one and carried the same type of gun.

"Aiden," she said.

"I'll deal with this," he snapped.

"You're going to deal with absolutely nothing," said the first man with the gun. He reached down and pulled Ella off the floor by the collar of her lab coat.

"Hey!" barked Aiden, stepping forward.

"No," said Ella, but it was too late. The second man hit Aiden on the back of the head with his gun butt.

Aiden – Third Floor

Aiden regained consciousness with a jerk. He couldn't remember where he was. That wasn't a good sign. He was laying on the floor and every instinct screamed to get up. Whoever had hit him was probably going to do it again. That was usually what happened anyway.

He tried to put his hands up to cover his head but realized that his hands were trapped. Someone was holding them? No, they were tied. Why was he tied up?

"Oh, thank God. Aiden. Aiden, get up."

Someone knew his name. Was that good or bad?

What the hell had happened to him? He opened his eyes and stared at a single foot in black spike-heeled bootie. That shoe belonged to Ella. He twisted his head and looked up Ella's leg.

"Aiden, get up," she said again. Her face was a blurry spot on the far side of her knees.

Was there a reason he was supposed to be mad at her?

He rolled to his side and tried to do as she asked. His attempt was only partially successful. He made it as far as sitting up and collapsed against Ella's leg, his face pressed against her inner thigh. He closed his eyes again, feeling the world spin. Hello, concussion.

He tried to sort out what had happened and why he was tied up, but he was having to think really hard and what he really wanted to do was rest here against Ella.

"Aiden!" Ella's tone was pleading.

So they were on opposite sides of a court case. Did that really matter? How could that matter when her skin felt so good against his cheek? She still smelled like something he couldn't quite place. Something that reminded him of summer? Heat? Mexico?

"Your skin is really soft," he thought and then realized that it hadn't been a thought so much as a verbalization.

Ella sighed in exasperation. "This is not how this fantasy is supposed to go," she muttered.

"How does it go?" he asked, trying to keep up with events. He opened his eyes and realized that he was sitting more or less between her thighs. He looked up into her big brown eyes and suddenly grasped exactly how the fantasy was supposed to go.

"Does it go like this?" he asked, tilting into her and kissing her thigh. She shivered and he leaned further in and kissed again.

"Aiden," she said, her voice going up, "this is not the time." He'd reached the hem of her skirt, and he kissed just under the edge of it and she let out a little gasp and her legs widened, stretching the fabric of her skirt taut, but making room for him. This was going to be difficult with his hands tied, but he was willing to try.

"Aiden!" Her voice was high and strained. "Aiden, I am tied to a chair!"

That wasn't good.

"Right," he said, pulling back and blinking up at her. "Right."

"Can you go around and try to untie me?"

"Yes," he said, attempting to catch up to current events. "Yes, that is totally what I'm doing."

It took him several more minutes to get up, make it around the chair and work through the knots with his teeth. He stood up as the last rope fell away and found the world spinning again. He closed his eyes and leaned against the wall. He could feel Ella untying him and when he finally opened his eyes again, she was in front of him, hands on his face.

"Don't look so worried," he said. "I'm fine."

"No, I don't think so," she said, her hand caressing his cheek gently.

"No. I promise," he said. "Or at least I will be." Then he leaned down and did what he knew he shouldn't do. He kissed her.

He was twenty-one again, a hot Mexico night just outside the door. His head was on fire and his fingers were cold. Blood pounded in his ears with a dull roar like the ocean, and the girl in his arms tasted like chocolate and smelled of spices. Everything was melting away. It didn't matter who was outside the door or where they were. The only thing—the only person—who mattered was right in front of him. Then reality, both realities, hit him and he let go, stumbling back, his eyes still closed. He put his hand up to his lips trying to capture the ephemeral taste that was singular, distinct and only belonged to one person.

"Cinder," he opened his eyes, and saw her, "Ella."

She had one hand on the back of the chair that she'd recently been tied to. She looked nervous.

"Number Nine?"

He remembered suddenly why he was mad at Ella. She had broken into DevEntier and was stealing evidence. He looked around the room. They were locked in some sort of office. It was full of janitorial supplies and an ancient and grimy computer on an equally grimy desk.

The door opened and, before Aiden could register who it was, Ella had picked up the chair and flung it at the man in the doorway. The chair crashed against him and he stumbled back. Ella sprinted forward and jumped into a front kick, stomping hard into his gut and groin. There was a ripping noise as her skirt gave up against the force of her legs and split along the front seam. The man yelled in surprise and pain, falling backward through the doorway. Ella grabbed up the chair again and smashed it over him.

"Come on," she yelled back at Aiden, waving urgently. He moved away from the wall, head pounding and feeling shocked, as if he were thinking through Jell-O. The man ignored Aiden and rolled over, grabbing Ella by both ankles and yanking. Aiden's thoughts sped up as Ella toppled over. With a quick step, Aiden landed his knee on the man's back and grabbed his hair with both hands, smashing his face into the floor. Ella scrambled to her feet and grabbed his hand, pulling him across the wide expanse of open warehouse area and toward the elevator.

"I tried to tell them you worked for DevEntier," she said. "They said they didn't care and that the boss would deal with you."

"Who's their boss?" asked Aiden.

"I don't know," she said. "Our research said that there were only two security guards. I don't know who these guys are, but they are not nice people."

"What does that mean?" asked Aiden. His head hurt. Aiden reached back to rub the source of the pain and found it matted with blood.

"How are your ribs?" she asked. She still hadn't let go of his hand.

"What?"

"They kicked you while you were unconscious."

Now that she'd mentioned it, his ribs did hurt. And he now was not even a little bit sorry he'd just broken that guy's nose.

"And," she continued, still talking fast, "that one said he was coming back to have a private conversation with me. Call me crazy, but I don't think he was going to do much talking."

He pulled up short with a growl. "I will kill him."

"Yes," agreed Ella, reaching back and grabbing his wrist. "Very upsetting. Kill later. Leave now."

"But…" Aiden let her pull him along and tried to work through the soup that was currently his brain. He still felt like he was going to puke a little. "You broke in here," he said, clinging to the facts he did know. "You stole evidence."

She reached for the elevator button, but the readout above the door said it was already moving. "No, I didn't." She pulled him toward the stairs.

"How am I supposed to believe you?" he asked. He looked at the moving elevator numbers and felt a kick of adrenaline. Now wasn't really the time to be having this discussion with Ella. Also, at the moment he felt like Ella could have whatever she wanted.

"Seriously?" she demanded, still holding onto his wrist and pulling him like a balloon on a string. He tried to quicken his pace. He needed to step up. "If I had time to slap you, I would," she said, opening the door to the stairs. "But you clearly can't take anymore brain damage."

There was a bellow from the man they'd left on the floor behind them. Ella pulled Aiden into the darkened stairwell. It took a moment for his eyes to adjust to the light of the streetlamps coming in from the high, multi-paned windows at the end of the stairwell, but it was a relief from the buzzing fluorescents in the room they had just left. They had barely gone half a flight when they saw flashlights coming up toward them. Aiden took a deep breath and rolled his shoulders. Time to get back in the fight.

"Um," said Ella, freezing on the landing and watching the flashlights come up toward them.

Aiden swung open the window next to him and looked down into the open maw of the dumpster two and a half stories beneath them.

"Too bad you're not wearing your Cinderella dress," he said. "What?"

He picked Ella up and threw her out the window. She went out with a small shriek and he watched her land. Just as he was about to go after her, he felt a hand on his shoulder. Without turning around, he pushed back and elbowed at the same time. The man grunted and stumbled, taking a step off the landing so Aiden could turn and sent him all the way down with a kick. The man behind him avoided the flying body and lunged at Aiden. Aiden side-stepped and punched. The first man came back and grabbed at his arm, but managed to snare only his sleeve. Aiden heard a rip as sweat-shirt tore. He kicked out again, then punched. He heard the door above him slam open. This was not going well. He grabbed the first man, head-butted him and then threw him into the second. Then he kicked them both down the stairs. He sprinted toward the window and was over the sill and falling just as the third man came running down the stairs, hand out-stretched to grab him.

He landed in something unidentifiable and disgusting, but at least Ella's ass was in front of him. She was trying to climb out of the dumpster but seemed to have one foot stuck in a garbage bag. He put his hand on her ass and pushed, noting the firm yet soft qualities of his handful and trying to ignore it. He climbed out after her. There was paper in her hair and she was missing a shoe.

"Next time," she said, yanking off the other shoe, and waving it at him, "a little warning would be nice."

"There's not going to be a next time," he snapped.

There was a shout from the front door of the building and Aiden grabbed her hand and began to run.

"Did you bring a car?" she demanded.

"I took a Lyft," he said as he attempted to shake off his pound-ing head. Headbutting that guy really hadn't helped the headache situation. "Shut up and run."

They ran four blocks before they found a street busy enough

to have cabs on it, though it took another block before they found one willing to stop for them.

"Rough night?" asked the cab driver suspiciously as they climbed in.

"You could say that," said Ella. "Can you go to—"

"Trios Hotel," cut in Aiden and she looked surprised. He glared at her, daring Ella to argue.

"Sure," said the cabbie.

"Aiden," she began.

"We'll talk at the hotel," he said.

She threw her hands up in a clear gesture of frustration, but said nothing. Aiden sat back in the seat and ignored her. Then he looked at his sleeve and her ripped skirt. Her single shoe was still clutched in one hand. He took out his phone and dialed Claude.

"Hey, Claude," he said. "It's Aiden."

"Ah, Aiden. What can I do for you this evening?"

Claude was the Deveraux dresser. He was French and possibly a saint, or at least a genius. And he was probably one of the few non-related people that all of the Deveraux trusted. Aiden had occasionally tried to pry secrets about Evan and Jackson out of him and had gotten nowhere. He assumed that the same veil of secrecy applied to him.

"Clothes," said Aiden.

"What else would it be?" replied Claude.

"Usual mix. At the hotel."

Claude clucked disapprovingly. "Should I include a first aid kit as well?"

"No. I'm fine. It's just the clothes that took a beating this time. But I'm going to need a second set for…" he glanced at Ella, "a woman. Size two?"

"Usually," she said, looking surprised.

"What size shoes?" Claude asked.

"Shoe size?" asked Aiden.

"A six and a half," she said, looking perplexed.

"A six and a half," repeated Claude, not needing Aiden to say it again. "Any preferences I should be aware of?"

"She looks good in green," said Aiden. "And she likes dangerous shoes."

"They come in handy," said Ella.

"I can work with that," said Claude. "It'll take an hour or two."

"No problem," said Aiden. "She and I have a lot to talk about."

That was the understatement of the century, but he felt so fucking confused that he didn't know what to think, let alone what to say. The cab dropped them off and Aiden went directly to the elevator. Ella followed, looking mystified.

"Shouldn't we have checked in?" she asked.

"No," said Aiden. "I have a room on permanent reserve. I use it for all of my fight-related business and recovery time."

"You can't just go home?"

"I can never confirm, but I assume Jackson has informants at my house. Because, you see, no one is supposed to know about my hobby."

"OK," she said, seemingly oblivious to the bitter note in his voice. "You can't just get a second apartment?"

"It would show up on a property search and on my taxes."

"Oh. That makes sense."

They arrived at his floor and he took the key card out of his wallet and let them into his room. He held the door open for her and then shut it behind her—perhaps too forcefully.

She turned back to him. "Why are you so mad?"

"I don't know. How about the fact that you lied to me!"

"No, I never have."

"So you just stole and faked evidence?"

"No!"

"And if that didn't work out, you were what? Just going to blackmail me with the fact that I do illegal fighting?"

Her eyes went wide, and she stared at him, her face filled with hurt. He wanted to take it back. He wanted to hug her. He honestly didn't know what he was supposed to do. What part of Ella was he supposed to respond to? When had everything gotten so complicated?

"I'm going to take a shower." He didn't wait for her to reply. He walked through the suite and into the bathroom.

Ella – Trios Hotel

He was mad at her and that hurt. Even in their most heated exchange in court she had never felt the cold anger that he exuded now. It was everything the Deveraux were famed for and just as unpleasant as reported.

Ella stood in the middle of the room and smelled the garbage in her hair. Did he just expect her to stand around and take this?

Angrily, she began to yank off her clothes. The shower was a multi-headed walk-in affair, which, she decided, left him plenty of room to share. His back was to her as she entered, exposing his ass and well-muscled back. She could see the scrapes from the fight in Jersey. How had she not known it was Aiden?

"You're not being fair," she said, snatching the soap out of his hand.

He turned around, confusion evident on his face. He made one gesture as if to cover himself, then stopped, folding his arms across his chest.

"In what way?"

"I did not steal that evidence. I was approached by a jani-tor from DevEntier. He said he had something I might want and showed me one page. It had my father's name on it. I paid him for the rest. I expected a handful of papers that he'd fished out of the garbage. I did not know that he would steal an entire box from file storage."

"But once you had it, you had to assume it was stolen!" he protested, flapping his hands in exasperation. He never flapped in court. Ella felt like she was getting somewhere. He was clearly very flustered. Maybe that was it. It had been a rather hard evening. Maybe he just needed a moment to wrap his head around everything.

"I had to assume nothing," she said calmly.

"So, you decided to just break-in and get the rest?"

That accusation annoyed her. She scrubbed angrily at her hair and tried to ignore the way water was dripping off various parts of him. She watched his gaze drift down her body and then yank back up to her face.

"No," she said sweetly. "You pointed out the Berdahl-Copeland report was a fake. Since I know I didn't fake it, someone in DevEntier must have. We've been arguing over whether or not DevEntier even employed my father. I've always thought that the missing paperwork was suspicious. That's why I pushed so hard for the bank records!"

"Wrap it up here, counselor." Aiden's eyes narrowed, and he took a step toward her. God, he was chiseled. "You're not exactly helping your case."

"Depends on which case I'm trying to win," she said.

"What?" He looked confused again and Ella realized that if she wanted to win any of her cases with him, she was going to have walk him through it with her. He wasn't usually this slow. She was putting it down to the bump on the head.

"Assume for a moment that DevEntier destroyed any records of my father's employment."

Aiden was silent, which made her think he'd already contemplated the thought.

"So why, if they did that, would someone go out of their way to prove not only his employment, but with the Berdahl-Copeland reports, that he'd been reviewed by the DOD? What do they gain? And was it only one year? If it was one year, then someone at DevEntier set me up with that one box. Give me the box, and I'd submit the evidence. Suddenly the evidence is spotted as a forgery and I'm discredited. I had to know if you were setting me up!"

"If I was setting you up, then why would I come to you in the first place?"

"Well, as you recently said to me, 'I didn't think it was you. I thought maybe it was someone on your team.' As it turns out, it was not a set up. Those Berdahl-Copelands show up in multiple years."

He hesitated. "I know. I looked before you came in. There was a DOD audit five years ago. That's the last date on all of those boxes. I think whoever did it, must have done it for the audit."

She frowned. "Dad wasn't a citizen. He was going through the process, but he was in country on a marriage visa. Mom used to say that was the only reason they stayed married. I thought she was just being a bitch."

"Even fifteen years after the fact, the DOD would care about a Chinese national working on one of their projects. Fake Berdahl-Copelands would make it look like he'd been vetted."

"OK," said Ella, "but who could do that?"

Aiden ran his hand through his hair, leaving it in damp shark fins that made him look sexy as hell.

"I don't know," he said.

She put the soap down and rinsed out her hair. The chunks of whatever seemed to be gone. She probably ought to switch to real shampoo and conditioner, but she had to focus on the more important facts—she was naked in a shower with Aiden. And, unfortunately, she had now gotten him to focus on the case. She needed to put his focus back where it was supposed to be: on her.

"I wouldn't ever use your *hobby* against you," she said, mad that she even had to be saying it.

"When did you know?" he demanded, still sounding gruff.

"Yesterday. At the bank."

"Oh," he said. His shoulders relaxed and he took a step closer to her. "I didn't want to leave you, but your uncle…" He trailed off, his eyes intent on hers and she breathed a sigh of relief. He had felt it. Even if he hadn't known who she was, he'd felt the moment the same way she had. "I kept telling myself it was the right thing to do. We're on opposite sides. We're supposed to hate each other."

"I know we're on opposite sides about DevEntier," she said. "But you helped me when I needed it most. How could I use that against you? How could I *ever* hate you?"

He let out a lungful of air and she took a step toward him. They were within inches of each other—close enough that she could feel the warmth coming from his skin. She put her hand up to his face. His sweet, stupid, perfect, beautiful face.

"Oh, Ella," he sighed and did what she wanted him to do—he kissed her. Aiden had been her first kiss, and unlike every other girl she knew, her first kiss had been electric perfection. Now, six years later, nothing had changed.

Or rather everything had changed. Now there was nothing between them.

She wrapped her arms around his neck. Water cascaded over them, hot and stinging where she had been scraped in her escape from the dumpster. But none of that compared to the sensation of his lips on hers. He pushed downward, kissing her neck, and she ran her hand down his side, feeling the hardness of muscle and bone and the softness of skin. His cock was rigid against her leg and she felt an answering heat between her thighs.

Abruptly, he pulled away and she uttered a noise that wasn't a word, just vocal disagreement.

"Right," he said. Then he snapped the water off and picked her up, bending to scoop her up as if he were carrying her across the threshold.

He carried her into the hotel room and lowered them onto the bed, their legs tangling as they tumbled across the bed spread. His fingers and mouth were on her breasts, and she gasped as her nipples sprang erect and taut. His tongue teased across one as his hand drifted downward, grazing across her clit. She gasped again and he transferred his attention to her mouth, kissing her while his fingers caressed and stroked her sex. She was wet everywhere from the shower, but under his fingers she became slick with desire.

"Aiden," she moaned. She reached down, feeling along his body like she was blind, unwilling to stop kissing him long enough to look. Finally, she reached his cock. It was thick in her hand, heavy and hard. She ran her thumb down the shaft and he groaned.

"Aiden," she murmured, as she stroked again, insistently.

"I don't have any condoms," he mumbled, around her lips.

"I have an IUD," she said.

"Oh, thank God," he said quite clearly, before kissing her hard.

He pushed her onto her back and settled his weight onto her. His cock rested at the entrance and she felt an almost painful ache of desire. He eased into her and she found herself gasping. The utter sense of satisfaction from having him inside her was unlike anything she'd ever experienced. She moaned as he began to move.

"More," she gasped, and he thrust into her, gently at first and then with more urgency.

She clutched at his sides, trying to pull him into her further. Everything he did seem to make her want more. This was far better than any of the fantasies she'd had about either of his personas.

"Number Nine," she purred into his ear, nibbling his earlobe. He responded with a growl and harder thrust that made her gasp. He continued on and she panted, digging her nails into his sides. She wanted him like this, wild and hard. She moved her hands inward toward his spine and he groaned.

"Right there, Princess. Dig in."

She did as he asked and sank her nails into the soft ridges of muscle on either side of his spine. She arched back, giving him everything.

"Say it again," she begged. "Call me—" she broke off, moaning, unable to contain herself.

"Princess," he growled into her ear. "My princess."

She was so close, hovering on the brink, each thrust edged her nearer, and she found herself arching, wanting him to go even deeper. He reached down and scooped a hand under her ass, lifting her leg up higher, allowing him to do what she wanted—to fuck her deeper. He drove into her and she said something, but couldn't remember what. She came then, in an all-encompassing orgasm that tightened every muscle in her body and then released her. He came just as she did, collapsing onto her with a groan.

She clung to him, burrowing her head into the space beneath his chin, planting soft little kisses on his chest, unable to keep her mouth off of him.

"Princess," he whispered, happiness coloring his voice, "I'm so glad I found you."

"No, I found you," she whispered back.

"Stop arguing, counselor," he ordered, and ducked his chin down so he could kiss her mouth.

Aiden — How the Fantasy Goes

Aiden woke up and blinked to focus his eyes on the bed side clock. It was nearly three in the morning. Ella was sitting naked on the desk, watching the city and eating grapes off a fruit plate. It was the sexiest way to eat grapes he'd ever seen.

"How are you awake?" he groaned.

"I don't have a concussion," she replied. "Also, I was hungry. Also, they brought up our replacement clothes."

"Great," he said, stumbling from the bed and into the bathroom. He came back out and leaned against the desk with her, stealing grapes out of her hand as she picked them up.

"You are going to get that checked out, aren't you?" she asked, running grape-cooled fingers over the goose egg on the back of his head.

"Yeah, I've got a guy."

"A guy? You leave your medical care to *a guy*?"

"A doctor guy. He deals with all of my fighting-related injuries, since I'm pretty sure the GP I go to would just rat me out to Grandma."

"Oh." She leaned over and gently kissed his bump, then nibbled his ear. He turned his face down to catch her lips and kissed her.

"Mmm," she said, pulling back with a smile. "You make me want to do that all the time."

"I don't mind," he said.

"I would get hungry," she said. "And at some point, it would get awkward."

"You're too practical," he said. "Where's the romance?"

She giggled at him.

"I knew you thought I was funny."

"No, I don't," she promptly disagreed. "I have no idea what you're talking about. You're distinctly unfunny."

"Liar," he said, breathing the word heavily into her ear, and she flinched away, laughing. He moved to be in front of her and dropped kisses like tickle bombs around her neck and she laughed harder, her breasts bouncing against his chest. He looked down at her, sitting on the edge of the desk, legs dangling and a thought occurred to him. "You know," he said, picking up one of her hands and dropping a kiss on her wrist, "you're not tied up now."

"True?" she agreed, looking a little confused at his change in topic. He kissed her neck more seriously this time and began to work his way down. Then he knelt down in front of her and she made a little noise that sounded half-nervous, half-excited.

"So tell me," he said, kissing along her inner thigh, "how is that fantasy supposed to go?" He reached up and grabbed her by the hips, pulling her to the edge of the desk.

"I think you've got the general idea," she said, her voice fluttering slightly.

He looked up at her as he slowly licked her thigh. She leaned back on her hands as he stroked her with one hand. Her breasts heaved with every touch, her body rocking against his fingers. He finally put his mouth to her, and she gasped his name. He circled her clit with his tongue, and she moaned, grasping his hair with one hand. He slid his finger inside her and she moaned something in Chinese. He tried not to smile, knowing that would throw off the rhythm, but if she had switched to Chinese, he knew he was close. He found the spot on her clit that seemed to get the largest reaction and then circled, driving into it with his tongue.

She repeated his name and clutched at his hair in the same

rhythm that he touched her. Her breathing became ragged and she said something with his name in it and then came with a final, body-shuddering gasp.

He looked up at her and found her staring down at him with a beautifully stupefied expression. He stood up and popped a grape in his mouth.

"So… like that, more or less?"

She let out a warm purring groan. "Yes, exactly like that."

He laughed and pulled her off the desk and they tumbled back into the bed. "I can't stay Aiden," she said as he wrapped his arms around her and prepared to snuggle back to sleep. "I have to be back home before Uncle gets up."

Aiden felt a leaden sense of disappointment.

"How long do we have?" he asked.

"I have to be back before six."

"Then we've got a little bit of time," he said, and he held her tighter.

Ella – Home Again

Ella stood on the corner across from the building that was the temporary home of the Zhao family and tried to make herself let go of Aiden's hand. Dawn was a soft light behind some buildings, painting everything in the eerie glow of a black and white movie. The October air was cold, and she shivered. Aiden suddenly pulled her around and hugged her tightly.

"Don't go in there. Come home with me."

"Aiden!" she protested, even as she burrowed deeper into his coat. "Don't ask me that."

"Why shouldn't I?" he demanded. "Why should I have to let you go again?"

"Because if you ask me, I'll say yes. And we both know that's a bad idea. At least until we settle the DevEntier matter." With her ear to his chest she had no trouble discerning his growl of discontent.

"And what about after? What then?"

Ella was silent.

"I don't want you to go in there," he said, his voice quiet. "He yells at you."

Ella chuckled. "No, he yells at you. He's never yelled at me."

He heaved a breath that sounded like relief. "Why doesn't he like me? What did I ever do to him?"

"He was very concerned for my safety."

"That's ridiculous. I would never..." He stopped and she felt his hold on her shift slightly. "It's not us, is it? Jackson and Evan and me, I mean. It's Randall and Owen. My uncles."

"Probably," agreed Ella. "He didn't say. He's just very clear that your family is not to be trusted."

Aiden sighed. "It's been fifteen years since they died. How do they find ways to keep screwing us from beyond the grave?"

Ella looked up at him in surprise. She had assumed that her uncle's hatred of the Deveraux was somewhat overblown from insults long past. She hadn't expected Aiden to agree. "They were really that bad?"

"They were horrible fucking people. From peeing on the Christmas tree in front of the mayor, to sexually harassing anyone—and I do mean anyone—within a ten-foot radius, to physically abusing my cousin. They were grade-A assholes who literally no one alive misses."

"Oh," said Ella, feeling an enormous swell of sympathy for Evan. "That's horrible," she said quietly. "I'm sorry. Is Evan OK?"

"He has a very nice therapist who is apparently some sort of miracle worker. I need to ask Jackson where her office is so I can send her a giant Christmas basket. But anyway, I guess if your uncle knew my uncles, then yeah, I shouldn't be surprised that he hates me."

"I'll make him like you," said Ella, with more confidence than she felt.

"Mm," he said.

She looked up at him. How could she not have known instantly that he was Number Nine? His jaw was right there. On the other hand, she hadn't spent a lot of time looking at him from this angle previously.

"You'd better go," he said. "The longer you stand here, the harder it will be for me to let go."

"You really are a romantic."

"No, just freezing."

Ella laughed and stood on tip-toe to kiss him. He let go and she walked across the street. She tried not to look back but couldn't help it when she got to the door of her building. He waited until she was all the way inside.

She slipped inside the apartment and slid off the total fuck-me pumps that Aiden's person had procured for her. They were going on her NSFW shelf. No one in a professional situation would take her seriously in those shoes. But the emerald green silk top was probably going into standard rotation. She tip-toed into her room and did a double-take. In the gloom of half-morning, it looked like someone was in her bed. She gingerly moved the covers, assuming it was Lilly, and then realized it was just pillows and a shirt mushed together to look like someone. She put on her usual sleep tank-top, rearranged the pillows, and climbed into bed. Her eyes felt as though they had barely been closed when she felt someone bouncing on the bed.

"Ah!" She struggled to sit upright and found Lilly snuggling into bed next to her.

"I put pillows in your bed," whispered Lilly. "Where did you sneak out to? You were gone all night! Was it a boy? Ooh! Was it that guy from the elevator? The really nice one. Because if it wasn't, you should seriously consider that."

Ella stared at her little cousin who was taller than she was. "Go back to bed, Lilly. I'm tired."

"Just answer the question! Was it the Aiden guy?"

"Yes, sort of. At least mostly."

"Really?" Lilly's face looked like it might split in two from her grin.

Ella sighed. "Yes."

"Did I tell you about Nora and Kacey?" asked Lilly.

"No?" Ella was confused by the change in topic.

"I remembered what Aiden said."

"What did Aiden say?" asked Ella, adjusting her head to try and get her cousin in focus. She'd only left the two of them alone for a few minutes. She didn't think Aiden could have managed anything earth-shattering in that time.

"He said that Kacey was injured. Like an injury that can't be seen, and she was doing the best she could, but she was injured. I don't know how, but after the puking, that was still with me. So the next day, I sent a text and said we were fine and if she needed to talk, I was here for her."

Ella wanted to cry for both Lilly and Kacey, and she wished she'd had a Lilly when she'd been their age.

"Anyway, Kacey apologized, and we're cool. But even weirder was Nora."

"Isn't that the girl—"

"Yeah, it was her party and her dad who yelled at us. She said that when she heard what happened later, she told her dad about last summer when Brett and Chet tried the same shit on her. And then she went out of her way to sit with Kacey and me at lunch and now everyone knows what happened and no one will talk to Brett and Chet."

"Holy shit," said Ella.

"Pretty sure they aren't getting invited to anymore parties for at least a year," said Lilly. "I'm not delusional. Their families have a lot of money, so it probably won't last forever, but it will last awhile."

"We'll go shopping," said Ella.

"What?"

"You're new," said Ella. "So probably they haven't realized it yet, but your father can buy and sell most of them. We'll do a little strategic shopping and send you to school with enough new stuff that the kids figure it out."

"Dad hates that shit. He's going to go on a rant about not growing up with indoor plumbing."

"I'll take care of it," said Ella.

"Well, all right!" exclaimed Lilly, her voice raising in volume and she added a little fist pump.

"What's all the fuss?" asked Nai Nai in Mandarin, poking her head around the door.

"Ella was out with a boy," said Lilly. Her Mandarin was a little rough, but when it came to gossip, she was clearly willing to step up.

"Snitch," said Ella, mildly outraged by her cousins turn-coat behavior.

"Ah!" exclaimed Nai Nai, coming all the way into the room. She carried her tea mug in one hand. It said, *World's Best Grandma* and had a kitten on it. "The sweet boy who likes my candy?"

Ella sighed. "Aiden, yes."

Nai Nai settled herself onto the other side of Ella, wedging her into the bed.

"Ew. He ate Grandma's cricket candy?" Lilly looked horrified.

"He didn't even gag. He said it tasted *crickety*," said Ella, and Lilly laughed.

"That's bad ass."

"I know, right?"

"Lilly, you're not bothering your cousin, are you?" said her aunt sticking her head around the door. "Oh." She looked suspiciously at Nai Nai and Lilly. "What are we plotting?"

"Nothing," said Lilly. "We're fine. No plotting."

Nai Nai laughed. "Ella is being courted by a boy Bai does not approve of."

Liu rolled her eyes. "When does he ever approve of any of the boys any of you date? Ignore him." She disappeared back into the hall but was back a second later. "I mean, assuming he's a nice boy and is respectful and there's nothing actually wrong with him."

Ella laughed. "He's very respectful and I don't think there's anything wrong with him."

"Well, then, carry on. Let me know if you need my help bludgeoning Bai into being polite."

"Thank you, Aunt," said Ella.

"Of course. Now really, Lilly. Stop pestering Ella and let her sleep."

"Nai Nai is pestering Ella," complained Lilly, getting up reluctantly.

"Nai Nai is old and can do whatever she wants," said Liu, and Nai Nai beamed smugly over her mug of tea. Lilly stomped off, rolling her eyes.

"Nai Nai, you know it's more than just disapproval," said Ella.

"Yes," agreed Nai Nai.

"Why does he hate the Deveraux?"

"You'll have to ask him," said Nai Nai.

Jackson – The Storage Unit

"What do you mean: he's not there?" demanded Jackson, barking at Garcia.

Mateo Garcia was a thirty-six-year-old ex-beat cop who had gotten fed up with his job and his wife at about the same time. He ranted about divorce attorneys periodically and Jackson thought he probably lived in an apartment with one La-Z-Boy and a massive TV. He was also a reliable employee and Aiden's assigned minder. Not that Aiden had known that until recently. Once the Zhao mess was cleared up, Jackson was probably going to have to rotate Garcia out.

"I mean," said Garcia, "that I am standing in his place right now and it is empty except for a note that says: Hey Garcia, if you pop in feel free to help yourself to the beer in the fridge."

Jackson growled in frustration. "Why are they so determined to get themselves killed?"

"I don't know," said Garcia. "Probably because they're related to you?"

"Ha fucking ha," said Jackson.

"What do you want me to do?" asked Garcia.

"Well, first, put the beer back."

"Damn it."

"It's six o'clock in the morning."

"Nothing wrong with morning beer."

Jackson sometimes felt like he was running fraternity or reformatory for wayward boys.

"Uh-huh. Except I don't really want him to know you can get into his house. Put it back, then head back to the office."

"What are you going to do?"

"I'm going to go ahead and look like a putz and call him," said Jackson. "He agreed to have you follow him around. Not answering the door means I can call. I just don't like doing it."

"Sorry," said Garcia, sounding sincere. "I really don't know how he got past me. I swear he was in for the evening last night."

"Yeah, I know. He's a sneaky bastard. Talk you in a bit."

With a sigh, Jackson hung up and dialed his cousin.

Aiden picked up on the first ring. "Oh, good," he said before Jackson could speak. "You're up."

"Yes," said Jackson, "I am. Where are you? You're not home."

"How would you know? I wiped your software off my phone."

"My guy is supposed to make sure you make it to the office. He calls when you don't answer the door."

"Right," said Aiden. "Forgot about him."

"Mr. Deveraux," said a female voice, chiming through clearly from Aiden's side of the phone. "We're ready for you to head back into the dressing room."

"The dressing room?" repeated Jackson.

"Yeah, I'm getting an MRI," said Aiden, with the sound of rustling fabric.

"Would you care to explain why?" asked Jackson, pushing one finger against his eye to keep it from twitching.

"Got conked on the head," said Aiden. "It's fine. Teeny concussion. They just want to make sure I'm not going to throw a blood clot or something."

"Aiden, what the fuck? What the hell happened?"

"No time to explain," said Aiden. "I've got to go get changed and I need you to do me a favor."

"And what would that be?" demanded Jackson.

"I need you to get Evan and go out to the storage unit."

"The storage unit?"

"Yeah, that's where Grandma dumped all of Owen and Randall's shit that no one wanted to go through. There's some DevEntier boxes in there, and I need you to bring them all back to the house. I'll be over to go through them after I get done here."

"Aiden, is this really important? Shouldn't you be—"

"Figuring out why someone at DevEntier is falsifying documents about Bo Zhao and, you know, also whacking me on the head? Yes, this is what I should be doing. And I'm asking for your help. Evan will know where everything is, but he'll need the moral support. Can you please just do this?"

Jackson took a beat to assess if this was something that he argued about even though he was going to do it anywhere.

"Yeah, of course I'll go," said Jackson. "And you'll bring the MRI report home from your doctor."

There was a second of dead air. Jackson guessed Aiden was taking a moment to assess if *he* was going to argue.

"I will do that," said Aiden. "And I'll bring you up to speed on everything else when I get back to the house. I should be done in a couple of hours. Maybe faster since it's early and it shouldn't take them that long to look at the results, but I feel like I say that every time."

"And how many concussions have you had?" asked Jackson.

This time Aiden was only silent for a fraction of a second. "Just the normal amount," he said cheerfully. "See you back at the house. Bye."

Jackson hung up the phone and reached for his shoes. He wasn't sure he wanted to broach the topic of storage units with Evan over the phone. He jogged down the stairs and found Theo holding his coat for him. Jackson could never figure out how Theo managed to predict his movements.

"We're going to need some space for laying out papers," said Jackson. "Aiden's sending Evan and I out to the storage unit."

"I can put extra leaves in the dining table," said Theo, "or we can put the cover on the billiard table upstairs in the games room."

"Dining room," said Jackson. "No reason to tote boxes upstairs."

"Jackson," said Eleanor, coming out of the solarium where she usually liked to eat breakfast, "what on earth are you doing up so early?"

"Errand for Aiden," said Jackson with a smile.

Eleanor frowned as if trying to parse his meaning. "Aiden is taking the DevEntier matter very seriously."

"Yes," agreed Jackson.

"That seems like an unexpected development," she said.

"Aiden likes to be full of surprises," said Jackson and a smile quirked up the corners of Eleanor's mouth.

"Indeed, he does. Well, I'm glad you can support each other."

It was a smooth, political kind of sentiment that should have been meaningless, but for once Jackson sensed the sincerity behind it. "We do what we can," said Jackson. Which was a meaningless phrase of his own, but he didn't know what else to say.

Thirty minutes later he was standing at Evan's door with a coffee in each hand. Evan opened the door and looked at him with raised eyebrows. "Why do I feel like whatever you're about to say is going to suck?"

"Because I come bearing gifts?" Jackson suggested hoisting the coffee.

"Clear indication of suspicious behavior," agreed Evan. "Come on in. I've only got five minutes though. I was about to leave for work."

He went to the table where the newspaper and the remains of

breakfast could be seen and picked up his suit jacket off the back of the chair, pulling it on.

"Yeah…" said Jackson.

Evan sighed and began to take the jacket back off. "What is it?"

"I just talked to Aiden. Apparently, sometime last night he discovered new evidence that DevEntier falsified records."

"Charlie," growled Evan.

"Don't know at this point. Aiden promised to fill us in later. But, um, he also said he got hit over the head."

"Jackson!"

"What?"

"You're supposed to prevent this kind of thing."

"I can't help him if he sneaks out of the house and intentionally avoids my guy." Evan snorted. "Anyway, he sounded OK and he said he was getting an MRI, but…"

"Wait, that wasn't the bad news?"

"No, the bad news is that he wants us to go out to the storage unit and bring back any DevEntier records."

Evan groaned. "I hate that place. It's like someone dumped my entire childhood into one horrible tin can and shook it up to frothy badness that will explode in my face at any moment."

"Sorry," said Jackson, trying not to smile at the metaphor or reveal how excited he was that Evan felt safe enough to give voice to the feeling. "Um, I brought coffee?"

"Fine," said Evan with a sigh, grabbing the coffee. "I'm going to need to change and to call work."

"Cool," said Jackson, eyeing the remains of Evan's breakfast.

Evan looked sourly from his breakfast to Jackson and back. "Do you want some eggs?"

"If you have some already made…"

"You and Aiden," said Evan, rolling his eyes and going into the kitchen. "I swear you're bottomless pits." He retrieved the pan from the sink and tucked his tie into his shirt.

"You don't have to make more," said Jackson, watching in fascination as Evan pulled ingredients out of the fridge.

"It's eggs," said Evan, "not rocket science. It takes two minutes, and it will keep you from whining when I make you climb over all the crap to get to the boxes."

"Well, that does sound like me," agreed Jackson, sitting down at the kitchen bar and sipping his own coffee. Evan called his office while he cooked, managing the two tasks with practiced ease. Jackson was surprised but tried not to show it. Evan being a responsible, self-feeding individual seemed unexpected.

"Thanks for cooking," said Jackson around a forkful of scrambled eggs, when Evan hung up on work.

"Again, it's eggs. That barely qualifies as cooking. I don't understand why you didn't get breakfast when you got coffee."

"There was a line and I was in a hurry."

"Uh-huh," said Evan. "Going to go change. Back in a minute."

Jackson finished up his eggs and then washed the breakfast dishes while Evan changed. When he came back downstairs Jackson laughed. "You in jeans. I didn't know it was possible."

"Fuck off," said Evan. "Let's go get this over with."

The storage unit was in midtown and had more security than some celebrities. When they finally unlocked the door to the unit that housed the unwanted Deveraux items, Jackson had to admit to a feeling of let-down.

"With that build up, I was expecting the Arc of the Covenant."

"Nope, just shit that Grandma can't let go of," said Evan, frowning at the pile of furniture and boxes. "If you ask me, we should take a flame thrower to all of it."

"Some of it is probably worth money," said Jackson with a shrug.

"Who gives a shit?" demanded Evan. "All right, back this way. I wasn't kidding about the climbing. I think the DevEntier shit is behind an entire set of wicker furniture."

"Wicker…" said Jackson.

"It's woven wooden furniture," said Evan, leading them back further into the maze.

"I know what it is. It's rich people furniture."

"I don't think so," said Evan.

"It's furniture specifically for the outdoors, right? When I was growing up, outdoor furniture was the couch that someone left on the street corner."

"Why would someone leave a couch on the street?" asked Evan.

"To get rid of it. Usually after the cat irreparably peed on it. Or someone set it on fire. Or the recliner function broke."

"I always liked the idea of a recliner," said Evan wistfully. "Grandma never goes for them. She says they're low-brow."

"My dream was to get one of those movie theater seats that uses the buttons to recline."

"I could be into that," agreed Evan. He paused and turned to face Jackson as if coming to a sudden realization. "I *could* do that. I have a media room. I could have recliners. I'm going to have recliners."

"OK," said Jackson. "Sounds good. Can we watch *The Matrix*?"

"Yeah, all right," agreed Evan, with a careless shrug that was so Aiden that Jackson almost laughed. "But not two and three. They sucked."

"Sweet," said Jackson. "I'll bring brats and some of that kettle corn shit that gives my tongue sugar burn but I can't stop eating. We should invite Aiden though, or he'll get super bummed."

"Oh," said Evan, blinking. Jackson guessed that he hadn't realized they were making a real plan. "Yeah. OK. Um… boxes are this way."

The back wall was covered by a long industrial shelving unit that was packed with carefully labeled boxes. As if someone had started the storage unit with the firm intention of being organized. Unfortunately, the gravitational pull of storage units had overtaken that intention at some point. In front of the shelving unit was a wall of wicker furniture stacked Jenga style to the ceiling. Next to it, there were three actual steamer trunks. And a clothing rack. Next to a wardrobe. More cardboard boxes. Giant plastic bins. Some had labels, some didn't.

"Ohhhhhkay," said Jackson, looking in dismay at the wall. "I can see why Aiden said it would take two of us."

"Yeah," said Evan. "The ones we want are the boxes with the yellow tags. Those are all DevEntier."

"All right. So…" Jackson found himself flipping through various scenarios of how he would steal the boxes without anyone knowing, and then realized that was unnecessary. "How about we take those trunks and we layer them up like stairs? Then we'll take off the top layer of wicker and then I can climb down the shelves to the boxes."

Evan gave him a look that said his suggestion was insane. Jackson thought about it again—it still seemed viable.

"No?"

"Whatever you think," said Evan with a shrug.

Jackson put his plan into action and soon was handing down a wicker coffee table and then a rocking chair. The chaise lounge took a bit of levering, but they managed it. Jackson then went over the summit and crawled along the shelf to the DevEntier boxes.

"OK," he called to Evan. "I think I can get it out the side, can you wedge over there and grab it from me?"

"Working on it," called Evan.

Jackson shoved the box along the lids of the row of boxes and then out to Evan's waiting hands. Evan grabbed the box and Jackson was just about to go back and grab the next one when he saw an orange folder poking out from between two boxes.

"Huh," said Jackson, bracing himself and pulling the folder out.

"Huh?" asked Evan, his head appearing over a piece of furniture.

"It's a Pete folder," said Jackson, flipping it open. Evan made an inquiring noise and then belly flopped further over the end of a wicker couch, perching there like some sort of awkward red-headed bird.

"Pete gives everything to Eleanor in orange folders. FYI—in case you're ever trying to get a read on her desk. Huh. This must be how they found me."

"What do you mean?" asked Evan, craning to look.

"They're custody papers from Randall. It looks like he was filing for custody and requesting a paternity test. It looks like he never got around to filing them." He looked up at Evan and saw that his cousin's face looked stricken. "What?"

"I knew," said Evan, his voice hoarse. "Randall, he came over one day and said he was going to bring me a brother. Which, I know, I know, sounds insane." Jackson hadn't said anything, so he suspected that the commentary was a reaction to someone else, most likely Evan's therapist. "But Randall always assumed he owned everything of Dad's, so that probably included me. I think that's partly why Randall freaked out when Dad moved us out." Evan looked as if he weren't sure how he'd ended up at this fork in the conversation.

"When did you and Owen move out of Randall's?" asked Jackson, trying to slide the question in without disrupting Evan's tumble of thoughts.

"When I was like seven? It was about the time Dad left DevEntier, which probably was the real reason for the freak out. I mean, it was another unit in the same building, but you would have thought Dad had moved us across the country."

Jackson smiled. "Why do you think Owen left DevEntier?"

Evan hesitated. "Randall said it was because…" Evan's cheeks flushed.

"What?"

"When I was six, I came to work with Dad, and I was wandering around doing whatever. And then I went to Randall's office. Only Randall was not alone."

"Oh, ugh," said Jackson, sympathetically.

"No, I mean, really not alone. Randall had someone bent over a desk and Dad was watching them."

"Ohhhh," groaned Jackson. "I won't be able to wash that out of my brain."

"And you think I can? Anyway, Randall said Dad was overreacting. And Dad said some separation would be better for me. He did try sometimes. I mean, not very often. But he had periodic bouts of fatherliness. He wasn't horrible all the time. It's just that the scales on horrible and not-horrible don't balance out."

"Sorry," said Jackson, and Evan shrugged.

"In hindsight, I think he also wanted his own life. I think that's probably why he had me to begin with—he wanted something that was only his. And why he sent my mom away. I think he wanted freedom from Grandpa and Grandma and eventually even Randall. Only I think he had no fucking clue how to do that."

Jackson nodded. That sounded about realistic.

"Anyway," said Evan, looking guilty again, "Randall said he'd bring me home a brother, but nothing ever came of it and then they all died."

Jackson tried to work out the math on the dates of the paperwork to their lives. "These would have been about nine months after Mom died. Nice to know he at least intended to come get me."

"But I never said anything!" Evan sounded anguished.

"*Brat moya*," said Jackson, which was Ukrainian, the shared nationality of their mothers, for *my brother*. "Did he ever tell you my name or where I was or anything?"

"No. And to tell the truth, I thought it was just one of his bullshit things he did to wind people up and make them react. But if I'd said something, Grandma would have at least known to look for you."

Jackson thought about that. Life had sucked pretty hard after Mom died, but on the other hand, growing up at Deveraux House hadn't done his cousins a lot of favors. He could have done without the stint in juvie, but overall, Jackson thought he'd done all right. Sometimes life just was what it was. He shrugged.

"I was pretty pissed after Mom died. Chances are I would have told you all to fuck off. I wasn't ready for a family." He tucked the folder back where he'd found it. He was going to have to come back here at some point and do a true inventory. Family secrets were probably buried here in between the furniture and the dusty hat boxes.

Evan laughed. "Because you're such a settled adult family man now."

"As far as anyone knows," said Jackson with a grin. "Now stay there. I've got two more DevEntier boxes and one that looks like it might be, so we might as well just bring it."

"You're really not mad?"

"Nah," said Jackson. "Water under the bridge. Do you think there are actually hats in those hat boxes?"

"Grandma used to have a top hat she let me wear. So, maybe. We'll look after we get the boxes," said Evan.

Jackson grinned. "God, I love being a Deveraux."

Aiden – The Dinner Table

Aiden looked at Evan and Jackson bent over the various piles of paper and smiled. This was how it was supposed to be. He had expected Evan to return from the storage unit in one of his dark thundercloud moods, but instead he and Jackson had come back with silly hats and boxes of paperwork. Grandma had said the hats were part of a costume box from one of the relatives. Jackson had them hung on the deer antlers in the hall over the fireplace. Theo had frowned, of course, but Aiden noticed that he had made no efforts to relocate the hats.

When Evan ducked off to the bathroom, Jackson had managed a quick run-down on his trip to the storage locker with Evan which had been eye-opening as to why Evan didn't want to attend the DevEntier board meetings. In return, Aiden gave a condensed version of his previous evening that left out Ella entirely. He didn't think now was the time to mention Ella or why he trusted her. As usual, Jackson looked suspicious, but Aiden was beginning to think that was just Jackson's default setting. The rest of the day passed in sorting through the boxes. Grandma looked in at lunch time, declared that family dinner was cancelled, and took herself off to Le Bernardin. Aiden didn't blame her. Crowding all of them into the breakfast room for family dinner didn't sound nearly as much fun as fancy French seafood and to-die-for wine.

The dining room doors opened, and Dominique came in. "I feel like I *should* be a part of this," she said, scrutinizing the room. "But, in fact, I have no desire to."

Jackson looked up, his eyes dancing. "Probably wise."

"Although, Aiden, I think it's rather annoying of you to pre-empt my big announcement."

"Big announcement?" asked Aiden, frowning.

"Max is moving in with Nika," said Evan, without looking up.

"What?" Aiden felt blindsided. "When? Did I… What?"

"Didn't you read Jackson's text?" asked Evan, staring at him. "He said we had to make supportive noises tonight at dinner. I had a whole *that's great* thing I was going to do."

"Did you?" asked Dominique, looking amused.

"That's great!" said Evan, faking a cheerful face, which made Jackson laugh.

"I'm slightly horrified," said Dominique. "Although, I appreciate the effort."

"When did you send it?" asked Aiden, grabbing for his phone. "I swear I didn't see that."

"Like on Wednesday?" Jackson looked like he wasn't sure. "I don't know. Evan and I were watching the Granger coverage and drinking wine."

"And you hit send. I remember," said Evan, "because you had more than I did." He sounded smug.

"You were pouring," said Jackson.

Aiden looked up at Dominique. "Sorry. I didn't see it. I mean, I remember a text coming through, but I thought it was about Granger and I never went back to it. Congratulations. I think that's great. I really like Max."

"Thanks. Now remember to say that when I tell Grandma. Jackson says she's being weird about the idea."

Aiden rolled his eyes. "When is she not weird about one of us doing something she didn't personally plan?"

Jackson and Evan both grunted an emphatic agreement, and Evan went back to flipping through his pile.

"Agreed," said Dominique. "But it's happening one way or another. I was just hoping to do it at dinner when I had all of you with me."

"I'm open Tuesday and Wednesday," offered Aiden. "If you want to do a replacement dinner."

"Wednesday would work for me," said Dominique, looking cheered. "Guys?"

"Whenever," said Jackson, and Evan nodded.

"Well, all right. I'll email Grandma," said Dominique. "Has Theo plied you with food and beverages?"

"We are well stocked in the sandwich department," said Aiden around a yawn. He waved at the sideboard with the depleted tray of sandwiches. They had been reading papers for the better part of the day. Most of it was boring, with the occasional searing reminder of what dickheads his uncles had been.

"Well, in that case I will go away and pretend I never saw this mess. Good luck!"

She ruffled Aiden's hair, and he winced as her fingers found the goose egg on the back of his head.

"Are you all right?" she demanded, poking the lump.

"Hey!" Aiden batting at her hand.

"Why is your head lumpy?"

"Pretty sure it's been that way for years," murmured Evan, and Jackson sniggered.

"My head may not as spherical as yours," Aiden said, "but I don't really think being shaped like an egg is something to brag about."

Jackson laughed harder.

"You're only encouraging them," said Dominique to Jackson.

"Like they need encouragement," said Jackson.

"That is entirely my point," said Dominique.

"Aiden," said Evan, frowning at him.

"It's not really shaped like an egg. I just needed a come-back."

"What? No. I wasn't… That wasn't what I was going to say."

"Oh. What then?"

"I think this is what we're looking for."

"What is it?" asked Aiden, reaching for the paper Evan was handing across the table.

"It's a print-out of an email from Randall. It was in Dad's stuff. Dad used to paperclip his to-do piles. I think that's what this group of stuff is. It was next to a dry cleaner tag."

Aiden looked at the email. The ink was faded, and the paper had yellowed, but it was still legible.

"The signs are unmistakable," read Aiden. "We're losing confidential data. Particularly on the Frixion…" Aiden trailed off and read ahead. "Where is the rest?" he asked, flipping the page over.

"It was just the one page," said Evan, flipping through his stack.

"Let me see," said Jackson, and he grabbed the sheet. "I might have a matcher. I've been sorting mine by category and date. All my email print-outs are over here."

"I've been sorting mine by Dad vs. Randall," said Evan.

"I'll take the Owen pile," said Dominique. "Maybe he sent a reply."

"What's the date again?" demanded Aiden as he took the sheet back from Jackson. He checked the subject line and looked around the table. "Pull anything about a project named Frixion."

"I know I have some of those," said Evan, switching piles.

There was tense silence as the cousins tore through the stacks of documents.

"Frixion," said Dominique. She placed a stapled report in front of him and went back to her stack.

"More Frixion," said Jackson, adding a single sheet.

The pile grew, and Aiden tried to skim each item as it arrived. Frixion had been a Department of Defense project looking into energy storage. It was essentially giant batteries. Aiden didn't understand the techno-babble, but he got the concept—storing energy was the holy grail of the energy market.

"Got it," said Jackson, holding up a single piece of paper.

Aiden grabbed it from his hand and read the contents. The others gathered around him, reading over his shoulder.

"Industrial espionage," said Evan.

"Wait," said Jackson, "is he talking about Bo Zhao?"

"Yes," said Aiden.

"That's not industrial espionage then," said Evan. "That's regular espionage. Randall is saying he thinks his data is being sold to the Chinese."

"Why didn't we ever hear about this?" asked Dominique, looking to Evan. "It seems like this would have been a big deal. Did you hear about it?"

Evan shook his head. "I don't remember Dad ever mentioning it. I would have been about thirteen or fourteen?" He checked the date. "I feel like I would have remembered if he'd said something. DevEntier was important to Dad, even if he wasn't working there."

"So what happened?" asked Jackson as he read the email. "He suspected someone was stealing info. Why didn't Randall do anything?"

"Because Bo Zhao died," said Aiden. "And then Randall and Owen died the year after."

"Where's my phone?" asked Jackson.

"Sideboard," said Dominique. "Hot date to cancel?"

"No. I'm going to get the case file on Zhao's murder. I said I was going to do it earlier, but I got side-tracked."

"Jackson, maybe not..." said Aiden, trailing off too late.

"Why not?" demanded Evan, his voice harsh.

"Not relevant to the current case," said Aiden with a smile.

"You think Dad or Randall killed him."

"No," said Aiden, but it didn't sound convincing even to himself.

"Doesn't matter if they did or not," said Dominique. "That's what the Zhao's think. That's why they're here, isn't it?"

"Yes," said Aiden. "I think Bai does, at least."

"Bullshit," said Evan. "This is bullshit. Dad didn't kill anyone."

"I didn't say he did," said Aiden. "Sometimes a mugging is just a mugging."

"Then why didn't you want Jackson to get the file?"

Aiden hesitated. He knew that was a mistake, but he didn't have a good lie ready.

"Right," said Evan. "Right." He pushed away from the table, knocking over a pile of papers and heading for the door.

"Evan! Evan, it doesn't mean anything!" Aiden tried to go after him but found himself hemmed in by boxes. By the time he reached the dining room door, Evan was already leaving the house. "Damn it!" Aiden ran his hand through his hair and winced as he got to the sore spot.

"Let him go," said Dominique.

"I realize you hate him," snapped Aiden, "But *I* want him in this family."

The dining room was silent.

"I meant that he would be better with some time to cool down," said Dominique. "Something that might be good for all of us." She grabbed her purse and followed Evan.

"Fuck," said Aiden and clunked his head against the door jamb. "Ow."

"Aiden," began Jackson.

"What? You want to tell me how I'm screwing up too? You think I haven't figured it out?"

"I think you're doing a great job," said Jackson.

"Really? Because everyone was here and everyone was happy, and I blew it, just like I always do. I get Evan in a good place then I piss off Dominique. I can't ever keep everyone happy."

"They don't need you to," said Jackson. "Dominique is fine. What she needs is for you to stop feeling guilty about liking Evan. And Evan needs you to tell him the truth. You can't wrap up everything in a bow for him."

"And what if that pushes him back into drugs? I can't do that. I need—"

"Aiden, Evan's happiness is not on you. Neither is Nika's. They are both incredibly strong individuals. They can handle their own shit."

Aiden rubbed his head. "God, my head hurts."

"So go upstairs and grab some shut eye," said Jackson. "We can take a fresh look at this in the morning. And maybe by then I'll have the Zhao police file."

Aiden looked longingly up the stairs to where he could just see the edge of his old bedroom door. "I should probably go home," he said, but didn't move.

"Why? You'll just be back over here in the morning. If you spend the night, you know Theo will make you pancakes."

Theo came out into the hall from the kitchen and surveyed them both with his trademark frown.

"Your bed is turned down, Mr. Aiden. Shall I put you down for flapjacks in the morning?"

"Blueberry?" asked Aiden hopefully.

"Of course," said Theo primly.

"Oh, all right," he said to Jackson. "But only because there will be pancakes."

"Theo really *is* my secret weapon," said Jackson. "Your lumpy noggin needs the rest anyway."

Aiden rubbed his egg-shaped lump again. His head hurt and he'd been up far too late last night. What he really wanted to do was wrap his arms around Ella and fall asleep for about a hundred years. "You'll get the case file, right? We need to prove that Randall and Owen didn't kill Bo Zhao."

"Don't worry about it," said Jackson. "I'll take care of it."

"Thanks," said Aiden, and he stumbled toward the stairs.

One more time, he felt stuck between people he loved. Would Ella hate him if he told her the truth? How had everything gotten so complicated? How the hell was he going to explain to Ella that her father had been selling DevEntier secrets to the Chinese?

Ella – Consider the Facts

Ella stared at the case board in her office and tried not to smile at Aiden's stupid head shot. After a minute, she went out to the lobby where Wei Nuwa sat patiently. Aiden's visit to the apartment had resulted in the head of Bai Zhao's security team being more present. Wei Nuwa was a veteran of the Chinese military system, but Ella always thought her uncle had hired the forty-ish woman specifically because Wei Nuwa hadn't excelled there. Nuwa was far too creative for the rigid system imposed by the military.

Ella leaned in the doorway of her office and Nuwa looked up questioningly, her sharp black bob barely moving. "Are we following Aiden Deveraux?"

"Not anymore," Nuwa said.

"What happened?" Ella asked.

"Which time?"

"There was more than one time?"

Nuwa sighed. "The first time, Aiden caught Chang and told him to stop. The second time we put Yang on him. That time, Jackson expressed the same opinion, but with more emphasis."

"More… physical emphasis?"

"Yes," said Nuwa. She didn't look concerned about it.

"Was Yang OK? I thought he was good at following people."

"He is good at following people. And he'll be fine. Jackson just seemed to think that we shouldn't need two warnings."

Ella shrugged, and Nuwa nodded. The unspoken agreement being that Jackson wasn't entirely wrong. "So we don't have eyes on Aiden at all?"

"We've got someone watching his house."

"Hm," said Ella.

"Do you need something?" asked Nuwa.

Ella shook her head. What she needed was to see her boyfriend without getting caught. "Not really. I was just hoping for a convenient answer to a question. Doesn't matter. Is my uncle in the building?"

"He's expected in about twenty minutes," said Nuwa.

Ella looked back at the board, looking at Aiden again. "You'll probably want to talk to him," she said.

"Why's that?"

"Because I want you to bring me my mother's phone number."

Nuwa was silent.

"I don't need my mother's entire file," she said, looking back at him. "But I need her number. You can bring it, or Uncle can bring it. Either way."

Ella went back into her office and shut the door.

A half hour later, her uncle entered. He had the cautious look of a man entering a lion's den. She looked up from the stack of documents she was going through.

"I'm not going to bite your head off," she said.

"Are you sure?" he asked with a smile. She didn't reply and he went over to the board and looked at the pictures. He was a naturally slender man. Her father had been built along similar lines. Their faces were distinct, but Bai made occasional movements and gestures that reminded her of Bo.

"Uncle," she said, leaning back in her chair, "why DevEntier?"

"It's owed to us," said Bai.

"Is it? Are you sure?"

"You've seen the email," said Bai. "There was an agreement."

"And we don't think that maybe…"

"Maybe what?" asked Bai, turning around.

"I'm not stupid, Uncle. Utah? California? Are you telling me you didn't make those agreements based on contacts that Dad provided? Or maybe those were actually agreements he made, while he was still at DevEntier? He was setting up to be their competitor while he still worked there, wasn't he?"

Bai sighed. "Not exactly. I mean, yes, he made those contacts and hammered out verbal agreements with people while he still worked here. But DevEntier was primarily Department of Defense contracts in those days. They hadn't shifted toward public sector and energy. So… it's not like we would have been their direct competitor."

"But he was using their network to build Zhao Industries?"

Bai sighed again. "Yes," he said, looking a little guilty. "But that doesn't change anything. He was promised shares. We should own part of DevEntier."

Ella stared at her uncle, wondering just how far to push. "You hate the Deverauxes. Why do you want to be in business with them?"

"Because they owe us," said her uncle harshly, his eyes snapping with anger.

"Do they?"

"Randall was your father's boss. If the offer of shares came from anywhere, it was from him. And he…"

"He what?"

Bai didn't respond, but instead pivoted to look out the window.

"I asked Aiden about them—Randall and Owen," she said, and Bai wheeled around in surprise. "He said they were horrible fucking people. I figure they have to have been pretty bad if their own family describes them like that."

"They were," said Bai.

"Do you know what Aiden calls me in court?"

"No?" Bai looked confused by the shift in topic.

"Ms. Zhao, his esteemed colleague."

"What's wrong with that?"

"Absolutely nothing," said Ella. "But in the year and a half that I've been playing in your sandbox, I've had opposing counsel call me everything from child-lawyer, hysterical co-counsel, and in one instance just plain idiot."

Bai made a face.

"I've never had an opposing counsel argue with me and not make the argument about who I am. Of course, I've never been this close to losing before, but the point remains: Aiden treats me with respect."

"You're not going to lose. And I don't care what he does in court. He's still a Deveraux. I'm sorry I yelled the other night, but they are dangerous."

"Lots of people are dangerous," said Ella. "Hell, I'm dangerous if I want to be. But he's not Randall."

Bai's head hung down a bit. "I really am sorry about yelling."

"I'm not the one you should be apologizing to."

"Well, I'm not apologizing to him! I repeat, the Deveraux are dangerous."

"And they owe us?"

"Yes," he said sharply.

"Hm." Ella scrutinized her uncle, tapping a pen on the desktop. "I can't believe I'm having to point this out, but if it weren't for him, it's possible that those bank robbers would have shot me."

"Why are you doing this?"

"Because I would like you to acknowledge that the Deveraux are possibly not who you think they are. Your anger toward them is clouding your judgement."

"My judgement is fine," he snapped. "Maybe it's yours that has skewed."

She'd made him angry. He was clinging to it.

"You think Randall or Owen killed Dad, don't you?"

"Yes, I do!"

They stared at each other. She'd never gotten him to be this honest before. Bai spoke first.

"He told Randall he was leaving to start Zhao Industries and the next week he was dead in an alleyway mugging? I don't believe it for a minute. They took your father from us and now I'll take something from them."

Ella took a deep breath. She wanted to argue with him, but she had no evidence and all of her theories were based on information she'd gathered with Aiden. There was no way to refute his theory without revealing Aiden and she guessed that doing that now would be a disaster. She tapped her pen on the desk again.

"Did you bring me Mom's number?"

He groaned. "Ella, don't call her. Whatever you want to ask her... It's not worth it."

"I want to ask her about Dad."

"I can answer whatever you need to know," he said firmly.

"No, you can't. You weren't here when Dad died."

"We just need DevEntier," he said. "Leave your father's death out of it."

"I wish I could," said Ella. "Unfortunately, if you want DevEntier, I need some questions answered and I think Mom can provide them. That's your choice, Uncle Bai. What's it going to be?"

He stood for a long moment, fidgeting with the contents of his pants pockets.

"Fine," he said. He pulled a print-out from the inside pocket of his jacket. "Just… whatever she says about your father, only believe half of it. And whatever she says about you, don't believe any of it."

Ella smiled. "Useful advice," she said. "Thanks."

It took her twenty minutes after Bai left to work up the courage to call.

"Bai," said her mother on the third ring, "go to fucking hell."

"Hi, Mom," said Ella.

There was silence on the other end of the line. "Well," said Sabine, "this is a surprise. The caller ID said Zhao Industries. I thought it would be your uncle."

"Just me," said Ella.

"You know," said Sabine, a complaining note in her voice, "you could have called after you left. I thought you'd run off with that fighter in the black mask."

Ella laughed. "I nearly did."

"It's a good thing you didn't," said Sabine. "I saw him a few years ago at a different fight."

Ella couldn't stop a small noise of surprise from escaping her mouth.

"He told me to go fuck myself. And then I'm pretty sure he threw the fight because I bet on him. Such an asshole."

Ella laughed again, the chuckle bursting out of her in an uncontrolled gust.

"You can laugh, but it cost me a lot of money."

"I don't think he cared," said Ella.

"Apparently not. Well, to what do I owe the pleasure of this call? Or have you suddenly come to your senses and realized that your uncle is a humorless automaton and you want me to rescue you?"

Ella tried not to let that idea enter her consciousness.

"I want to ask you about Dad," said Ella, and Sabine groaned.

"God, I should hang up on you right now."

"Just answer a couple of questions and I'll go away again," said Ella soothingly. "If you don't, I'm sure I could get someone to hack your email and send your entire address book your real age."

Sabine made a squawk of outrage. "You want to play dirty? Fine. Let's play questions. You want your questions answered, then I get mine answered. A question for a question."

"Sure," said Ella, with the confidence of someone who had no secrets. "I'll go first. When Dad worked at DevEntier, what exactly was he doing?"

"Project Management. Who are you dating?"

"Aiden Deveraux."

There was silence on the other end of the phone. "Honey, don't do that. That's not funny."

"What's not funny, Mom?"

"Don't joke about that."

"I'm not joking. I'm dating Aiden Deveraux."

"Honey, stay away from the Deverauxes. They're not nice people. And Randall and Owen are… out of your league."

"Randall and Owen are dead, Mom. They died in a plane crash with their sister and her husband about a year after Dad. Aiden is Genevieve's son."

"Hm," said Sabine thoughtfully. "Genevieve was always a boring little twit, so that's probably OK. And he probably has lots of money if his parents are dead." Her tone brightened significantly on the last sentence.

"Glad to have your seal of approval," said Ella drily. "Back to Dad. He was working with Randall, who we have all established was not a nice man, but was Dad working with anyone else?"

"Who have you been talking to?" demanded Sabine.

"Lots of people," said Ella. "Answer the question."

"You need to leave this alone, Ella," said her mother warningly.

"Mom, after Dad died, we had a break-in and the place was trashed. But they didn't really take anything, and you never called the cops. We left after that and you took a gym bag full of cash with us. It doesn't take a genius to think that maybe Dad was doing a little more than working for DevEntier."

"No, he was working for DevEntier all right. Or at least someone at DevEntier," said Sabine.

"Who? And what was he doing?"

"I don't know," said Sabine.

"I think you know something," said Ella. "Just tell me."

"Why? So you can get yourself killed like he did?"

"I have a security guy following me around," said Ella. "And on the apartment. Right now, sneaking out is even harder than when I lived with you. I'll be OK. I think Uncle believes that one of the Deveraux brothers killed Dad. What do you think?"

Sabine sighed and Ella could hear the sound of her acrylic nails tapping on a hard surface.

"How big is his cock?"

"What?" asked Ella.

"Questions, remember? Answer my question and I'll answer yours."

Ella was silent. This was textbook Sabine—she always used sex as a weapon. How badly did Ella want this?

"Honestly," said Ella, "it's really thick. I mean the length seems normal to big-ish, but he is so fucking thick I kind of come a little bit every time he goes into me."

"Oh," said Sabine.

"Right," said Ella. "Now that we've established that I'm not fifteen anymore, can you answer the fucking question?"

"I don't know who killed your father. He was working with

someone at DevEntier. I don't think it was Randall, but I don't know. I think your father and this other person were selling information. Bo was funneling most of the money to Bai to start Zhao Industries. And when your father said he was thinking about going to work with Bai, I think that person killed him."

"Who were they selling information to?"

"I don't know, but I mean, at the time, the Chinese seemed obvious. He did a lot of traveling back and forth and he was born in China. And it could be that the Chinese killed him. I really don't know. All I know is that Bo said he was planning on exiting DevEntier and the next week he was dead. Then I got a couple of threatening phone calls and the house was trashed. I took the hint. I packed up and I left before something happened to us too."

Ella leaned her head into hand. This was exactly what she'd been afraid of. She'd been avoiding this in her head like a quarantined house. But her mother's words brought everything back—the sense of fear, the mysterious urgency, Sabine's face when she had cheerfully announced that they were going to be playing a fun new game of pretend where they had new names.

"Thanks, Mom," said Ella tiredly. "I really appreciate you answering."

"Ella… you're not going to do anything crazy, are you? Like trying to figure out who did it or something? You'll just get hurt."

"No, of course not," said Ella. "I've just been digging through some old contracts for Uncle and, what with dating Aiden, some stuff has come up. I needed to know."

"Oh, OK." Sabine sounded doubtful. "I know you thought he was a saint or whatever, but nobody's perfect."

"That's true," agreed Ella. "Anyway, thanks for your time. I'll let you go."

"OK," said Sabine. "Um, you could call again. If you wanted. You don't have to wait another six years."

"Yeah, maybe," said Ella. "Bye, Mom."

"Bye, baby."

Ella dropped the phone and found her head dropping down to the top of the desk. Finally, after resting there for more minutes than she cared to count. She picked up her phone again and dialed Aiden.

"Hi," he said, his voice gravelly with sleep.

"Were you asleep?" she asked guiltily, checking the time. It was barely nine.

"Yeah," he said, and she could hear the smile in his voice. "Someone kept me up late last night."

"Can I keep you up a little late tonight?" she asked. "At least for a couple of hours? If I promise to have you back before midnight?"

"That's my line for you, but yes. Although, I'm not at home. I crashed out after dinner and Jackson put me to bed at Deveraux House."

"That's probably for the best," she said. "Uncle has someone watching your place, and my *Like Aiden Campaign* hasn't made much of a dent yet. I don't want to get caught."

"Meet you at the hotel in a half hour?" he suggested.

"That sounds great," said Ella, feeling relieved. "See you there."

Ella picked up her bag and went out to the lobby. "I'm going out for a drink with Aiden Deveraux's secretary," she announced and Nuwa looked up in surprise.

"I should come along," she said.

"No, if she catches wind of you, it'll spook her. I don't think it's a big deal. I'll be back home before midnight."

Nuwa nodded reluctantly and watched her leave. Ella still switched cabs twice before going to the hotel.

Aiden – Trios Again

She arrived at almost the same time he did, and Aiden found himself catching his breath in excitement when he saw her in the hallway. It was as if they'd been parted for months not hours. He swept her up in his arms and kissed her. They practically fell through the door and onto the bed.

"I actually do need to talk to you," she said as he stripped off her clothes.

"We can talk," he replied, between kisses.

She giggled as he pulled her into his lap. "Later," she said.

Her skin was silken soft and every bit of her called to him. He found himself exploring her body all over again, as if last night had never happened. Her breasts in his mouth, the little curve of her jawline that was meant for kisses, the indulgent wetness of her mouth as she sucked his fingers. He took those same fingers and pressed them to her clit, and she moaned his name. His cock was hard as she slid back and forth against it, rocking against his fingers. Soon he was wet from her body.

"Aiden," she moaned again. "Put it in me."

He pushed her back slightly, trying to make room and his cock sprang upward, seeking her out. She settled against the tip, her face inches from his, and sank down onto him. She was tight and wet, and the sensation made him gasp. Ella rocked back, closing her eyes with a moan of pleasure.

Aiden seized her by the hips and fell backward onto the bed, keeping her tight to him. She gasped as he settled more deeply into her. She pushed herself up, her hands on his chest, and began to fuck him. Her breasts were round and perfect, and he caressed them as she rode him. He slid the other hand down to her hip, putting his thumb between them, finding the clit and letting her rub against it. She moaned as he did and began to go faster.

"Aiden, God, Aiden, I need—" she gasped, and her rhythm faltered. He grabbed her by the hips and began to force her back down. "God, yes! Aiden, yes!"

She was going faster now, her eyes closed, and he found it almost right for him, but not quite there. She was going to come before him. He slid one hand up a little and tugged her waist, making her arch more. The result was a fountain of Chinese ending in his name. He made her go faster and thrust up into her, lifting his hips off the bed as he pulled her down. She came with a shout of delight. He pushed her knee out and rolled her onto the bed, still inside her, putting his weight onto her, giving her a moment to recover.

"God, you feel so good inside me," she whispered and pulled him down to kiss her. "Your turn?" she asked letting him go and he grinned.

He pushed into her, slowly at first, and then picked up speed, and she moaned. He pushed faster and harder and her body seemed to tighten around him, her breathing hard and ragged in his ear. "God, Aiden, I'm going to come again. Keep going. Faster. Harder." She moved one leg higher on his side and adjusted the other one and whatever she did was perfect because he found himself gasping. She slid one hand down low on the base of his spine and pressed as if urging him inward. "Aiden, almost there. Please don't stop. Please don't stop." He thrust into her with a force that worried him, but she groaned with a frenzied joy. She came again and this time her body seemed to tighten so hard around his cock that he came with a jerk and collapsed into her.

Her arms wound around him, holding him tight to her, and he submitted completely because it was exactly where he wanted to be.

He was laying in brain-dead happiness, snuggled against her when she spoke.

"I talked to my mom tonight."

His heart rate took a leap upward. "Why?" he asked, struggling to sit up and see her face. "Are you OK?"

"I'm fine," she said, pulling him back into the snuggle. "She told me a hilarious story about you though."

"What?" This time he did sit up, staring down at her, partially illuminated by the half-hearted glow of the city outside the window.

"She said she saw you at a fight a few years ago and you told her to go fuck herself and then threw the fight, so she would lose her bet."

"Oh," said Aiden. "Right. I did do that. I wasn't going to help her win money."

Ella chuckled. "Yes, but you had to lose!"

"And it kind of hurt. I think I broke some ribs on that fight. Josh was so pissed."

"Aiden!"

"What?" he asked.

She pulled him back down again and this time he didn't resist. Wrapping his arms around her, holding her close.

"But you're OK?" he asked again.

This time she didn't respond right away.

"No," she said quietly. "Not really."

Ella – In the Room

"What did she do?" asked Aiden. She could hear his heartbeat in her ear, and she could tell it was faster than it had been a few minutes ago. She'd ruined their post-sex cuddle. "Actually, she was… Well, she was herself, but it wasn't anything I couldn't handle. Which is kind of nice to know, I guess? I thought I'd be more upset, but mostly it was tiresome. And then she sounded sad."

"Good?" Aiden sounded like he wasn't sure what his response was supposed to be.

"Yes, I guess. But that's not what I'm…" she hesitated and went for a less fraught word than *devastated*, "freaking out about."

He was quiet, but she could feel the tension in the arm that she was laying on. She shifted, trying to figure out how to bring it up, knowing that he had to already know. "It's my dad," she blurted out. "I know we talked about the idea that someone at DevEntier was covering up whatever it was my dad did for them. But until I talked to her, I just kept thinking there would be another explanation. But there isn't. I'm pretty sure my dad was collaborating with someone at DevEntier to sell information from his work on the DOD projects with Randall."

Aiden sighed, and in the dark, she could hear him running his hand through his hair. "Yeah," he said. "I didn't want to tell you, but yeah. This morning I had Evan and Jackson pull Randall and Owen's files from storage. I found some emails between the two of them. Randall thought that someone was leaking information on his project to the Chinese. He suspected it was your dad specifically, but maybe it wasn't him…"

"We left the country with a gym bag full of money and Mom

took us straight to Brazil and took money out of a bank account. Knowing what I know now about tax shelters and off-shore banking, it seems obvious why. She says she didn't know who he was working with, but after he died, she received some threatening phone calls and that's why she moved us."

She pushed herself away from Aiden and got up. She took a bottle of water from the mini-bar and cracked it open. She thought she probably ought to turn on the light, but she wasn't sure she wanted to see Aiden's expression.

"I'm so used to thinking of Dad as the good parent. Only it turns out that he was just the better parent. I mean, way, way better in the parenting department, but just as fucked up of a human being. I mean... treason. What the actual fuck?"

She moved the curtain so a little light came in from outside, outlining Aiden as he sat up in the bed and draped his arms over his knees.

"I'm sorry. If it makes you feel any better, one of my uncles was physically abusive, and I kind of think the other one was a rapist."

"That doesn't actually make me feel better."

"Oh." He looked disappointed.

"That just makes me want to hug your poor cousins. And what about your grandmother? What the hell did she go through with those two sociopaths in the house?"

"A lot," said Aiden. "Grandpa was probably worse than either of my uncles so... yeah. I don't know, my point is that we're OK people and our relatives were pretty shitty. Who they are doesn't define us."

"But it does, doesn't it? I mean, aren't there ways you do your best to not be like them? Don't you define yourself in some way by being the opposite of them? And even if you don't, doesn't the rest of this city judge you by who they were?"

Aiden rubbed his head again.

"I'm not saying you're a shitty human being. I'm saying that our families indelibly stamp us in one way or another. And all this time I've been thinking my stamp said one thing and now maybe it says something else."

"But no," he said. "This is my point. You thought your stamp said your dad was a good guy who was unfairly murdered by a mugger. Are you telling me that isn't what started your interest in law? That you're not just a little bit turned on by the idea of justice, and solving mysteries, and making a difference and all that big idea stuff we went into law school with?"

Ella found herself smiling at him. His hair was sticking up and he was only half covered in a sheet, his skin strangely glowing in the light from the window. He was so handsome when he was passionate about his argument.

"Yes," she admitted.

"The circumstances of his death don't change who you are," he said. "I'm sorry for you if it turns out that he was selling secrets to the Chinese because I know you care about it. But it doesn't change..." He trailed off, looking sort of wide-eyed, "how I feel." He finished with a rush.

Ella tried to figure out how to respond to that. Just giggling happily was not really an answer. She went over to the bed and kissed him. He pulled her onto the bed and kissed her back until her toes tingled.

"Of course," she said, pulling away from him, "the other problem is that this means I'm going to lose my case."

"Well, shoot," said Aiden. "That is just terrible. Allow me to comfort you."

Ella giggled as his version of comfort ended up with his face on her boobs.

"Aiden," she said, and he looked up inquisitively. "It's possible that, um, we may have to prove that your uncles didn't kill my dad for my uncle to like you."

He grimaced. "Yeah, that's a thing for my family too. I've got Jackson working on it, but… You know, just once I would like to be able to tell Evan something good about his dad. I mean, 'your dad wasn't a murderer' is a pretty low bar, but to be perfectly honest, I'm a little bit worried about clearing it."

"Sorry," she said.

"Your family really hates me?" he asked, looking pained.

"No! Nai Nai—"

He looked confused.

"Grandmother thinks you're a sweet boy. And Lilly thought you were cool. And Aunt just wants us to date nice, respectful boys. So really, it's just Uncle. Sorry," she said again.

"We'll figure it out," he said, kissing her, this time gently and softly. She sighed in contentment as he transferred his attention to her neck. Then she opened her eyes and caught sight of the clock.

"Oh," she said, coming down to earth. "Oh, I should start getting dressed."

"We've got a little more time," he murmured.

She giggled as he rubbed the scruff on his chin gently over her nipples, tickling her. She rolled away from him, trying to escape, but not trying very hard. They wrestled until she was breathless with laughter, and in his lap, her back to his chest, on the edge of the bed.

"Struggle snuggles," he laughed into her ear and she giggled, but it turned to a moan as he slid his fingers inside her. His other hand caressed her breasts and she groaned in pleasure. She could feel him getting hard beneath her.

"Aiden, we don't have time," she gasped.

"We could be fast," he said.

She tried to assess how late she could be before Wei Nuwa started looking for her. His fingers were rubbing her clit and she rolled across his hard cock. God, she wanted him inside her. "Yes, OK, yes!"

He picked her up and she suddenly found herself on all fours in front of him on the bed. She looked over her shoulder at him. "Fast, yes?"

He grinned, his fingers curved over her hips and she could feel his cock pressing against her.

"Fast?" he repeated and thrust into her hard.

"Oh God," she gasped. Previously, he had entered with a gentle push that left her moaning in satisfaction. This time he gave her no time to adjust and his speed and thickness left her reeling. She could feel her orgasm building like a deep, overwhelming need inside her. She said his name again and again. Her legs were shaking, and her breath came in short gasps.

"Come for me, Ella," he said, his voice hoarse.

He was filling her, giving her every inch of him and all she could do was scream his name as she came, every muscle in her body seeming to quiver and clench.

"Oh God, Ella!" He came moments later, and they dropped onto the bed. They tangled together, and she wrapped her arms around him, clinging to him.

She had almost drifted off to sleep when he cleared his throat. "Ella, my darling, I don't want to say this, but you were trying to leave."

She groaned unhappily. "I don't want to!"

"Well, I don't want you to either, but you said I wasn't supposed to ask you to stay."

She opened her eyes and glared at him. "We have to figure this out soon," she said. "My willpower is only so strong."

"Well, mine is non-existent, so I'm sorry, but it's down to you."

She groaned and got up. Stomping around the room, she re-dressed and pulled herself together. She knew she shouldn't feel so pouty, but she felt like she'd waited six years for this. She felt in some way that she was owed Aiden. She had been patient and good and everything that anyone could want, but she and Aiden were meant to be together and she sure as hell wasn't going to put up with some sort of bullshit international conspiracy and family drama keeping them apart.

They walked down to the lobby, and Aiden hailed a cab for her.

"We'll file for a continuance on Monday," he said.

"I could drop it," she said.

"No, I want to keep the pressure on whoever's behind this. The continuance will work."

She nodded. He was right. She went on tip-toe to kiss him.

"I'll see you tomorrow then," she said.

"Tomorrow," he promised.

Aiden – Trios Bar

Aiden shut the door on the cab and watched as it pulled away.

"The opposing counsel," said Jackson's voice behind him, and Aiden jumped. "Aiden, you traitor."

He turned around to see Jackson grinning gleefully.

"I have been sneaking out of that house since I was fourteen," said Aiden. He supposed it was the wrong thing to focus on, but it was all he could think of. "How the hell did you know?"

"You may have been doing it since you were fourteen, but I'm the one who lives there now. Let's just say you're out of practice." Jackson was chewing gum and that gave his smug tone an even cockier lilt. "You do realize the Zhao's hate us, right?"

"No, Bai Zhao hates us. Grandmother thinks I'm a sweet boy. Cousin Lilly thinks I'm cool. And Ella is… obviously very fond of me."

Jackson laughed. "I did notice the way she was stuck to your face. So you two thought in the middle of a court case was really the time to start dating?"

"No!"

"And yet…" Jackson gestured in the direction of the departed cab.

"It's a bit more complicated than that."

He nodded but looked unconvinced. "You gonna tell me what's going on, or are you going to make me guess?"

Aiden sighed and rubbed his hand through his hair and then realized it was the same gesture that Jackson used when frustrated. "Yeah, come on into the bar. You can buy me a drink."

They settled in at a back table where the lights were dim and even the bartender and waitress left them mostly alone. "All right," said Jackson, stretching out his legs under the table. "I knew there was more to that story about last night. Ella was there?"

"Yeah," said Aiden with a nod. "Since she knew that she didn't fake the Berdahl-Copeland reports, she decided to investigate. I… uh… bumped into her at the records warehouse."

"Uh-huh." Jackson's eyebrows had gone up higher than a kite. "What?"

"So… what? You squeezed in making out between looking at files, getting conked on the head and fleeing for your life?"

"No! It was… after. And a little bit during." Jackson laughed. "You know what? Shut up. You don't see me commenting on your string of bad decisions and definitely not-girlfriends."

"Uh-huh. And what makes Ella not the worst decision you've made lately?"

"Ella is always the right decision," said Aiden. "But that's beside the point. So is the court case, I think, but we'll see what Ella says."

"You're being purposely mysterious," said Jackson.

"No, not really, I just haven't had to lay it out yet." Aiden stared into his glass for a moment, trying to figure out where to start. "OK, twenty odd years ago, Bo Zhao, his wife, and Ella were all living in here in New York. We'll ignore for the moment that he and his wife were probably headed for divorce, but hey, you know, more or less everyone was happy, and Bo was working for DevEntier."

"I thought that was in dispute? Or at least whether he was a contractor or an employee was in dispute."

"He was definitely an employee. What we found proof of today at the house was that he was working with Randall on, among other things, a Department of Defense project called Frixion. It's just, that is not all he was doing. During his business trips I think he was also networking and setting up the foundation for the solar power production pipeline that Bai Zhao is currently trying to muscle into place."

"I've looked into that," said Jackson. "It's too bad Zhao is set on a hostile take-over because they'd be a natural ally for DevEntier."

"Agreed," said Aiden. "But we'll get to that in a minute. Aside from using his DevEntier business trips to network himself into a new business, Bo Zhao was also financing his dream by working with someone inside DevEntier to sell military secrets, probably to the Chinese."

"And then Randall caught wind of it. That email was him and Owen discussing what to do about it, right?"

"Right," agreed Aiden. "But then someone killed Bo and scared his wife so badly that she took Ella and fled the country. And while industrial espionage is a pretty good motive for murder, we're really, really hoping that Randall, Owen, or anyone else we're related to wasn't responsible."

"I can help with that," said Jackson, pulling out his phone and flipping open an email. "The police eventually labeled it a mugging gone wrong, but the detective at the time was less than happy about that. He suspected that it was a targeted attack. Bo Zhao had ligature marks around the neck and two stab wounds in the back, and to cap it off, a bullet to the temple."

"Other than overkill, what does that mean?" asked Aiden.

"It means, someone grabbed him around the neck, and stabbed him twice in the back once through the ribs into the heart and once down low into the liver area. It's immobilizing and a good way to kill someone. But the killer wanted to be extra-super-duper sure. They drug him back further into an alley and used a silencer to finish the job."

Aiden grimaced. "That doesn't sound like a mugging."

"That's because it's not. It's a hit. Sure, they tossed the body and took his wallet, watch, et cetera. But no, that's not a mugging."

"And we don't think Randall or Owen could have done that?"

"Not saying they couldn't have," said Jackson. "But the body was found in Chinatown where a couple of tall blond dudes would have stood out. The police turned up zero witnesses and no one even admitted to having seen Bo that day. The detective at the time thought it was a triad hit."

"Randall and Owen could have hired out," said Aiden.

"Plausible. However, one of the giant piles of bullshit we unearthed from the boxes was all of Owen's bank statements and his tax filings for about five years before his death. They looked pretty legit. I'm currently having a guy go over them to look for any cash withdrawals, because that kind of hit is a good solid ten grand. If he paid for it, it will show up."

"Even fifteen years ago?"

"Yeah, a hit is like a blow job. The prices have been pretty consistent through-out history. Just adjust for inflation and the Romans were paying about the same."

"I…" Aiden didn't know where to go with that. "I'm going to pretend you didn't just say that. So it probably wasn't Owen, but it might have been Randall?"

"Might have been," said Jackson, "but I mentioned having someone go over Owen's taxes to Eleanor and she said the reason he'd probably kept all of them was because Randall was undergoing an IRS audit at the time. Kind of hard to make money go missing when someone is going over all of your receipts."

"This is good," said Aiden. "This fits."

"Fits what?"

"Evan surprised me. I should have been able to walk through it with him, but my brain was fuzzy and talking to Ella helped."

"Yeah, talking. I'm sure that's what helped."

"You are such an asshole."

"I truly am," agreed Jackson with a grin.

Aiden decided to ignore him. "OK, so from the email we discovered, we're pretty sure that Bo was selling secrets to the Chinese. Ella's mom says the same thing. But from the same email, we know that person *wasn't* Randall, otherwise he wouldn't have been surprised by it. But Ella's mom says it *was* someone at DevEntier."

"OK, I'm with you so far."

"Then everyone died. The problem appears to go away. But five years ago there was a DOD audit on DevEntier before they awarded a new contract. They went back twenty years and examined every fucking document in the place and DevEntier passed with flying colors."

"OK?"

"Except they shouldn't have. Bo Zhao was born in China and he never completed naturalization. He was here on a marriage visa. Those points alone should have thrown up red flags, and his subsequent murder should have tripped some alarms too. Having a Chinese national employee working on a DOD project even ten years before the audit should have been enough for them to dig deeper."

"So why wasn't it?"

"Because someone falsified records showing that Bo was previously DOD vetted and no one noticed the anomaly."

"And that couldn't have been Randall or Owen?"

"No," said Aiden, shaking his head. "Their plane went down the year after Bo was murdered. Whoever faked the documents did it, I think, right before the audit."

"That means whoever was working with Bo and whoever faked the reports is still at DevEntier," said Jackson.

"Most likely, yes."

"But who is it?"

"We don't know yet."

"Ella has security, right?" asked Jackson, spinning his glass around in a circle.

"Yeah," said Aiden. "She had to ditch them to come see me, but usually, yeah. Why?"

Jackson took a deep breath as if preparing to make a large statement. That didn't bode well. "The bank robbery was a targeted hit," said Jackson.

"What?" The words didn't make sense to him.

"The bank was a set up. The thieves left a bomb wired to the building's electrical system. The bomb squad pulled it out yesterday. They say it would have wiped out the bank's servers and any records stored locally."

"Oh fuck," said Aiden. "That would have been any of the DevEntier information on Bo Zhao. They didn't want to let Ella go. Or any of her team. Shit. Who knew?"

"Who knew what?"

Aiden focused on Jackson. "Who knew what records we'd turn up at the bank? It would have to be a limited number of people. There can't be that many who have been at DevEntier this long."

"I can think of one," said Jackson. "Same guy who could hire new security for the records warehouse."

"Charlie?"

"That was Evan's gut reaction when I told him someone had falsified records. What do you think?"

Aiden took a sip of his drink and thought about it. "I'm not sure. It's selling information on his own company. How does that make sense?"

"I ran some background on him," said Jackson. "At the time of Bo's death, Charles Senior was still in charge."

"Evan did say that Owen and Randall talked about forcing Charles Senior out," said Aiden. "And Randall's email made it sound like it was Department of Defense info that was getting leaked."

"Agreed," said Jackson. "What if Charlie and Bo were collaborating? They would make a ton of cash—enough that Charlie could oust the old man."

"Charles was going to leave the business to Charlie anyway," said Aiden. "It was implied in the partnership agreement and I'm pretty sure it was in Charles Senior's will."

"Does Charlie seem like the kind of guy who would sit back and wait for his old man to die?"

"Not especially. And if he decided that he didn't want to leave like Owen, then yeah, maybe selling information seemed like getting one over on Charles. But then what?"

"Then Randall and Owen die. You, Evan, and Dominique are all kids. Eleanor wants no part of the company. Charles Senior had a stroke two years later, and Charlie took over for him. That left him in charge with no one to oppose him. All he had to do was make sure no one caught on to what he and Bo had done. A convenient server crash for HR. Forged records before a DoD review. Easy."

"The bank is a lot harder," said Aiden.

"And once I find those guys, I'll be a lot more certain of my theory."

"Yeah," agreed Aiden. "The problem is that with the bank being a crime scene, we won't be able to get those records, so Ella and I were going to file for a continuance. Charlie or whoever is behind this will realize that it's only a delay, not an end to the case. If he's willing to hire some thugs to rob a bank or kill Bo, what's to stop him from going after Ella?"

"Not a damn thing," said Jackson. "I told NYPD to call them, but you might want to reach out in a... uh... more personal way."

"Oh, my God, you are such a pain in the ass."

Jackson laughed. "Yeah, I am. Sorry."

"No, you're not."

"Yeah, not really."

Aiden reached in his pocket and pulled out his non-work phone that he used for all of his Number Nine business.

Bank was a hit job intended to take out DevEntier records. Stay close to your security team. Explain later.

"What I don't know," said Aiden, setting the phone down, "is what to do next. So we have a theory. We don't have any proof. And I'm not sure how to get it."

Jackson's eyes flicked up from the phone on the table, but he shrugged. "What about the guys who knocked you out last night? Why don't we just go have a chat with them?"

"Tempting, but no. We did appear to be trespassing and it's not as though I identified myself. Plus, if I question them, then I'm going to tip my hand. At the moment, whoever is behind thinks I know something, but they don't know how much I do or do not know. If I question those guys, he's going to know exactly how much I don't know."

Jackson grunted in dissatisfaction and slid his glass from hand to hand across the smooth tabletop.

I've only been gone twenty minutes. What the hell are you doing?

Talking to Jackson. We're busted, FYI. Will fill you in later.

Is that… Is everything OK?

Aiden considered that. Jackson was glaring at his drink as it passed in front of him. Aiden wanted to ask what Jackson thought about Ella. Was everything OK? But if he asked, then Jackson would know that it was important.

EVERYTHING'S FINE.

He debated for a moment and then added a kiss emoji. He got back a kitten with heart eyes that made him laugh.

"The easiest way to find out who's behind this," said Jackson, sardonically eyeing Aiden's texting, "is to find the guys at the bank. And ask them who hired them."

"The easiest way," argued Aiden, "is to prove that the records in the warehouse were forged and who knew about it."

Jackson looked unimpressed. "You can't do it for the same reason we can't talk to the security guys. You'd have to do interviews and chase down paper trails. Someone would go back and talk to Charlie."

Aiden thumped his glass down on the table. "Well, I can't do nothing while the police sit around with their thumbs up their asses. They haven't exactly been super helpful in any of our previous dealings."

"They do not move swiftly," agreed Jackson. "But they usually get there in the end. In the meantime," he held up a hand, forestalling Aiden's commentary, "I will find them. We don't have to wait on the police."

"How fast?"

"I don't know," said Jackson. "First I have to make sure my cousin isn't sneaking off to a hotel room to meet his girlfriend."

Aiden laughed. "We really do have to hurry up and figure this shit out, so I can stop monkeying around with hotel rooms."

"It's not really monkeying around, is it?" asked Jackson. "Not when you've had it on permanent reserve for the last three years. Right, Mr. Casella?"

"Stop prying," said Aiden.

"I try not to," said Jackson.

"Not very hard," said Aiden.

"Surprisingly, yes, I do try very hard, actually. I can never decide if I should rip into everything to figure out what all of you are up to, or if I should sit back and wait for you to ask for help, or for it to blow up in your faces and force my help on you."

"We don't make it easy, do we?"

"No, you do not."

"You don't have to worry about me," said Aiden. "I really am fine."

"Hm."

"Besides, I tell you about… most of my stuff. I told you about the Zhao guy who was following me!"

"You want a gold star?"

"Yes?"

Jackson laughed. "Does Ella know about your stuff?" He made air quotes around *stuff*.

Aiden barked out a surprised laugh and Jackson raised an eyebrow. "Sorry. Yes, she does."

"And we're not worried about her exposing it?"

"No," said Aiden, with a grin. "We're really not. Besides, Ella practically is my stuff. Don't worry about Ella."

Jackson stared at him measuringly. "OK, then."

Jackson – Bodies

Jackson loved his car—an Audi R8 retailed for somewhere north of a hundred grand and damn did it go fast. But it wasn't a brand that screamed small-dicked show-off the way a Porsche or Lamborghini did. It was almost subtle enough to be able to drive into the shittier neighborhoods without getting immediately targeted. Almost. But not quite. Which was why today Jackson was driving his other car—a dinged up 2015 Shelby GTO. It looked fast, but it also looked like it was being driven by some fucked meth head car-jacker. He got more tickets in the GTO, but no one tried to boost it when he went to Hunt's Park.

Garcia was waiting for him in the shelter of a fire stair on the outside of a one of the big food warehouses. The kid next to him looked strung-out and squirrely as fuck. Jackson had been shoveling money and resources at the problem of where to find bank robbers like cash and overtime were going out of style. Two days might not seem like a long turn-around time to the cops, but Jackson had started to sweat. Anything longer than twenty-four hours and it was even money that his bank robbers were either dead or had skipped town.

Jackson's money was on the skip. When he'd first started taking scores, a driver had told him to never be confused by the idea that a gun gave him power. Power was what the string-pullers and the planners had. Guns were for the guys at the bottom. And cash was for survivors. The lesson had stuck with Jackson. If he'd been on the bank crew, he would have been across the state line to just about anywhere by now.

Garcia looked like he was holding onto his temper by a thread. Babysitting junkies would do that.

"Cash," said the kid as Jackson approached. "Cash only."

"I have cash," said Jackson, evenly. "Tell me what you have."

The kid swiped as his nose and itched his head and then shoved his hands up into the opposite sleeves. "How do I know you won't stiff me? Dingus said this guy was legit, but I don't know you."

Jackson took a fifty out of his pocket.

"It's supposed to be two hundred," said the kid. He looked like he was maybe seventeen. He was filthy, had cracked sores on his lips, and his shoes were held together with duct tape.

"Spill, T.J.," growled Garcia. "We're not going to stiff you."

"Fifty up front," said Jackson, holding it out. "Good faith."

The kid took the cash and then went through the ritual of nose wipe, head scratch, fingers back up his sleeves. "OK. Um, so sometimes I squat in this warehouse and then a couple of days ago, I rolled up and went in through the back, like usual. Only it was already occupied, and they weren't the kind of people that wanted company. And they were carrying a lot of serious hardware."

"Handguns or rifles?" asked Garcia.

"I don't fucking know," said T.J. "Do I look like I can afford *Call of Duty*?"

"How many guys?" asked Jackson.

"Four," said the kid.

"OK, that's great," said Jackson, handing over another fifty. "Can you take us back to the warehouse?"

The kid took the money but gulped nervously, and there was an extra round of nose-wiping. "I already went," he whispered.

"What'd you see?" asked Jackson.

The boy shifted nervously and looked around. "Dingus said you weren't cops. He said you were cool."

"We are definitely not cops," said Jackson. "You're not going to be in any trouble. We don't rat."

More head scratching. "I went back. They didn't look like they were going to be long term residents, you know? And it's fucking cold out. I thought I'd just go take a peek. I saw them. I didn't know what to do. I got warrants out on me, you know? And then Dingus said you was lookin' for four guys." T.J. looked freaked and like he was thinking about running or crying or both.

"What'd you see, T.J.?" asked Garcia, leaning in, as if sensing that the kid was about a half-step from running.

Jackson held up another fifty. T.J.'s fingers crawled out of his sleeves and reached for the money.

"They're dead," he said, and the bill disappeared. "All four of them. They're still in the warehouse. I can't call the cops. I got warrants. I can't be involved in this shit."

"And meanwhile, you can't squat there," said Jackson sympathetically, and T.J. nodded. "Show us where the warehouse is, and I'll give you an extra hundred. Then you can disappear, and we'll take care of calling the cops."

T.J. nodded eagerly. "Yeah, OK."

T.J.'s route to the warehouse avoided traffic cams, but it was a lot more walking through needle-infested scrub grass and along train tracks than Jackson wanted to do. Finally, they got to a dilapidated warehouse that had faded *no trespassing* signs across a chain link fence and a padlock on the gate.

"There's a split in the fence along there," said T.J. pointing. "I don't wanna go in again."

Jackson took the cash out of his pocket. "You could take this down to the shelter. You could sleep there and get fed."

"Yeah, that's totally what I'm going to do," said T.J. and Jackson gave him a look. "The shelter sucks. Someone's always trying to fuck you. If it's not the staff, it's the other residents."

"I know one of the social workers," said Jackson. "I can vouch for her. She can get you into a program."

"I'm fine," said T.J. reaching for the cash, and Jackson sighed.

"Ration your shit," he said, handing over the cash.

T.J. looked annoyed. "I'm not going to O.D. I know what I'm doing."

"Everyone always says that," said Jackson. "Everyone always lies."

T.J. hesitated, but took the cash and backed away, then turn and ran without another word.

"I don't know why you try," said Garcia.

Jackson shrugged. "You never know, and it doesn't cost anything."

"It will if someone ever says yes," said Garcia, heading along the fence.

"I'm fine with that," said Jackson.

"What do you think we'll find in here," asked Garcia, looking up at the crumbling cinderblocks and grayed wooden-slat siding. He fingered the gun on his hip. "It could be a trap or something."

"I think we're going to find dead bodies," said Jackson. "I think I'm going to have to call Nowitsky, and I think it's going to suck."

"Yeah," said Garcia, touching his gun again.

They crept in through the back door that had every appearance of being padlocked, but just had the chain looped deceptively. The warehouse was full of hulking machinery of indeterminate use covered in dust and cobwebs. The spaces were tall and echoed at the quietest of their movements, which only served to underscore that there was no other movement.

The smell reached them before they reached the front of the warehouse where the cold fall sunlight filtered through grimy windows.

"Yup," said Garcia, covering his nose and mouth with his scarf. "Sucking."

The four bodies were sitting each in a chair facing each other as if marking out the points on a square. Each of their belongings was behind them in neat bags. None of them had been shot. Jackson crouched down and scrutinized the scene.

Each of the four had a shot glass or a cup near their chairs. He looked around and spotted dead rats a few feet away.

"What the hell killed them?" asked Garcia.

"Poison," said Jackson. "Then the rats licked up the drinks."

"There's a bottle of scotch over there," said Garcia, pointing to a banged-up metal desk. Jackson nodded. It was an eighteen-year-old bottle of single malt Oban. He could read the label from where he was standing. He could also see that the top had been dipped in red wax.

"Do you see any phones?"

"No," said Garcia. He walked closer to one of the bodies. "Could be in a pocket? Hmm."

"What?" asked Jackson.

"This one actually has his jacket pocket inside out. Like he pulled something out of it."

"Don't think it was him," said Jackson, circling to check out another body.

"You think whoever killed them took the phones."

"I would," said Jackson.

"How would someone get these guys to drink something?" asked Garcia, inching closer and holding his scarf tighter.

"He faked the bottle."

"What?"

"Oban doesn't come sealed in wax. But it's an expensive bottle so he took a chance on the fact that none of these guys would know that. He opened the bottle, poisoned the bottle dipped it in wax and then let one of them open it again and pour it."

Garcia looked at the scene again. "And they're all here, politely not shooting each other, getting everything divvied out. They're ready to split town. They waited to talk to this guy, and then he offed them."

"Yeah," agreed Jackson. The smell was starting to get to him. He wished he'd worn a scarf like Garcia.

"Then he took the phones," said Garcia. "Meaning we've got fuck all unless he kindly left fingerprints on the damn bottle."

"Yeah," agreed Jackson. And then a phone rang.

They both turned to look at the black duffle bag of the guy closest to the door. The phone rang again, and Jackson pulled on his gloves. Moving carefully, he unzipped the bag and carefully felt around the inside of the bag. He finally retrieved a black, boxy, distinctly utilitarian phone.

It rang for the final time, flashed a missed call message and went dark. Jackson attempted to flip it back on, but it came up as fingerprint locked. Trying not to think about what he was about to do, Jackson breathed on the screen of the phone leaving a warm mist on the screen. Due to the cold weather, rigor mortis hadn't yet released, and the bodies were all still stiff. Gingerly, Jackson pushed the screen against the thumb of the dead body in front of him. The phone registered the fingerprint and unlocked.

"Come on," said Jackson as he stood up and jerked his head at Garcia. "Let's get out of here."

They left through the front door this time. Once outside, Jackson inhaled deeply, enjoying the stink of fresh diesel and wet ground.

"God, that was gross," said Garcia. "I do not know why I don't go get a nine-to-five job in an office somewhere."

"You don't like to get up that early," said Jackson, flipping through the phone settings. It took a moment or two of poking, but he found the security and turned off the screen lock.

"Get anything?" asked Garcia.

"No, that's going to be your department. Take it back to Pete. Have him call Kerschel—see what she can get out of it. I'm going to call the cops and hope they don't do something weird like try and pin this on me."

Garcia grinned. "You know at least one of them is going to suggest it."

"Probably," said Jackson. "Go on, get gone. I want answers by the time I get back to the office."

He was barely off the phone with Nowitsky when his phone burped out a text from Aiden.

SOMEONE BROKE INTO MY OFFICE.

Today was seriously sucking.

Aiden – Murdock Esq.

Aiden bounced up the stairs to his office. Last night had been surprising. There had been some rough patches with both Ella and Jackson, but they had surprised him. They both had his back and he was starting to feel like maybe he wasn't out here battling all on his own—like maybe he had a little bit of an army behind him. A tiny army, but powerful nonetheless. And tiny armies could take down dragons.

He happily tapped the vintage light fixture beside the door as he exited the stairwell. He still hadn't gotten over the joy of having his own office—he couldn't believe Evan had made the effort for him. The thought gave him pause and he took out his phone as he reached the landing.

I REALLY DON'T THINK YOUR DAD KILLED ANYONE. CALL ME.

He'd only gone a few steps when he got a text back.

YOU HAD THE THOUGHT. IT WAS THERE. YOU THOUGHT IT.

Aiden made an unhappy noise that echoed in the hallway.

OK, YES, BUT IN MY DEFENSE, I DID GET HIT ON THE HEAD EARLIER IN THE DAY AND I WASN'T THINKING STRAIGHT.

He waited for a response, but it seemed to be taking a long time. He tried again.

I'M SORRY.

There was more silence. Aiden thought about chucking his phone down the hall. Every time he thought Evan was coming back, it was exactly this: radio silence. He took a few more steps toward his office when his phone rang.

"It's shitty," said Evan without preamble when he picked up. "It's shitty that you even thought that."

"I'm sorry," said Aiden. "They did a lot of shitty stuff. I leapt to a prejudicial thought without considering the evidence."

"You always think they're evil!"

"Yeah," said Aiden, "I do. I look at you and I want to punch Owen and Randall in the face."

"Not everything they did was bad!"

Aiden felt like he'd just put his foot down in a bear trap only to realize it too late, and if he lifted it up in the wrong direction or speed, he was going to lose a limb.

"No," said Aiden. "No, I suppose not everything was bad. But I don't have a lot to go on. I only have you."

"I'm not like that!"

"I'm not saying you are," said Aiden speaking slowly, trying to get each word right. "I'm only saying that they treated you badly, so I tend to think badly of them."

Evan didn't respond.

"Maybe that isn't right. But I do. However, even if they had done something—"

He heard Evan's sharp intake of breath.

"I said *if*. Even *if*, they had done something like that, that's not you. I know that isn't you. I don't think that about you. We are not our parents. They don't affect us."

"That's easy for you to say. Your parents weren't shitty."

"Really?" demanded Aiden. "Then why didn't they—"

"Why didn't they what?" snapped Evan.

"Why didn't they come get you?" said Aiden, not knowing if it was the right thing to say, but unable to hold it in anymore. "They should have taken you away. Why didn't they do that? Why didn't Grandma do that?"

Evan didn't respond.

"Sorry," said Aiden, when the silence had gone on too long. "I just… They failed. OK? They were good parents to Nika and me, but they failed you. And I have a really fucking hard time looking you in the eye sometimes because I… I know it would have been different if you had been with us."

There was a ragged breath from the other end of the phone and Evan gave a weak, watery chuckle. "I thought you said our parents didn't affect us."

"I'm probably wrong," said Aiden. "Ella says I'm wrong anyway, and she's right a lot." Aiden realized he was standing in a public hallway trying not to cry, and he started to walk more swiftly toward his office.

"Aiden, I'm not your fault."

"I don't want you to be anyone's fault," said Aiden. "I want you to be OK."

"I'm working on it," said Evan. "I'm kind of asshole, so it's not going that great. But I'm working on it."

Aiden laughed. "You and Jacks—Damn it! They broke my Daredevil window!"

"What?"

Aiden stared at the ruin of his door. "Someone broke into my office. They broke my Murdock Esq. window!" Now he really did feel like crying. He loved that stupid sign.

"I'll be right there," said Evan. "Call the cops and text Jackson."

"I… Yeah, thanks," said Aiden.

Aiden called 9-1-1 and was told that unless it was burglary in progress, he should call the non-emergency number. He hung up and dialed 3-1-1 because it wasn't like he knew the non-emergency number and the 9-1-1 operator wouldn't give it to him. Because apparently arguing about giving out the non-emergency number took less time than giving out the number?

Evan arrived just as he finished his phone call with the police.

He'd gone through the office and was standing in the front desk area. He looked glumly at his cousin.

"They broke my Daredevil window."

"Sorry," said Evan.

"I really liked that sign."

"You can get it replaced," said Evan.

"It's not the same," said Aiden with a sigh. "Replacing it means I'm trying too hard. Before I could just pretend I hadn't gotten around to it."

"But," said Evan, "if I buy it for you, then you can't replace it without offending me because it's a gift."

Aiden chewed on that. "Yeah, OK. That could work."

"Did they take anything?" asked Evan as he looked around.

"Nah, they just rifled through all the papers. I keep most of it on my laptop, which I take with me, and the important shit is at the house."

"Your house?"

"No, our house."

"Right," said Evan, correctly interpreting that to mean Deveraux House.

Aiden had the feeling that he wasn't making as much sense as he should. He rubbed his head. It still hurt. "I hate concussions."

"How many concussions have you had?" asked Evan.

"Just the normal amount," said Aiden with a smile, trying out the line for a second time.

"That works on Jackson, not on me," said Evan calmly. "Try again."

"Five," said Aiden. "Don't worry about it."

"Why am I not worrying about it?" asked Evan.

"Because I'm dating Ella Zhao and that's probably more

important?" Aiden couldn't believe he'd said it out loud even after the words were out of his mouth.

Evan looked like he was processing that. "Huh," he said after a moment. "I'm suddenly not feeling good about my odds with the case."

"No, it's fine," said Aiden. "We're going to win. Which is kind of bumming me out because she'll be sad. And also that's only going to make her uncle hate me more."

"Aiden," said Evan, looking at him sternly, "exactly how big was that concussion?"

"I'm fine," said Aiden sitting down on the desk, and rubbing his head again. "I'm just short on sleep and I'm kind of… There's a lot going on and I'm not sure I can fix everything."

Evan laughed and sat down next to him on the desk. "I'm in therapy," said Evan. "You know that, so if the next shit I say sounds stupid or like something you already know, then forgive me, because I feel like half the stuff I learn in therapy is only an epiphany for someone who's behind the curve."

Aiden looked at Evan and waited. In childhood, Evan had always made everything better, and if he could produce even a little of that magic now, then Aiden thought that maybe he might believe in miracles for once.

"You can't fix everything," said Evan. "And we don't expect you to."

Aiden snorted. "Jackson already said that. Or something like that. But I'm in charge of this DevEntier mess. I'm supposed to figure it out. So far all I've figured out is that I'm in love with Ella, her dad was a spy, someone killed him, tried to cover it up and now that same someone is trying to prevent us from figuring it out before it blows up in their faces because there's no statute of limitations on treason."

Evan began to laugh.

"You're just happy because you're not responsible for this," said Aiden.

"Yes, I am," replied Evan between chuckles. "Giving this to you was the best decision I ever made. But that actually isn't what's funny. Aiden, does it ever occur to you that you're really smart?"

"Nah. I mean, I'm smarter than some people. But jeez, I mean, Jackson catches me at shit all the time, and it's not like he even went to college. I don't think prison classes count, do they? But the two of you always seem one step ahead of me. I expect you to be, of course, but it's annoying when it's both of you. And if I had one tenth the social understanding that Nika does, I'm pretty sure I could be president or something. I'm always behind."

Evan looked like he thought Aiden was full of shit.

"I'm not saying I'm total moron," said Aiden. "I'm just saying I feel like I'm always playing catch up. I'm lucky Ella thinks I'm cute. She'll probably find out I'm faking it sooner or later though."

"You're not faking it," said Evan. "Jackson is… an anomaly. I don't think you should use him as a point of reference for anything."

"He caught me sneaking out of the house!"

Evan looked like he was holding back a laugh.

"I specialize in sneaking out that damn house!"

"Yes, I understand. What I'm trying to say is that we all have strengths and leaving houses in unusual ways is one of Jackson's strengths. Comparing yourself to him may not be your best bet. Perhaps you should try comparing yourself to the people at say… Axios Partners."

Aiden snorted. "They're idiots."

"So you're epically smarter than a bunch of snooty Harvard Law grads, but not Jackson?"

"Yeah?" Aiden tried to think about that. "It feels like that."

"Perhaps you should try out the idea that you *and* Jackson are both really smart, but good at different things."

Aiden mulled that one over. "What about you?" he asked, looking sideways at Evan. How far was his cousin willing to go to cheer him up? "Am I smarter than you?"

"Obviously, I'm still *way* smarter than both of you," said Evan. Evan's tone was as arrogant as Aiden had ever heard it, but his eyes twinkled, and Aiden laughed.

"Obviously," he agreed, then rubbed his head again. "Ev, I'm *really* not sure how to fix this mess. I'm pretty sure it was Charlie, but I don't have any proof."

"Sounds right," said Evan. "He used to try and get me to smoke Dad's cigarettes when I was ten. Thought it was funny. I guess that's not relevant. But my point is that he's someone who thinks that rules are for other people. If you want to get him, you have to offer to let him help you take down the Zhao. Tell him you want to do something illegal and you need his help. He'll believe it because hc thinks we're like that. He thinks he knows us."

Aiden looked at Evan and felt himself grin. "He doesn't know us at all. And he sure as fuck doesn't know Jackson."

Jackson – DevEntier Corporate

Jackson stood in the lobby and waited for the information of his presence to filter through to Charlie. He noted that a dark-suited gentleman seemed to be loitering conspicuously near the front door. Jackson pretended not to notice. Eventually, a secretary showed up to escort him upstairs to the CEO's office.

The DevEntier offices had moved multiple times over the decades and currently resided in a shiny glass-and-steel midtown building. It was everything that was modern. The original DevEntier building with the records storage and junior researchers still existed on the outskirts of Brooklyn with its pseudo-futuristic and dated eighties architecture. Jackson had sent teams out to do recon on both locations. They had reported heightened security provided by an outfit called Unified Coverage. Jackson wondered if there was a marketing firm somewhere that specialized in generating vague business names for barely legal jack-boot operations masquerading as security firms.

Unified was run by an ex-Marine, Joe Foss. Foss had managed to retire one step ahead of an investigation into criminal misbehavior in Afghanistan. Not that anyone was supposed to know that—everything public was black bar redacted. But knowing the right people who drank with the right people meant that the black bars could slip a little. Jackson was unimpressed by both Foss's reputation and his hiring practices. At least three of the operatives Jackson's team had identified had felony convictions and white power affiliations.

Jackson knew he was the last person who should be judging someone else on prison time and he didn't hold it against anyone for running with the right color gang in prison—that was just how prison was. But that didn't mean you had to associate on the outside. Particularly not with white power asshats who probably couldn't spell Nazi without some guidance.

The secretary, who was of the old school variety in a tight skirt and heels and looked like she didn't know how to type, but probably took dictation, led him into MacKentier's office. It was expansive and dominated by an enormous desk that was probably a master-work of furniture design, but Jackson thought would be a bitch to get through the door.

"Jackson!" said MacKentier, coming forward to shake his hand. "Color me surprised."

"I gave up coloring," said Jackson. "I could never stay in the lines."

Charlie laughed, but Jackson saw his eyes narrow as if searching Jackson's face.

"Trying to decide if I look like Randall?"

"Yes," said Charlie. "I'm not really seeing it."

"Got a cigarette?" asked Jackson. It was half a joke. His cousins were convinced that smoking made the family resemblance stronger. He thought it was the reason they had wanted him to quit. But Aiden had also said Charlie was a closet smoker and Jackson thought that if he was here to do his best Randall impression, then he might as well start with the one thing he knew for certain about either man.

"Now, at least, I'm hearing the resemblance," said Charlie, laughing again. "Randall would never admit he had a habit. I swear he stole more cigarettes than those bums down on the street."

Charlie returned to the massive desk and rummaged through

a drawer for a moment before tossing a pack and lighter over to Jackson. Jackson caught them and took a seat in the chair across from the desk.

"My brand," said Jackson, feeling surprised, and flipping open the gold box of Sobranie cigarettes with the double-headed eagle embossed on the cover.

"And there it is," said Charlie with a nod. "This is all Owen's fault."

"What is?" asked Jackson, pulling out the black bodied cigarette, trying not to inhale it like a damn junkie. He rolled it between his fingers, feeling the familiar, smooth black paper, and he went through the ritual of tapping it on the box before lighting it. Charlie pulled a shallow dish off a shelf and plunked it down at Jackson's elbow. It was a crystal cut bowl with a plaque on it that said Business Man of the Year 2011.

"The Sobranies. He started dating that model."

"Evan's mother?" asked Jackson as he breathed out his first lungful of smoke in three years. He tried not to look like he was having a mini-smokers' orgasm. He'd forgotten how fucking good nicotine was.

"Yeah. I forget her name," said Charlie, returning to his desk.

"Sofia," supplied Jackson, who had an entire file folder on her back at Cheery Bail Bonds.

"That's right," said Charlie. He sat down in the tall, ergonomic, high-tech chair that was at odds with the dark wood desk. "Anyway, she smoked 'em. She was a model. And she was Russian, so she liked smoking Black Russians."

Jackson tried not to sigh. Sofia was Ukrainian. He didn't understand why people couldn't get it straight.

"Owen liked them too, so he switched. And since Randall wouldn't buy his own goddamn pack, he smoked them too. Which meant that then he wanted everyone else he bummed cigarettes off of to buy them as well. He said switching brands led to smoker's cough."

"Sounds like bullshit," said Jackson.

"Of course it was, but Randall liked to make people do things."

Jackson nodded. That had worked out for his mother, who liked to have people make her do things. "I guess I should send Sofia a thank-you note then."

"What do you mean?" asked Charlie.

"My mother was also Ukrainian, where Sobranie is a popular brand even though they are made in England. Apparently, she was the only one at the hotel Randall was staying at who knew where to get Sobranies."

Jackson didn't add that that the cigarettes were only popular with the kind of person who wanted to look rich. To his mother's ultra-conservative religious family, they had just been one more sign of Nataliya's degeneracy.

Charlie gave a sharp bark of laughter. "Life is a funny thing."

"Generally true," agreed Jackson, flicking ash into the business man of the year award. "But I didn't actually come here to reminisce about my DNA donors."

"I didn't think you did," said Charlie, leaning back in his chair and watching Jackson carefully.

"I don't know if you've managed to get the update, but since the bank with the financial records is still a closed crime scene, the Zhao were forced to file for a continuance yesterday. They've got a week's stay."

Charlie's face twitched in displeasure. "That's disappointing. I was hoping Aiden could press the judge to dismiss it."

"He tried," said Jackson. "Judge didn't go for it. But it's going to be a bit of a problem for us in about a week."

"What do you mean?" asked Charlie sharply.

"Well, you and I both know those financial records are going to show that Bo was an employee."

"Do we know that?" asked Charlie. "I can't say that I do."

Jackson gave him a look and took another drag on his cigarette.

"DNA donors indeed," murmured Charlie. "Is there anyone else who shares your opinion?"

"Aside from you? No, not at the moment," said Jackson. "And Aiden assures me that even if the files Charlie gave us were somehow wrong," Jackson infused his voice with as much Aiden-esque enthusiasm as he could and saw MacKentier's lips twitched in an almost smile, "we have plenty of precedent to show that the Zhao still shouldn't get any shares. Bo died before stocks were distributed, yada yada yada. We can trust Charlie!" He took a moment to ash his cigarette and assess MacKentier's reaction.

"That would seem to be true," said Charlie.

"Is it?" asked Jackson.

"Of course you can trust me," said Charlie, smiling.

"Uh-huh," said Jackson. "I meant the other part about the stock."

"That's what the files show, isn't it?" asked Charlie, side-stepping.

Jackson gave him a look. "I don't care if Bo Zhao was an employee. I don't care if he had a written promise of stocks in one hand when he died. Fucker's dead. He doesn't get dick. And his daughter and brother certainly don't get it twenty years later. That offer has expired."

"The Zhao probably don't believe it either," said Charlie with a shrug. "Aiden is right—this is a power grab. It's business."

"Nah," said Jackson, leaning forward, putting his elbows on his knees. "It's personal. There's plenty of other company's working on solar stuff they could target. This is about Bo, and it's about Randall."

Charlie frowned, seeming to chew on the idea.

"They want DevEntier. And here's the thing, Chuck. I may be new to business and to being a Deveraux, but I have never in my life let someone take something that was mine, and I don't intend to start now."

Charlie smiled and Jackson thought it was the first time he'd seen a real smile on the man's face, but it faded quickly. "It was my impression that Aiden was handling this matter for you."

"He is. Aiden's great. He's got lawyer brains coming out his ears. He can lawyer shit all day long." Jackson leaned back and flicked ash into the bowl again. He couldn't help thinking that Eleanor would have some sort of fit of hysteria if she saw him do such a thing. "But I know enough about business to know that sooner or later the lawyers get tired of hearing themselves talk in a courtroom, and then they suggest we go listen to them talk in arbitration."

MacKentier grunted in displeasure.

"And not only does it annoy the fuck out of me to cave on any point at all, it pisses me off to think that this shit is going to meander on for another six months. We've already got Granger and Absolex for that. I don't need two pending court cases."

"I see your problem. I'm not sure I see how I can help," said Charlie.

"As I said—Aiden's handling this. But the thing about Aiden is that he really is Prince Charming. He fights fair, above-board and legal."

"And you don't?"

"No percentage in it," said Jackson, stubbing out his cigarette in the bowl. "But here's what I've been thinking about—Bo's daughter, the pretty little Ella Zhao."

"What about her?"

"I've done some research. She's also got lawyer brains coming out her ears, but she's got some funny little hobbies."

"My research didn't turn up any hobbies," said MacKentier, and Jackson grinned.

"I may have a slightly more far-reaching…" he paused as if searching for the right word, "research team."

"I take it these are hobbies that she might not want to have everyone know about?"

"Exactly those kind," said Jackson.

"Do tell."

"She likes to attend illegal fights and she likes illegal fighters to attend her, if you know what I mean."

Charlie's eyes sparkled and he smiled a shark toothed grin.

"It's exactly the kind of thing that could get her disbarred and would upset her meal-ticket uncle a great deal. I want to make her an offer. Basic carrot or stick options. If she takes the carrot, then she'll cave on the case and everyone goes home. And if she takes the stick, well…" Jackson shrugged. "I don't think she'll test me. But either way I can't have Aiden know about it. So I can't use any of the people I would usually use."

"I'm not funding your buy off," said MacKentier.

Jackson waved his hand and reached for the cigarette pack again. "Don't worry about that. Evan runs the finances, and he's with me."

"Of course he is," said Charlie with a nostalgic expression.

"No, coming up with cash isn't a problem. What I need is someone to speak to her for me. Someone who knows the problem and has an interest in making sure everything goes right."

"Ah," said Charlie. "And you were thinking that could be me?"

Jackson shrugged as he went through the ritual of tapping out a cigarette and lighting up. His fingers remembered the movements with a happy familiarity, but his lungs were already starting to protest. Quitting was a better decision than he'd realized.

"I'm not sure I'm the man for the job," said MacKentier, and Jackson laughed.

"Charlie, you're the only man for the job. Do you really want me to suggest to Aiden that you should go on the stand and testify under oath that Bo wasn't an employee?"

"Dad was in charge back then," said Charlie easily. "I really wouldn't remember everyone's employment status."

"I found a great picture of you and Randall the other day in the Deveraux storage unit," said Jackson. "Or should I say a picture of you, Randall, and Bo. It seemed like you all knew each other pretty well."

"I suppose we did," said Charlie icily. "That doesn't mean I kept track of their projects or status."

"Mmm-hm. You know," continued Jackson, "it was amazing how many old DevEntier records they had stashed away in that storage unit."

Charlie's eyes narrowed. "If you have DevEntier records, you need to return them. They're DevEntier property."

"It's also amazing how many DevEntier records from those days have *accidentally* gotten destroyed," said Jackson. "I think they're probably safer if they stay with me."

Charlie's fingers drummed on the desktop.

"I mean," said Jackson, exhaling, "I haven't gone through them all yet. Seems like they're mostly Randall's files. Lots of stuff about some project called Frixion."

"I would like those files back," said Charlie through gritted teeth.

"And I like making people do things they don't want to do," said Jackson.

Charlie stared at Jackson as if attempting to gauge his seriousness. Jackson added a smile and let the smoke trickle out through his nose.

"Fine," said Charlie, standing up. "I'll arrange a meeting with Ella Zhao, and I will speak with her, but you will be there too. We're both in, or this doesn't happen."

"Fair enough," said Jackson, stubbing out the cigarette with relief. He stood up to match Charlie's posture.

"And after it's done, you will give me all of Randall's files."

"Of course, Charlie," said Jackson with a smile. "It's not like I actually want the damn things."

"You're mistaken about one thing though," said Charlie as he walked to the office door and opened it.

"What's that?" asked Jackson, allowing himself to be herded out the door.

"I suspect that you have been a Deveraux your entire life."

"Could be," said Jackson with a shrug. "I'll be in touch."

"You do that," said MacKentier, and he swung the door shut behind him.

Ella – Aiden's Office

Ella paced around Aiden's office suite, waiting for Jackson. Aiden was on the phone in his office, which left her to her own thoughts—something that she was not happy about. Her own thoughts were not productive. After filing the continuance the previous day, she had attempted to suggest to Bai that not only was the case not likely to break their direction, that Aiden might not actually be the devil. That had not gone over well. Unable to explain about the things she had discovered with Aiden without also explaining Aiden, she hadn't been able to put forth a convincing argument. She wasn't sure that Aiden's half-whispered plan after court was the right decision, but it was starting to seem like her only option.

Ella sometimes liked to picture cases like trains—law and logic dictating that events moved along in a straight track toward a fixed destination. It was her job to spot where junction points were so that she could divert the train to the station she selected. She had always been better at predicting where and how to turn the train than others. But in this instance, she felt like not only was she riding a driverless train, but that someone had ripped the brakes off and moved the station.

Aiden was the only one who seemed certain of what to do next, and while she found that almost as sexy as his incredible ass, it was not a feeling that she was used to. Trusting someone else's judgement before her own was disconcerting at best. She had told her security detail that she was going for a massage and then paid the therapist to smuggle her out the back door. And now she was in Aiden's office, and what she ought to be thinking about was the plan and the next steps, and instead all she could think about was that Jackson would arrive shortly.

Jackson, who had caught them with apparently hardly an effort at all. Jackson, who had explained to Yang that following Aiden was not an option. Jackson, who Aiden thought was the best cousin ever, who made his family better by simply by existing. Jackson who now knew all of her horrible family secrets, and who might not like her or that she was dating Aiden.

In the time that she had spent strategizing about how to make Bai like Aiden, it hadn't occurred to her that Aiden's family might not like her. At this point, that really seemed like a glaring oversight. She fidgeted with the tiny scarecrow bobble-head on the secretary's desk and the woman looked up at her with an expression that said she was being incredibly patient.

"Would you like a glass of water?" asked the secretary.

"No," said Ella. "If I drink anymore water, I'm going to spend the next hour running for the bathroom. I might float away. I am totally and completely hydrated."

"Yes, but all I have for snacks is dark chocolate and that has caffeine."

Ella looked at the secretary. Leave it to Aiden to have someone smart and also slightly sarcastic.

"I'll stop touching the scarecrow."

The woman laughed. "It's OK. You're just starting to make *me* nervous, and I don't even know what we're waiting for."

"We're waiting for Jackson," said Ella.

The secretary looked perplexed. "Is he bringing bad news or something?"

"I've never met him," said Ella.

"Oh!" The secretary instantly relaxed into her chair. "Well, don't worry about that. He's great. Really nice. You'll like him."

"Oh," said Ella trying to square *really nice* with someone who explained things to Yang with emphasis.

"Actually, it turns out they're all nice. I thought the red-headed one was possibly a demon in an Italian suit, but he's actually kind of a sweetie too."

"Oh," said Ella, trying to square that with the man whom Eizo Matsuda described as an ice-cold bastard. "I'm sorry," she said to the secretary, "I feel like I should know your name, Aiden probably said it, but I don't remember."

"I'm Jenna."

"I'm Ella."

"Yes," Jenna said with a smile that said she was trying not to laugh, "I know."

"I feel like his family is going to freak out that I'm here."

"I don't know," said Jenna. "I kind of get the feeling that they don't freak out a lot."

"Huh. Wonder what that's like?"

Jenna did laugh. "I wouldn't know. My mom is currently freaking out that my sister is dating a Jewish guy. Like, hello, it's New York. But Mom skipped straight to *how will they raise the children*! Even though my sister's only been on like three dates with this guy. Then my brother is freaking out because his kid got called to the principal's office for the second time and we're all freaking out because my dad started seriously dating someone for the first time since the divorce—which was a decade ago, by the way."

Ella laughed. "I have three cousins—all girls. My uncle kind of loses his shit any time he finds out any of us are dating."

"Yeah, it's a dude thing. It's like they think about their daughter having sex and they freak out and start talking about shotguns and how we can't trust boys. Which, and you may never repeat this with my father in the room, kind of tells me more about how he thinks than about what other men think."

"What do you mean?"

"Well, I think he thinks women are things to have sex with, but daughters and wives are actual people. But the idea that some other guy is trying to treat us like he's been treating women freaks him out."

"Oooh," said Ella. "You can't tell him that—he'd have to believe he wasn't the good guy. You're right. I don't think we can repeat that in public."

"It does make the menfolk and their fragile egos uncomfortable," said Jenna, just as the door opened.

Ella saw Jackson pause on the threshold with a wary expression. She had his picture posted on her case board, so she was familiar with his appearance. But the photo, which had been a rather expressionless family portrait after his formal name change, didn't capture his intense energy. "I can go back out and wait five minutes," he offered, and Jenna chuckled.

"No, we're probably done discussing feminist theory for a bit," said Jenna.

"Well, whatever the conclusion was, I, and my fragile ego, fully support it," said Jackson. The twinkle in his eye made Ella think of Aiden.

"Good choice," said Jenna with a grin. "Jackson, this is Ella Zhao."

"Nice to meet you," said Ella, taking a step forward and holding out her hand.

"Nice to meet you too," said Jackson, shaking her hand. He managed the nice feat of giving a firm handshake that neither crushed in competition or dead-fished in condescension for her delicate femaleness. She could feel him assessing her and wondered what conclusions he came to.

"Jenna," he said turning back to the secretary, "do you have any gum? I had to smoke at the last place and if Aiden smells it on me, he's going to flip a bagel."

Ella tried to assess what that meant. She understood the general implication of bagel flipping, but not necessarily as it applied to Aiden. Was Jackson really worried about what Aiden would think? That seemed out of character for someone whose entire persona seemed based on not giving a shit about what anyone thought.

Jenna pulled open a compartment on her desktop organizer. "I have mint, tooth whitening, and Hubba-Bubba."

"You do not!"

"Oh, yes, my friend," she said, pulling out the pink package. "I do."

Jackson grinned in delight and took the pack of gum, then he caught Ella's eye, and a faint blush crept up his cheeks. "I mean, maybe mint would be good."

"The Hubba-Bubba is for Aiden, isn't it?" asked Ella.

"Yes," said Jenna, flashing her dimple. "He likes to chew it before court. He says it reminds him not to get too serious."

"Oh, good. I'd hate to think he was taking me seriously," Ella said.

"I always take you seriously," said Aiden, coming out of his office. "The gum is for me. So that I remember that I'm not a god among lawyers, and that I can be as bone-headed as the next kid on the block, and that I should also remember to have a good time."

"*Momento Mori,*" Ella said. "Remember that you too will die."

"Cheerful," said Jackson, blowing an enormous pink bubble.

"The Roman emperors had someone ride behind them in their

chariots and whisper *momento mori* to them between the cheers of the crowd," explained Ella.

"Got it," said Jackson. "Don't get a huge ego." He hefted the Hubba-Bubba pack in his hand with a chuckle. "This is probably cheaper than a guy and a chariot."

"Also, it comes in travel size and by the foot," said Jenna, which made Aiden laugh.

"Thanks Jenna. If Jerome calls, tell him I'll call him back. And after these two leave, we'll go over the contracts."

"I'll set them up," said Jenna with an understanding nod.

Aiden jerked his head and Ella and Jackson followed him into the conference room.

"What do you need Jerome for?" asked Jackson.

"If this goes down, then so will Charlie," said Aiden, taking a chair at the far end of the conference table. Ella made a quick choice and sat to his right. "That will be a huge shift in management at DevEntier and I need to make sure we're prepared. How *did* it go with Charlie?"

Jackson didn't answer right away, busying himself with taking off his coat and settling into the chair across from Ella. Ella looked at Aiden, trying to assess how to take Jackson's silence. Aiden was watching his cousin intently but didn't appear to be impatient.

"It went about as we expected it would," said Jackson, finally sitting. "He agreed to everything but admitted to nothing."

"So I can be expecting a call from Charles MacKentier sometime this week, then?" asked Ella, and Jackson nodded.

"I think so. He'll say he wants to talk and invite you to an in-person meeting."

"I would take that meeting," she said. "It's not a stretch."

"Yeah," agreed Jackson with a nod. "I'm supposed to meet you there and I'll offer you cash, and when you don't go for it, I'll threaten to expose you. Charlie's job is to lure you to the meeting and to help with the negotiating—extra pressure."

"Expose her to what?" asked Aiden with a frown. "That wasn't part of the plan."

Jackson cracked a bubble. "Yeah, I had to improvise. You were right about him. He doesn't believe in straight arrows, because he's never been anything but bent. He had to believe that she had a string to pull."

"OK, fine," said Aiden, sounding annoyed. "And what did you say her string was?"

Jackson popped a bubble and looked… Ella couldn't tell if it was sly or smug. "I told him she likes illegal fights and illegal fighters."

"Oh," said Ella. "I'm not really sure that's a big enough threat. I mean Uncle already knows I go sometimes. Although, I suppose MacKentier won't know that. And of course, I never did tell Uncle about…" She trailed off, catching sight of Aiden's face. "You didn't tell Jackson about Number Nine, did you?"

"No," said Aiden.

"Oh," said Ella.

Jackson chuckled. "My favorite part is when you claimed you were a pacifist and let Dominique hit that guy with a baseball bat."

"She clearly had some pent-up frustration. I think it was good for her."

Jackson laughed again, but Ella felt shocked.

"Dominique hit someone with a bat?"

"It's a long story," said Aiden.

"Yes, a long story in which Aiden claimed to my face—this face right here—that he didn't know how to punch people."

"Aiden!" she exclaimed. "Who is going to buy that?"

"Everyone!" snapped Aiden. "Everyone buys it. Except Jackson. And possibly also Evan," he added as an afterthought.

"Dominique is also suspicious of your winter tans," said Jackson and Aiden made a disappointed noise. "Did you really think we were never going to notice?"

"You haven't for the last six years. So yes, I thought that."

"Well, I've only been here for four, so I don't think the first two years should count. Also, thanks."

"For what?" asked Aiden, looking surprised.

"Well, I just realized that my review hearing took place during the high-season. Getting me out of jail must have been extremely hard on your fight schedule."

"Meh," said Aiden with a shrug. "You're not going to tell Grandma, are you?"

"What am I—high?"

Ella watched Aiden's shoulders relax slightly.

"No, what we're going to do is have a much longer conversation about your security arrangements. But unless you're planning on taking this pro, I think your secret identity should probably stay secret."

Aiden was quiet and Ella wasn't sure what to make of his expression. "Thanks," he said at last, sounding a bit shell-shocked.

"Although, at some point, I would also like the inside scoop on you," he said, pointing at Ella. "You don't have to tell me, but I do like to have a complete story."

"Well, I guess it's not exactly a secret," said Ella, trying to assess how much to sanitize her mother's behavior. "My mom threw this Day of the Dead party and I was dressed as Cinderella—"

"No," said Aiden firmly. "We're not telling Jackson."

Ella frowned at him in confusion. Jackson obviously already knew most of it and he obviously wasn't upset. On the other hand,

Aiden seemed to compartmentalize quite a bit—maybe he wasn't ready to break down all the walls. "Well, all right," she said. "If that's what you want. But I don't see why he shouldn't know."

"You just said you never told your family!" objected Aiden.

"Well, yes, because I thought my uncle would stop me from trying to find you, and I wasn't going to let that happen."

"It *was* you who talked to Josh!"

"Yes, of course. I've been looking for you for the last six years!"

"Really?"

Aiden looked so touched that she impulsively leaned over and kissed him.

"Well, now that Cinderella has found her Prince Charming, can we come back from happily-ever-after-land and work on nailing Charlie to the wall?"

Ella blushed at Jackson's amused expression.

"Yes," said Aiden, blatantly reaching across the table to hold her hand. "We should do that."

Jackson looked like he was two seconds from rolling his eyes.

"So what do we do when MacKentier makes me an offer?" asked Ella. "The goal is to get him to admit that he's responsible for forging the Berdahl-Copelands?"

"The goal is to get him to admit he's responsible for your father's death," said Jackson.

"But I'll take whatever I can get," said Aiden. "The destruction of records, the forgeries, the bank robbery—any of it works."

"The deaths of the bank robbers," added Jackson. "Although, it's my bet that he had Joe Foss and Unified Coverage handle that."

"What?" Ella looked from Jackson to Aiden. "When did that happen?"

"Oh," said Aiden with a grimace. "Yesterday. Sorry. Forgot to mention that when you came in."

"Four dead people slipped your mind?" she demanded.

"Well, yeah. We've been busy. And I didn't want to cover it over text."

"What the hell happened?"

"Most likely, whoever hired them met them in an abandoned warehouse and poisoned them," said Jackson.

"Son of a bitch." Ella stood up angrily, unable to sit still any longer. She walked the length of the conference room. "I don't like this. I've pressed my uncle as far as I can on what happened to my father. He believes it was one of your uncles." She held up a hand, forestalling commentary. "I realize that you disagree. I also realize that it was far more likely to have been whoever he was working with selling Department of Defense information. What I have not been able to get confirmation of is whether or not my uncle knew that's where Dad's money came from."

"You're worried that if what your father was doing comes out, it could bounce back on your uncle?" asked Jackson.

Ella took a deep breath. "Yes. Mom knew what Dad was doing. She didn't know who he was working with, but she knew enough to get us out of the country. I always thought that she was… controlling and that Dad's family didn't approve of her because of her…" She looked at Aiden for help.

"Lifestyle choices," he supplied.

"Yes. And I thought that was why she didn't go to Bai for help. Because even back then, Bai had money and connections. He probably could have protected us. In retrospect, it's telling that she didn't go to him, even for money."

"You think your mom thought Bai was involved somehow?" asked Jackson.

"I don't know. I didn't even think to ask her about it when I called her." Ella tried to ease the rubber band holding her ponytail. "I guess I could call her again."

"No," said Aiden.

Ella wanted to argue or say it was fine, but the truth was she didn't actually want to.

"I can't guarantee that it won't come out," said Jackson. "We can put the brakes on. The two of you could drop the lawsuit and we all walk away. It sounds like that would be unpleasant for you personally, but we could explain the truth to your uncle."

"He won't believe me," said Ella. "He's really convinced Randall or Owen killed my father. He's set on DevEntier because he wants revenge."

Jackson and Aiden exchanged a look that spoke volumes about both their opinions on their deceased relatives and their own relationship.

"I understand that idea," said Aiden. "I'm also used to thinking of my uncles as doing everything evil. And I'm not suggesting that he was ever like them, but I think I can walk Bai through the evidence that strongly suggests that it was not them."

Ella smiled at him but wasn't cheered up by his sweetness. "I doubt I could even get him to meet with you. If I can't prove it was someone else, I don't think…" She trailed off, breaking eye contact.

"Got it," said Jackson. "You have to come back with someone's head on a platter otherwise Aiden's not going to be welcome at the dinner table. But if it comes out that Zhao Industries was built on profits from industrial espionage, it could be a serious problem for your uncle."

"Am I right in thinking," asked Aiden, "that as long as your uncle knows who killed Bo, and that it wasn't our family, that we don't have to pursue prosecution for that? We could focus on the bank robbers?"

"Yes," said Ella, running that through the matrix of what she knew about Bai. "I think he would be satisfied. As long as there was some measure of justice."

"I still can't guarantee it won't come out," said Jackson.

"I think we have to risk it," said Aiden. "Bai would have to be crazy if he thought he could pursue DevEntier without having the past dug up. He had to know that there was a chance that Bo's activities would come to light. If anyone is going to get what they want, let alone everyone, I think we have to move ahead."

Ella could practically feel the train surging forward as she nodded. "What do you want to do?"

"Exactly what Jackson's set up: a meeting with you and Charlie and Jackson. I want the two of you to get him on tape admitting to something. Anything. But preferably, the bank robbery."

"I'm at a massage," said Ella.

"What?" Both Jackson and Aiden looked like she had taken a side-step out of reality.

"I have exactly twenty more minutes before I have to meet my security detail at the front of Tranquility Day Spa. Since the bank robbery, even without your less than explanatory message, Uncle has been freaking out about security. Getting out for an extended meeting and, presumably, interaction with the police is not going to be easy. And I doubt that if I propose this to him that Uncle will be inclined to go along with it."

"What if we have Evan call him up and offer to discuss things face-to-face?" suggested Aiden. "If he's distracted and taking security with him, presumably it will be easier for you to disappear for a while?"

"That could work," she said. "He probably would want to at least hear what Evan would say."

"You think Evan can do it?" asked Jackson, looking worried.

"Be in a room with a guy who hates him? Neither of us will be able to be there."

"I know," said Aiden, nodding and seeming to contemplate the skin of his knuckles. "But I think you were right. I think he's stronger than I've been giving him credit for, and I think we can count on him."

For a moment, Jackson's face flashed with an expression that Ella characterized as triumph, and had she been in court with Jackson on the witness stand, she would have pursued it for an explanation.

"I think we'll also need some of your police friends," continued Aidan, finally looking up at Jackson.

"They are definitely *not* my friends," said Jackson.

"Ella." Aiden ignored Jackson's interjection and turned back to her. "Can you meet with Charlie? If Jackson's there as back-up? Is that going to be OK?"

"I don't need back-up," said Ella.

"I'm starting to think we all need back-up," said Aiden, and Ella thought Jackson looked surprised.

The plan was simple: gain the assistance of the police, and she and Jackson would wear wires and hopefully catch Charlie saying something incriminating. If he didn't, then Ella would appear to go along with Jackson's offer, and everyone would go home and regroup. There really wasn't much danger to it.

Other than facing her father's murderer.

Jackson insisted on walking down to the cab with her. She wasn't sure how she felt about that. It was either chivalrous or demeaning, depending on which way she thought about it. She was fully capable of getting in her own cab.

"I wanted to talk about Aiden," said Jackson as the elevator doors closed.

Or perhaps it was an excuse to talk about Aiden and she should stop noodling on feminist theory.

"What about Aiden?" she asked, trying to keep her face impassive.

"He…" Jackson trailed off, seeming to search her face. She waited. "He's very important to me. My cousins are the only family I have." His tone seemed intentionally soft, as if he were making an effort to not sound aggressive.

"That's good to hear," she said, since some response seemed to be called for.

"Aiden doesn't often admit to wanting things," he said, and Ella frowned, uncertain of what he was trying to say. "If he admits that something is important to him then that makes it *very* important."

Ella felt a blush creep up her cheeks.

"I'm simply asking if he is as important to you as you are to him? Because if he's not, I would really prefer that you leave now."

"Aiden is very important to me," she said, feeling that she sounded silly. "I'm not going anywhere," she added raising her chin. "And I assure you that I'm extremely hard to get rid of."

"You're used to getting what you want." Jackson didn't sound angry. Again, she sensed that he was trying not to aggravate while asking extremely aggravating questions. He was not succeeding.

"Yes, I am," she snapped.

"And Aiden is what you want?"

"Aiden is everything I want," she said firmly.

Again he searched her face, but she thought he looked pleased. "Good," he said at last. "I have the feeling that you are going to run circles around him. It will be hilarious."

"Aiden is very smart. I don't think anyone runs circles around him," said Ella, still annoyed. The elevator doors opened, and they walked out into the lobby.

"But if anyone can manage it, I'm sure it will be you," he said, still smiling. He held the door open for her and she saw the cab waiting for her.

"You are annoying," she said, going for a direct assault.

"Yes, my cousins tell me that often," he agreed amiably. "But I think they secretly enjoy it."

"They probably only enjoy it when it's pointed at someone other than them."

Jackson laughed. "That may be true. But I won't bug you again. It's just my job to look out for them."

She glared at him but was once again struck by his tone. He was attempting to walk the very difficult line between giving her the third degree and letting his cousin get rolled by someone he wasn't sure he could trust. She had a sudden flashback to the moment she'd first met her cousin Rushi's fiancé and his nervous face and nerd's misunderstanding of fashion. She had not been nearly as delicate as Jackson was being.

"It's difficult," she said, her hand on the cab door. "It's hard for them to trust you when you've missed their entire childhood and all the trust that goes with that. They stick together and you're on the outside. They don't mean to, but they do. But it's hard to trust them too. Particularly, when an entire lifetime of experience says not to trust anyone but yourself."

For a moment Jackson's expression was bleak, then he smiled. "We're all getting better," he said. "Slower than I'd like, but we're getting there."

Ella nodded. She remembered that feeling of impatience. The summer before Rushi's wedding had been hard and culminated in a vase-smashing fight and night of binge drinking that had solved more than any of the previous years of careful behavior ever had. "You're right—you'll get there. But it's not them you have to worry about," she said.

"What do you mean?"

"Look at me," said Ella. "We have learned to trust each other—it's not my cousins that are the problem."

"It's your uncle."

"Yes. I'm fighting on two fronts because he can't let go of the past."

Jackson nodded, but didn't look concerned. "Eleanor is happy," he said. "I don't think we have to worry."

"I hope you're right," she said with a shrug. Then smiled at him and reached out and touched his arm. "Aiden really is what I want. There isn't anyone else like him and I'm not leaving a second time. It was the right decision back then, but not this time."

Jackson's face softened and he smiled at her in a way that reminded her strongly of Aiden. "Then he's lucky."

"We'll see," said Ella. "If we can't sort this out then it's going to get ugly."

"Nah," said Jackson reassuringly. "We got this."

Ella opened the cab door and prepared to enter. "Are all the Deveraux so cocky?"

"Um…" Jackson appeared to think it over. "Yes."

Ella laughed and got in the cab. "See you soon," she said, and he nodded and shut the door for her, sending her off with a wave.

Aiden – Hanson's Furniture

Aiden stood next Detective Nowitsky in the defunct furniture store a few blocks from the old DevEntier building and tried to pretend he wasn't nervous. He timed himself between sips of coffee to make sure he wasn't drinking too fast. He could do this. Everything was fine. Totally, absolutely, fucking fine. It was no big deal that the girl who was possibly the love of his life and the cousin who had almost single-handedly managed to turn his family into an actual family were walking into a room full of armed thugs. Totally normal. Totes norms. He was sooo chill.

It had been one minute and fifteen seconds. He was allowed another sip of coffee.

Jackson had not wanted to wear a wire. Ella had been fine with it. Aiden thought Jackson objected on philosophical grounds. The look he gave Aiden while they were taping it on was one of a man making a great sacrifice for King and Country. Which made Aiden feel a tiny bit smug. After four years he shouldn't really need proof of Jackson's loyalties, but it still felt good. Except that now Jackson and Ella were inside the old DevEntier building on the edge of Brooklyn and all Aiden could think was: what if that tiny little microphone and recording device was what got Jackson or Ella killed? He tried to dismiss the thought. Charlie was autocratic, narcissistic and a total asshole, but he wasn't crazy enough to think that he could get away with killing or hurting either Ella or Jackson. Right?

"So," said Detective Nowitsky, who seemed like he probably

had *Property of NYPD* stamped on his ass, "Jackson says you do corporate law."

"Generally," said Aiden. "But I have been known to dabble in criminal law."

"Hm," said the detective. "My kid's at Brown. She's thinking about law. Not really sure. She was thinking about applying for an internship at your grandmother's office over the summer. Jackson said she could do that."

Aiden tried to wrap his head around this statement. He had not previously suspected that Jackson said anything to cops beyond *fuck off, you pig*. It was an entirely new side of his cousin.

"It's a good opportunity—if she's at all interested. You can learn a lot about politics and government that way. It's not the same as legal experience, but it teaches a lot about how the law gets made in a very hands-on way. If Jackson is recommending her, I'm sure Grandma will listen."

Nowitsky nodded. "I like the idea of sending her with your grandma. All this *me too* bullshit… Every other senator sounds like he's sending dick pics to people. I mean, I made sure Hannah knows where to find the off switch for guys, but how am I supposed to protect her against online bullshit like that?"

Aiden nodded. "People like working for Grandma. Jackson does all the staff vetting. And neither of them stand for shit like that. I worked on a bill she was writing one time and there was an after party and like three people told me what a relief it was that they didn't have to worry about any after-hours *misunderstandings* with co-workers or bosses because Eleanor didn't hire people like that."

"OK, yeah. See? I think this is a good plan. Hannah said she was interested in interning in DC over the summer and I started to freak out. Those fuck-heads on the hill can't seem to keep their hands to themselves. You'd think they were running some sort of capital sleep-away camp for horny teens up there. But I like the sound of this. This sounds like a safe environment."

"Well, it's still DC," said Aiden. "I can't promise that one of the other fuck-heads won't say something."

"She's a big girl. She can handle herself. But it's a lot harder to handle something when you're in it every day, all day. As long as there's a safe place to work from, she can take on the world."

"And you think it's your job to make sure she's got a safe place from which to take on the world?"

"Yeah. I'm her dad. That's pretty much the definition of the job."

Aiden laughed and Nowitsky looked surprised.

"Sorry," said Aiden. "But I think your definition of parenting needs to be put on little cards and passed out at hospitals upon birth. I think there's a lot of people who may have missed that memo."

Nowitsky shrugged and then looked at Aiden appraisingly. "You have any specific people in mind?"

"One or two," said Aiden with a shrug. "But it doesn't matter. How long until we worry about Ella and Jackson?"

"At least thirty more minutes," said Nowitsky. "And really, it's Jackson, so it's not like we're really going to worry anyway."

"Excuse me?" demanded Aiden, bristling angrily. "I think I would prefer that the NYPD worry about my cousin's safety."

Nowitsky stiffened, his face hardening. Then he seemed to consciously force himself to relax. "I meant that Jackson is a guy who can roll with whatever punches get swung his way. I'm not worried about him because he's a tough kid."

"Right," said Aiden. "Right. Slight deviation into the rude dimension there. Sorry."

Nowitsky laughed. "Don't sweat it. Although, I have to say I didn't really see the family resemblance until just now. I guess you two really are related."

"Don't let the hair color fool you," said Aiden sourly. "We're all Deveraux."

Aiden's phone rang, and he tried not to jump. "Shit," he said, looking at the face on his phone. "It's Evan."

"Isn't he supposed to be with Bai Zhao?" asked Nowitsky.

"Yeah, he is." Aiden thumbed the phone to green and felt the coffee churn in his stomach. "Ev—"

"Get them out," said Evan, cutting Aiden off. "They're fucked."

"What?" asked Aiden, knowing it was a stupid comment, but he was unable to have another thought. Nowitsky was leaning in, clearly listening to every word.

"Bai talked to MacKentier," continued Evan. "Get them out." There was the sound of someone on the other end, speaking angrily in Chinese.

"Evan?" There was the sharp and, to Aiden, unmistakable sound of a fist hitting flesh. "Evan!" Then he heard the sound of footsteps and a door slam. "Evan!"

"I'm fine. Get Jackson and Ella out of there. Bai thought Jackson was working a double-cross on Ella. He ratted them out to MacKentier. I'm on my way."

The line went dead, and Aiden stared at the phone. His first instinct was to sprint the few blocks to the DevEntier building and grab Ella… His plan petered out there.

He had sent Ella in there. He was supposed to protect her, and this was what he'd done. He thought about throwing up, but that wasn't going to be productive and he didn't have any gum. He needed very much to get her the fuck out of there. What was going to make that outcome happen?

He looked at Nowitsky. Who was now yelling at some of the other police officers to report. Yelling was about as productive as throwing up. Who could help him? What assets did he have? Where was Jackson when he needed him? Jackson was right where Aiden had told him to be—next to Ella.

"Nowitsky," he said, and the detective turned around and looked at him. "Shut up. I need to call Jackson and they can't hear you."

"You're going to call him? No. We can't do that!"

"*You* can't do that," said Aiden. "I'm his cousin. I can call him anytime."

"MacKentier—"

"If he's smart, he'll make Jackson put it on speaker. I have to assume that he's listening to every word."

"Well what are you going to say?"

"I'm going to pretend that I don't know where he is. Jackson said he told MacKentier that I was out of the loop. I'll support that. Then I'll tell Jackson to meet me out at the old DevEntier building because I think I've found something suspicious and I want to go through the old records. That way Charlie knows that he can't expect to sweep this under the rug if Jackson disappears."

"You're going to paint a target on your ass," said Nowitsky.

"Yes," agreed Aiden. "But they'll let me in the building. Meanwhile, you're going to take your team and go in the side door of the records warehouse. It's not alarmed."

"We don't have a warrant or any firm evidence of imminent threat."

"As Jackson is a top shareholder with the company and I'm his lawyer, I'm giving you permission to enter now. You need to post someone here to stop Evan from going straight to DevEntier when he arrives."

"Got it," said Nowitsky. "Give me five minutes to put the team together before you call."

"Five…" Aiden glared at Nowitsky angrily.

"Don't go all Jackson on me, kid. These things take more than a minute, and you're changing the plan on the fly."

Aiden waited. He knew Nowitsky was moving quickly. He could see it in the hurried gestures and the running feet as everyone reacted, but it didn't feel fast enough. His pulse was jackhammering, and he could feel the adrenaline making his hand shake.

Carefully, he put down his coffee on one of the police department's folding tables. He'd been amused that the police had brought their own furniture to a furniture store, but as the computers unfurled and the bulletproof vests began to stack the tables, he realized that the police were working from experience. He walked out to his car and took off his overcoat, laying it in the passenger seat. He leaned against the roof and stretched out his calves and then rolled his head around on his neck. He needed to be loose for this. Then he bounced on the balls of his feet and tried not to throw warm-up punches. He didn't need to look like a total idiot. But he longed for Josh and his pre-fight routine. He felt unprepared to be Aiden Deveraux. Being Number Nine was so much easier—go, punch, punch again, leave. Aiden Deveraux had to think and plan and always have a smile. Never let them see you sweat.

He checked his watch. It had been longer than five minutes. He tried to calculate how long it would take Evan to get here. Tried to calculate how long Jackson and Ella had been inside. There were too many damn calculations.

Ella – DevEntier

"Charlie," said Jackson with a smile, "what the fuck are you talking about?"

Ella looked from Charlie MacKentier to the three men with guns and back to Jackson. This was not going well. When she had arrived, carefully timed to be a few minutes later than Jackson, she had been patted down and then, in a show of good faith, handed over her phone to MacKentier's security. She had been quite happy that the little microphone threaded through the lapel of her jacket to an inside pocket had not been discovered. She hoped that Jackson had escaped similarly unscathed. She had then been escorted along an echoing hall in a distinctly empty portion of the building to a conference room.

The security guard who escorted her was wearing a nice, fresh black eye that she guessed was courtesy of Aiden. It hadn't occurred to her that she might run into the security guards who had attacked them over the weekend. She added their presence to her list of things to worry about—along with the echoing and abandoned corridors. When questioned, the guard had said this portion of the building was about to undergo renovations. The décor looked original to the building, so it certainly needed renovations, but she wasn't sure the story was true. When she had arrived in the conference room, Charles MacKentier sat at one end of the table with Jackson's gun in front of him and three security guards behind him. Jackson had chosen to stand and was loitering by the big windows that looked over the parking lot. She hoped it was so he could see when the police arrived to rescue them because Charles MacKentier had promptly accused them of trying to screw him over.

"Seriously, Charlie," said Jackson, feeling his pockets. "Sorry, did you bring cigarettes? I really can't talk about anything serious without smokes."

MacKentier looked annoyed and then yanked a pack out of his pocket and slid it down the table toward Jackson.

"You're double-crossing me," said Charlie as Jackson began tapping out a cigarette and lighting up, "and I don't appreciate it. You and Miss Zhao." He sneered her name. "I shouldn't be surprised, I suppose. Like father, like daughter."

"What's that supposed to mean?" demanded Ella. She had chosen to seat herself in one of the rolling conference chairs. She was currently wondering how she could use it as a weapon. Being seated was a bit of drawback when it came to self-defense. At least she'd worn pants today.

"Your father would have sold out his own mother if it got him what he wanted. I'd say he was two-faced, but that number isn't high enough." Bitterness sparked bright in Charlie's voice.

"If he'd try to sell out his mother, she would have beat him with her cane," said Ella. It didn't need to be said, but she thought it might disrupt the full steam of anger that Charlie was building up to.

Jackson snorted in amusement, but that only seemed to make Charlie angrier. Jackson held up his hand as Charlie seemed about to speak. "Charlie, relax, would you? You and the goon squad over there are a little too uptight. No one is here to sell anyone out. We're here to make a deal, remember?"

"That's right," said Charlie. "You and Miss Zhao."

"That's right," agreed Jackson.

"Then why do you need me, again?" asked Charlie.

"I needed you to make the meeting, and I thought an adult in the room might help," said Jackson. "You're persuasive when you want to be, and Miss Zhao is known to be stubborn." The sky outside the window was bright white with a foggy mess of clouds that illuminated the room with a cold fall light and put Jackson into stark relief against the window, making it difficult for her to see his facial expression. She wished she knew him better. She felt like she was playing doubles tennis with a partner she'd only just met.

"I'm known for steamrolling idiots like you," said Ella. "Having MacKentier here isn't going to stop me from doing that."

"You can both stop lying," said MacKentier. "I know you already met yesterday."

Jackson paused, the flame of MacKentier's lighter flickering before the end of the cigarette. "And who told you that?" he asked, without lighting up. She noticed that he didn't put the lighter back down though.

Charlie chuckled. "Bai Zhao."

"What?" Ella demanded, deciding that this was an emotionally plausible time to stand up.

Charlie chuckled. "Apparently, you've given his security detail the slip one too many times recently, and he thought you needed additional protection. You were seen coming out of an office building with him yesterday. And security also flagged my number on your phone."

"Just your number?" asked Ella.

"Are there other numbers they should be worried about?" asked Charlie archly.

"I used a burner phone to call you," Jackson swiftly replied. "They won't peg it as Deveraux."

"Oh," said Ella, and she realized that he was telling her that information for Aiden's sake.

"So you admit it," said Charlie, sounding smug. "What did he

do? Tell you that the two of you could get rid of me? A win-win for
the Zhao and Deveraux?"

Ella was about to respond when a phone began to sound with
the William Tell Overture.

"That's Aiden," said Jackson. "If I don't answer, he'll just keep
calling. He thinks now that he's unemployed, the rest of us have all
the time in the world too."

Ella tried not to give Jackson an angry glare for his utter mis-
characterization of Aiden. She realized he was doing it for MacK-
entier, but it still annoyed her.

One of the goons took the phone out of his pocket and looked
at. "It is Aiden," he said.

"Answer it," said Charlie calmly, "put it on speaker."

Jackson did as instructed. "Hey, Aiden," he said.

"Jacks! Good, you're available. Where are you? No, never mind,
I don't care. Can you meet me out at the old DevEntier building?"

Jackson looked up at Charlie. "Yeah, I could probably do that.
Why?"

"I had a total brainwave. What if Ella Zhao is right?"

"Right about what?" asked Jackson, still eyeing Charlie. Ella
held her breath, wondering what Aiden was up to. None of this was
according to the script.

"What if Charlie really did cover up the fact that Bo was an
employee? I mean, it is in his own interest for us to win, so that
wouldn't be terribly shocking."

"Not terribly shocking, no," agreed Jackson.

"Actually, kind of nice of him, really. Not that I endorse that
in any way, of course."

MacKentier smiled smugly.

"I mean, it's also totally stupid," continued Aiden. "He couldn't
possibly get away with it."

MacKentier snarled in silent anger.

"But, whatever, here's the thing—I looked up the Zhao Industries's incorporation date. I want to go plow through some back records at DevEntier because I am willing to bet that Bo was setting up Zhao Industries contracts while he was still at DevEntier. And I know for a fucking fact that Charles Senior was running some damn stiff non-competes. I've totally copied off of those before. And if Bo was an employee, and he was working for Zhao at the same time, then we've got enough for a countersuit. Which should be enough to get the Zhao to drop their lawsuit."

"Sounds genius," agreed Jackson. "What do you need me for? I'm kind of busy."

"You can't possibly be that busy. Just meet me out there. Because I think if I go digging in the warehouse, security is going to get a tad squiffy. But you're an actual owner and whatnot."

"Ah, yes, the whatnot that I'm responsible for," murmured Jackson.

"And the other things," said Aiden, and Ella could practically hear his smile through the phone. "I fully intend to rely on you for the other things."

"I *am* great at gum-chewing," agreed Jackson.

"It's either you or I have to pretend to be Evan and I can't be that big of a dick. Anyway, I'm on my way over there now. Just meet me out there, kay?"

"I will definitely do that," said Jackson.

"Cool. See you in a few," said Aiden.

Jackson shut the phone off and looked at MacKentier. "Was Bo an employee?"

"Of course, he was," snapped MacKentier. "How else do you think I ever got information on what Randall was up to?"

"The Deveraux are notoriously secretive," agreed Jackson with a nod.

"The Deveraux are notorious liars," said Ella, feeling that now was the time to spin a new narrative. Maybe they could still get the answers they needed. "You said if I helped you, I could get the shares out of MacKentier's portion."

"I may have exaggerated," said Jackson.

"Feeling the sting of betrayal?" MacKentier hissed at her.

"Oh, don't take the high road," snapped Ella. "My entire family knows that you and Dad were selling Department of Defense secrets to the Chinese."

"And then Bo thought he could just quit," growled MacKentier. "You don't get to just quit!"

"He used you," said Ella. "Is that what you're pissed about?"

"I used him," said MacKentier.

"If you say so," said Ella with a shrug. "I don't really give a shit. Homeland Security probably will, of course, but that won't be a problem if one of you coughs up the shares I need."

"Did you tell anyone you were coming here today?" asked MacKentier pleasantly.

"You just said you talked to my uncle," she retorted. "Don't be an idiot. If I don't turn up in one piece, they will come straight here."

"You sound just like your father," said Charlie. "He thought he could walk out too. Never quite made it home though, did he?"

"Charlie," said Jackson, "I think maybe we're all getting a little ahead of ourselves here."

"You don't get to have cold feet now," said Charlie. "You wanted this problem to go away. You asked for my help, you don't get to decide what kind of help I give."

Out in the hall, they heard a door slam open and the sound of someone whistling in an off-key cheerful way. Ella had never heard Aiden whistle, but she would have bet a stack of greenbacks that it was him in the hall.

"Sounds like our favorite lawyer has arrived," said MacKentier. "Foss, go fetch him."

Foss jerked his head at the other two security officers and then left the conference room with a cracking of knuckles and an eager look on his face.

"If you hurt him, you're going to regret it," said Jackson, flicking the lighter off and on with hard ratcheting clicks. He had finally lit the cigarette, but she noticed that he hadn't actually taken more than a drag on it. The tip was a glowing red dot.

"They're not going to hurt him that much," said Charlie. "Probably. But I'm sure it's no more than you've wanted to do."

"Think you've got us all figured out, don't you, Charlie?" asked Jackson, taking a drag with a smirk.

"Yeah, I've had awhile to figure out what a Deveraux is most likely to do."

"This is ridiculous," said Ella, walking closer to MacKentier, while Jackson's lighter went click, flame on, click, flame off, click, flame on. "Whatever you have in mind, Aiden isn't going to go along with it."

"I think Jackson can manage Aiden," said MacKentier. "And Aiden might like to play at being Prince Charming, but all princes know that the money has to come from somewhere. I think he'll listen to sound financial reasoning."

Jackson had gone back to the windows, but this time it was closer to the remaining security guard.

There was a surprised yell from the hallway. Then a crash. The security guard behind MacKentier tensed, looking from the hall to MacKentier, uncertain of whether or not to stay or go help his friends. There was another yell, this time angry and pained. More thumping. Another crash, with extra splintering sounds. Then silence.

"Or maybe Aiden will listen to a good old-fashioned fist in the face," said MacKentier with a smile.

"Shit!" exclaimed the security guard as the window curtain went up in flames. The man stepped toward the curtains and Jackson flicked his cigarette into the man's face.

MacKentier sprang to his feet, reaching for Jackson's gun on the table, just as the conference room door burst open and Foss was thrown through it. Aiden stepped through after him and kicked Foss in the face. His expression was hard and angry, and she recognized the look from his fight with Dulce six years ago.

"Randall!" MacKentier barely said the word, more exhaled it in shock. He began to swing the gun away from Ella and toward Aiden. Ella reached out and clamped her hand down on top of the gun, hopefully preventing the slide from moving back and discharging. With the other hand she formed a fist, middle knuckle out and punched MacKentier in the back of his hand.

His hand sprang open and he yelled in pain, leaving her holding the gun. She immediately shoved her hand forward and slammed the gun into the side of his face. He raised his hand as if to hit her back, but he never made it past the idea. Aiden stepped forward and grabbed him by the neck and arm. MacKentier found himself shoved forward, then tripped and his face was rammed into the conference room table. He bounced back and Ella thought that he wasn't really conscious anymore, but Aiden hauled him up and punched him twice.

There was a squawk and then a gasping breath and Ella and Aiden turned to Jackson. The smoldering window curtain had been pulled down and partially wrapped around the security guard. It was unclear what had happened after that, but Jackson now had his arm around the security guard's neck, and he looked thoughtful and a little embarrassed as the man struggled for another few moments and then passed out.

"Hey," Jackson said, dropping the security guard and stomping on the remains of the curtain. "Nice timing."

Aiden stepped across MacKentier and swept Ella into a hug. "Are you OK?"

"Yes," squeaked Ella through his boa constrictor hug.

"You're going to squish your girlfriend," said Jackson with a laugh, coming around the table.

"Whatever," said Aiden turning to Jackson, "you're next."

"I don't—" Jackson's opinion was cut off as Aiden wrapped his arms around him and hugged him hard enough to boost him off his feet and bounced him.

"Yeah, OK," said Jackson, sounding annoyed, but Ella thought he looked pleased. "We're fine. You can put me down."

"Aiden!" someone was yelling down the hall. "Jackson!"

"Evan?" said Jackson as Aiden returned him to his feet.

"Ev?" asked Aiden, sticking his head out in the hall. "How fast did you fucking drive? And didn't I leave police persons to intercept you?"

"I ignored them," said Evan, coming into the room. "And I set the meeting for Brooklyn. I didn't want to be that far away. I'm not a total idiot. It sounded too easy for something *not* to get cocked up. Why are there bodies in the hall? Where are the police? Hi, I'm Evan." The man who had been described as an ice-cold bastard, smiled at Ella and held out his hand. He was a smidge taller than Aiden, but where Aiden always appeared slightly disheveled, as if he'd just run his hand through his hair, Evan's red hair seemed carefully regimented.

"Hi, I'm Ella," she replied, uncertain of just how much to take Evan at face value.

"Nice to meet you," he said with a smile that Ella thought was completely genuine. He looked around the room. "Jackson, did you smash Charlie's face in?"

"No, that was Aiden. And, also, Ella."

"He shouldn't have pointed a gun at Aiden," said Ella with a shrug.

"Oh," said Evan. "Well, you couldn't have waited for me? I would have liked to have seen that."

"Believe it or not, Evan, I do not actually schedule my face-smashing to suit your timetable," said Aiden in exasperation.

"Josh schedules it for him," said Jackson.

"Jackson!" snapped Aiden, glaring at him.

"Who's Josh?" asked Evan.

"Aiden's trainer," said Ella.

"Ella!"

"What?" said Ella and Jackson at the same time and Evan laughed.

"You're going to be fun to have around," said Evan approvingly, and Aiden looked flummoxed.

"I don't think that you get to—" Aiden began.

"Jackson?" yelled someone in the hall, interrupting Aiden.

"Yeah, Nowitsky, come ahead," Jackson yelled back. "We're in the conference room." Jackson seemed about brush past them, and then paused to check his pockets. "Ah," he said and held out his hand to Ella.

"Oh!" exclaimed Ella, realizing she was still holding his gun. "Sorry." She handed it over and Jackson tucked it away before going out to the hall.

"Jackson, what the fuck did you do?" demanded the police detective, his voice echoing off the tile of the corridor.

"It wasn't me! Why does no one ever believe me? Although…" he stepped back in and looked around the room. "Aiden, I give up. Where did you put the third one?"

"Hm?" Aiden turned to look at his cousin.

"Three went out. We've got Foss here. And then there's the one in the emergency eyewash fountain. That's two. What'd you do with number three?"

"Oh. There's a janitorial closet down the way. Shoved him in there for safe keeping."

"Ah." Jackson disappeared out into the hall again.

"Are you sure you're all right?" asked Evan, looking at both of them sternly.

"Ev, stop worrying," said Aiden. "Between Ella and Jackson, we've got the badass angle covered. I don't think—"

There was more yelling in the hall and Ella grimaced.

"Tamade!" she swore and grabbed at the pocket square in Evan's suit jacket pocket.

"I can't finish a sentence," said Aiden. "What are you doing?"

"That is my uncle," she hissed, swiping at his face. "And you've got…"

"Got what?" he asked, leaning down to make it easier for her.

"You've got blood on you," said Evan. "Although, I don't see why my pocket square has to suffer for it."

"I don't have one," said Aiden. "I left my jacket in the car."

"Always underdressed," said Evan, shaking his head.

Ella scrubbed at a tough spot and Aiden chose that moment to kiss the tip of her nose, just as her uncle walked in.

"Ella! What the hell is going on!"

Ella looked into Aiden's eyes. He looked like he was trying not to laugh.

"Oh," said Ella, straightening up and snapping the pocket square to make a nice popping noise. She really was going to owe Evan a new one. "Is it not obvious? Aiden and I are dating. Charlie MacKentier killed Dad. And Jackson and the police are trying to get everyone handcuffed before they regain consciousness."

Bai looked from Aiden to Ella to Evan and then back to Ella. "I think I need to sit down," he said.

"Aiden has that effect on people," said Evan. "However, I believe this is about to be a crime scene. Perhaps you and I should go back down to the first floor. I think we could possibly find a decent conference room, potentially with coffee and chairs that don't date from the nineties."

Ella wanted to take a moment and congratulate Evan on managing to sound like a gracious host in the least civilized situation she could think of, but Bai's eyes were fixed on her face. She knew that her joking recap hadn't done her uncle justice. He needed to know. He deserved the truth.

"Ella… That man killed Bo?"

"Yes," said Ella, deciding to state matters as clearly as possible. "He and Dad were selling Department of Defense secrets to the Chinese, and when Dad tried to quit, Charlie MacKentier had him killed."

"I thought it was Randall," said Bo, blinking. "I, wait, Department of Defense? No. It was… Bo said it was just private sector insider knowledge. He never said…" Bai looked at all of them again, chagrin and horror filling his face. "Bo said he would make Zhao Industries happen. It wasn't supposed to be at any cost."

A lump formed in Ella's throat, and she found she was blinking back tears. She didn't know what to say. She had wanted to find out who killed her father, not hurt her uncle. But the pain in Bai's face was clear. Aiden put an arm around her shoulders, and she leaned into him. He smelled of soap and sandalwood, and she felt a wave of relief knowing that he would never let her go again.

Jackson – Granger

Jackson watched as his cousins trooped into the house. Aiden, particularly, was beaming, but even Evan looked happy. Theo opened the door for them, and Aiden began to divest himself of his outerwear, still talking a mile a minute to Evan, working through the possible options for the DevEntier board. Jackson saw Nika waiting for them in the hall and she gave him an inquiring look. He gave her a smile and a nod. She looked relieved, but not as much as he might have thought.

"Nika," bellowed Aiden, handing over his coat to Theo.

"I'm right here," said Dominique, coming forward. "You don't need to yell."

"Truly," said Eleanor coming out of the office and scrutinizing the trio. "I assume whatever it was the three of you were up to has gone well?"

"Went perfectly!" Aiden exclaimed.

"That may be stretching it," said Evan.

"Perfectly!" reiterated Aiden, wrapping an arm around both Evan and Jackson and forcibly hugging them. Dominique laughed at them. "We are well on the way to resolving issues with the Zhao. I got to punch Charlie in the face and—and!—I found out that Jackson offers college advice to police officer's daughters."

"Yes, Ms. Nowitsky," said Eleanor. "She's doing very well at Brown."

"Oh," said Aiden, looking disappointed to have his news flop. "Well, I told her father that she should apply for a summer internship with you over the summer."

"Oh, good," said Eleanor. "She seems quite bright."

"Can we go back to the part where you punched Charlie in the face?" asked Dominique.

"Yes," agreed Eleanor. "Why did you punch Charlie in the face? I don't object, necessarily. One usually does want to punch him in the face, but it *is* frowned upon."

"Turns out," said Evan, handing over his coat to Theo in turn, "that Charlie and Bo Zhao used to sell DoD secrets from Randall's projects to the Chinese. Bo was leveraging DevEntier contacts and the cash he was making with Charlie to found Zhao Industries. Only when he tried to quit, Charlie had him killed."

"Good grief," said Eleanor, looking shocked for once. "I don't know what to say to that."

"Well, we've got him admitting to it on tape," said Aiden smugly. "Thanks to Jackson and Ella."

"Do we have to mention that?" asked Jackson. He hated the idea of wearing a wire. He'd always sworn he'd never snitch and while getting Charlie MacKentier to admit the truth wasn't snitching—particularly since he and MacKentier had never been remotely close to allies—wearing a wire was still one of the things stand-up guys didn't do. When he'd joined the Deveraux family, he'd fully intended on leaving the criminal life behind, but he occasionally still found himself bumping into these remaining vestiges.

"Losing street cred?" asked Dominique, her eyes twinkling.

"Yes," he agreed, and she smiled sympathetically.

"Don't care," crowed Aiden. "We got him and he's going away for the rest of his life."

Eleanor made a tsk noise. "I shall have to have a word with Buffy."

"Buffy?" asked Dominique with a frown. "Sanders or Sorrento?"

"Sanders. She's friends with Charlie's current wife, who is in Aspen at the moment," said Eleanor. "Someone should warn her."

"Ah," said Dominique, nodding. "She'll probably want to get a divorce lawyer."

"I suspect she has one already," said Eleanor. "One doesn't generally go to Aspen this early."

"Oh," said Aiden. "I hadn't considered that. Should we do something more? I just want Charlie to go to prison. I don't want to hurt his family."

"She'll be fine. She's screwing Teddy Van Burstein," said Jackson. "Who I think is also currently in Aspen."

"Really?" asked Evan, looking surprised. "I hadn't heard that."

"It's amazing what you can find out about a person when you really want to look," said Jackson, glancing at Aiden. Aiden glared at him, which made Jackson chuckle. Knowing Aiden's secret was really the most fun ever.

"Can we return to the topic at hand?" demanded Aiden.

"I don't think I care to spend more time on who Teddy Van Burstein is screwing," said Evan.

"No! The topic of how awesome today is and how I saved the day and…" Aiden appeared to be searching for additional superlatives.

"Whatnot?" suggested Dominque with a giggle.

"Are all of you quite done trying to ruin my moment?" demanded Aiden.

"No," said Eleanor. "We're not really trying to do that. But I'm about to and I'm sorry. I would wait to tell you, but you'll probably see it on the news."

"Tell me what?" asked Aiden, and Jackson felt a quiver of concern. He glanced at Dominique, who grimaced unhappily.

"It's Granger. They dropped the majority of the charges against him."

"What? Why?" demanded Evan.

"Homeland Security has decided that the mercenaries who attempted to harm us are no longer available to testify—that they are too valuable to the national defense. Which means that the charges against him regarding us are no longer… viable."

"Son of a bitch!" swore Evan.

"Grandma!" exclaimed Aiden. "How could you let this happen? Let's get a press conference going or something. We've got to have enough juice to put Granger away."

Eleanor sighed. "I'm sorry, darlings, but at the moment I'm using my leverage for something else. If I focus on this, I lose other things that are more important to me. And there are other charges on the table against Granger."

"I really feel there must be other ways we can make his life hell," said Dominique thoughtfully.

"Didn't we already decide that I don't do horseheads, Nika?" asked Jackson.

"Don't be ridiculous! I'm against animal cruelty. I had something… I don't know… more social and financial in mind."

"Nika," said Aiden, "as your lawyer, I'm advising you to let the courts handle this. I don't think we need another Suzy Fletcher."

"She had that coming," said Dominque.

"Didn't Suzy Fletcher get arrested for drug possession and have to go to the women's correctional facility in Pennsylvania or something?" asked Evan with a frown.

"I have no knowledge of that," said Dominque. "What I do know is that her sister is no longer has an eating disorder because Suzy doesn't harass her every moment of every day."

"I worry when you go Godfather on us," said Aiden.

"Nonsense," said Dominique. "I don't go Godfather. It's not like those drugs weren't Suzy's. She didn't have to slap that cop. Or try to drive off in his patrol car. She did that all on her own."

"And no one called in a tip to the police on her car or anything?" asked Aiden.

"I really wouldn't know," said Dominique. Jackson felt a qualm of misgiving when he saw Eleanor watching Dominique with an expression of thoughtful interest. "My point is that Granger should not be allowed to get away with these sorts of things."

"Well, at the moment," said Jackson, hoping to pull Eleanor's attention away from his cousin, "he's not. Right? There was a stack of indictments, wasn't there? Even if you take away ours, he's still got the fraud charges, right?"

"Yes," said Aiden, nodding. "I'm sure that they'll get him on something." Aiden smiled, but Jackson thought it wasn't as genuine as it had been a moment ago.

"My favorite part," said Evan, "was when they picked up Charlie and all this nose blood came out and splatted on his suit. He's going to have to sit through arraignment in a gunky suit. Thanks for that." He patted Aiden's shoulder, and a little of Aiden's sparkle came back. "Can we have wine now?"

"Of course, Mr. Deveraux," said Theo. "However, dinner will be in the breakfast room as Mr. Aiden has *still* not removed his papers from the dining room."

There was a chorus of groans of the family.

"I believe," said Eleanor, and the cousins turned to see what she would say, "I believe that we should go out to dinner. Today seems like it needs a bit of celebration."

"Yes!" agreed Aiden. "Plus, we need to toast Nika and Max for moving in together."

"What?" Eleanor said, turning to Dominique.

"Finally convinced him," said Aiden. "Although, I hope he gets along with Ella. That will be weird if our S.O.'s don't get along."

Eleanor turned back to Aiden. "What?"

"I'm going out with Ella Zhao. Did I not mention that?"

"Mention… No, Aiden. No, you distinctly did not!"

"Mentioned it to me," said Evan with a carefully careless shrug.

"I knew," said Jackson. "I thought everyone knew."

"I…" Eleanor looked at all four of her grandchildren and Jackson watched her cave. She really couldn't stand against all of them. It had taken him awhile to get them all aligned, but today was the day. "I did not realize that you liked her that much," said Eleanor, trying to regain her composure.

"Oh, I love her oodles," said Aiden. "She can kick ass in multiple languages. Could not be hotter."

"I don't think I need to know that," said Eleanor.

"Oh. Sorry. But honestly, she's absolutely brilliant and gorgeous. And she makes us look multi-ethnic. Great for the newsletter, Grams."

"That is a very calculating thing to say. Stick with the"—she waved a descriptive hand—"*oodles*."

"Easy," said Aiden cheerfully.

"I'm going to get my sweater from the office," said Eleanor as she eyed them sternly.

Jackson waited until she was out of eyesight before letting his smile show. Evan made a mime of wiping sweat off his brow, which nearly made Jackson laugh.

"Thanks," whispered Dominique, hugging Aiden.

"Any time," Aiden whispered back.

Jackson looked at his family assembled in the hall and found that he could not stop grinning. Today really did deserve a celebration.

Aiden – The Right Decision

Aiden opened the door to his brownstone and looked at Ella, who was adorable in leggings and a slouchy shirt under a puffer coat.

"I was starting to worry you weren't coming," he said, breathing out a sigh of relief.

"Sorry. I had to help Lilly. There's some class presentation thing and Lilly wanted to do hers on how feminism has helped women of today. I was pulling stats on women in sports and Title IX for her."

"Credit cards," said Aiden.

"What?"

"Women couldn't hold credit cards in their own name until 1974 and the Equal Credit Opportunity Act."

Ella took out her phone and began texting.

"Forgot about that one?"

"My degree focused on a lot of European law," said Ella, hitting send. "I've been working overtime to keep up with you and all your..." She waved at him in annoyance.

"Damn, you're smart," said Aiden, grinning.

His neighbor's ficus, evicted during a house cleaning purge, still sat on the front porch and leaned drunkenly across the railing between the properties. It chose that moment to droop its leaves into her hair. She batted back at the sudden attack.

"Ficus," said Aiden. "This is Ella. The girl I've been telling you about."

Ella gave a surprised giggle.

"It's been a stressful couple of weeks," said Aiden. "I've had to find comfort where I could. Ficus is very good at listening."

"You may need to get a pet," said Ella.

"Josh said he'd get me a Roomba with ears. Personally, I was thinking more along the lines of getting a girlfriend."

"I don't vacuum," said Ella.

Aiden laughed. "I didn't think you did. Come on in."

Ella entered cautiously and surveyed the stripped-back brick entryway and dark-stained staircase with the abstract painting of a Chinese style bird hanging above it.

"That—" she pointed at the painting.

"I got it when I got the house. I really liked yours," he said, suddenly feeling embarrassed. "Although, now that I'm thinking about it, I can see why you wouldn't tell me the real translation of your middle name."

"What?" she frowned at him.

"You said your middle name meant *bird*," he said. "And I believe the artist told me that the bird in that picture was a swallow."

"It's not first date material," said Ella, pinking up. "I didn't think I needed to tell a half-naked man I just met that my middle name meant swallow. Particularly not with porn playing in the next room."

Aiden chuckled. "What *is* your middle name?"

"Yan," she said. "After Nai."

"Good source material," said Aiden.

"I could do worse than to be like Nai," she agreed with a grin.

"You're in my house," he said, feeling a bubble of happiness well up inside of him.

"And everyone knows it," she said, taking a step closer. "Uncle still wasn't happy about it, but he just went off to his study in a huff and Aunt said she would take care of him."

Aiden inched closer and slid his arms around her waist. "Ella, the answer to this better be no, but are we crazy?"

"The answer is absolutely yes," said Ella, dropping her purse and wrapping her arms around his neck.

"Do you have to argue with me about everything?" he asked, even though he knew he was beaming.

"Yes," said Ella. "I'm the opposing counsel. That's my job."

"No," he said and pulled her close. "Not anymore."

"Oh, well, then maybe I just like arguing with you."

"Argue with this," he said, and he leaned down to kiss her.

She pulled back after a minute and looked up at him with a wide grin. "OK," she said. "Here's my counter argument." She kissed along his neck with delicate lips that made him shiver.

"Your counter argument is so persuasive," he murmured, nibbling along her ear, "that we might not make it to dinner."

"I have a granola bar and a change of clothes in my purse," said Ella. She leaned back to look him in the eye. "We don't have to go anywhere until tomorrow."

"Ella," he said, laughing, "you are the easiest person in the world to fall in love with."

"So, I win then?" she asked, lifting her chin.

"Yes," he agreed, going back to her lips.

"I'm not easy," she said between kisses with a giggle. "You're easy."

"I think I'm being misquoted," said Aiden.

"I want to see the rest of your house," said Ella, and she pushed him through the nearest doorway, her hands finding their way under his t-shirt.

"Right," he said, trying to kiss her while moving backward into the living room. "Living room, couch." He waved blindly.

"Mmm, lovely couch," she said, pulling his shirt over his head and pushing him down onto said couch. She landed on top of him and grinned at him, her black hair falling like a curtain around him. "I suppose we might actually be crazy, but I don't think so," she said, kissing him gently. "I have actually given this careful thought. And I'm fully convinced that this"—she slid her hands down his chest and stomach and found the button on his jeans—"is the right decision."

"Ella," he said seriously, "you are always the right decision." Then he did exactly what he knew he should do and kissed her.

EPILOGUE: THE DEVERAUX CHILDREN

Jackson Deveraux

"Hey," said Nowitsky as he looked up from his pie. "How's the Deveraux household? Sunshine, lollipops, and balloons?"

"More or less," said Jackson, taking his seat next to him at the diner counter. "Aiden's pretty pleased with himself. He's managed to divest DevEntier of Charlie without too much of Charlie's bull-shit bouncing back on the company. There's a new joint venture with Zhao Industries in the works and Bai Zhao even invited Aiden to dinner."

"The kid's too bright to be that heavy of a hitter," said Nowitsky, shaking his head.

"Tell me about it," said Jackson. "What's up? I would have thought we could be meeting at the station."

Nowitsky grimaced. "We probably could, but I'm about to be more open than I suppose my co-workers would approve of."

"Intriguing," said Jackson, waving at Priscilla and pointing to the pie.

"Yeah, that's one word for it. So we took the screws to Foss with some of the stuff you turned up for us. They rolled on MacKentier as predicted. But here's where it gets weird—sorry, intrigu-ing. Foss said that they were *not* responsible for the bank robbery or the bank robbers. Said they didn't hire them. Foss even went so far as to say MacKentier did it himself—that he got a contact from an associate, and that he did all the hiring and, ahem, firing. Foss says he recommended against the plan, but that MacKentier went ahead with it anyway."

"That's four counts of murder if you can get him on it," said Jackson thoughtfully. "Not to mention conspiracy on the actual bank robbery."

"We'll see. CSI is chasing down some angles. We might or we might not be able to connect him. Foss is not exactly an all-star witness, and he has no first-hand knowledge, so…" Nowitsky made a shrug gesture with his hands. "The recordings you guys got are more sure-fire and gets us straight to Federal time. Anyway, the point was, Foss wasn't the connection, but that made us wonder who was. So we took a stroll through MacKentier's phone records during the time Foss says the bank robbers were hired. There was only one name that has a history of suspected criminal activity on the list."

"Now I'm dying to know," said Jackson, accepting the pie and a smile from Priscilla.

"J.P. Granger."

Jackson looked sharply into Nowitsky's face.

"There's that Deveraux look," said Nowitsky with a nod. "It was only one phone call and it lasted less than five minutes. But I figure that's long enough to get a name and a number. Granger hired mercenaries to go up against you guys, right? If MacKentier wanted to get a connection that could help him hire a crew, it seems plausible that he'd dial up Granger."

"Yeah," said Jackson, "it does."

"Anyway," said Nowitsky, "I know they've got Granger up on charges. But he's a rich guy with a lot of lawyers and it looks like he's still interested in causing trouble for you. If I were you, I'd stay on my toes."

"Yeah," said Jackson, "I think we should."

"Fortunately," said Nowitsky, turning back to his pie, "all three of you boys seem to be able to punch your way out of trouble."

"It's Dominique you have to look out for," said Jackson. "She's got a baseball bat."

Nowitsky laughed. Everyone always did.

Dominique Deveraux

Dominique entered her grandmother's office and tried not to show her trepidation. She always felt like she was being called on the carpet when she went into Eleanor's office.

Eleanor was standing by the window, the pale autumn sunlight gilding her hair a silvery gold.

"Hey, Grandma," said Dominique, flopping into a chair in front of the desk. She knew the casual pose would drive Eleanor nuts, which was rather the point.

"I do not understand how you and Jackson can be so much alike," Eleanor said.

"Are we?" Dominique asked, surprised.

"Yes, you're both very careless about posture."

Dominique laughed and sat up in the finishing school pose that Eleanor preferred. "Is this better?"

Eleanor came to the second chair and sat down there instead of at the desk. Her pose mimicked Dominique's own.

"It's not that it's better," she said. "It's a matter of audience. One must select the audience in which to be casual."

"Yes, Grandma," said Dominique. "I know."

Eleanor's eyes narrowed and her chin tilted down, assessing Dominique. "You do it on purpose to annoy me then?"

"Yes," said Dominique, relaxing and leaning back in the chair. "Of course."

Dominique expected some sort of rebuke, but instead Eleanor's head tilted, still assessing Dominique. "Jackson says that I baby you too much," said Eleanor.

"No, not enough," said Dominique. "I would prefer to be much more spoiled, really."

A surprised laugh escaped from Eleanor, but then her face grew serious. "Your mother," Eleanor paused as if picking her words, "needed your father very much."

"I hope so," said Dominique. "She had two kids with him."

"No, I mean… I think, she frequently felt overwhelmed by life. Your father provided a buffer and a… safe place, I suppose?"

Dominique frowned. Getting Eleanor to talk about their parents was like pulling teeth. She could see what Eleanor was talking about now that it had been said, although she had never previously been able to state it. "Dad loved her," said Dominique, uncertain what Eleanor was getting at.

"Yes! Yes, of course. It's just that needing someone is sometimes dangerous. You can't rely on people."

"Yes, you can," said Dominique. "I rely on Max and Jackson all the time. And Aiden. And even Evan," she added as an afterthought. "I mean, I usually only rely on him for financial and wine advice. But he does a bang-up job at those."

"Yes, I rely on them too," said Eleanor. "I'm not saying this very well." She paused and Dominique waited. "Jackson keeps telling me that you have a plan and you're fine and that I should just let you have your..."—she waved her hand and Dominique took that to be the sign language equivalent of *silly*—"job. But you are very much like Genevieve, and I worry that you'll get out there and you'll get hurt."

"Oh," said Dominique. "Well, I suppose I might, to be perfectly honest. Max could break up with me or I could get fired or… I can't think of anything else horrible, but either way I would recover. And then I would probably wreak horrible vengeance upon them."

Eleanor looked skeptical. "Vengeance takes a bit of effort."

"Yes, but sometimes I believe it to be worthwhile."

"Granger for instance?" suggested Eleanor. "You seemed to have some specific ideas."

"Well, I have, actually," said Dominique. "Of course, what I really would like is for Granger to go to jail. But it is looking less and less like that will happen. It's very upsetting. So I was thinking that the next best thing would be to ruin him. Just find a way to make him poor and take away everything that he likes about life. I haven't made any efforts until now though. And I'm pretty sure I can get him blackballed from certain events and restaurants, but I think in order to bust open his piggy bank, I'd have to know a great deal about his finances."

"Don't worry about that," said Eleanor. "I've already done the research. I'll have a word with Evan."

Dominique looked at Eleanor in surprise. "You've thought about this already."

"Of course," said Eleanor. "We can't have anyone trying to hurt the family. It really will not be tolerated. The problem is, of course, that what I will ask Evan to do may not be precisely legal, and you have just announced that the very lovely, but morally upright, U.S. Marshal Maxwell Ames will be living with you."

"Ah," said Dominique.

"Yes," said Eleanor. "And while, of course, I respect law enforcement and adore Max, he is a bit of risk factor. If this is the kind of thing you're uncomfortable with, I think we need to discuss it now."

Dominique knew she had a split second to make a decision. From her grandmother's point of view, there was only one right answer. And if she wanted her grandmother's confidence, then Dominique had better say the right thing.

"No, Grandma," said Dominique sitting up straighter in her

chair. "I'm not uncomfortable with it. This is a family issue. There's no reason to discuss it with Max."

Of course, what Eleanor didn't realize was that Dominique could stand up to Max about zero percent. If he asked, she would tell him the truth. She was just going to have to make sure he didn't ask.

"Good," said Eleanor, smiling.

"Is this why you have been concerned about Max moving in with me?"

"Co-habitation produces a great deal of proximity to information that you may not want shared," said Eleanor in a beautiful blend of jargon and message. Dominique felt like she should be taking notes.

"He leaves his cases at the office, and I leave all of the Deveraux business here," said Dominique. "It is why I use my old bedroom as a spare office."

A smile flickered over Eleanor's face. "Jackson said I was wrong. I really ought to listen to him."

"I recommend it," said Dominique. "He's very smart."

"You're all so young," said Eleanor plaintively. "I dislike taking advice from people your age."

"You'll have to get used to it eventually," said Dominique. "We know how to change the passwords on everything."

"You really aren't Genevieve." Eleanor said with a soft little laugh. "That's probably for the best." The phone on the desk rang and Eleanor stood up. "Thank you for coming today, Nika. It was so good to catch up."

Dominique knew when she was being dismissed and stood up herself.

"Yes," said Dominique thoughtfully. "It was nice to see you too."

Evan Deveraux

Evan stopped the dolly at the door of the storage unit. He could do this. He'd gone in with Jackson, and he hadn't freaked out. Dr. Nicholas was right—he was strong enough to face some of the things he'd been avoiding. The DevEntier issue had gone well. Having Aiden pummel Charlie MacKentier had been satisfying on a level that probably meant that Evan was a bad human being. But it was like having all the old memories get slam-dunked into the conference room table. And, well, if enjoying that meant he was a bad human being, then so be it. Jackson said it just meant that he *was* a human being. And Jackson was right about a lot of things, so maybe it was fine.

Evan opened the door and drove the dolly with the cartons through and into the unit. He ignored his childhood bed, which was separated into pieces and tied into a flat package that leaned against the wall. He hesitated at the vintage brass cigarette holder shaped like a globe that used to sit on the coffee table. He remembered flipping the lid on and off a million times and being in charge of restocking the cigarettes. He pushed the boxes back toward the shelves. He wasn't sure he had Jackson's climbing ability, but he thought if he just shoved them somewhere onto the shelf it would be good enough.

He grabbed the first box and stepped on a piece of wicker to lever himself up. Box one: away. Box two went the same way. Box three was almost on the shelf when the piece of furniture he was standing on gave way. He dropped abruptly and the box came crashing down on him in a flurry of papers. He lay on the floor, blinking at the now paper-obscured vision of the ceiling. He should have known better than to think this would all go according to plan. If it involved his dad or uncle, it was pretty much guaranteed to suck. With a sigh he sat up, shedding papers. He plucked one out of his hair and reached for the box. The papers were all a mixed bag. The back half of the box hadn't had anything DevEntier related. He hadn't bothered to look through most of it once they found the email and information on Frixion. The headings on the papers flipped through his view.

SOLAR MARKET SEGMENT ANALYSIS

GDR INDEPENDENT LAB: AUTOPSY REPORT

HISTORIC RATES OF RETURN ON TECHNOLOGY STOCKS

Evan's fingers stopped as he pushed the first group of papers into the box. Going back, he retrieved GDR Independent Lab: Autopsy Report and scanned further down the page.

EXHUMED BODY... HENRY EVAN DEVERAUX... UNUSUALLY HIGH LEVELS OF CYANIDE.

Evan found his hands shaking as he read the report. He flipped to the next page and then the next, angry at the nonsensical charts, finally making it to the last paragraph.

RESULTS ARE INCONCLUSIVE, BUT INDICATIVE OF A MEDICATION OVERDOSE.

Evan didn't have many memories of his grandfather. Henry had been ill for most of Evan's infancy and then died suddenly after Evan's fifth birthday. What he did remember was that Owen and Randall had thrown a party after the funeral. A good many people had attended. Evan remembered thinking how happy everyone had been. After Henry died, Evan had been able to spend whole weeks at Deveraux House with Grandma and Aunt Genevieve. Those had been good times. But it was Grandma who had cared for Henry in his final days—managing the nurses and medications and chemotherapy with her customary calm.

He flipped the report closed and stared at the front. The date on the report was three weeks before the plane carrying all of the Deveraux children went down.

Evan carefully folded the report and put it in his jacket pocket. Then he shoveled the rest of the papers into the box and put it back on the shelf. He had no idea what to do next.

ABOUT THE AUTHOR

Bethany Maines is the award-winning author of action adventure and fantasy tales that focus on women who know when to apply lipstick and when to apply a foot to someone's hind end. When she's not traveling to exotic lands, or kicking some serious butt with her black belt in karate, she can be found chasing after her daughter, or glued to the computer working on her next novel.

OTHER WORKS BY BETHANY MAINES

CARRIE MAE MYSTERIES

Bulletproof Mascara

Compact With The Devil

High-Caliber Concealer

Glossed Cause

THE DEVERAUX LEGACY

The Second Shot
PNWA 2019 Literary Contest Award Winner

The Cinderella Secret

The Lost Heir
A Deveraux Legacy Novella

GALACTIC DREAMS

When Stars Take Flight Vol. 1

The Seventh Swan Vol. 2
A Book Excellence Award Winner

SAN JUAN ISLANDS MURDER MYSTERIES

An Unseen Current

Against the Undertow

An Unfamiliar Sea

SHARK SANTOYO CRIME SERIES

Shark's Instinct

Shark's Bite

Shark's Hunt

Shark's Fin

Peregrine's Flight

Wild Waters
A Paranormal Romantic Suspense

BLUE ZEPHYR PRESS

THE FAARIAN CHRONICLES: EXILE
by Karen Harris Tully

Fifteen-year-old Sunny Price dreams of being an Olympic gymnast, but thanks to the worst custody agreement in the universe, she finds out she's half-alien and is exiled to her absentee-mother's home planet. She has to give up her friends and elite gymnastics career to live with a mother who only wants to give orders? This. Sucks.

THE CHRISTMAS SPIRIT
by J.M. Phillippe

In this award-winning dark comedy inspired by Charles Dickens A Christmas Carol, Charlene Dickenson's untimely death in a Christmas-related accident means she must do whatever it takes to become a Ghost of Christmas Past, Present, or Future or spend her after-life in chains. Can she learn to embrace the Christmas Spirit?

bluezephyrpress.com